the innocent

Also by Taylor Stevens

The Informationist

the

taylor stevens

innocent

A Vanessa Michael Munroe Novel

 crown publishers   new york

Published in the United States by Crown Publishers, an imprint of the Crown Publishing Group, a division of Random House, Inc., New York.
www.crownpublishing.com

CROWN and the Crown colophon are registered trademarks of Random House, Inc.

Library of Congress Cataloging-in-Publication Data is available upon request.

ISBN 978-0-307-71712-2
eISBN 978-0-307-71714-6

Printed in the United States of America

Book design by Lynne Amft
Jacket design by Jarrod Taylor
Jacket photograph © 2005 by VisionsofAmerica.com/Joe Sohm/Getty Images

10   9   8   7   6   5   4   3   2   1

First Edition

To those who didn't survive. May you find in your forever sleep the peace that escaped you in life.

the innocent

Prologue

*She moved in a crouch, blade between her teeth, all four limbs con-
nected to the earth. She cocked her head, listened, and then continued on again, through the undergrowth and past the body at her
bare feet.*

*Along the jungle floor, shadows cast against shadows, playing
tricks with light, and unnatural stillness replaced the buzz and chatter
of the canopy, as if nature held its breath while bearing witness to the
violence.*

*She paused at the whisper of air that alerted her to movement from
behind.*

They'd been smart to track so silently.

She shifted, ready to face them when they came.

And they would *come.*

The knowledge brought with it a surge of adrenaline.

Euphoria followed.

*Two emerged from the verdure, dressed in shoddy camouflage and
rubber shoes, carrying no firearms, only knives. They came steadily,
circling, hunting, eyes glazed with bloodlust, lips turned up in snarls.
They wanted her dead, and so they must die.*

*She breathed deeply, focus pure, measuring the strength of the
threat. Awareness came in waves, a feral instinct that returned nuance*

with radarlike clarity. Understanding their weaknesses, she launched forward for the first strike.

Connected.

A scream shattered the calm.

Off balance, the first attacker toppled, and in a fluid movement she twisted, pushing off his body to propel herself into the second man.

He shifted to avoid impact, and the twist of his neck met the slice of her outstretched blade.

He fell.

She landed in a crouch and without pause returned to the first. Hand to head. Knife to neck. Swift, through tendons and sinew.

The fight had taken only seconds, and now in the silence the kill was finished. She stood over the bodies, the sound of her own heartbeat loud in her ears, and after a moment of hesitation she swore. It had been too fast. Too easy.

Her chest heaved in hatred of the skills that kept her alive, skills that drove her to win, skills that inevitably brought death.

She dropped to her knees and there, for the first time, stared at the face of the nearest hunter. A vise of recognition gripped her heart. She fell forward onto the body.

His open eyes were green. His hair was blond, his face longingly familiar.

Her soul pounded a rhythm: Please not him. Not him. Not him.

In death, his eyes fixed a piercing accusation. She gaped in mute horror at the liquid of life that had, in seeping from his neck, painted her skin crimson.

She couldn't breathe.

Dizzy. Suffocating. Nausea.

She found air. It came as a burning rush into collapsing lungs, a scream that started from the depths of her soul and ripped through her vocal cords, shattering the stillness, sending a flurry of beating wings through the canopy.

Head tilted upward, and with the primal shriek of rage and pain still rising, she opened her eyes. Not to the jungle roof but to her bedroom ceiling, patterned, whitewashed, and tinged with the color of dawn coming through the window.

Vanessa Munroe gasped. Curtains in the room rustled lightly. The call to prayer sounded from minarets across the city and her hand was still gripping the handle of a knife plunged into the other side of the king-size mattress.

Awareness settled, and she let go of the knife as if scalded, rolling off the bed in the same movement.

She stared.

The blade had struck twice and stood in silent witness to the increasing ferocity of the nightmares. The sheets were soaked with sweat. She glanced at her tank top and boxers. Drenched. And Noah, had he not left for work early this morning, would have been dead.

Chapter 1

Casablanca, Morocco

At last, the crowd moved forward.

He picked up the duffel bag and slipped the strap over his shoulder. Aching and nauseous, he placed one deliberate foot in front of the other, part of the collective escape from transatlantic captivity—down the aisle, out of the belly of the plane, along the Jetway and through the sunlit terminals of Mohammed V Airport.

Three days of little sleep had brought him here, three days and three lifetimes since that call in the wee hours that had, without warning, provided long-awaited news. He'd sat in the dark, rigid on the edge of the bed, searching his way through possibilities until, certain there was really only one option, he'd picked up the handset once more and placed the call to Morocco.

I need a favor.

Those had been his only words. No introduction, no explanation, only the plea.

"Tell me," she'd said.

"I'm coming to you."

And that was it. No good-bye, just his unspoken fear wrapped into those words and whispered into the night, across the wires. He'd put down the phone and then, with palms sweating and hands shaking, sat in front of the computer and purchased a ticket.

He needed that favor and had flown halfway around the world to ask it.

Now, without thinking, he moved with the throng while inside his head the words of entreaty came and went; rewound and started over; front to back, end to beginning in the same perpetual loop that had not stopped since the call.

He slowed. Stood in front of a plate-glass window. Stared out over the naked runway while those behind him hurried past.

Even if he tried he could never count the number of airports and train stations that delineated his youth; a collection of visa stamps and endless moves that defined his life as one of eight siblings hopscotching the globe with cult-member parents, together a ragtag group of economy-class vagabonds.

Into the glass he whispered his name, strange as it was even to him. The sound drifted in a low and hushed tribute to the past that had brought him here, the past that refused to die no matter how long or how often buried.

Sherebiah Gospel Logan.

His name was Logan. *Only* Logan. *Always* Logan. And to those few who knew the rest, he blamed it on drugs and hippies, which was so much easier than trying to explain what most could never comprehend.

Desperation had compelled him here, to the one person who did understand, the one capable of burying the past for good. If she so chose. He needed that favor, needed her to say yes, and instead of arriving with something to barter, he'd come a beggar, hat in hand with nothing to offer but their shared bond and the secret dread that her answer would be no.

His eyes tracked the last of the thinning stream of passengers and the airline crew as they trailed luggage down the hall, and finally his feet again followed.

He moved through customs and the whole of the border crossing on autopilot, until he came at last to the waiting area, and there among the sea of faces searched hers out. He passed over her once, twice, before finally spotting her with arms crossed and leaning into a column with a grin that said she'd been watching him for a while.

Vanessa. Michael Munroe. Best friend. Surrogate family. Personal savior.

She looked nothing like the battle-hardened woman who'd returned from Africa's west coast eight months ago, now nearly unrecognizable, in flowing pants and delicate head scarf, everything about her soft and feminine and the opposite of what he'd expected to find. But seeing her, he could hope again.

He stood in place while she shoved off the pillar in his direction, smirk indelible, slicing through the crowd nimble and catlike, her gray eyes not once breaking contact until she was within arm's length.

And then, in a movement that would have resulted in a broken nose for anyone else, she reached out and tousled his blond hair, laughing that deep carefree laugh of hers that said she was genuinely happy to see him.

The inward rehearsal and stress that had consumed him the last few days was replaced by the possibility of hope. Logan grabbed her in a bear hug, which she halfheartedly attempted to escape; he spun her full circle, and when he'd finally let go and there was a second of awkward silence, she tousled his hair again.

"Jesus, Logan," she said. "From the look on your face, you'd think you'd come to ask me to marry you."

He ran a hand through his hair to mitigate the damage and, unable to contain the ear-to-ear grin, said, "Maybe one day I will."

"You should be so lucky," she said dryly, then with a light punch to the shoulder that held his bag, "That all you got?"

He nodded, the stupid grin still plastered on his face.

She smiled, hooked her arm in his and, shoulder to shoulder, nearly equal in height, led him away from the crowd, saying, "It's really good to see you."

The lilt of her voice, the uncharacteristic enthusiasm of her touch, gave him pause, and as they continued arm in arm, he turned to catch her eye. She grinned, impishly squeezed his biceps, and then placed her head on his shoulder.

"You hungry?" she asked. "We've got a long trip ahead of us."

"I ate on the plane," he said, and then confused, he hesitated. "How long could it possibly take to get into Casablanca?"

"Not Casablanca," she said. "Tangier."

The last map of Morocco that he'd seen showed Tangier nearly two hundred miles northeast. He grasped for reasons. "You and Noah broke up?" he said.

Munroe shrugged and turned ever so slightly, so that she walked backward as she spoke. She flashed him another smile, and in that smile Logan saw a glimpse of the same, odd, telltale stupefaction that hadn't washed over her face in more than half a decade.

"Hard to call something that could never be whole, broken," she said. "But no, things haven't changed, we're still together."

She smiled yet again, went back to walking side by side, and in the wake of this last, the burden Logan had come to share grew that much heavier.

He understood from that look what she'd not said with words, and he fought for composure, to prevent the shock of knowledge from escaping to his face. He kept beside her, matching her step for step across polished floors to the lower level, where they'd catch a train into the city.

Logan said, "Why the move to Tangier?"

"I like it there," she said.

Her words came blank and deadpan. No humor, no sincerity; her unusually indirect way of saying *none of your damn business*, and so he let it go for now. He'd find another way to probe the extent of the damage behind the smile, to come at it from a different direction, because both as friend and as supplicant, he had to know how hard he could push, how solid the chassis, how twisted the wreckage.

They reached Casa Voyageurs, the regional train station, and there, Munroe led him through the cool, high-domed terminal to the ticket counter, where she segued into an exchange of Arabic.

Logan handed her his wallet and she pushed it back. "I've got it," she said. "This isn't breaking the bank."

Tickets in one hand, she took his hand in the other and moved beyond the clean and tidy interior to the outside, to the tunnel and its confusing array of tracks, to the train that would take them north. They were still walking the corridor to the first-class compartment when the car lurched and the train began a slow crawl out of the station.

Logan paused and, as he'd done so many times in years past, stood watching the platform shrink into the distance. Tracks and walls and city structures began to blur, and he turned toward the empty six-seat berth that Munroe had entered.

She sat beside the window with her head tilted back and eyes closed, so he dumped the bag on his assigned seat and took the spot opposite her. She opened her eyes a sliver and stretched so that her legs spanned the aisle, resting her feet between his knees.

Logan said, "I could have flown to Tangier, you know, saved you the trip down and back."

She nodded. "But I wanted to have the time alone with you," she said.

He faltered and left the unasked "why" hanging in the air.

She'd handed him an opening, presented the opportunity to unburden himself and say in person what he'd flown across the Atlantic to say, but he couldn't. Not now. Not with her like this. He needed time to think.

Munroe paused. It was a small hesitation, but enough that he understood she'd given notice. She was aware he'd parlayed the opening gambit and was willing to go along with him.

"Noah's there right now," she continued. "He's edgy, jealous." She turned her eyes back to meet his. "I didn't want you to have to face that right off the bat."

"Doesn't he know that I'm gay?"

She flashed a cheesy grin and crinkled her nose. "He knows. But he also knows that I love you."

"So that makes me a threat?" Logan said.

She nodded.

He sighed.

The only way his arrival could be deemed a threat was if something else wasn't right. Under ideal circumstances Logan would ask for details and she would tell; their conversation would flow in that bonded way of confidants that had defined years together. But this wasn't ideal, not anything close to ideal.

They settled again into small talk, then gradually into silence as Logan, lulled by the peace of her presence, the rhythm of the wheels against the tracks, and fighting three days of being awake, drifted into the oblivion of sleep.

It was the subtle exchange of metal on metal that gradually pulled him back. According to the sun's path, hours had passed.

Dazed and disoriented, he turned to Munroe. She was smiling again, that odd telltale smile. She flipped the knife from her palm, her eyes never leaving his as she played the blade across her fingers.

Logan cursed silently, fighting the urge to stare at the weapon, and said, "Been a while since you've carried them."

She nodded, eyes still to his, still grinning, the steel continuing to play.

Logan leaned his head back and closed his eyes—his way of shutting out the pain of seeing her in this state. The knives and all that they symbolized spoke volumes to how far she had fallen.

The sky was dark when they arrived in Tangier, Morocco's gateway to Europe. Tangier Ville was the end of the line, and the station, with its clean and polished interior was in turn its own gateway to nighttime streets that birthed life and motion into the humid air of Africa's northern coast.

Their destination in the eastern suburb of Malabata was close enough that they could have walked, but instead of footing it as Logan had expected, Munroe flagged a petit taxi. In the glow of the terminal's fluorescent lights she bantered with the driver over the rate, and Logan sensed disquiet in her haste.

The ride was but a few minutes, and the vehicle stopped in front of a three-story building that faced the ocean. The apartment block, like most of the others Logan had seen on the journey, was whitewashed, stacked, and topped with a flat rooftop that he knew to be as much a part of the living space as the rooms inside.

He stepped from the cab and sniffed the salt-tinged breeze.

Parked against the curb not far from the building entrance was a black BMW, and Munroe swore quietly as she took note of it.

"He's already here," she said.

Logan lifted the strap of his bag to his shoulder. "I've wanted to meet him anyway," he said.

She stared at the car and after a long pause walked through the front door with Logan following close behind.

The stairs from the entrance led to a tiled mezzanine that amplified their footsteps, and they went up again, another half floor, stopping in front of the only apartment on the landing. Munroe turned the key and swung the oversize door wide to a deep and sparsely furnished living area.

"Home," she said with a flourish, and Logan grinned at the joke. Six months in Morocco and she'd already jumped cities. For her there would never be anything so permanent as home.

The apartment was quiet and dim, the silence made larger by high ceilings, patterned floors, and a light current of air that billowed through open windows into gauzy curtains. Footsteps echoed from the hall and Logan turned in their direction as Noah entered the living room.

Noah Johnson, a Moroccan-raised American, had been a chance encounter on Munroe's last assignment, an encounter that had eventually evolved into her latest and possibly final departure from the United States.

Although Logan knew much of the man from pictures and conversations, this was the first time he'd seen him in person, and it was clear why Munroe had taken such a liking to him. He was an easy six-foot-plus, black hair, fair skin, and a rock climber's physique.

In a gesture proprietary and tender, Noah pulled Munroe close and kissed her on the forehead, then extended his hand to Logan in greeting.

Munroe ran interpretation between Noah's rudimentary English and Logan's broken French, and in the easy exchange Logan sensed a fracture in the closeness the two had shared. He wondered as he stood there now, making small talk through Munroe, what it must be like in Noah's shoes, to helplessly watch the woman he loved withdraw emotionally, to fear she would soon walk away, while extending a hand of friendship to the man he suspected to be the cause.

Munroe returned Noah's kiss, said softly, "Let me show Logan around. I'll be ready in twenty minutes," and with that took Logan's hand and led him toward the hallway.

Three bedrooms and two bathrooms made up the bulk of the one-level apartment, and a narrow staircase beyond the kitchen led to the laundry and work area on the rooftop. Like so many places in the developing countries in which Logan had once lived, the apartment was bare and rustic, the kitchen and bathrooms minimalistic, and as a whole the flat went without many of the standard fixtures found in even lower-income homes of the United States.

The brief tour ended at the guest bedroom, and when Munroe had shown Logan what little he needed to know, she left to dress for the evening.

He turned off the light and in the dark dumped his bag on a chair.

The room was enveloped in the quiet of night, and in that quiet there was a form of peace. Here, alone in the dimness, he could think; he could process and plan and try to figure out how to dig his way out of a hole that had, in less than a moment of clarity, doubled in size. He'd come to Morocco focused on nothing more than begging for Munroe's help, a yes or no answer, and had instead been blindsided by the complex series of hoops he'd have to jump through to get it.

The sound of running water filtered from across the hall, and in the streetlight glow he sat on the bed, elbows to knees, methodically forcing calm; waiting.

A shift in the light under the bedroom door announced her presence before the footfalls. Logan lay back on the bed, hands behind his head, ready for the knock that came a second later.

She was stunning in silhouette, the loose and modest clothes replaced by a very short, figure-hugging dress that accentuated a long, lean, androgynous body and brandished sensuality. In heels, she had at least an inch over Noah's height, and together they would make a visually intimidating pair.

With a hug and then a house key placed in his palm, she was gone.

The front door echoed a thud and Logan rose from the bed to watch from the window as the BMW peeled away from the curb. He waited until he was certain they would not U-turn for a forgotten item, then headed toward the living room where he'd spotted a telephone.

Chapter 2

Ten in the evening local time meant late afternoon in Dallas, still within the office hours of most businesses, although Logan expected that Capstone Consulting kept the phones running far later than the standard nine to five.

He picked up the handset, exhaled, and dialed a call he'd never expected to make.

Capstone was owned and operated by Miles Bradford, former Special Forces turned private contractor, the man who'd been by Munroe's side when the world had turned upside down. If there was ever a person who'd want to know about her current state, who'd be willing to get involved in a nightmare predicament for no other reason than that it involved *her*, that man was Bradford.

Anticlimactically, Logan was put on hold. During the frustrating wait, he moved methodically about the room, scanning surfaces and opening drawers, careful to leave everything as he'd found it while the phone to his ear provided background music. He was checking beneath the sofa when Beethoven's Ninth was clipped short by a cheery voice announcing Capstone, as if it were some high-stakes New York marketing firm instead of the bullets-and-blood mercenary outfit Logan knew it to be.

According to the receptionist, Bradford was out of the country.

"I know you have a way to get in contact with him," Logan said.

"Tell him that Michael's in trouble and that if he wants to talk to me, this line's only going to be clear for the next three or four hours."

He recited the apartment's phone number, and after a routine reassurance that someone would get back to him, he hung up and moved on to the meager pantry.

He was violating Munroe's space and her privacy, a deed not done lightly, hunting for what he knew was hidden somewhere nearby. He didn't need a visual to confirm his suspicions, but he did want the specifics in order to assess the damage.

He was in the middle of Munroe's bathroom when the phone rang. Logan fumbled and then recovered. The wait had been thirty minutes, not a bad measure of Bradford's concern.

There was static on the line and a few seconds' delay, but even through that Logan could hear the clipped, impatient quality of Bradford's tone.

"I just got your message," he said. "What kind of trouble is she in?"

Carefully scripted, Logan said, "The self-inflicted, oops-look-at-that-I'm-dead kind of trouble."

There was a pregnant pause and Bradford said finally, "Suicide?"

Logan closed his eyes and exhaled slowly. "No, she's very much alive. But she's self-medicating. And she's started carrying knives again."

Silence, and then, "How long has this been going on?"

"I have no idea. I flew into Morocco this morning and she met me at the airport. The signs are all there, she doesn't try to hide them—flaunts them, even—she's poking at me with them, like she wants me to know. I'm going to take a guess and say it's only been a few weeks. She just moved to Tangier, and it could be related."

"Any idea what she's taking?"

"Not sure," Logan said. "I'm trying to find out. Never thought I'd see the day she started this shit again, but if history's any predictor, it'll be legal and she'll have a fake prescription."

Logan searched the nightstand drawers. "Anyway, she's out with Noah right now. I'm ransacking her apartment."

Bradford exhaled a low whistle.

"She won't know," Logan said. "Been there, done that, won't get caught."

There was another pause and then Bradford said, "Logan, I'm in Afghanistan. There's no way for me to get out of here for another week and until then I'm at a loss as to what I can do."

Logan knelt to look under the bed. "I'm not sure either," he said. "I just figured you'd want to know. You're the obvious intervention partner of choice—I mean, you were there, you know better than any of us why she's doing it—and really, Miles, I think you're the only other person who cares the way that I do."

Logan opened the doors of a large armoire and glared at a small box barely visible under a pile of clothes. "I think I've found it," he said.

From the box he pulled a smaller box, opened it, and shook free a bottle of syrup. He read off the label, "Phenergan VC."

"Is that the codeine version?" Bradford said.

Logan searched the label, lips set tight. Bradford knew his pharmacopoeia. "Yes, codeine," he said. "The box holds twelve and two are missing."

"If we're lucky, that's the first box," Bradford said. He hesitated. "Okay, look, I understand why you called and I thank you for it. The earliest I can get out of here is next Thursday. Do you think you can find an excuse to get her to the States?"

"You know how she is about returning."

"I could come to Morocco," Bradford said. "But I really don't think that's a good idea." There was a long silence, and although Bradford never verbalized it, Logan understood the reason. Noah and Bradford around Munroe at the same time brought far too much potential for conflict.

"Best would be to get her to the U.S.," Bradford said. "Or really anywhere out of Morocco."

Logan nodded agreement to the empty room. "I'll figure something out and let you know how it goes," he said, although in truth his favor already required that he take her from here.

"I'd give you a number," Bradford said, "but it's pointless, I move around too much. Call the office. They'll be able to reach me. If you can't get her to go back, I'll come to you, but I need at least a week."

The call over, Logan continued to stare into the armoire at the box and all that it stood for. Codeine wasn't the heaviest stuff she'd taken, nor was it the worst to be abused; the issue was that she was self-medicating at all.

Heavy, burdened, he replaced the bottle and rearranged the clothes.

He could work this thing. Getting Bradford involved was a definite step forward, and pulling him in had been rather easy.

Logan shoved away the stab of guilt.

He would have made that call even if he didn't need Munroe's help, and Bradford wasn't offering to do anything he didn't want to do.

Logan returned to the bedroom and the weight of two days' travel pressed against his eyelids. Intent on remaining alert until whatever godforsaken hour Munroe came back, he closed his eyes for a second and opened them to bright sunlight streaming through the curtains.

He bolted upright with no recollection of falling asleep or of Munroe returning, or with any concept of how much time had elapsed. He fumbled for his watch.

Seven in the morning, local time.

God, he was tired.

He rolled his legs over the side of the bed and listened, shook his head in an attempt to clear the fog that wrapped around his brain. There was no sound or movement in the apartment, so he stood and padded to the window. Parked along the curb were a few cars, but no BMW.

Logan opened the bedroom door and, with the stealth of a kid preparing to sneak into the kitchen to grab a cookie, peered down the hall.

Munroe's door was slightly ajar, definitely not closed the way he'd left it the night before. Barefoot against the tiled floor, he moved toward her bedroom, and there, hearing nothing, pressed his palm to the door.

She was alone: sprawled across the mattress, face in a pillow and tangled in sheets that trailed to the floor. The knives sat on the nightstand and against the foot of the bed lay the clothes she had shed before climbing into it. The armoire doors were partially open, and although there was no visible sign that she'd helped herself to the contents of another bottle, crashed out and dead to the world as she was, Logan had no doubt that she had.

He left her room for the guest bathroom, irritation and anger washing over him. He needed her right now, needed her to be herself, lucid, aware, not this—brain- and emotion-numbed, and half-alive. No matter the reasons, what she was doing was such a goddamn fucking waste of brilliance.

He turned on the shower and let it run. There was no point in keeping quiet; the insomniac woman who would normally go from a dead sleep to a fighting stance over less than a whisper had drugged herself into a state of unconsciousness.

It was afternoon when the light tap of footsteps first echoed down the hall. Logan waited until they passed, then left his room in search of Munroe and found her in the kitchen filling a coffeepot with water, dressed in a tank and boxers and sporting a case of bed hair so bad he would have laughed if things had been otherwise. He didn't see the knives, but then she'd never needed them to kill, and that wasn't why she carried them anyway.

"Want coffee?" she said.

"Sure," he replied. "Where's Noah?"

She yawned and scratched the back of her neck. "He's at his holiday house. What time is it?"

"Around three o'clock," he said.

Munroe placed the pot on the stove and lit the burner. She sat at the kitchen table, then tilted her head up and smiled. A real smile. And in spite of himself and the frustration and anger, Logan smiled back.

"I needed the sleep," she said. "And thought you might need some too, what with the jet lag and the long trip. I won't make you wait on me like that again."

This was as much of an explanation as she'd give, but Logan knew she did it with calculated reason. The sleep and making him wait had been as much a deliberate display as the knives on the train. She wanted him to know her state of mind, to take it all into account should he continue toward whatever favor he must ask.

Logan said nothing, and she smiled again—that killer smile.

"Have a seat," she said. "I'll make you lunch."

He nodded toward the empty cupboards. "From what?"

With a straight face she said, "Coffee," and the heartbeat of silence was followed by commingled laughter that came as a welcome release of tension.

Logan couldn't help but grin, so good was it to see her lucid and to have her again, the real her, the Michael that he knew and loved; and he relished the moment because he knew it would be short-lived.

As if she'd read his mind, she said, "Tell me why you've come—what is it you need?"

He froze.

The coffeepot percolated on the stove, but Munroe made no move to get it. She nodded toward the seat opposite. It wasn't an invitation, it was an instruction. There was no point in arguing, so Logan sat in the proffered chair. Forearms on the table, he shifted forward, and as he opened his mouth to speak, she put a hand on his wrist.

"Hold the thought," she said. She stood, stepped to the stove, and turned off the burner.

She'd so perfectly disarmed him. He watched her move about the kitchen: fluid, methodical, neither hurried nor pausing, much like a well-trained dancer. She turned to catch his eye, smiling conspiratorially as she set out the coffee mugs.

She placed a cup in front of him and held her own while she sat, her posture taut, her face relaxed. "Go on," she said, blowing steam as she held the coffee to her lips.

He reached for his wallet and slid the faded photo with its beauty and tragedy, memories and heartbreak, across the table. Munroe paused to look.

"Is that Charity's daughter?"

Logan nodded.

Charity.

The person he'd loved longer and truer than any other being. Charity, who was his fellow childhood survivor. She'd lived the life, knew the pain and trauma better than he, and shared the burden: the lies, the secrets, and the scars.

Logan gazed down at the photo of the little girl with the blond ringlets and bright green eyes, traced his fingers along the edge of it, and then stopped. All reason, all argument, all the words that had been turning around in his head for the past three days fled, and he was left vacant. Logan looked up and staring into Munroe's eyes said only, "I've found her."

Chapter 3

Logan didn't need to say more because, without explanation, Munroe understood why he'd come and, if not the specifics, at least the essence of what he wanted.

She reached across the table and placed her hand on his.

In the quiet he wished more than anything to plead his case and argue reason. But he kept silent.

Munroe knew the cost, knew what it meant, and he could see the calculation reflected in her eyes. Finally, she shifted her gaze toward the windows.

"I don't know, Logan," she said. "I just don't know."

He paused, waiting, allowing the stillness to swallow them, and then, with a lump rising in his throat, said, "Would you at least listen to what we know? The details? Would you hear us out?"

She gave no response.

"Come with me," he said. "Just for a week—just to meet the others."

"Return to the States?" she said.

"They can't all come here," he said. "It's too expensive and there's not enough time, but that doesn't mean you have to return home. It can be anywhere—New York; how about New York? We go for a week, stay at a nice hotel, talk to some interesting people, and when all is said and done and you've had time to think about it, then you make a decision."

She stood, refilled her coffee mug, and continued to stand, staring at nothing.

"Please," Logan whispered. "For me."

In the silence, sounds of traffic and occasionally pedestrian chatter filtered through the open windows. She remained motionless, eyes distant, vacant, unreadable. Finally, she turned to him.

"I'll go," she said. "For you."

He exhaled, realizing only then that he'd been holding his breath.

"Logan, I can't promise you anything," she said. "I'll go. I'll listen. But I make no commitment, and I won't stay, you know?"

He nodded. She'd offered enough: a start.

She was still standing at the kitchen counter when she said, "I need a bit of time before I can leave."

"Noah?" Logan ventured.

She nodded and made no pretense at hiding what he could so clearly read in her face. In the heaviness of the moment, he felt sadness at the inevitable and understood why she hadn't fought harder against his request to go with him. She braced for good-bye, hating it, hurting from it, and feeling no way out.

Logan said, "He thinks it's him—or maybe me. Noah has no idea, does he?"

She shook her head and turned slightly so that she stared again at some invisible point. "I've tried to explain it," she said, "but how could he possibly understand?"

No matter how well Noah believed he knew Munroe, there was so much he would never grasp, undercurrents that would, Logan or no Logan, inevitably pull her away, all of it guaranteeing pain and confusion as the natural course of things. The man had given Munroe laughter and a reason for happiness, and for this Logan wished it were possible to offer reassurance that things would be okay. But they weren't and might never be.

"It's better this way," he said.

Munroe's eyes shifted back, a long and languid gaze until finally she whispered, "I know."

The pain in those words left him speechless. She'd offered a brief glimmer, a crack through which Logan saw beyond her eyes, past her soul, and into the torment of her private hell. Then, without warning, as if a switch had been thrown, Munroe's face shifted and the glimmer ended. She said, "Tomorrow we race on the water," and Logan, still struggling for words, responded with a tired smile.

She bartered her time for his. A week in New York for a week in Tangier, and beyond the emotional tension that accompanied Noah's reaction, the days were action-fueled and driven by an undercurrent of laughter that continued through the return flight home. If Munroe was medicating, she hid it well, though Logan had woken often in the night to the sound of her footsteps passing in the hall and knew that she slept little.

They entered the United States through JFK and took a taxi into Manhattan, to The Palace, where Munroe had reserved one of the hotel's triplex suites. Even with his racing career and celebrity status as an adrenaline junkie, Logan's bank balance wasn't high enough to defend splitting such a bill, and so he didn't argue when she insisted on covering it.

At the top of the towers, the suite was three bedrooms spread over three floors and five thousand square feet, a direct and opulent contrast to the sparse conditions Munroe had lived in during the last several years. On the second floor she opened the door to the master bedroom and fell backward onto the king-size bed, arms splayed, laughing at the ceiling.

To Logan, she said, "You like it?"

He was wearing an ear-to-ear grin, staring out across the skyline. "It's insane," he said.

"This is your room," she said. "You'll need the space for your friends. Take the upstairs areas, spoil them a little; my treat. I'll stay downstairs."

Logan held her smile for a long while. In the joy of that moment, words were unnecessary, because without doubt this was the proverbial calm before the storm.

*   *   *

At nearly one in the morning, Munroe stood staring out the living room window. Logan had gone to bed over an hour ago, and she had lingered this long, observing the city streets, listening to the heartbeat of the suite, waiting for the night to lengthen, if only to be sure he was truly down for the evening.

For her, rest—sleep—would come much later, if at all, because to be awake when darkness threw a mask of beauty over the world was to be alive.

Munroe turned from the window, from her ghostly reflection, headed back through the room and out the door. She took the elevator down to where midnight air refused to let go of the day's humidity, down to civilization and asphalt, gas fumes and garbage, the mix of odors that only the heat of a big city could produce, New York in the middle of summer.

She'd left the hotel to breathe outside air, to walk out the body kinks that were the by-product of too many hours of air travel, and so stayed on foot, moving fast, heading west to nowhere in particular.

It was a mewling sound that turned her from passing a service entrance and drew her into the blackened depths where the outlines of trucks and parked vehicles filled space: it was a sound out of place in the city night, the cry of a lost kitten, or, as became evident as Munroe's eyes adjusted to the deeper darkness, the abject terror of a girl pinned to the ground by two men.

The young woman was eighteen, tops, still partly child, a perfect representation of the innocent, hopeful and naïve, who, on a quest for something more, streamed steadily into the metropolis only to find themselves sacrificed to the fires of Moloch.

The men hovered over her body, every movement menacing, brisk, and hostile. Munroe couldn't hear their words, only the raw threat of intent, which carried to her on the still air. The woman had given up fighting and appeared paralyzed. She'd not come to the oil-stained and garbage-strewn area willingly. Dragged, perhaps. Her shoes were missing. Her dress was torn and hiked up around her waist. Her chest heaved with silent crying.

Munroe stopped and, for a second that passed like millennia, stared. She felt no surprise or horror at having been guided into the arms of the wicked, only an unquenchable burning rage against the violation of innocence, an unbridled anger that surged from inside depths, up, up, into her head, pounding out a rhythm of retribution and destruction. Even if she'd wanted to, she couldn't have turned away, so strong was the drumbeat of war.

Not once did her eyes wander while she placed one foot in front of the other, moving forward, each step slow, certain, deliberate, until her toe thudded against something soft and pliable.

Munroe paused. Looked down.

The woman's purse with contents strewn.

Eyes ahead, she continued on, unseen and unheard, until she was within feet of the men, and they, taking notice, hesitated in their violence.

The larger of the two, leader of the pair, stood to face Munroe.

Time and space slowed into sharp focus, and in her vision he was a target narrowed into a shadow of gray against the night. Her hands remained relaxed at her sides, her body calm, almost nonchalant, while her eyes darted from one spot to the next within the enclosed area, judging distance, surfaces, weapons.

The man stepped close, invaded her personal space.

He was rank breath and flared nostrils; he was eyes that didn't see and air without oxygen. He looked down at Munroe and inhaled, trailing his nose around her hair.

Inside her core the percussion beat harder, louder: marching orders to every cell in her body.

"Look what we have here," he said, and his partner chuckled, a nervous bark, while holding tight to the victim still on the ground.

The big man ran his fingertips along the edge of Munroe's hair.

"Don't touch me," she said. "Not if you want to live."

Her voice was low, monotone, and although the man couldn't

know it as the sound of impending destruction, his partner understood the threat, and in a form of solidarity came forward to stand next to his leader.

The girl on the ground scrambled upward and, with the men's backs to her, and only a second's glance in their direction, bolted behind them to the street.

In silence the three watched her run, and then, with the little figure fading in the dark, the leader turned again to Munroe.

"Now see what you've done," he said.

He was smiling a row of clean white teeth.

Munroe, motionless, turned her eyes back to him and said nothing.

"You owe me a fuck," the man said.

The smile was gone.

"I'd advise you to walk away," she said. "If you touch me, I'll kill you."

He laughed. Hard. A loud boom against the walls that rose up on either side, and then, in an instant, he stopped.

A fight was inevitable, and with Munroe's realization came the rush. She pulled it all in and closed her eyes in a slow, extended blink.

A heedful observer would have noticed the twitch in her hands, would have wondered at the lack of fear, would have been cautioned against the level of self-assurance. But overconfidence had blinded these men from observing much.

There came a moment of silence, of deliberation, as if this man and his partner might, after all, be smart enough to recognize a form of insanity greater than their own and back down.

But no.

The big man grabbed a fistful of her hair. Yanked. Dragged her to her knees.

"Fuck you, bitch," he hissed.

Munroe's eyes smarted, and in response the corners of her lips turned upward.

Time passed in microsecond gaps, movement in nano-slices of

space, intense clarity, which like a flash flood through a gully rushed in a torrent through her blood.

His left hand still gripped her hair. His right arm pulled back for a strike, and this man with his smile, his laugh, his breath, became a familiar enemy who had to die. She was no longer in the middle of a sweltering city but in the heat of the jungle with its pervasive raw earthliness.

Hands still to her sides, her fingers reached for the knives sheathed against her shins. Skin connected with metal. Instinct followed. The internal percussion rose to climax screaming the order to survive, to win, to avenge: commanding the order to kill.

The bedside clock read eight in the morning. Logan glanced at the digital readout and in a half breath understood the fear that had brought him awake.

He threw off the sheets and headed down the stairs at a near run, calling Munroe's name as he went, stopping short at the ground-floor bedroom.

The door had been left slightly ajar, and as he had done that first morning in Tangier, he placed his palm to it and the hinges swung inward.

In a shock of déjà vu, Logan stared, open-mouthed.

She lay sprawled across the bed, knives on the bedside table, dead to the world. He remained for a moment, pushing down the frustration and resentment, and then, turning to go, eyes adjusting to the dim of the room, recognition settling, stopped midstep.

Heart pounding, stomach churning, he moved closer to the bed, closer to her. Knelt. And being careful not to touch her, followed the trail of crusted blood that smeared and streaked across her forearms.

He had never heard her leave the suite, hadn't heard the sounds of the private elevator as it came or went. He drew a quiet intake of air and clenched his fists. In a few hours the others would begin to arrive.

They would come to provide bits and pieces of an eight-year-old story that she needed to hear, and there she was, the one person who could turn it into a goddamn happy ending, strung out in a drug-induced haze.

He wanted to wake her; to find out what the hell had happened last night, what she had done; to yell and smack some sense into her. But he knew better, and so he returned to the kitchen to try to bolt down something against the returning nausea.

Over the course of the morning and into the afternoon, the others came, and against mounting anxiety over Munroe's condition, Logan played host.

Amused at their reactions to the opulence of the place, he walked them through it and answered their questions about how the suite was paid for.

An odd, mixed lot, they congregated on the rooftop terrace amid wrought-iron furniture and wooden planters that provided a quiet, Old World feel in contrast to the city chaos below.

Their looks, tastes, and styles, the directions of their lives, were as far removed one from the other as any group of random strangers, but childhood, the common thread that banded them together, was tighter still than any difference. They shared easy conversation, the camaraderie of soldiers bonded through the trauma of war, until the glass doors to the terrace slid open and Munroe stepped out.

She'd cleaned up: The blood was gone, and at the door's threshold now she stood a picture of demure innocence in a girlish dress and flat shoes.

She returned Logan's glance, and there was a touch of mischief in her eyes.

Logan sighed.

Whatever else she might be, naïve and pure she wasn't. She'd deliberately assumed this likeness, this facade of diffidence and modesty that so easily became a veil to the unlearned, and as was evident in that glance, she knew that it frustrated him badly.

He broke off eye contact, and her smile widened, as if to say, *Yes, Logan, I know what you're doing.*

His heart pounded heavily.

It was always a mistake to underestimate her, and although he'd not lied to or misled her, there was much that he hadn't mentioned.

Logan glanced again at Munroe's girly clothes, hesitated, and then introduced her to the others.

"This is Michael," he said, "the one I told you about."

In addition to Logan, there were six around the table: real estate agent, lawyer, project manager, IT director, photographer, and medical student, all in their late twenties to mid-thirties, each one having fought to where they were now in life at such personal cost and private sacrifice that there were spouses who didn't know the details.

Munroe took a seat, and one by one they introduced themselves. There wasn't much small talk, albeit a measure of flippancy, while each in the little group told a variant of the same story: one of a life controlled and structured from birth, of consecration to God and The Prophet, of poverty, servility, and eventually a gamble—family, social structure, and their entire known world wagered on the hope that there was another life, a better life, out here in the Void.

Logan could hear the desperation that lay behind each measured word and wondered if they could hear it too. They were gauging her, uncertain if she was capable of comprehending the gravity of what was at stake, wondering how this timid *girl* could be the one to make wrong right, doubt written clearly across their faces.

Looking at her now, Logan found it difficult, even knowing her as well as he did, to visualize how such apparent innocence could be the harbinger of so great a justice. He understood their disbelief and pushed his own doubts aside, because he needed that favor.

Chapter 4

Buenos Aires, Argentina

The trees and buildings and parked cars rolled by, and Hannah stared out the passenger van window not really seeing, but definitely listening.

She was badly curious about why she was here, but knew not to ask, and so sat silent in the farthest back row, trying to catch clues in the discussion between the two adults in the front seat.

Not knowing made her stomach queasy. At least when you knew a thing, even if it was bad, you could prepare for it. It was better to know something bad than nothing at all, and right now she knew nothing at all.

It was very odd that they'd brought only her and none of the other kids, and although it didn't seem like she was in trouble, sometimes it was hard to tell, because like a slap upside the head, trouble had a way of coming out of nowhere.

Until Hannah knew one way or the other, there wasn't really any way to get rid of the sick feeling, but right now the best way to stay out of trouble was to keep quiet. If she was quiet, they would forget about her, which meant that at least for a while they would leave her alone and she could listen.

They were very serious in the front seats, Uncle Zadok and Auntie Sunshine, calling on the Golden Verse for protection and wisdom, and for guidance, and the matter must have been Secret, too, because they didn't make Hannah come to the first row and join them in prayer.

Zadok's eyes were open, they had to be so he could drive, but Sunshine's were closed and her mouth was moving, and Hannah could tell that she was Spirit Talking, which was boring, so she only half-listened.

Having the whole back of the van to herself, with no one to mind her, felt amazing—almost as good as it did that time when she got a real present on her birthday. And since Zadok and Sunshine were too occupied to rebuke her for idleness, Hannah spent the stolen moments staring out the window while her thoughts went far, far away into the forbidden and hidden daydreams that helped time fly and made everything else better. And then the van swung wide and the pull of the turn brought her back.

She'd no idea how much time had passed or how long she'd been in fantasy, and because of this her stomach flipped in a pulse of fear. For such disobedience, there was certainly trouble waiting.

But Zadok and Sunshine hadn't noticed that she'd been daydreaming, and so she calmed. Hannah recognized a building and knew that they were now somewhere in the business district, not too far from the ports. They came here sometimes to raise money in the offices.

Sunshine's eyes were open again, and she seemed a bit more relaxed. That was good, because relaxed adults meant better moods and less chance of getting in trouble. Maybe the Spirits had said nice things would happen, although to Hannah it seemed the Spirit Words were forever vague and the adults always ready to believe the excuses for why predictions didn't come true. What was the use, really, of dead people talking if you could never count on what they said?

Sunshine was speaking to Zadok again, real words, not Spirit Words, so Hannah turned her eyes toward the book of Instructives in her lap, and her ears to the front. The sounds came in pieces. *The Lord's will. Small packet. United States. Prophet will be pleased. Only a few times a year.*

None of it really meant anything for certain, but Hannah could guess; that was the good thing about being quiet and listening when they forgot about you—you could learn things.

This same kind of special outing had happened before, in late summer, right before Auntie Sunshine went on a two-week visit to another place. That last time, Sunshine had taken Teen Rachel on the trip into town, and Hannah had to fill in on Rachel's work duty so that she could go. It had seemed that Rachel was special for being chosen, and even though it was wrong, Hannah had been a little jealous. On that day, just like today, everything had been Secret and hush-hush—more than the usual—so maybe today was the same kind of thing, whatever that thing was, and this made Hannah feel good, because maybe it meant she was special too.

Zadok parked the van, but he didn't get out when Sunshine did, which probably meant that he was staying behind, which was kind of unusual.

Sunshine motioned for Hannah, so she slid out of the far back and made her way to the door and then the sidewalk.

They were in front of a five-story building, old and very expensive it seemed, and that made Hannah's clothes feel all the more awkward and embarrassing. The dress was borrowed, a bit too small and pretty in a girly way that was uncomfortable. But Sunshine had told her to wear it, and there wasn't room for possible discussion, so that was that. At least it was new-looking and not as worn out as Hannah's own hand-me-downs.

Sunshine took hold of Hannah's hand and led her forward, and this made her feel even more uncomfortable than the clothes, but she knew better than to squirm, so she endured the bad feelings, shoving them away.

Sunshine said, "Sweetie, you want to serve the Lord and be a good little soldier for Jesus, right?"

Hannah hated that word *little* and everything that it implied, hated the way Sunshine talked down to her as if she were a two-year-old, but she nodded.

"That's good. It means God can bless you. He can only bless us when we're obedient to Him and to The Prophet, yes?"

The uncomfortable feeling was growing and made it hard to talk, so Hannah just nodded again.

"Being here is a very special privilege and The Prophet wants your dedication and your obedience," Sunshine said. "He needs you to be completely yielded, and to be Secret—talking about today is disobedience, you understand?"

Another nod, this time solemnly.

Sunshine's voice grew sterner, if that were possible. "What happens when we're disobedient to the Lord and The Prophet?"

"God can't bless or protect us," Hannah said, and her words came out in a hoarse whisper.

Sunshine nodded as if she was satisfied, and although Hannah should have felt relieved that Sunshine was pleased, she didn't. Instead she felt worse, though she didn't understand why, because Sunshine wasn't behaving as if Hannah had done something wrong or as if there was trouble coming.

It's just, things didn't feel right, which meant the uncomfortable was very strong and growing worse—that sick feeling that started in the pit of her stomach and worked its way outward until everything was irritating and it was difficult to think or breathe. The only thing she knew to do when this happened was to obey and then get through whatever it was, one moment at a time, until it was over and the uncomfortable went away.

They'd reached the building, Sunshine had pushed the front door open, and as they stepped inside she looked down at Hannah, a stern and unforgiving look that Hannah didn't have to think about to understand. *Be very obedient, because Sunshine could make a whole lot of trouble happen.*

On the second floor, a hallway spanned in both directions off the stairwell, and along the hallway were solid doors, each with a brass plate and the name of a business.

Sunshine still gripped Hannah's hand, and the heat and sweat of the close contact made Hannah want to scream or tug away, but she held quiet.

Sunshine went to the farthest door, which had a plaque with no name and opened onto a room with a desk backed close to the shaded windows, like it was supposed to be an office reception, but there wasn't anybody at the desk.

To Hannah the furniture, lamps, and wall coverings were more like a rich person's house than any office she had seen, and on each side of the room was another door, but those were closed, and the whole place was very quiet.

Sunshine pointed at a divan. "Sit there and don't touch anything," she said, and then she walked to the door on the right and knocked. A voice called out, then Sunshine opened the door, stepped inside, and returned a few moments later with two men following. One man was older, like Sunshine, the other was like the young adults at the Haven.

While Sunshine stood aside with the younger, the older man came to Hannah and knelt so that he was at eye level. Not unkindly, he asked her name, and after she answered, he took her hand and lifted it gently. Hannah looked to Sunshine for assurance, and Sunshine nodded. Understanding the man's intention, Hannah stood.

His eyes went from her head down, down to her feet and then back up again. He touched Hannah's hair, just a little flick against the strands by her ear, and then turned to Sunshine.

"Much better," he said.

Sunshine said, "Hannah, I need to run some errands; you stay here with Mr. Cárcan, and I'll be back in a bit."

Hannah felt a spike of panic, not because she was afraid of this man or that she minded being away from Sunshine—definitely not that—but because she was being left alone with an outsider from the Void, and that was very much against the rules. Everyone kept a buddy in the Void, everywhere and always. It was one of The Prophet's principles of obedience, and to break this meant God couldn't protect you.

But Sunshine said to do it, and Hannah could only do as instructed.

When Sunshine had gone, the man said, "Do you like ice cream?"

Hannah nodded, and his eyes moved kind of funny. "Come," he said. "I have a freezer in my office."

She followed him into a room that could only be called an office because of the big desk, but everything else about it made it look like a living room. The man's phone rang and he took the call while opening the little freezer. He pulled a frozen bar from inside, handed it to Hannah, and motioned her to sit while he nodded to the voice on the other end, and then he laughed.

"Yes, of course," he said, "they're too simple and naïve to know better, but they are very close to God and I like to have God on my side." He'd switched to Spanish without appearing to care if Hannah understood; he probably assumed that she didn't, because he didn't bother whispering or stepping outside the room.

Still on the phone, the man laughed again and said, "Yes, but in any case it's like having your own personal priest, and I can't help that I like them. Religion, sex, and a simple mule, it doesn't get any better than that."

Hannah didn't understand the meaning of the words, but just as when listening to Zadok or Sunshine, it was always best to look dumb and pretend to not care.

She was on the couch, face toward the wall, fully focused on the ice cream bar, tasting it slowly to make the rare treat last as long as possible, when she realized that the room was silent and she couldn't remember for how long. She turned to look around.

The man was off the phone, sitting on the edge of his desk, studying her, rubbing his thumb slowly up, slowly down, between his legs. All the feelings of discomfort and trouble, and the uneasiness that she couldn't pinpoint, which had gone away a little with the ice cream, came back even more, and the knot in her stomach made it impossible to take another taste.

Hannah felt like she might throw up, so she just held the bar, unsure of what to do with it.

The man continued to stare, continued to do what he was doing, and finally, when slow drips began to trickle down her hand, he stood, took the mess from her, and said, "Take off your dress."

The words were like a smack across the face. Like trouble. Bad trouble. And the uncomfortable feelings were so bad now that Hannah couldn't move.

"You love your Prophet?" the man said.

Hannah nodded.

"And your auntie, she told you to obey, yes?"

She nodded again.

"Then do the will of The Prophet, and obey," the man said.

The words were right, but they were confusing coming from this outsider in the Void, and the uncomfortable feelings were now both inside and outside. It wasn't fear, but yes, it was fear. She should do what he said, she needed to obey, he might hit her, or worse he might tell Sunshine, but Hannah still couldn't move.

The man tossed the ice cream into a trash can and wiped his fingers on his pant leg. He reached for her hand and, more roughly than he'd done in the reception room, pulled her to her feet.

"Come," he said. "I will help you."

His hands were impatient as he turned her around so that her back faced him. It was not new, what he was doing, even if this experience outside the Haven and with this man were new. He tugged the dress zipper and Hannah closed her eyes. Behind her lids the tears burned hot, but she would never let them surface. She breathed long and slow, and let her mind run away, far away, to the hidden and forbidden daydreams where nothing bad happened, where there was no trouble, where she was special and wanted, and always, always safe.

Chapter 5

Logan pulled the picture from his wallet and placed it on the table. The photo had been taken when Hannah was five years old, just three days before she'd been walked out of class, down the hall, through the school's front doors, and, as they'd later learned, driven over the border and into Mexico.

From across the table, Gideon, the IT director, pulled a printout of a scanned photograph from his computer bag. He placed it on the table next to Hannah. The photo was old, dated in the way most photographs are—by hair and clothing, and the odd color it assumed over time.

"David Law," he said.

A breeze caught the edge of the paper, lifting it slightly, and Gideon placed his glass on the corner to hold it in place.

Munroe's eyes came alive, and she reached for the page, David Law's picture, that spark the first hint of hope that Logan had sensed since she'd arrived on the terrace.

She'd seen the photo of Hannah now three times, but this was the first time she'd been shown David Law's, and even a casual observer would have spotted the intensity with which her eyes roamed over his picture.

Her glance darted back and forth between David and Logan and their striking similarities: blond hair, green eyes, similar bone structure.

"David and I aren't related," Logan said to her unasked question, "at least not that I know of. David was Charity's boyfriend at the time—a cult baby, like us. He's the one who kidnapped Hannah and took her back inside."

"Where is Charity?" Munroe asked. "Why isn't she here?"

"She wanted to be here," Logan said. "But she couldn't make it and so asked me to speak on her behalf. She says 'hi' by the way."

Munroe nodded.

Logan paused, mentally framing the context and where to continue. Over the years Munroe had heard snippets of this story, and twice her path had briefly crossed with Charity's. Munroe knew vague details of Hannah's kidnapping because during an unusual outburst of frustration Logan had railed against the injustice of it all, but beyond that, he'd told her little.

"It took me four years to coax Charity out," Logan said. He tapped his head. "For many of us the thickest bars are in here. It takes time to overcome the fear and the guilt that a life of conditioning has put into you—especially when all you've ever known has you terrified of the outside. Anyway, I had an apartment ready, a job lined up for Charity and day care for Hannah, and when Charity finally made her break, David came along. Five months after they'd gotten settled, David took off with Hannah and went back."

"What do you mean, 'he came along'?"

"David was Charity's boyfriend, not Hannah's father," Logan said. "And he and Charity hadn't been together long—maybe a year total, if that—so he kind of just hitched a ride, so to speak."

"You're certain he wasn't Hannah's father? No chance at all?"

"Not according to Charity."

"Then why did he feel he had a right to take her?"

"No idea," Logan said. "Because he didn't have one. He got hold of her passport and then forged a power of attorney, took her across the border, and from there hopscotched into South America."

"So this wasn't a custody issue of two parents fighting over who keeps the kid?"

"Not at all," Logan said. "It was out-and-out child abduction." He paused and tried to find the words. "It's hard to find the ground under your feet when you leave," he said. "Life comes at you so fast, there's so much you weren't prepared for, and it sometimes feels like every day is a new attempt to break up to the surface for air. But since I'd already made the way for Charity, David didn't have that problem. If he'd really wanted to do something with his life on the outside, he had more opportunity than any of us did, had it very easy by comparison—"

Heidi, the project manager who was sitting next to Gideon, interrupted. "David never really fit in though," she said.

Munroe said, "You knew him?"

Heidi nodded. "He didn't seem to care much, didn't make much of an effort to do anything, just kind of mooched off Charity, really. Not everyone can make it out here. Some go back. A lot of it depends on why they left in the first place."

"We don't know why he left—why he came with her," Logan said. "He could have loved her for a while, or it could have been curiosity, or maybe he didn't like being ordered around every day . . ."

"Never a good reason," Heidi said.

"Or it could be that he was asked to leave with Charity and then bring Hannah back."

"Would the leaders do that?" Munroe said. "Order him to find an opening to take her back?"

Logan shrugged. "They don't feel society's laws apply to them."

Heidi said, "Their views on the children born into the group are more like property ownership. Even if they didn't order it, even if he got the idea and planned it on his own—which we doubt—they've done well at protecting and hiding him ever since. That's why it's taken us so long to find her."

"And now that you've found her?"

"We want you to get her out."

Munroe returned the photo to the table and slowly placed Gideon's glass back on top. She sat back and then grinned. "You want me to kidnap her."

She'd made a statement, not asked a question, and Logan knew with certainty that she'd said it for his benefit and no one else's. It was classic Munroe. *Have you really thought this through?*

There was silence around the table.

Munroe said, "Now that you know where she is, wouldn't this be the time to go the legal route?"

"It's not that simple," Logan said.

Eli, the med student, said, "We've already tried that. If David returns to the U.S. he'll be arrested. He's also wanted by Interpol, and we figure that's why he keeps to less-developed countries—less technology, harder to find him. But even still, none of it does any good when it comes to actually getting to Hannah."

"And we're trying to get to her with minimal collateral damage," Logan added.

Munroe said, "Collateral damage?"

"We know where she is, we know the country and the city. We don't know specifically which commune. There are at least three in the immediate area. If we get law enforcement involved, in order to find her they will raid the communes. All of the children will be taken into protective custody, and events have a way of spiraling out of control. There's also a good chance that in the confusion we'll lose Hannah again, especially if they've forged her documents using a different name."

"Don't misunderstand," Heidi said. "We definitely think it's an unhealthy environment, and it's not that we don't care about the other kids, but at the same time, ripping them away from the only structure they know and putting them in South American juvenile centers isn't the solution."

Munroe paused and then said, "I assume this has happened before?"

"Yes," Logan said. "And then some. No matter how we may feel about The Chosen and its leaders or even about some of the individuals within it, the children are our brothers, sisters, and cousins. Right now, this is about Hannah. Charity has full legal custody, there are warrants out for David's arrest, and it's just a matter of getting close enough. The cleanest way to do it is to get behind their doors."

"None of us can do it," Gideon said. "They know us. As soon as we get close, they'll know what we're doing, and they'll move her again."

"So what you're saying is that in order to get her out, I've got to get in."

"Pretty much."

Munroe was silent for a moment, and Logan could see analysis written on her face.

"This happened eight years ago," Munroe said, "so Hannah is what? Twelve? Thirteen?"

"Thirteen," Logan said.

"In the United States, children's passports are only good for five years, and parents have to be present in order to renew them—a situation like this, renewal in a foreign country, only one guardian who's not even a parent—it's going to raise serious questions. If the alerts are out, as you say they are, why hasn't she been picked up at a consulate or embassy when her passport expired?"

"It's happened before," Heidi said, "with another family. So now the leaders are wise to that and won't let it happen again. As best as we can tell, she's no longer using an American passport, but we're not sure which country she carries."

"So, what you're saying," Munroe said, "is that for all intents and purposes, in whichever country she's living, she's not an American citizen." She paused for effect. "Which means that essentially you want me, an American, to go into a foreign country, kidnap what may possibly be a citizen of that country, and bring her to the United States?"

"If you want to put it cut-and-dried like that, then yes."

Bethany had spoken, the real estate agent, and her tone had a sarcastic edge. "We're looking for someone who has the acting ability to get inside, the fortitude to endure it, and the skill to get her out."

"Okay, look," Munroe said. "Assuming that I'm capable of doing it, assuming that I even want to do it, I can see Logan's point in all of this—Charity being his childhood friend and his having been involved in searching for Hannah all these years. But what's in it for the rest of you? You didn't fly in from around the country and offer to put money in a pot just because of an arbitrary connection to a thirteen-year-old girl. Are you each related to Charity or Hannah or Logan in some way? There's got to be more."

"Eli is Charity's half brother," Logan said. "And although we each have our private reasons—certainly some of this is about us and our personal issues with the past and the people who were responsible for what happened—it's primarily about Hannah."

Munroe said, "Or revenge?"

Logan said, "If we want to avoid semantics entirely and call it by its most simple definition, then yes."

She stood and said to Logan, "I need to think about it."

After Munroe left, there was a momentary silence, and then one on top of the other the opinions and comments flowed, a mesh of conflicts and agreements that grew in volume.

"Goddamn it, Logan," Gideon said, "the way you described her, described the plan, the whole thing seemed plausible, but seriously, who are we trying to kid? We *might* be able to get Michael in, but how the hell is she supposed to get herself, much less Hannah, out?"

"She can do it," Logan said.

"Just because you like her and trust her doesn't mean we do. Just because she's willing to do the job—assuming she's willing to do it—that doesn't mean she *should* do it. We get one shot at this. If she screws up, it's game over."

"She can do it."

"It's not just about Hannah," Heidi said. "You *know* that if this goes wrong, it's going to come back to burn us."

Logan rolled a bottle of water between his palms, then set it down on the table and stood. "Eli, how much are you putting into the pot?"

"About three grand."

"Ruth?"

"Five."

Bethany held up two fingers and the others did as she had, fingers speaking the words, as Logan's eyes went from one to the other.

"That's what? Twenty-five grand between us in order to pull this off, right? Anyone want to venture a guess on what Michael's last contract paid out?"

Gideon said, "I dunno, fifty thousand?"

Logan paused, waited a beat, and then said, "Five million dollars."

The table fell silent.

"Yes, Michael is my friend," Logan said. He paced. "She's my friend, which is the only reason this project even registers on her radar screen. Twenty-five grand won't even cover expenses on a job like this. Michael's not looking for crazy, she's here because I asked her to come. If she does this, it will be for me. We can sugarcoat it as much as we like, but she's not stupid, she's been down this road before and knows that even the cleanest of ins comes with a complicated out."

"How's her Spanish?" Bethany asked.

"Last count, she spoke twenty-two languages." Logan sat and leaned forward, elbows to knees. "I don't know, it could be more by now. But yeah, she's fluent."

Bethany continued, "So, assuming she gets in and locates Hannah, assuming she's able to get her away from the commune, does she even know what it's like dealing with corrupt officials—and what if things go wrong and she ends up having to take the rural routes out of the country? Can she do it?"

"Let me put it this way," Logan said. "If it came down to pulling a trigger to protect Hannah and get her safely out of the country, Michael wouldn't hesitate." He paused and held his hands up in a form of backed-off caution. "I'm not saying she would go in guns blazing, I'm just saying that she's capable of doing it if necessary. And she's spent more of her life navigating shit-hole, despot-run countries than any of us, including Gideon."

"I have a hard time seeing it," Gideon said.

"Hey, don't take my word for it," Logan said. "She's downstairs. I dare you. I dare you to go pick a fight. No wait, you don't even have to do that. I dare you to lay a finger on her. Touch her shoulder, grab her wrist, anything."

"I liked her," Ruth said, putting a pause on the tension. Ruth, the lawyer, who had until now remained silent. "She's smart, very smart, and I think she actually gets it."

"I'll agree to that," Heidi said. "She gets it. But can she do it?"

"The question is not can she do it," Logan replied. "It's will she do it."

Chapter 6

Munroe pulled down the cap that shadowed her face, shoved her hands into the pockets of cargo pants, and with a furtive glance over her shoulder crossed the street.

Even in the early morning, that cooling time marking the close of day for some and the beginning for others, the city remained wrapped in a familiar heat, torrid and sticky. She inhaled the aroma of civilization and moved up Fifth Avenue, in the direction of Central Park, hoping against the inevitable, for an evening without mishaps.

Mishaps. Like last night.

It would be easy to plead innocence, to say that she'd been in the wrong place at the wrong time, to say that it had been self-defense. But excuses were for cowards. Excuses couldn't bring the dead to life or undo the damage wreaked by a second of instinct. Blood was blood, no matter the reason shed.

She pushed back the thoughts. It was over and couldn't be undone.

She strode forward, one foot in front of the other, reaching the southeast corner of the park and following the illuminated paths, without regard to where she was or where she was going, focus turning from what had already transpired in this city to where she would go from here.

She was glad to have made the trip, if only to meet Logan's friends, to hear what they had to say and from their collective stories glean a clearer insight into Logan's past—although she was far more familiar with his history than he gave her credit for.

How could she not be? No matter the details that he'd conveniently left out over the years, he was her best friend and, like her, had a childhood marred by trauma. With the glimpses and tidbits he'd shared, she'd done what any good informationist would do. She'd looked.

Like his friends, Logan had been birthed into The Chosen of God, a movement spawned in the late 1960s that attracted thousands of teenagers and young adults out of society, the Void, and into the arms of The Prophet, a modern-day Moses who promised to lead his people out of Egypt.

They cut ties with family and friends, severed relationships with anyone who didn't believe as they did, creating instead a collective new family bound together by loyalty to The Prophet.

The Chosen established communes—Havens—around the globe, and like Logan's parents, those thousands of young people birthed even more thousands of children into the life of The Prophet, separate from the outside world. There was no consideration that the children might want another path, no possibility that the world might not end in their own lifetimes, and when, like Logan, the children grew and began to leave, they were cut off, demonized, and abandoned to fend for themselves in a world they didn't understand.

Logan's story, like that of so many of his friends', told of falling through the cracks of a society unaware that children like him existed, of watching many of his childhood friends succumb to drug abuse and suicide, of experiencing anxiety and stress disorders, of being clueless about social mores and customs, of fighting the prejudice and social stigma that followed, and then of clawing his way upward one exacting day at a time.

In one way or another, the stories, no matter how different or with how much levity they might be told, were still the same, and without intervention, it was this same story that little Hannah would be telling in ten years, if she was alive to tell it at all.

Munroe came to a fork in the path, flipped a mental coin, and then

Check Out Receipt

Ovitt Family Community Library
909-395-2004
www.ci.ontario.ca.us

Wednesday, May 27, 2015 5:31:42 PM

Item: 3252009108949
Title: The innocent : a Vanessa Michael Mu
nroe novel
Call no.: STEVENS, T.
Due: 06/17/2015

Item: 3252007979948
Title: The secret servant
Call no.: SILVA, D.
Due: 06/17/2015

Item: 3252009376249
Title: Sniper's Honor : a Bob Lee Swagger
novel
Call no.: HUNTER, S.
Due: 06/17/2015

Total items: 3

Renewals: 909.395.2042

HOURS:
Sunday: 1:00 pm - 4:00 pm
Monday - Thursday: 10:00 am - 9:00 pm
Friday - Saturday: 10:00 am - 6:00 pm
----

left the lights and the trail for an area that promised darkness and seclusion. A breeze swept through the treetops, and the moon, ripe above them, lit the way.

She was a child of the night, and nocturnal movement was familiar and cathartic—far better than remaining inside, cooped up, unable to sleep and cautious of stanching the tide of dreams one time too many.

But letting her mind wander, seeking solitude and getting away from Logan and his friends, wasn't the main reason for this foray into the park. She'd come here tonight because, just as had happened when she'd left the hotel the night before, she was being followed.

Her nature would have her make a game of it—keep up the guise of oblivion as long as possible for no other reason than that she could. But tonight wasn't the night for games. She needed to bring the pieces together.

She came at last to a bench, stopped, and waited, listening to the darkness. Certain he was there, she sat and, after another moment, spoke to the shadows.

"Come and join me," she said. "I'm tired of being stalked."

She heard his approach before she saw him, the bulk of his outline materializing from the dark as he drew near. His stride was casual, his shoulders squared, and his hands relaxed in a summer jacket's pockets. He stopped within a foot of her and gazed down with a subtle smirk, and she smiled in exchange.

Head tilted up and in his direction, she said, "Hello, Miles."

He nodded, returned the smile, and with arms crossed remained standing for a moment before joining her on the bench.

Silence.

"How long have you known?" he said finally.

"I spotted you at the airport," she said, and he chuffed.

In the full light of the moon she noted the way the months had left their mark. There were a few more wrinkles around his eyes and a three-inch sliver that traced from the base of his left ear across his jaw. She touched his face, ever so slightly, to tilt it away for a better view.

"I took a hit of shrapnel," he said. "I'm one scar closer to catching up with you." There was a longer silence and finally Bradford said, "Why didn't you say something and save me the hassle of playing surveillant?"

"And ruin the illusion of Logan's little"—Munroe paused and finger quoted the air—"intervention?"

"He's concerned—says you're medicating."

"Yeah, I am. But not for the reasons he thinks."

"Should I be worried?" he said.

She shifted forward, elbows to knees, face to the darkness. "Maybe." And then in the silence she struggled to find words that would adequately explain the veritable nightmare the land of dreams had become.

"Does it have anything to do with Africa?" he asked.

She glanced back toward him. "Who knows," she said. "I'm sure it didn't help." She turned again to face the darkness and, with half-shut eyes, said, "I've made my peace, Miles. I can't rewrite the past no matter how much I wish I could, and nothing I could have done would have changed anything."

She was quiet for a long while, and if Bradford wished to hurry her, he gave no indication of it.

"It started about a month and a half ago," she said. "Began as the occasional really bad dream and progressed into full-fledged violence. While I'm asleep, I have no awareness of what's going on, I only see the destruction after I've woken." She paused, turned toward him again. "It's bad enough to have a death on my hands when I'm awake," she said, "but now it can happen in my sleep. I don't trust myself, I have no way to control it, and so I knock myself out." She shifted back to staring at the dark. "I can only go so many days without sleep before I start to break down," she said. "Damned if I do, damned if I don't."

"Have you seen a doctor? At least gotten a proper prescription?"

She cut a glance in his direction. "We've already had *that* conversation."

It had been at their first meeting, a discussion about the value of psychiatric evaluations after Munroe had learned that Bradford was the one responsible for pulling together the research on her past on behalf of her employer.

She let the weight of her words settle and said, "Has Logan told you about the favor he's asked—his reason for bringing me here?"

"He hasn't. I'd assumed he got you here for your own sake."

"He wants me to make a trip to South America," she said, "to infiltrate some bad guys and steal his childhood friend's daughter back home."

Bradford said nothing and Munroe remained silent, allowing him to piece together the extent of Logan's altruism. Bradford let out an audible sigh and with a protective edge said, "Where in South America? Is this thing drug cartel related?"

"Argentina," she said. "Not drug related, religion related. It's kidnapping, it's complicated, and probably the right thing to do. Truth is, even though the reasons behind it are sound, it's a crapshoot, and if anyone but Logan had asked, I'd have already said no."

"If you knew this," he said, "why did you come to New York?"

"I have my reasons."

"Noah?"

She nodded, although truthfully Noah was only part of it.

"Will you be going back to Morocco?" Bradford asked.

"I don't know," she said.

He was quiet, and Munroe knew that as much as he wanted to pry, he wouldn't. In time, perhaps, there would be reason to bare her soul, expose the pain, to put into words what Bradford already instinctively knew. But not now.

After a pause, Bradford said, "Besides the lack of sleep and the drugs, how are you really?"

She shrugged. "Messed in the head as ever—you saw what happened last night."

"Some of it," he said. "I lost you around a corner, and by the time I caught up with you there was one dead guy at your feet and another limping away."

"It happened fast," she said. "Sadistic fucks."

"Defending yourself isn't messed in the head," he said.

She turned to him. "Isn't it? No one makes me walk the streets at two in the morning. I don't have to lurk in the dark alleys, or the lonely trails, just waiting for trouble to invite me to play." She looked out toward the path they'd taken to the bench. "What's the difference," she said, "between seeking out a victim and playing the victim, knowing that predators will seek me out?"

"There's a huge difference."

She opened her mouth to say something and then stopped. This was another topic for another time. "How long are you in town?" she said.

"That depends," he said. "How long are you in town?"

She let out an involuntary laugh. "You can't be serious. Is Logan paying you?"

"Don't be an ass, Michael. No, Logan's not paying me."

"What then?"

A pained look crossed his face. "You have to ask?"

She exhaled audibly, slowly, stretched back and stared up at the sky. "I apologize," she said. "I know what being here for me costs you." She turned toward him and then back to the night. "I truly appreciate it—more than you might ever know—I just don't think it'll do much good."

"Maybe, maybe not," he said. And then after another pause, "You know I respect you, right?"

She nodded.

"Good," he said. "Because I think you're insane to carry those knives while you're impaired. You intend to medicate consciously and you're trying to master the usage, but it's like driving drunk, you think you're in control and you're not. Michael, you're dangerous enough clean and weaponless."

"I'm not off on some loony drug-induced binge," she said.

"I understand that," he said, "but we both know you don't carry those knives for self-defense—you don't need them. Kill someone with your hands and you might have a plausible reason to escape jail for the rest of your life. With a knife, you're screwed, and you know it. Why take the risk?"

Risk. A word bandied about so easily by people who had no clue as to what risk really meant. From anyone else those words would have been trite and easy to brush aside, but this was the man who had saved her life, a man who knew the truest meaning of what it was to risk everything.

After another space of silence, she pulled three knives from their hidden places. Without ceremony, she placed them on his lap.

He reached for the blades and held them in his hands. "Would you also let me take the drugs away?" he said.

"If you can take the nightmares with them."

He didn't reply, and she let him have the silence. In time, perhaps he'd understand. She tilted her head back and looked east, where the sky had turned purple. She stood.

"I need to get back to the hotel," she said. "Walk with me? You can stay in the suite if you like—it'll be more comfortable than holding vigil on the street."

"Don't you have a full house?" he asked.

"It's a big place," she said, "but either way you'd stay with me."

His brow furrowed, and, understanding the source of his confusion, Munroe hooked her arm in his and led him forward. "I'm trying, Miles," she said, "really trying. If you want to help and I'm willing to allow it, then let's do it right. Stay with me."

The sun had fully risen by the time they returned to the hotel, and when Munroe opened the door Logan was striding toward it. His face held a mixture of anguish and relief, as if he'd been pacing until her return and expected that it would never come. Then he saw Miles.

Logan blanched and stopped short. Shock replaced everything else.

Miles nodded and Logan continued frozen for a half-second before turning speechless toward the television, then to Munroe, back to the TV, and to Munroe again.

Tiring of his indecision, Munroe said, "What is it, Logan?"

In a disjointed movement he motioned toward the television, which, now muted, flashed pictures of the local news. "An NYPD officer was murdered night before last," he said. "This morning someone pulled the body out of a Dumpster."

He stared at Munroe's hands and arms, long since washed clean, and whispered, "Was that your doing?"

Mental dissonance filled her head. She couldn't reconcile what Logan said with what she'd experienced. *Police officer.* Wordless, she turned her back to him and, with the world moving in slow motion, joined Miles in front of the TV.

The sound was still off and a breaking news banner streamed, beneath a looped clip. She watched in silence, and after a moment Logan asked again, this time his question an accusing hiss. Munroe shifted away from the flat screen to face him and then, without a word, leaving him bewildered and panicked, turned and strode to her bedroom and closed the door.

She stood by the window, morning light reflecting onto her hands, and she gazed at the invisible macula of death that marked them. There was a quiet knock and the door opened. Bradford stuck his head inside the room and then, without waiting for a response, entered fully. He closed the door and walked over to her, staring out over the city.

"Did you leave evidence behind?" he asked.

She turned her eyes slowly to him and said, "Not that I know of."

Bradford reached forward, touched his thumb to her chin, and said, "Maybe taking this assignment would be a good thing."

She leaned her head into his hand. "If those men really were police, there's sure to be fallout, and I won't run from my mistakes."

"That would only be a side bonus," he said. "God knows you've needed a break, and I'm sure you've kept busy, but have you considered that the extended downtime might be part of your problem?"

She turned again toward the window, to the ants and toys that crawled along the city streets. There was no doubt that she needed to work; it had been almost eight months since Mongomo, and the internal pressure was steadily building—a violent tension that could only be eased by the pure focus of an assignment. But this thing that Logan offered? This was a form of madness.

"Death follows me," she said. "I can get the girl out, but I can't guarantee that others won't die, and one way or another, those people are all connected to Logan." She turned again toward the window and the city streets. "Logan is blinded by desire and need, so much so that he's ignoring the possibilities, ignoring the potential for"—she found Bradford's eyes—"the potential for savagery.

"There's something he's not telling me," she said. "He wants this far too badly for it to be as simple as what he's explained."

"But still, you go."

She nodded. "I'm bracing for it and the many repercussions."

Muted sounds of laughter filtered in from beyond the door, and they both turned toward it. "The rest of them are awake," she said. "It's time to play the game."

She pulled an ankle-length dress off a hanger in the closet and said, "Excuse me for a moment," and then stripped down, not caring if Bradford stared or averted his eyes, knowing he would want to do the former but do the latter.

Having shed the fatigues of the night and reverted once more to harmless and demure, she paused with her hand on the door handle.

"Coming?" she said.

Seeing her manner of dress, Bradford raised an eyebrow, and she grinned in reply, then closed her eyes, a brief flash in time while she shifted from one mode to the next. When she opened her eyes, she had become the girl who would walk out the door.

The four who had stayed the night had joined Logan in the living area, and as far as Munroe could tell, the lively discussion centered on breakfasts of times past. The television had been switched off, and although Logan interacted little, he did well at masking the undercurrents of stress that had so recently played across his face.

Munroe entered the room with Bradford beside her, and as had happened the day before, the conversation hiccupped when a stranger joined the mix; it was not so much a closing of ranks as a concern that the newcomer might misunderstand what he'd heard.

With a mischievous grin Munroe introduced Bradford. "Soldier of fortune," she said, "mercenary for hire, and sometimes my bodyguard."

Hands were shaken, small talk made, and Gideon said to her, "The way Logan tells it, you shouldn't need a bodyguard."

His words, spoken lightly, held the undercurrent of challenge, and Munroe, finding no reason to defend or explain, turned from him. She reached for the phone intending to order room service for the group, and Gideon stopped her, hand to her shoulder.

Gideon was thirty-five and bore himself with the assurance of a man who had experienced hand-to-hand combat and lived to tell about it. At six-foot-four and 240 pounds, he held a six-inch, hundred-pound advantage, and by his behavior seemed to believe that Munroe, in her late twenties, light, lean, and innocent, would be easily schooled.

Munroe froze. The room went silent. Her vision faded, the world turned gray, and her mind ran a series of rapid calculations. In that moment of suspended time, she yearned for the catharsis and soothing relief of pain, for the exhilaration of spilled blood.

Logan should have warned Gideon; he should have known.

She'd taken on larger men and feared nothing of it. To strike was instinct; second nature. She could move with devastating speed, a frightful sense of crazy that bordered on true insanity and became, not shock-and-awe, but shock-then-die; a drive to kill that had been carved into her psyche one savage knife slice after another.

Standing straight, her back still to him, her voice low and monotone, she said, "Remove your hand."

In minute calculations that reported back like echolocation, she placed each person in the room and readied for what was to come. Bradford had stood up from the sofa and then stopped. Logan had stayed seated. Neither would dare move for fear of triggering a violent reaction. The others had remained where they were, and Gideon's hand was still weighted on her shoulder.

Forcing down the urge to strike, her back still to him, she said, "I don't want to hurt you."

Gideon's fingers tightened. He pulled. "I'm talking to you," he said.

Darkness descended. Time ceased. Movement blurred. Instinct without thought, and then Gideon was on his knees, hands to his throat, gasping for air, and she was standing over him prepared to strike again.

Munroe's eyes darted to Logan, and instead of finding horror on his face, as she expected, he was smirking.

She understood then that this was Logan's doing—Logan and his stupid, dangerous games, proving points that didn't need proving. She stood upright, reached a hand for Gideon, pulled him to his feet, and gave him a gentle jab to his arm.

"Give it a few minutes," she said. "You'll be fine."

Conversation in the room slowly resumed and gradually the moment passed as if nothing had occurred. When breakfast arrived, the discussion turned again to the issue of bringing Hannah home. Logan said little and his eyes hurried often to seek Munroe's, as if begging assurance. She smiled in reply, but under the circumstances the gesture was probably more confusing to him than not.

In the stories of the children of The Chosen, in the sincerity of their pain, she understood the insanity of accepting the assignment and exactly why she would. There was no logic in it, no list of pros and cons; it defied the calculation and the meticulous exactness that had thus far defined her career. This desire to accept welled from deep inside; a child's innocent yearning from years long past; the prayers for rescue never answered.

In this round of discussion, Bradford asked the questions, and while the others answered, Munroe withdrew in order to observe body language and facial cues. As it had been yesterday, there was a collective aura of disbelief. And rightly so.

Unlike typical clients who wore expensive suits and made decisions with businesslike detachment, who had millions of investment dollars at their disposal, who plotted outside of board meetings, and who knew Munroe only by reputation, this assignment was being run on a shoestring and intensely personal—everything was being staked on the commitment and ability of a stranger.

The conversation increased in volume, and Munroe watched amused as the silent battle lines were drawn. Bradford's questions were direct, tactical, had less to do with sentiments and feeling than with logistics. He was a soldier ignoring emotion in order to calculate risk. His detachment wasn't personal, it was the way of war, and of those around the table only Gideon and Logan, each former military men, seemed to grasp it.

Munroe stood. A long and slow movement that pushed the chair back fully and stopped the conversation cold. She shifted forward, palms against the table, and said, "I'm ready when you are."

Chapter 7

Buenos Aires, Argentina

Hannah snuck down the stairs and tiptoed toward the kitchen. It was terribly disobedient being out of bed at this late hour, but she had to look, she couldn't sleep until she found out, and since she hadn't been in any trouble lately, if she got caught, it shouldn't be too bad.

Compared to her room, which was crowded and never really quiet, the house was very dark and very lonely, and the schedule board seemed at first just a blob along the hallway wall. Hannah stood in front of it, squinting at the marker print, looked for her name, and found it under the kitchen crew.

She groaned.

Normally she liked kitchen duty. It was way better than going out on the streets or to offices and stores in order to raise money, and definitely better than scrubbing floors and cleaning toilets. But if she was assigned to the kitchen, it would make it very difficult to find Rachel alone, because unlike Hannah, who rotated between the ministries, filling in wherever she was needed, Rachel had a full-time one. Rachel was a whole year older and stayed with her children's group all day, nights too, every day except on part of Sunday.

If Hannah was in the kitchen, she'd need a really good excuse to get to the toddlers' area to talk with Rachel, so tomorrow would have been a good day for cleaning toilets.

To tell what happened was disobedience, but Sunshine hadn't said anything about asking. And if what had happened to Hannah yesterday had also happened to Rachel, then nobody was really telling anything to anyone because they both already knew, and that made it sort of a gray area. Maybe. But the only person that Hannah could possibly go to, the only one who might understand, was Rachel.

Hannah would try, because sometimes the only way to feel better, when forgetting didn't work, was to talk to someone who knew how bad the thing could be.

It had taken Sunshine three whole hours to come back yesterday. The more time that passed, the meaner that man had become, and it had been harder and harder to stay far away in her mind and to hold back the tears. But she had.

And it seemed like Mr. Cárcan knew exactly when Sunshine was coming, because he'd let Hannah get dressed and then sent her to the reception room to be alone right before Sunshine walked in the door.

Sunshine had taken her back to the van, where Zadok was still waiting, and nobody said anything. If ever by accident you were alone with someone in the Void, the adults wanted to know everything, every word, to be sure you hadn't been spiritually poisoned or said something Secret to the wrong person. But this time they didn't seem to care, and maybe it was better that way because Hannah was ashamed and embarrassed and really, really didn't want to talk to them; she wanted to forget.

She understood that Sunshine had said it was Secret and that to talk about it was disobedience, but Sunshine needn't have bothered. Hannah would never talk to another adult about it; even without the warning, she knew better than that. If any of the Representatives found out, they would blame her, just like last year in Chile, when she'd told about Uncle Gabriel and they'd said that it was Hannah and her influencing demons that had tempted him, and it was she who had been shamed in front of the entire Haven, and then later punished more.

Hannah turned from the schedule board and tiptoed back down the hall, snuck up the stairs and then into bed, all the while trying to figure out how to arrange a way to talk to Rachel—Rachel, who had not so long ago been a good enough friend that the Haven leaders forbade them contact.

That was the way things were—you could be friends but not get so close that you were the best of friends. Best friends, like married people, might put another person above the Lord, or The Prophet, or the Haven, and tempt her to keep secrets. Sometimes, even if you were just good friends it might appear like best friends to the Haven leaders, and since you couldn't explain, you had to be careful, which they hadn't been.

Things were better now, at least they were allowed to talk to each other again, but the leaders still kept an eye on them, and that's why they'd moved Rachel into the toddlers' room and her full-time ministry, so there wouldn't be many opportunities.

In morning devotions, Hannah sat as still as possible, staring at the pages even though she wasn't reading. Her own conscience rebuked her, but she gave up trying to focus, because no matter how hard she tried, the words just filtered in and filtered out, and whole pages would pass before she realized she hadn't really read a single word.

The Instructives, the words of The Prophet, were important for her spiritual health and absolutely necessary to keep the Devil and his demons at bay, but her mind kept jumping. She tried not to fidget, tried not to look at the clock until, at last, the two hours ended, and the living room emptied.

More than a dozen people, some of them adults, but mostly young people who were rotators like Hannah, went to the schedule board to find their assignments for the day. Hannah already knew where she belonged but followed anyway, and after an appropriately long glance, went to the kitchen, where lunch preparation would soon go into full swing.

She found an opening in midafternoon when Hezekiah, the kitchen leader gave her a fifteen-minute break before dinner prep started. She liked Uncle Hez because he was easy on the rules and he wasn't serious and strict like most adults. As long as you worked hard and didn't disrespect, he didn't care about much else, and sometimes he even joked around.

Hannah knew the schedule, knew Rachel would be outside with her group, which wasn't as good as if they were in the toddlers' room, where no one would pass by and see them talking, but it was the best she would get. As long as nobody got very interested, and as long as neither Hannah nor Rachel went to the leaders about it, there shouldn't be a problem.

Today, Rachel sat on a makeshift bench, and nearby the six little ones played while Mercy, Rachel's eleven-year-old helper, stood watch over them.

When Hannah approached, Rachel scooted over on the bench to make room, but she didn't say anything. That was how it was when you got in trouble and were separated; it was hard to know how to start again.

Hannah sat down, but still Rachel stayed quiet, so Hannah watched Mercy play with two of the kids. The ten- to twelve-year-olds had it so much easier than the thirteen and ups—they worked only half days, still got to see their parents after dinner, and, best of all, still got to have a few hours of school. Hannah missed the school, mostly, and the fact that she never got a chance to learn how to do fractions.

Mercy moved a little closer to the bench, and Hannah could see on her face that she was curious about why she'd come. Even though Hannah would be very careful with what words were used, she didn't want Mercy to get close enough to hear the conversation, so quickly and quietly she said to Rachel, "Did he hurt you too?"

Rachel didn't look up, but after a while she nodded. The good part was that, without really having broken any rule, Hannah had learned something, and without being specific, they both knew what they were talking about.

But it was too risky to say more unless Rachel contributed. Hannah waited, but Rachel kept quiet, and before long Mercy was there right next to the bench like a nosy eavesdropper waiting to hear anything they said.

Hannah's time was up, and it had been mostly wasted except that now she knew she wasn't the only one—but because Rachel had been so quiet, she was a little worried that Rachel might say something to the leaders. With her stomach swirling, Hannah went back to the kitchen, and since her hands could work without her really needing to think much, and Hez wouldn't say anything as long as she kept up the pace, she let her mind wander through most of the afternoon.

It was late that evening when Uncle Elijah came for her.

He stuck his head into the girls' room and asked her to step out for a bit. He needed to talk to her, he said, and that was enough for Hannah to feel she'd have to throw up. There was never anything good that came from a talk.

She'd been careful, she'd not technically broken any rules, but in the end that didn't matter because apparently Rachel had reported her, and there was no way to know whether what she'd said was true or not.

Elijah took Hannah to his little office, put a sign on the handle, and shut the door. That was worse. Elijah was the main leader of the Haven. If he said don't come in, nobody would come in, and that meant anything was possible.

He told her to sit on one of the folding chairs. She did, and he sat opposite. He was quiet for a minute, staring down at her, and even if she wanted to look back at him, she just couldn't. Inside and out, her body was shaking, and the best she could do was to just hold back the tears that always came when she was afraid.

"The Lord has shown me that you've been disobedient," he said, "and we just can't have that. It's an opening for the Devil into our ranks."

Elijah didn't say what she'd done, they never did, and she was afraid to ask, because she might make it worse if she were to offer something he wasn't already aware of. And even though Hannah hadn't truly disobeyed today, she couldn't explain herself and so had to accept whatever he measured out.

It was so frustrating never being able to explain, to just swallow the punishment without at least having a chance to change things.

Hannah's eyes smarted.

"You'll be on probation for two weeks," Elijah said. "I've asked Morningstar to be your Keeper for that time, and you'll be on silence restriction until I feel your heart is right with the Lord again."

Hannah nodded, and though she tried to fight back the tears, she couldn't. The fear, the things that happened on that trip into town, Rachel reporting her, this punishment—all of it was too much, too fast, one thing on top of another without anything in between to help dull the effects and no time to process and shove them away.

And there was relief too. Two weeks of being watched full-time by Morningstar and not being allowed to talk to anyone else wasn't so bad, not nearly as bad as being paddled in front of all the members of the Haven until she begged for mercy.

But the tears came, and once they started, they just kept coming. A few were okay, they showed she was repentant, but too many could mean more trouble, and still she couldn't stop them. Big, huge racking sobs until finally Elijah reached for her hand and pulled her onto his lap.

"Maybe I've been a bit harsh with you," he said. "The Prophet teaches that punishment without love is against the laws of God, and it's important that you know how very much the Lord loves you."

Elijah's hands wandered up to the inside of her nightshirt and rested on her bare legs. His touch made her uncomfortable and even more nauseous than when she walked with him to the room knowing that the talk would bring something bad.

Elijah said, "Perhaps the problem . . . perhaps the reason you were led into disobedience is because you haven't been receiving enough of the Lord's love, sweetie."

Hannah tried to stop crying, she knew where this was going and wanted to get away. But until the tears were gone, she had no excuse. Elijah had put her here on his lap and she couldn't just get up without inviting a whole new bunch of problems.

"Being reproved is the Lord showing his love for you, sweetie. Sometimes God has to hurt you so that you can learn to behave. But yes, maybe I've been too harsh, and tenderness is what you need."

Hannah wanted off Elijah's lap, and even if it made Jesus angry, she didn't want this kind of love. She fought back the tears, fought them, but they wouldn't stop, and the only thing she could do now was to go to that other place, to let her mind run far, far away again so she wasn't here in this room, with this man or anywhere near anything to do with the blessing of love.

Chapter 8

John F. Kennedy International Airport,
New York

Against every principle of work and survival, Munroe boarded the flight to Buenos Aires with a three-person entourage. She hadn't asked Logan and his friends to come, and didn't waste energy refusing when they insisted. In her own time and on her own terms, she'd have her way.

She worked alone. Information was a solitary job. She was a shadow, a ghost, blending to become whatever was necessary to get the assignment done. She endured no partners or tagalongs, no buddy to screw things up, and relied on and worried about no one and nothing but herself. This was the policy that kept her invisible and kept her alive.

Aside from the stint in Africa with Miles Bradford at her side, the closest Munroe had to a partner was Logan. From a distance, Logan watched her back. If she needed help, he ran the other end of the assignment. He was the supply source, the go-to guy, the one who fed the air hose when she descended into the trench.

And at the moment he was quickly moving from being useful to being a liability.

She'd assumed that saying yes would have calmed him, that knowing her as he did, he would have relaxed, handed the job to the professional and allowed her to do what she did best. Instead, Logan hovered, micromanaged, and, so typically difficult to faze, had become obsessive in his need to run updates, opinions, and information.

He was one of the three who'd demanded to be a part of this circus, and now Munroe followed him along the dry interior of the plane, through economy class, scanning the faces of those already boarded, and, as was her habit, touching seatbacks in a silent count from the nearest emergency exit. Behind her trailed Heidi, then Gideon, all of them waddling down the aisle like hatchlings after a parent.

Nonstop from New York to Buenos Aires meant eleven hours of flying time, and the short-notice ticketing meant that the best they could do for seating was groupings of two, separated by fourteen rows.

Halfway through the cabin, Logan paused to lift his carry-on into an overhead bin, and Munroe stopped him, slipping the boarding pass from his hand as she did.

She'd humored him and tolerated his incessant interruptions and questions as long as she could, but having him in the seat next to her overnight would likely find him murdered in the morning.

"I'm sitting with Heidi," she said.

In a moment of quiet confusion, Heidi looked to Logan for assurance. Logan hesitated and then nodded, lips drawn tight. By way of rapport, Munroe gave his shoulder a playful jab, and his eyes returned gratitude.

She stepped aside. Heidi slipped beyond her to the window, and Munroe moved out of the aisle to let Gideon pass. The boys continued toward the rear of the plane, and as Munroe stared after them, her original suspicion that Logan was withholding something turned to certainty.

Luggage and paraphernalia stowed, Munroe tossed a thick manila folder onto the open seat tray, all of it overnight reading.

Heidi said, "You don't sleep much, do you?"

Munroe opened the folder, an assemblage of documents that Logan had handed her shortly before boarding, and said, "You noticed."

Heidi smiled, radiating warmth. "It's hard to miss, and it always seems that brilliance accompanies lack of sleep. Being one of those eight-hour-a-night people, I envy the extra hours of living."

At five-foot-six, Heidi was a brunette with baby blues, a few extra pounds, and a magnetic personality that belied her thirty-six years. She also had the ability to articulate complex ideas with concise simplicity, and although this surely made her an excellent project manager, to Munroe, this capacity was a portal to be tapped—a temporary window into life as a child of The Chosen.

Munroe paused at the subtle compliment, tried to discern flattery, felt only sincerity, and said, "Don't envy it too much. Sometimes the price isn't worth it."

Heidi pulled a book from her purse and creased it open. "Logan says you were raised a missionary kid, kind of like us."

Munroe nodded. "Born in Cameroon," she said, "West Africa."

"Is that why you have a guy's name?"

"In a roundabout way," Munroe said. "When I was seventeen, I bribed my way on board a freighter headed to Europe—didn't want to invite trouble by looking like a woman, so I shaved my hair, bound up my chest, and wore boy's clothes. I needed a name to go with the look, and that's where Michael came from."

"Did it work?"

"The name?"

"The look."

Munroe gave Heidi a sideways glance. "If I did it again today, you'd think I was a guy."

Heidi raised a chiding eyebrow, and Munroe didn't begrudge the disbelief. You had to see it to understand.

"Why'd you choose Michael?" Heidi said.

Munroe said, "It seemed appropriate. She was King David's wife in the Bible, and she couldn't have children."

Heidi smirked. The Bible was familiar territory. "The spelling was different," she said.

Munroe nodded. "And she wore girl clothes."

"So do you," Heidi said. "So why the guy's name?"

"I spend more time out of girl clothes than in them," Munroe said. "Work takes me to some pretty rough places, and quite like boarding that freighter, it's easier to get what I want done as a guy. My clients don't expect me to be a woman either, so the name fit, and it stuck."

"What's your real name?"

With a lengthening grin, Munroe said, "Vanessa."

As if sharing a secret, Heidi tipped closer. "My real name's Bathsheba," she whispered. "I hated it so much I had it changed after I got out of The Chosen—adopted my middle as my first."

"Michael and Bathsheba," Munroe said. "We should find us a David."

Heidi laughed and returned to her book, and Munroe to the papers in her hands. She removed a paper clip, shuffled pages, and phased from one mode into the next.

In the world of information, life depended on accuracy. Assumptions and familiarity were treacherous, and it was a far different perspective standing here on the precipice of infiltration and kidnapping than it was glimpsing snapshots of Logan's life while chugging beer and shooting pool.

The challenge of weaving herself into this particular assignment would be absorption without bias, to replace everything she thought she knew with what she must know. These documents, all of them background information on The Prophet and The Chosen, were vital to understanding.

She sat with highlighter in hand, notepad on the side, and takeoff, with its obligatory *seats to their upright position*, was a bleep on the periphery of Munroe's concentration, and the hours passed until she leaned back to stretch and realized Heidi was studying her.

Munroe ignored the overt interest, circled and diagrammed across the printed page, and finally put the pen down. At this Heidi said, "It's a lot to cover—you read fast."

"This is the first run," Munroe replied. "I'm laying tracks, building a skeleton. Doing it last-minute while en route makes it very easy to miss critical pieces—it's why I wanted you sitting with me," she said. "There's a lot inside you that will never show up on these pages."

Predictably, Heidi relaxed. Munroe said, "Was it like this for you also? This fifth- or sixth-grade education thing?"

"Very much so."

"You give the impression of having been well educated," Munroe said. "How, having been given so little, did you manage to get so far?"

"Education isn't the same thing as intelligence and drive," Heidi said, and she smiled again. It was a sweet seduction, so subtle that most would not have even been aware of it, perhaps even Heidi wasn't aware. It was a natural part of her charm, and in this, Munroe noted, Heidi and Logan were very similar.

Heidi said, "Back in the day, some of us craved input so badly that we'd sneak stuff to read. Dictionaries. Occasionally an encyclopedia volume—we sometimes had them in the Havens, we just weren't allowed free access to them. So we'd sneak them."

"Did you ever get caught?"

Heidi sighed, almost nostalgically. "Yeah. One time I ended up locked in a closet for three days without food while they prayed over me and tried to cast out the demons that would have caused me to yearn for knowledge from the Void." She laughed. "Guess it didn't do much good."

Munroe turned the last of a series of pages, flipped back, scanned her notes, and then returned again, searching for answers to a still formulating question. The haste with which the project had moved forward had left her dependent on Logan for details, and although nothing could replace the quality of her own work, he knew well the type of background she looked for and had handed her a thick stack of photocopies, internal documents, newspaper clippings, book excerpts, and hard copies of Internet pages. This had seemed enough to get her started, yet already she was stalled.

To Heidi she said, "Based on what's in these pages, it makes no

sense for The Prophet to live on the run or be wanted by Interpol. People aren't arrested for being different unless those differences break
laws."

Heidi's nose crinkled. She tilted her head, as if puzzling the question herself, and then after a second pointed to the documents and
said, "Can I see those for a moment?"

Munroe passed the pages over, and Heidi gave a cursory glance
through them. "There's a lot of stuff missing," she said.

"Why?"

Heidi shrugged. "You'd have to ask Logan, but it's not exactly
stuff that's easy to forget." And then, waiting only a half beat, Heidi
changed the subject, spilling in a rush the question that had undoubtedly been eating at her for the last several days.

"Michael, why are you doing this?" she said. She paused and started
again, slowly, as if she were measuring words, afraid that they might
be misunderstood. "Why have you agreed to this job? Not money,
that's for sure, and not for the cause. So why? Because Logan's your
friend? Is that enough?"

Munroe leaned back, the question of the missing documents
shoved away for the time being. How to explain what she herself barely
understood? She said, "I have a unique skill set, Heidi. I'm doing this
because I can."

Sliding doors opened to the shock of chill, and following the others,
Munroe stepped from the terminal into the overcast midmorning at
Ezeiza, Argentina's largest airport.

The hours in flight had taken them from the soggy heat of New
York to the middle of a Buenos Aires winter, and Munroe inhaled
deeply, taking in the mixture of diesel fumes, exhaust, and cold, mist-
ing rain: the fragrance of an airport, the same mixture of smells that
preceded every job, the perfume of assignment, of focus and concentration.

During the trip Logan and Gideon had mapped out an itinerary and, now that they were on the ground, had assumed a shared command of the little group. Heidi seemed to have no problem allowing them to lead, so Munroe nodded assent and, in apparent quiet acquiescence, said little.

How Logan could possibly believe that her skill was best served by taking orders from someone who hadn't even a fraction of her knowledge or experience was difficult to comprehend, and performing as a lackey, marching to someone else's pattern, was out of the question. She'd come on board to bring the little girl home, and her expertise had been called on because she could do a job that nobody else could. Any perceived compliance was only temporary and would never be genuine.

The others tossed luggage into the trunk of a taxi. Gideon, due to his size, rode shotgun, the three remaining sharing the backseat.

Unlike the rest, who had packed appropriately for the trip, Munroe had brought only a single change of clothes and a jacket barely warm enough to keep out the penetrating chill. She carried these in a small backpack that she now kept with her.

Traveling light came naturally after years on the job. Things had to be carried, concerned about, fussed over, and since they would only slow her down, were usually abandoned anyway. She would procure and shed as she went, holding on to only that which was critical to get the job done.

The taxi pulled away from the curb, careening directly into traffic. The driver sped forward, merging with kamikaze-like aggression in the direction of the airport exit and the freeway that would run them toward the heart of the country's capital.

Munroe gazed out the window, the cityscape passing in rapid flashes. Square block apartment houses and residential districts swapped with shopping areas and advertisements several stories high, and traded again. At its heart, the forty-eight districts of the city proper composed an urban area of three million people, but in reality the metropolitan mass stretched outward to the suburbs, tying together ten million more.

Half the population of Argentina lived in this vast urban sprawl, and when it came to needle searching through haystacks, Buenos Aires was one of the largest in South America or, for that matter, the world. Somewhere out there, among those millions, was a child, and in one of those many houses and high-rise apartment blocks, the Haven that hid her.

In the city proper the scene shifted yet again. It was for good reason that Buenos Aires had been called the Paris of South America. Old World–inspired architecture, tree-lined avenues, and sleek, modern designs bespoke not only the city's current sophistication but also a culture steeped in European history.

Chapter 9

San Telmo, Buenos Aires

Their hotel wasn't a hotel but rather a hostel, a small single story of shared and private rooms, a common kitchen, and a small living area, located south of the city center in the oldest neighborhood. The area was made up of colonial buildings and cobblestone streets, cafés, and *milongas,* all of it vibrant and alive with color, and here they would stay until Munroe had a better grasp of what the job entailed and the length of time required to pull it off.

Like Munroe, Logan was committed for the duration, but Gideon had only two weeks and Heidi three before they each had to return home. Without consulting Munroe, they'd developed their own set of expectations as to how quickly the project would progress, and as with everything else surrounding their involvement, Munroe ignored them, and ignored the expectations.

The little group had two rooms, side by side, and the boys' master plan and the minimal operating budget called for Munroe to stay with Heidi. The walls, though thin, were a continuation of the same barrier that fourteen rows of seats had thankfully provided during the flight, and although this arrangement was better than being cooped up with either Gideon or Logan, sharing a room did not provide the solitude Munroe so desperately craved.

She needed sleep, needed it badly. She'd promised Bradford that she'd at least try to go under without medicating, but none of this was possible while sharing a space with someone else.

Gideon had allotted a few hours to clean up, rest, and otherwise settle before reconvening in the late afternoon. Fighting the urge to drift off, Munroe lay down, waited until Heidi reached the rhythmic patterns of sleep, then slipped from her bed and headed out the door.

She was halfway along the corridor that led to the street when she heard the expected footsteps behind her. The predictability pleased her, and without turning she continued forward.

From behind, in a stage whisper that bordered on a hiss, Logan said, "Michael, please, wait for me."

She slowed, and he continued toward her, keeping pace as she turned onto the narrow avenue that fronted the hostel. Logan said nothing as they walked but stayed so close that Munroe wanted to push him back.

It was nearing two in the afternoon, that time of day when the city stopped for lunch, and she searched for a café, some populated place nearby, where conversation would be buzzing and she could listen and absorb. She wanted submersion in the local dialects, needed tone, inflection, accent, and *lunfardo*, the local slang of the *porteños*, the port dwellers, as the residents of Buenos Aires were known.

Five minutes from the hostel on a busy pedestrian corner, Munroe found what she sought. The café was crowded enough that conversation abounded and small enough to facilitate eavesdropping.

She sat with a steaming cup in front of her and, with Logan across the table, immersed herself in the ambience that filled the room. Language washed over her, through her, and in snapshot glimpses she drew in the soul of the local culture. It was the same inexplicable absorption and understanding of language that had been with her since childhood, the poisonous gift that both created and destroyed, an ability that made it possible for her to blend and become anything to anyone.

Conversation with Logan was a slow, interspersed interaction that allowed for gaps and pauses until the room slowly emptied and she turned to focus solely on him. "According to Heidi," she said, "I'm missing a few things from the document folder."

Logan paused and then chuffed—typical cover for a distasteful subject. "I've got some more stuff in my suitcase," he said. "I'll give it to you as soon as we get back to the room."

"Why'd you hold it back?"

He shrugged. "Just wanted you to read everything else first."

Munroe was silent a long while, irritation washing over her. The last thing she needed was evasion and truth bending from the one person she should be able to count on. She shifted forward, and tapping her finger against the table, Morse to thoughts, said, "What else are you holding back?"

He shook his head, a slow *nothing* to steady eye contact.

"You seem to have forgotten who I am," she said, voice low and monotone. "Seem to have forgotten what it is that I do, seem to believe that I've become blind and dumb."

She sat back, arms crossed, and stared at him, not with anger or malice, but with the neutral stare of analysis. "I agreed to do this job for you," she said, "but that agreement was based on years of friendship, Logan. A friendship based on honesty and trust." She paused, waited for effect, and then continued. "Without the honesty there is no trust, without the trust, no friendship. You're holding out on me, and unless you're willing to come clean, I will get up from this chair and walk out that door, and you know as well as I do that you will never find me unless I want you to."

She paused again and said, "I want the truth, Logan."

There was silence between them, a long and languid stillness that muted the last of the surrounding conversations into white noise.

Logan's eyes were on the table. Munroe waited, willing him to speak.

She would not, could not, be the first to break: not for love, not for friendship, not for any bond; not in this scenario. The only way she could proceed was if trust and friendship mattered more than protecting whatever secret he harbored.

The silence drew into moments, and knowing that he had made his decision, she stood to leave. Logan reached for her before she had fully risen, an almost desperate grab across the table, his hand on hers.

"Please don't go," he said.

"You leave me no choice."

"I'll tell you," he said. "Just give me a moment to collect my thoughts, okay?"

She sat again, and still silent, she waited.

When he finally spoke, his voice was a hoarse and broken whisper. "Hannah is my daughter," he said.

For nearly the entirety of her adult years Munroe had known Logan—knew him in a way that even his childhood friends did not—and never in all this time had there been any hint or whisper to confirm what he'd just said.

Maybe it was the succession of boyfriends filtering in and out of Logan's life that had blinded her to the possibility, or maybe it was because together he and she had shared everything else, and on trust alone she'd never expected such a secret, but either way, no matter how much she should have seen it coming, she hadn't.

The meaning of his words, as detached from reality as they appeared to be, somehow made sense of everything else. Logan's tenacity in finding Hannah, his connection to Charity, which went further than what he shared with the others, but most of all, his blind desperation for Munroe's involvement in retrieving the girl.

A hundred thoughts raced around her mind, synapses connecting, details placed and then replaced in rapid reorder, so as to put new meaning to past events, but as to the one piece to which she had no fit, the only thing she said was, "Logan, you're gay."

"Gay men father children," he said. "It happens all the time—men who stay in the closet, who marry and become fathers so that they appear straight to the world." He opened his wallet and pulled out the picture that he carried always. "Michael, look at her. Just look." He held the picture up next to his face, and the resemblance was so clear that Munroe wondered why she hadn't seen it the first time in Tangier.

"It was a confusing time," he said. "I was barely twenty. I'd gone from a homophobic cult to the homophobic armed forces, was still discovering who I was and what I wanted out of life. I'd just gotten back from a bloody tour . . ." He paused. "The shit I saw," he said. "Death was in my face, and I wanted comfort, sanity. I was questioning everything, and I returned to what was familiar. My family had moved to Mexico, so I went to visit their Haven.

"I didn't know if the Haven leaders would let me see them, didn't know if because I had been assimilated into the Void they would lock me out, so I brought five months' pay with me, a sacrifice, an offering of remorse. They let me stay for three days. Charity was there. We'd been very close friends throughout the years, and if ever I was physically attracted to a woman, it was her. I loved her. I knew that. And maybe I confused emotional love with physical love, I don't know, but one thing led to another.

"She got pregnant. If anyone had found out it was me—an outsider—an evildoer—a doubter—she would have suffered horrible consequences. So no one knew, no one could know. Even I didn't know until after Hannah was born. Charity couldn't tell me because her letters were screened and her phone calls monitored, and it wasn't until I'd returned for another visit that I learned.

"I visited as often as I could," he said. "Almost every dollar I earned went to the Haven, and even though it was against their rules, I snuck some to Charity too, so she could try to get things for the baby and maybe eat a little bit better. I built a facade of being repentant, and since I was still in the military I had a good excuse for why I couldn't return from the Void. I went through the motions of belief and gave them so much money that the Haven elders overlooked a lot of the rules.

"It wasn't a far step moving from the cult to the army, you know. I could take orders, knew how to keep my mouth shut and how to become invisible. I could march to someone else's drumbeat, and so I did a double march—in the military and in the Haven, juggling both worlds so that I could utilize the GI Bill and get the hell on with my life.

"When my contract ended, I had to stop visiting, and that's when I started planning for Charity to get out. You were with me, so you already know that side of the story. Up until then we'd had to keep a secret of everything in order to protect Charity. Once she got to Dallas, because David was with her and Hannah looked to David as a father-type figure, we wanted to go slow in broaching the whole thing. Then David kidnapped her, and one minute to the next she was gone."

Logan choked, struggled to regain composure and, with the words catching in his throat, said, "We knew he'd taken her back inside, and because I'd already done such a good job of buying my way in, it made the most sense that I would continue that way. While Charity has gone through the courts and the media and has done so well at keeping a spotlight on them that they hate her, I've done the opposite, keeping contacts and trying to get any piece of information I could from the inside. Nobody has any idea how connected Charity and I are, or how I truly feel." Logan paused. "You see then why we could never let on? Why it's been such a secret?

"For eight years those bastards have kept my daughter hidden and protected that fucking criminal ex-boyfriend. They've moved them from country to country to keep ahead of us, and now we finally know where she is.

"Please," he said, eyes imploring. "Michael, I need you."

Munroe nodded and squeezed his hand in a gesture of comfort and reassurance that only added to the burden she now carried. Failure had never been a viable option, but now it would come with the highest price. She understood Logan's torment, why this silent and buried obsession had driven him through the years, and how, by proxy, the weight was now hers. The child was no longer a random picture of a girl; she was the beating of Logan's heart.

Munroe slid her chair back and stood. "We need to go," she said. "The others are probably up and waiting for us."

Logan nodded and joined her. Hand in hand they returned to the hostel in silence.

Munroe stopped in front of her door, and Logan said, "Wait one second." She paused, and he went to his room, returning a moment later with another folder.

Eyes to the documents, holding them tightly, he said, "I held this back because, normally, once someone reads this, they ignore everything else." He paused. "You were right—I *had* forgotten who you are. Not forgotten so much as got swept up in the desire to finally get Hannah—overwhelmed by the fear and disgust and frustration of nearly a decade." He nodded to the folder. "I held it back because until now this hasn't done anything except to turn our pain into a media-circus freak show. Nobody really cares," he said. "The Chosen abused us, the media used us, law enforcement failed us, and justice is a farce. I was afraid," he said, "that maybe you would be no different." He looked up from the folder and met her eyes, and with tears welling in his, he handed it to her.

"I'm sorry," he said.

Munroe reached for him, held him tight, and said, "I'll bring her back, Logan. If it's the last thing I do, I'll bring her back. You have my word."

The information on Hannah's whereabouts had come from Maggie, Charity's sister, who was still a follower within The Chosen, her reticent confession a breaking of rank that had pinpointed the child's location to the city without going so far as to betray the details that could bring them to the doorstep of the Haven in which Hannah was hidden.

Needle in a haystack, and there were four ways to find it: dumb luck, taking the stack apart piece by piece, using a magnet, or burning it to the ground. On this assignment, luck was out of the question, time was at a premium, and destruction was not an option.

Gideon and Heidi would be Munroe's magnet.

They had each, at different periods, lived in Havens within or around Buenos Aires. But even if either one had a clear recollection of specifically where, even if they'd had an address, the information would have been worthless.

The Prophet believed that owning property tied The Chosen to the Void, and this meant that Havens were transient, relocating often, renting from landlords who had no idea that the couple who signed the lease agreement would the next day turn the property into a commune. When a stay had been worn-out, when neighbors had begun to complain, or the number of people attracted too much attention, the place would close down and The Chosen disperse.

Havens varied in size—some housed as few as thirty people and others upward of two hundred—but one constant was the necessity of clothing and feeding the many members. Havens needed cash to operate.

The Prophet also believed that working to earn money within the Void was the equivalent of serving Satan, and so The Chosen refused any form of work-for-hire that would enslave them to the world. What income the Havens did have was acquired, not through industry or providing any service to society, but rather by begging, by selling overpriced trinkets to the good-hearted under the guise of sponsoring humanitarian projects, or through donations.

But begging, although time-consuming, was not highly lucrative, and the resources required to feed and house so many far outstripped the supply. The solution to the disparity came by way of donated goods, clothing, shoes, and food—usually perishables too old and spotted to sell, and cartons or cans nearing or passed the date of expiration. There was a fine line between garbage and sustenance, and The Chosen walked it well.

Once a Haven acquired a donor, the members made a great effort to maintain a positive relationship in order to continue receiving the goods over the long term. Typically, donors knew little about The Chosen, often did not even know that it was to this group that they gave, but they knew the smiling faces that greeted them every week, knew the children who occasionally came to sing for them, and truly believed that by contributing they were, in a small way, making the world a better place.

A trip to visit a donor was a special occasion for the children; it meant seeing life beyond the confines of the Haven, and special occasions created clearly formed memories.

Gideon suspected that at least some of the donors who had been giving while he had lived in Buenos Aires would still be doing so, and Munroe believed that with the donors they would find the map to the Havens—the magnet.

Instead of renting a car, they rented a taxi, and the simplicity of having a chauffeur was amplified by the boon of having a driver who knew the streets and the landmarks and understood, in place of addresses and clear directions, the general idea of where the children of The Chosen wanted to go.

Across the city, one district to the next, far past dusk and into early evening, they drove, up and down, gauging distances from familiar landmarks and comparing notes, locating first a supermarket, then a bakery, and finally, a midsize grocery store. With the vehicle idling and the cabdriver waiting, Gideon ran off the little he knew about the grocer, and then, having finished, he reached for the door handle, as if to get out of the car.

Munroe stopped him. "I'd prefer that we don't make contact," she said.

"I remember the owner," Gideon replied. "I don't know if he would remember me, but he would know if they still come around, and even if he's not there, the employees will know."

"I'm sure they would," Munroe said. "But let this one go."

He looked at her, doubt written across his face, and she said, "You hired me to do this job and you need to let me do it."

Gideon's reply was a barely perceptible nod. He removed his hand from the door, and for this Munroe was grateful. If another confrontation had been necessary to establish the order of things, she'd have done it, but at this juncture a face-off would be a waste of time and energy.

She had what she wanted.

Chapter 10

*T*he docks were deserted, and Munroe crept through the night, moving past security checkpoints and into the shadows that preceded the shelter that was currently home.

Heavy machinery and conveyor equipment stretched out from the wharf like giant manacles onto the three ships that lay at port. Powerful lights illuminated the waterfront, creating lengthening darkness between the two- and three-story buildings that stood opposite.

The knife attack came without warning, out of the shadows, as if the man who wielded it had been waiting a long, patient time, knowing she would eventually pass.

He was strong. From behind he jerked her head back and forced her to the ground. Light crossed his face, and she recognized him from the dockyard. His skin was rough, scarred, making him look old, though she knew he wasn't. His body was taut and muscular from the daily physical labor.

He tightened his grip on her neck, kept the knife to her throat, and in microsecond gaps she calculated. Her vision shifted to gray. Adrenaline flowed, and the edges of desire crept toward her soul.

She dropped a knife into a palm from a pocket in her sleeve; smiled; relaxed. In an unconscious response the man loosened his grip, and in that second of error she slashed his wrist. He screamed an obscenity, let go, stepped back out of her way, and blended into the darkness.

Munroe closed her eyes. Other senses would guide her where sight failed.

A scrape. A movement of air. He lunged.

She sidestepped, and his blade missed widely.

She pulled a second knife from the small of her back. Flipped it open.

His breathing was heavy, and she followed the sound of it, knives in both hands, circling cautiously. The lust for blood was there, she could feel it welling up inside, a pounding in her head, in her chest, an overwhelming desire to kill.

And she fought it.

She was not to be a killer, an animal, a predator. She had fled to get away from this, to leave it behind.

"There's no need for this," she said to the night. "Put away your weapon, I'll put away mine, and we can walk away."

The attacker taunted her with obscenities, and she understood then that he wanted her body and meant to take it by death if necessary. With his mocking, darkness flooded in. She smelled the rankness of his sweat, heard the rasp of scorn in his voice, knew the fear of the knife. Her heart raced, muscles contracted, and instinct washed over her.

Survive.

Kill.

Light reflected off a blade.

She rolled to the right.

Instinct.

Speed.

She turned. Came from below. Plunged a knife upward, connected under his chin and thrust it deep. Euphoria flowed.

The attacker dropped to his knees, eyes wide.

Green eyes.

Her stomach reacted violently.

His face. Soft. Familiar. A shock of recognition ran through her.

She gasped for air. Slumped forward and then, head tilted upward, with the primal shriek of rage and pain still rising, opened her eyes.

Not to the midnight sky, but to the bland, off-white ceiling of the hotel room.

Heart pounding, Munroe slid her legs over the side of the bed and stood, looking down at the aftermath of slumber. The sheets and her clothes were drenched, the pillow beside her shredded. She rubbed her fingers, feeling tenderness where friction had burned them raw. For this she had purchased three hours of sleep out of the last forty-eight. So little rest invited trouble, and agitated as she was now, there would be no natural return to the slumber that she so desperately needed.

Munroe shuffled to her bag, pulled out a bottle, and tipped the contents into her mouth.

It was nearing nine in the morning, at the same corner place where Logan had followed Munroe yesterday, and the café was filled with morning traffic. He sat at the far end of the room, his back to the wall, listening to a language that he only half understood, observing the bustling crowd, and through the storefront window watched the passersby. Across the table Gideon sat dazed and sleepy-eyed, and the fragrance of coffee blended with the sweet scent of the pastries that filled the empty space between them.

Conversation was sparse, and any words spoken were only filler. They were both tired, having spent far too many hours during the night planning and then rehashing options, and if it weren't for the prearrangement to meet Munroe and Heidi here for breakfast, Logan would have been happy to steal another hour or two under the covers.

He glanced again at his watch and took a sip of coffee. The girls were ten minutes late. He wasn't familiar enough with Heidi's patterns to know how many minutes past an appointment defined her version of tardy, but he knew Munroe. She was her own woman and worked her own schedule, but if she committed to be somewhere at a certain time, she would show—on time—always.

Logan took another sip and then another glance at his watch. Gideon, noticing the movement, chuckled. Logan ignored him and, his face to the window, saw Heidi pass on the other side. She entered the café, eyes scanning the room, and seeing Logan, approached the table.

"Where's Michael?" Logan said.

Heidi's head turned puppy-dog sidewise. "I thought she was with you," she said. And then in response to Logan's deadpan expression, "I overslept—didn't hear the alarm—I just figured she left without me."

Logan blanched, and his heartbeat, fast and heavy, made it impossible to attempt conversation. To the others, Munroe's absence would mean little—a stroll about the neighborhood or the desire to check out a lead—they would assume she would return in her own time. But he knew better.

Her promise to get Hannah repeated in his mind, a mantra that was the calm against his panic. Munroe had given her word—her *word*—but perhaps now, in her current state with the medicating—the drugs—her word meant little.

"Heidi, I need your key," he said. She looked at him quizzically, and he remained silent, hand outstretched. Finally, after a moment, she pulled the room key from her purse and handed it to him.

"Don't go anywhere," he said. "I'll be back in half an hour."

He left for the hostel at a near run.

The room was as he'd expected, with Heidi's things on one side and most of Munroe's few belongings on the other. Stacked neatly on the bedside table were the documents he had given her, and he could see from the way things were laid out why Heidi assumed that Munroe had simply gone ahead.

He browsed through the stack of papers, heart still pounding, until he came to the end and saw that those he'd held back, the ones he'd finally handed over yesterday, were missing. For that, there was hope.

Frustrated and sick to his stomach, Logan left the room to find a pay phone. He didn't know what to expect, didn't even know what he hoped to gain by the call, only knew that he had to make it, and that if there was anyone who knew what Munroe was up to, it would be Miles Bradford. Using a calling card, he dialed Capstone Consulting.

He asked for Bradford, the receptionist requested he hold the line, and then, in less than a moment, Miles was on the phone. No transfers. No waits or stalls, no voice mail or notice of being out of the country, just the man himself, listening, while Logan ran anxiously through the reasons why he'd called.

When Logan had expended himself to the point of emotional emptiness, he paused, and in that space there was silence. Unsure if Bradford was still on the line, he was about to speak when Bradford broke the quiet.

"Michael left a message for you," Bradford said.

Stunned, Logan made no reply. Munroe had known that he would go to Bradford—had made preparations based on it. Realizing, finally, that Bradford was waiting for a response of some kind, he said, "I'm listening."

"She's made you a promise," Bradford said, "and intends to keep it. But she can't work with the three of you hovering. You need to take a step back, stay out of her way, and trust that she knows what she's doing."

Logan paused and then said, "That's it?"

"She wants you in Buenos Aires," Bradford said. "She might even need you at some point, so stay where she can easily find you. Just don't go anywhere near anything concerned with the assignment, okay? And Logan?" Bradford paused. "She means *anything*."

Logan nodded to empty space. "All right," he said. "If that's what she wants."

Courtesy of the bottle, Munroe slept, and in that sleep was peace from the living and peace from the dead. From sunrise around the clock to three in the morning she bathed in sweet oblivion, and when she woke, she checked the time and the day's date to get her bearings, then set the alarm for eight.

When the hours passed and the buzzer sounded, her feet hit the floor before her hand found the stop. The bottle's purpose had been served, and the go signal, like a checkered flag to a race-car driver, launched her forward. Today she would begin to dredge the road toward bringing Hannah home.

She showered and left the hotel in search of a salon already open. As with every assignment, there was a role to play, and with any role, illusion was everything. The human subconscious filtered out that which was familiar, and to err in any detail, no matter how subtle, was to jar reality and place a role at risk.

To become and to blend required more than understanding the language or speaking as they did, more than mannerisms and walk and copying dress. To become was to synthesize completely, and this illusion meant that everything—from hairstyle to shoes, even imports— had to be acquired locally.

Hair shorn into a neutral gender look, Munroe took a cab to Paseo Alcorta, one of the city's several upscale malls. She moved through stores and boutiques with the speed and efficiency of experience. Styles, colors, weights, and textures changed from country to country, but the concept of blending was the same. Suitcase, clothes, shoes, backpacks, jackets; several collections to fill the needs of the neutral gender, all of it on her own dollar.

The money Logan and the other survivors had paid, although an exorbitant sum by their own standards, didn't even begin to cover expenses on a job of this nature. What the others would never know was that in order to pull this off, she was contributing more to the project than all of their payments combined.

Shopping finished, Munroe returned to the hotel long enough to drop off the day's bounty, and took a cab to the airport. She had the driver wait while she left for the arrivals area to search out Miles Bradford, who by now should have cleared customs.

She spotted him against the far wall, one leg kicked back for support, arms crossed, as if he had all the time needed to discover the world and no plans to do so. Beside him was a luggage dolly carrying two oversize lockers that functioned as trunks, an oversize carry-on, and a computer bag. He scanned the room with that disinterested look of his, which so belied the focus with which he observed all.

He met her eyes as she found his, and a beautiful smile transformed his face. He greeted her with a hug and then a kiss atop her forehead.

"You okay?" he said.

The question, so clean in its simplicity, so strong in sincerity, held so many complexities that Munroe simply nodded and returned his smile.

"How was the trip?" she asked. "Tired?"

"I slept," he said. "I'm ready to roll."

"Did you get the list?"

"Whatever I couldn't bring, I can get here," he said. "I've got connections in the area—I'm owed and have already started pulling favors."

Munroe nodded, and as they walked to the exit where the cab sat idling, she hooked her arm in his. Though it was strange to have Bradford as an on-site partner, knowing he had her back felt good.

In the cab, Bradford briefed her on Logan's call, she updated him on what she knew of the Havens, and between them remained the unspoken issue of whether or not she'd slept.

Bradford pulled an envelope from his computer bag and handed it to her. "It's what I have on New York," he said. "It's not much, but I've got my ear to the ground, and it'll eventually come."

Munroe stared ahead, eyes on the road, thin envelope limp on her lap.

Bradford put a hand on hers, his touch cautious, gentle. He said, "The killing was justified, Michael. You did the only thing to be done, let it go."

This was that conversation for another time. Munroe inclined her head against the seat, turned to the side so that half of Bradford's face filled her focus, and studied him as he watched the passing traffic. The way he spoke, that mixture of concern and respect, love and equality, was very rare and came from an intimacy grounded in complete acceptance and understanding of who she truly was.

From the airport, the taxi took them into Palermo, the vibrant northeast corner of the city just beyond the wealth-filled stretches of Recoleta. Munroe had originally come here simply to be across town from Logan and lessen the chances of accidentally running into him, but the hotel, large for the area with nearly thirty rooms stacked upon nine floors, and with a restaurant and wireless Internet, had all that she needed for a command center for the rescue—or kidnapping, depending on the point of view.

The room was on the fourth floor, and together they lugged the trunks inside. The local décor, as clean-lined and modular as any that Munroe had seen in Europe, added a variant to what would otherwise globally be considered a standard hotel room: two beds, a bathroom, a windowed balcony, corner chairs, a TV, and a desk against one wall.

Afternoon sunlight streamed through the balcony window and the heater took the chill out of the air. Munroe and Bradford rearranged furniture and cleared a wall upon which they taped a large sheet of paper that would double for a whiteboard.

But for brief questions or the occasional sigh or exclamation, Munroe and Bradford set up shop in silence, pulling matériel from among the clothing, assembling one piece after the other until the small desk was covered with machines and wires that overflowed and bled to the floor.

When Munroe had done all that she could, knew that she'd reached the stage of helpfulness that bordered on inconvenience, she left Bradford on his own and turned to the door.

"I'll be back by dark," she said.

Preferring to work alone as she did, an assignment rarely called for this level of assistance, but what she'd always had and currently lacked was time. The information on Hannah's location was now over two weeks old, and with The Chosen—particularly Hannah—relocating often, Munroe couldn't risk losing her before they'd even found her.

She needed a lot of information as quickly as possible, and even in a city the size of Buenos Aires, getting it without alerting The Chosen of their presence meant depending heavily on electronics and on the wallet.

In the hallway, Munroe slipped a DO NOT DISTURB sign on the door handle, and as a way to ward off curious eyes and unwanted visitors who might take a special interest in the electronic assembly upstairs, she let the front desk know that housekeeping wouldn't be necessary.

With daylight hours fading, she returned to Nueva Pompeya, the neighborhood on the south side of the city where stood the midsize grocery store whose owner Gideon had so badly wanted to speak with the day before.

The grocery was on a narrow street, fronted by and set between a variety of smaller mom-and-pop shops. For this, the location was perfect. Far down the block, Munroe exited the cab and, zipping her jacket against the cold, walked toward the grocery, taking in the area and confirming what she had noticed on yesterday's first pass.

A portion of storefront matched what she had seen in the blurry background of two pictures nestled among the many pages of documents and internal memoranda given her by Logan.

Gideon was correct that the owner of the store, a close friend of The Chosen, was probably still here, but Gideon's urge to go to the source, while logical to the inexperienced, had great potential for ruin.

The photos were a dot-to-dot, pointing out who to avoid.

Unless she was able to move faster than the target—something she could only do once she was certain of where Hannah was located—to come so close had the potential to cause The Chosen to spook and scatter.

Munroe shoved her hands into pockets, crossed the street, and entered the shop opposite the grocery's sliding doors. From the outside, the shoe store had appeared to fit what Munroe was looking for, but a cursory glance around the interior told her otherwise. A nod to the proprietor and she returned to the street and moved on to the clothing boutique next door.

But for the girl seated behind the counter, the shop was empty, and judging from the merchandise, it was probably often empty. The clerk was young, late teens, possibly twenties, and she sat bored and disinterested, her eyes glued to her hands and what Munroe assumed was a cell phone. From her position behind the counter, the girl had a nearly perfect view through the display window and across the street.

Munroe surveyed the room and glanced at the clerk once more. Here, although she could get what she wanted as a female, instinct said that the girl would be more eager to help a boy. Experience had taught her that dressed as she was—no makeup, neutral gender hair, and neutral gender clothing—unless she assumed the role of one gender over the other, people inevitably projected whatever made them most comfortable.

What most never realized was that masculinity and femininity were never so much about looks as attitude, and to create the roles and slip between them, one gender to the next, was a tool of the trade that Munroe had utilized for so long that it had become as natural as blinking.

Munroe moved through the store casually, slowly, holding up the occasional garment, and by all appearances completely out of her element. She lingered an appropriate time, held two shirts side by side, dropped her voice an octave, and requested advice from the girl, who until now had barely taken notice of her presence.

"Che, ¿te gusta esta remera para mi hermana?" she said. "I need to buy a birthday gift for her and don't know where to start."

The clerk placed her phone on the counter and stepped beyond the glass to the small floor space. Munroe smiled bashfully, and the girl returned the grin.

"I'm Michael," Munroe said, "and thank you."

"Bianca," the girl said, "and how old is your sister?"

The banter between them was casual and friendly, a gentle rebound about the choices at hand, and personal conversation that veered just shy of flirtation. And then, with a decision made, Munroe stood at the counter and glanced beyond the window. She wondered out loud how boring it must be to spend the day watching the comings and goings of the street.

Bianca sighed and nodded.

"So you've noticed the van, then," Munroe said, "the one with the children?"

"The children don't come every week," Bianca replied.

"But the van does," Munroe said, and she leaned in and dropped her voice to a whisper, "the same day every week."

The Chosen's propensity toward multipassenger vehicles had been evident in the photos scattered throughout the documents, but other than that one fact, everything else Munroe said was based on guesswork. Right or wrong, it made no difference. Bianca, adhering to human nature, would contradict or fill in the blanks, whatever the case might be.

As if on cue, the girl added, "And always at the same time."

"The van is gray, no?"

"White," Bianca said.

"Yes, white." Munroe grinned, this time blatantly flirtatious. "But I'm not color-blind."

Bianca blushed, and then, either through embarrassment at the attention or from a desire to prolong the conversation, continued. She was an eager gossip, and Munroe plied the desire to share, questions intermingled with further flirtation and bashful smiles.

The van came weekly, always Tuesday around midmorning, and nearly always the same driver. He and his companion—usually a woman—would go inside for twenty or thirty minutes and then return with several filled crates. Bianca rattled off other details, but at this point they were superfluous. With a gasp at the time and a parting wave, Munroe left the shop for the hotel.

To pinpoint one Haven meant, with time and patience, locating all three said to be in or around Buenos Aires. When tomorrow rolled around, she would be ready. The magnet had served its purpose, and she'd soon have the needle.

Chapter 11

Munroe sat beside the bed with her back to the wall and two sets of documents on the floor in front of her. It was after midnight, and Bradford, having claimed the bed closest to the window, had already crashed, his gentle snores assurance that he was either sleeping or doing a stellar job of pretending that he was.

Trying to keep ambient light to a minimum, Munroe had pulled the desk lamp down and settled it in the space between the wall and the bed. She had yet to go through the last set of documents that Logan had handed her, and they sat beside the envelope that contained information on the New York killing.

Munroe ran her forefinger between the two, a repetitive pattern of long internal debate until the documents were separated by a perfect line of tile. In a slow, drawn-out movement, she twisted her palms so that they faced her and gazed at the invisible stain of blood that marked them, urging away the tarnish, knowing full well that removal was impossible.

She was a predator, a hunter, hating the bloodlust that lurked always just beneath the surface, disgusted by how easy it was to kill and how good it felt when it was done.

Did it really matter that she killed in self-defense or that her dead were evildoers? Every kill had been a son or brother, father or lover to someone else. Death was death, killing was killing, and the urge to draw blood and the satisfaction it brought was as fierce as any addiction. For this reason Munroe didn't begrudge the nightmares or the guilt she carried; these provided a form of proof that in spite of the euphoric rush of the kill, she did have a conscience, that she was yet human and alive.

On the flip side, concern that Logan's assignment would add to the body count had gone down considerably with the realization that for the most part, The Chosen were pacifists. Unlike Jonestown, The Chosen disavowed mass suicide, and unlike the Branch Davidians, they didn't stockpile weapons in preparation for Judgment Day—although they did believe that as the End Days approached, they would acquire X-Men-type superpowers.

The physical danger came not from The Chosen but from their Sponsors—connected individuals that The Chosen sought out and courted for protection and financial gain—military, police, or powerful local families. The details varied from country to country, city to city, and sometimes even Haven to Haven within a city and weren't worth troubling over until the local situation became clearer.

The most immediate concern was not violence but being discovered by The Chosen and watching helplessly as the Havens scattered and Hannah vanished again, like fog between fingers.

Munroe pushed the New York envelope aside. Miles was right. She had acted in the only way that she could have. To brood over it now would only interfere with bringing Logan's daughter home, and here in Buenos Aires, as long as it was merely the violence of the supernatural that she had to deal with, things would be okay.

Munroe picked up Logan's folder and pulled out the pages, and as she began to read, rage, like a fire in her belly that could only be quenched by blood, began a slow burn upward.

The cause of the seething came not only from the details but also from the impunity with which they were published, promoted, and documented: The Prophet, with his divine revelation proclaiming freedom from the laws of the Bible, said that to the pure, all was pure, and for The Chosen only one law mattered, that anything was allowed if done in love. The Prophet reiterated that love was the criteria, not age, or familial relations, or marital status. Taboos were removed, safe-guards erased, and the innocence and bodies of the children violated, and these violations were shown and written about in graphic detail.

The Prophet's doctrine was Saint Augustine saying, "Love, and do as you will"; it was Aleister Crowley's dictum "Do what thou wilt shall be the whole of the Law"; it was Saint Paul's "All things are lawful unto me"; it was The Prophet saying that there was no reason young children couldn't be fully involved sexual beings if love was the moti-vation.

The children didn't scream or protest; they had been taught to submit, to obey, to never question. They had no power, no place but to serve, and when the pedophiles came calling, who had they to turn to for safety? Their parents, those who should have stood between the children and harm, had abdicated responsibility in order to follow The Prophet and remain a part of The Chosen, and these acts against the innocent, no matter how extreme, were, after all, done in love.

Only halfway through the pages, Munroe stopped and set the folder aside. She had to pause, to breathe, to consciously force herself into a state of levelheaded calm. There was no point in continuing through further details; she'd gotten the idea, and the emotion conjured by what she read brought her as painfully close to flashbacks as anything the years had thrown at her.

Munroe understood now why Heidi had said the missing pieces weren't easy to forget, and what Logan had meant by the children's pain having been turned into a media-circus freak show. He was right. After reading about it, it was easy to overlook everything else that had come before it, to forget how much further and deeper their pain went, how their entire lives had been a travesty of justice and a failure of those responsible to treasure, protect, and respect the innocence of childhood.

She didn't need to read to know the rest of it; she'd heard it from Logan and caught glimpses of it from the discussions that had taken place in New York. Stories of abuse began to surface, governments began to investigate, and doctrines that The Chosen had once prac-

ticed in the open became secret. The Prophet and his Representatives rewrote history, burned Instructives, and to the public and the
courts repudiated and denied, while on the inside they defended the
Godliness of their beliefs. Only in the face of mounting evidence did
The Prophet's spokespeople grudgingly admit that some of the stories
were true, even while denying the role of The Prophet or his doctrine,
instead blaming rogue disciples and claiming things had changed.

Munroe sat for several moments, reflecting. Remaining free of
preconceived opinions and ideas was critical to understanding and
assimilation, but given the background on this assignment, remaining
objective was becoming increasingly difficult.

When the rush of anger had subsided and the rage was temporarily
quelled, she stood. Slowly, so as not to make noise or disturb Bradford,
she crossed the room, pulled the laptop from the desk, and retreated
to the nook between wall and bed. She powered up the machine and
turned off the desk lamp.

Munroe had until early morning to pull and draw, to suck the life's
blood from the veins of information that lay within her reach. Logan's
folders had been thorough and had provided history, facts, and reality.
What she wanted now was to crawl inside the minds of those involved,
to understand the way that members within The Chosen thought, and
if she could, acquaint herself with those in Argentina. She would learn
their dreams and aspirations, their fears and motivations, and these
she would find, not in history and data, but in blogs and comments,
stories and testimonials floating through the vastness of the Internet.

Once started, her focus became so intense that she wasn't aware of
Bradford having woken until he'd crossed half of the room. She broke
midsentence to acknowledge him and then turned again to the screen.

"Hey," Bradford said, and he sat on the edge of her bed, tipped
over so that his face was parallel with hers. "Not planning to sleep?"

Without looking up, she said, "Probably not a good idea."

"What?" he teased. "You don't think I could handle your sleepwalking with my eyes closed?"

She chuffed. "It might get messy."

"When you want to rest," he said, "let me know. I'll keep an eye on you." The playfulness had gone out of his voice and his tone was soft and serious.

Munroe paused, looked up, and met his eyes, which were only inches from hers.

"Thank you," she said, and she truly meant it. "I might take you up on that, but tonight I've got to get this research in." She checked the clock. Four A.M. "How are you feeling?" she asked.

"Depends," he said. "Are we still on for seven?"

She nodded.

"I feel like I could use three more hours of sleep," he said, pulling backward off the bed and winking that irresistible wink of his.

Munroe sat tall, eyes following as he recrossed to his own space; he with the drawstring pants slung loosely around his waist and the chiseled torso that showed two-toned in the darkened room. Bradford, knowing that she watched, turned back to catch her eye, and when he did, she almost laughed, continuing to observe until he had settled down.

The chemistry that had smoldered between them in Africa hadn't lessened with time, but if the flame was to ignite, it would be on Munroe's shoulders to fan it. Not for any lack of desire on Bradford's part, that had been clear for a long while now, but because of his respect for her boundaries and for their shared history.

Thoughts of Noah tumbled through Munroe's mind followed by the piercing pain that lately came with them. She pushed them back, returning her focus to the computer and another series of blog links, reached down and jotted another note on the pad that had by now been nearly filled.

They left the hotel at seven-thirty, Bradford accompanying Munroe as spotter and a second pair of eyes. Munroe expected the van to arrive at the grocery sometime between ten and eleven, assumed that the vehicle would approach on the side of the street with easiest access, but unwilling to risk waiting another week on wrong assumptions, she was attempting to cover all angles.

At eight, the streets were still waking up, and in this part of town, traffic was light. Still several hundred feet from the storefront, Bradford exited the cab, walked into a corner café, and took a seat along the window so that he had a clear view down the street.

The piece in Munroe's ear chirped. Bradford was testing signal strength, and she smirked, eavesdropping on his conversation with the waitress as he struggled with the language. Then, having confirmed that he'd settled into position, she moved on, parking the taxi not far from where she expected the van to show.

She had borrowed not only the cab but also Raúl's, the driver's, clothes. Over the past few days she'd tipped him well enough to ensure that this morning he would be content to let her have the black and yellow car for a few hours while he lingered around the corner.

Munroe idled at the curb and settled in for the duration. For those few who flagged the cab or attempted to ride, she told them the vehicle was waiting on a fare and, in the long hours that passed, conversed with Bradford. Their conversation was abstract, time-killing talk, the rambling that bonded partners. He made her laugh with witty retorts, his mind nearly as fast as hers, jumping topics from the inane to the obscure until, as if on cue, the Haven van turned down the street.

Munroe spotted the van in her rearview mirror at almost the same moment Bradford alerted her to the target's approach. Clearly visible through the advancing windshield was the male-female pair and a number of smaller faces in the backseat.

Counting cars and measuring speed, Munroe waited and, at Bradford's go, shifted into gear and slid the cab away from the curb and into traffic, allowing the van to fill the spot that she had left empty.

Around the corner, she left the car with Raúl, swapped jackets, and added a hat and sunglasses to avoid the possibility of being recognized by Bianca, the store clerk, and any potential scene that would come of it.

Munroe doubled back the way she'd come, Bradford's voice in

her ear, clicking off minutes, updating her on the target's movements. Bradford had left the café for the street and was slowly walking toward the van, backup if for some reason she should fail in her mission.

She passed the front of the vehicle, confirmed it empty, and, reaching the rear, knelt to tie a shoelace. At Bradford's clear, she slipped a hand under the chassis, a movement clean and smooth that left behind a magnetic disk. She remained kneeling, waiting, working on the shoelace, until Bradford signaled again.

She rounded the vehicle to the driver's side and, sure to keep her back to the clothing boutique, shimmed the door open, confidently and subtly. To the very observant she was the rightful owner returning for a forgotten item. She remained only long enough to drop a pen into the cluttered console and slip a booster pack under the dash. She locked and shut the door, turned, and continued on the way she'd come.

The battery on the listening device had a short life span; they could expect perhaps twelve to fourteen hours if they were lucky, but the tracker would last until they killed it.

Munroe slowed, allowing Bradford to shorten the distance between them, and after several blocks, she crossed the street to join him. Together they turned the corner and, with a nod to Raúl, who waited, climbed into the cab.

Their work here was done. Rather than attempt to follow the van through the city, they would allow the GPS tracker to do the work; every street, every turn, and every stop would be transmitted to the machines in the command center and then recorded and analyzed.

If the van functioned as Gideon and Heidi believed it did, they would have the locations of all three Havens by the end of the day. If not, it was inevitable that in time the others would be found, but time was the one thing Munroe had little to spare.

She expected the van would take at least three hours to make its rounds, so they returned to the hotel. With Bradford in front of the computer, comparing GPS information to local maps, and nothing further for Munroe to do but wait, she lay down. Exhaustion settled, her eyelids drooped, and although she feared another nightmare and the havoc the dreams would wreak, sleep took her hostage.

She stood along the expanse of empty road, useless Ducati at her side, and watched the Good Samaritan pull to a stop.

He stepped from the rear of his Escalade, spare gas can in hand.

The vastness of West Texas stretched in all directions, a barren and endless flat that melted into the horizon. Munroe had followed the roads at random, taking the bike to suicidal speeds, open throttle, screaming engine, and having misjudged the distance between towns after she'd found the last gas station unexpectedly closed, had ended up stranded.

The Good Samaritan approached. His hand rose in greeting; she nodded. She returned small talk to his questions. Unscrewed the bike's gas cap.

He held the can toward her.

His smile was wrong and something about his body language put her on edge.

She hesitated.

It would take less than a gallon to make it to some form of civilization, and she wanted that fuel. Desire overrode instinct. She reached for the can.

Her hand closed around the handle, and the barrel of his gun came full in her face.

Without moving, she raised her eyes to his.

The smile was gone, the safety off. He nodded toward his vehicle.

She sighed. Not this shit again.

She slumped in resignation. Did as he instructed.

He prodded her to the rear of the vehicle and followed.

If he'd wanted her dead, he would have already shot her, and so she moved forward, confident he wouldn't fire until he had what he'd stopped for.

Munroe waited until they were parallel to the Escalade, and with the tinted windows working as mirrors, she struck. The speed of attack sent the weapon flying.

She drove a fist toward his face, a leg to his groin, and inexplicably, he countered. Blow by blow, block to block, an incomprehensible speed that matched hers until, against all reason, she was on her back, arms pinned to her chest, unable to move.

Rage boiled, frustration mounted, and still she could not gain the upper hand. The man raised a fist and struck her face. Hard. The blow left her dizzy. She turned directly to face him, stared hard, looking into his eyes.

It was Miles Bradford who blinked back.

Munroe's heart pounded, head throbbed, and she struggled to catch her breath, crushed beneath Bradford as she was. "I'm okay," she said. "I'm okay, get off."

Bradford reacted instantly, letting go and sliding back. She sat up and drew her knees to her chest, wrapped her arms around them, and one long, slow inhale after the other forced her heart rate back down to a reasonable pace.

Bradford, still on his knees, was silent, staring. "I'm sorry I hit you," he said.

She took another slow drink of air and shook her head. He had no reason to apologize. The strike had been worth not having to relive another killing.

She leaned forward and curled into the fetal position, rested her head in his lap. He ran his fingers through her hair, traced the outline of her jaw.

"How long did I sleep?" she said.

"About five hours."

His touch was comforting, soothing, and she lay there just to feel it. "Has the van stopped moving?" she asked.

"About thirty minutes ago."

"What did we get?"

"It looks like we've got at least two potential Havens," he said. "Theirs and one other—but I'm not sure you're in any condition for the next phase."

Munroe sat up, looked him dead in the face, and after a long pause said, "The hell I'm not."

Chapter 12

Munroe stepped from the bed to the bathroom and in turn to the shower, where the water would help to clear her head and erase some of the emotional aftershock of sleep. She lost track of time under the flow, the water hot, just shy of scalding, the heat taking with it the memories, if only temporarily. She watched the water run and filter down the drain and, after what felt like an eternity, shut it off.

Clean and as clear as could be expected, she joined Bradford at the desk.

At her approach, he moved slightly, making room and behaving as if the violence that had transpired had never happened. If he wished to probe and understand—and she was certain that he did—he kept it to himself. He knew her well, knew that to wait and allow her space would in time bring him what he wanted.

With a half grin he handed Munroe a headset and slid out of the way so that she could listen to the recording that had been transmitted by the bug.

The device was voice activated, a feature designed to conserve battery life, and during the five hours that Munroe had been asleep, there had been just over an hour of recording. Nothing new had come in during the past hour, and that, combined with the van's current location, led them both to believe that these transmissions were the last they'd get from the pen.

Munroe listened, jotting down the occasional note, and after a short while she took off the headset and set it aside. For the most part the conversation was useless. She motioned for Bradford to rejoin her.

He paused from writing, set his notebook aside, and sat beside her, so close that she could feel the warmth of him against her skin. She blocked out the craving for the calm of his touch and focused fully on the information at hand while together they pored over the data the tracker had provided.

The van had made a circuitous route through the city, and Bradford had pulled the two locations he considered most likely to be Havens. Both were residential and fairly secluded. The property at which the van had come to roost was the smaller of the two and closer to its neighbors than the other.

Satellite images provided enough detail to get a feel for the locale, and Munroe mapped out routes to and from each property. Having finished, she stood, stretched, and rolled out the kinks from her shoulders. "I'm going to make a dry run of it," she said. "You want to come?"

Bradford stood and reached for his coat.

She had invited him along, not because she needed his help but because of the calm she felt in his presence, and because no matter how much he believed her capable of looking after herself, the protective soldier in him wouldn't be able to help but stress until he knew for certain she was safe. Keeping him close was a win/win for them both.

Outside the hotel, in the coming twilight, Munroe flagged a taxi. With the directions pulled from the GPS, she talked the driver through what little he didn't already know.

They traveled first to the far edge of city, away from the elegant colonial architecture and wide tree-lined avenues of the city proper. Out here there were still dirt roads, the buildings were modest and humble, and although this property wasn't the van's final destination, there was no other reason for the forty-five-minute stop in this remote area but to visit a sister Haven.

The property, spread out ranch style, was comprised of a greater two-story house, a smaller single-story annex, and what appeared to be a barn or large shed at the far back. The buildings were set far off the rural highway with a dirt road connecting it to the main road. Stopping wasn't possible without attracting attention, so they passed twice, photographed what they could in the dimming light, and moved on to the next location.

The van's home was in a suburb closer to the city, a neighborhood where houses were surrounded by high walls and accessed through sheet-metal gates and interspersed among mom-and-pop stores and microindustries. The first pass confirmed what the satellite images had shown: a three-story house with subconstruction in the rear that appeared to have been built as servants' quarters. Placement from the walls allowed for a large backyard.

Far down the street, Munroe paid the taxi fare, and she and Bradford exited, joining the pedestrian traffic. Unlike the first property, which they'd known was inaccessible, here Munroe hoped to see if there were any guard dogs or night watchmen, and to get a visual of the easiest access route over the walls.

Arm in arm, casually strolling, Munroe and Bradford walked until they had looped the entire area and she had seen what she wanted.

"How many bedrooms?" Munroe asked.

Bradford glanced over his shoulder and then turned his gaze toward the sidewalk as they continued. "I dunno," he said, "maybe five or six."

Munroe nodded. "That'd be my guess too. And I'm going to venture they've got at least forty-five people living in there."

"Based on what?" he said. "Gut instinct?"

"Mostly from what I've read," she said, "and from the things that Logan has told me over the years.

"At least two-thirds of them will be children," she added.

Bradford paused, and Munroe knew he was running the numbers. Finally he nodded toward the house. "Thirty kids in there?" he said.

"At least. Probably more."

He waited a beat and then deadpanned: "That's a lot of laundry."

*   *   *

At one in the morning the heart of Buenos Aires was just starting to bustle. For those out on the town the evening didn't truly begin until around midnight and would only start to settle after three or four. The night was different in the suburbs, where beyond the occasional late sidewalk chatter, the streets were mostly quiet, the silence broken only by the occasional car or a dog's bark or the wail of a cat in heat.

Munroe stood with her back to the wall, one leg casually braced against it, watching the street, waiting in the silence for the right moment to move. She had approached the property from the rear, following the side road that Raúl had used to drop her off. Once on her own she'd pulled off her outer T-shirt, tightened it into a roll, and stuffed it into a vest side pocket. She donned a balaclava, and in full-body black with the depth of night calling to her, followed shadow to shadow, a phantom in the dark until she reached the loneliest of the Haven compound's walls.

Munroe tossed a retractable anchor over and hoisted upward. On the other side, the property grounds were well lit, and although Munroe didn't see them, she knew from the first pass that several dogs had the run of the space.

She lay flat in the shadows along the width of wall, her left leg hanging along the outside for balance. From a vest pocket she pulled a Ziploc pack of meat and with a trainer's whistle summoned the dogs. Relying on the old tried and true, she dropped several laced chunks into the yard, and with the dogs self-sedating, set to work pulling equipment pieces from her pockets.

She reassembled and mounted a surveillance camera first, followed by a wireless long-range transmitter. Located as they were, she wouldn't expect the pieces to be discovered for a very long time, if ever. With Bradford's guidance in her ear, Munroe made minute adjustments until he confirmed visual contact. She then repeated the procedure with a laser sight, pointing it so that it reflected off the largest downstairs window.

The dogs were dozing now, and though not fully asleep, they were not alert enough to raise an alarm. Munroe crouched and scooted along the balance beam of wall until her readings showed the proper angle. Placing a laser mike required a bit of finesse, and tonight was her one shot at getting it right.

Munroe twisted a wing nut, tilting the receiver another half degree toward the laser, and Bradford, in her ear, confirmed sound.

Based on what he heard, there were at least four people still moving about the house. Voice verification, an unexpected boon, was an upside to the downside of having someone awake in the Haven she'd hoped was by now asleep.

Camera and audio were secure and mounted, and logic said that having gotten what she'd come for, it was time to leave. But from this place on the wall, across fifty feet of well-lit lawn, the open garage, with its three vehicles, beckoned.

Munroe hesitated.

Surveillance on one window would net them something, but how much activity that one room received—even if it was obviously the largest in the house—was anybody's guess. She wanted more, and if the lure of getting a visual on the comings and goings of the Haven wasn't enough to draw her forward, getting a tracker placed on a second vehicle was irresistible.

Munroe checked her watch. She hadn't planned on staying this long, and in wanting to avoid accidentally overdosing the dogs and spooking the Haven, she'd gone easy on the sedatives. There wasn't a lot of time before the pack started roaming again. Munroe scanned the windows for signs of movement. Finding none, she removed the balaclava.

She slid over the side of the wall and dropped inside the grounds, heard Bradford's sharp intake, and knew from her placement that she'd entered the camera's range. She ignored him, stood, and strolled casually across the yard, as if she were one of their own out for some late-night air.

Bradford's voice was in her ear again, low and businesslike. Whomever he had heard speaking had left the room and now moved through the house. Munroe reached the far side of the garage. Here, shadows loomed and allowed her to again blend into the night. She paused, listened, and continued inward.

Three vehicles sat two wide and two deep, the space where a fourth would have been was filled instead with several refrigerators, a chest freezer, and, from the draped hoses and electrical cords, what appeared to be two broken washing machines. Noting the door, Munroe chose the corner behind the farthest fridge as the ideal framing point.

She slid between the vehicles, knelt, and placed the extra tracker, then ambled onto a washer and from there climbed to a fridge top. In the dark she assembled a second camera and amplifier, working with adhesive to hold the unit in place. She powered it on and Bradford again confirmed visual, again guided her through placement.

And then, with fingertips tilting the camera for a final adjustment, Munroe froze. Bradford's warning hissed in her ear as he too spotted the crack of light leaking from the house into the black. A moment later, the door to the garage opened and a boy of about sixteen stepped out.

The light from within was blinding against the darkness, and Munroe, previously so well hidden in shadows was now most certainly a demonic outline crouched above him. Had he stopped and tilted his head upward, he would have looked directly into her eyes.

But he didn't. Oblivious to her presence, he searched for something, eventually found it, returned to the house, and shut the door, and the garage was once more enveloped in darkness.

Equivalent to an all-clear, the door lock tumbled. Munroe slid down from her perch, and from there, back the way she'd come.

The same fifty feet of lawn separated her from the wall, and now, on the far side of the area, the dogs, though still sluggish, were beginning to move. She'd gambled against this possibility and knew she'd lost. They were still wobbly, and the longer she waited, the more dangerous they'd become. Caring for little other than making it to the wall before they did, Munroe paused for a beat, tensed, and then bolted across the lawn at a full sprint.

Chapter 13

The pack leader turned in Munroe's direction. He yelped and, stumbling a time or two, gave chase. The others were at his heels, all four of them picking up speed as they loped the long stretch of grass. Munroe neared the wall at an angle. The leader closed the gap. At a full run she grabbed the anchor's tail and, with the momentum carrying her up faster than if she'd merely climbed, hoisted herself, then scaled the wall as she felt the snap of teeth behind her.

Munroe reached the top and in the same movement released the anchor and pulled it with her as she slid over and dropped ten feet into a crouch. Hands to her knees, lower back tipped against the wall for support, she pulled in one burning breath after the next. After a moment she stood upright, swore at the pain shooting up her leg, and began a gimpy walk to the end of the road where Raúl had originally left her.

Bradford was in her ear again, his voice a steady calm that belied his panic.

"I'm okay," she said. "I sprained an ankle on the way down. Call Raúl. I'll meet him at the drop-off."

The walk was a slow half mile, and although the temptation to bring the taxi driver in for a closer pickup lingered, Munroe pushed it aside. The last thing the operation needed was an overeager bit player approaching the occupants of the house in a bid to double his money.

The less Raúl knew, the better, and in this, as with any part of the assignment in which he was needed, she would keep him at a distance.

Munroe pulled the lightweight T-shirt from her pocket, unfurled it, and pulled it back over her head.

The taxi driver returned Munroe to the front of the hotel, and she took the elevator up. The door to the room swung open before she touched it, and Bradford filled the frame. His face was placid and, but for the subtle creases at his eyes, unreadable. He stepped backward so that she could enter, and as she passed, his eyes followed, though his body didn't move.

Munroe turned back long enough to roll her eyes. "Relax," she said. "It's a sprain."

Bradford nodded, shut the door, and leaned against it, exuding that natural calm that so deftly disguised his true thoughts.

Without turning to confirm it, Munroe knew that he watched her, and so made a slow show of removing the accoutrements of the evening. When she had ripped the Velcro of the vest, emptied each pocket, and left a small pile at the foot of her bed, she glanced over her shoulder.

Bradford's arms were crossed, his head tipped back against the door, eyes focused on her. Maintaining eye contact, she sat, unlaced her boots, and, with the same slow deliberation, pulled them off.

Bradford said nothing, and the moment filled the room like smoke rising from the floor until, without a word, he reached for the handle, opened the door, and left.

The reverberation took with it the tension. Munroe sighed. She'd pushed him, had mocked his concern, and then taunted him with it. She stood and turned toward the shower, shed her clothes for the water, heat and regret washing over her until under the burning stream she lost all track of time. She would have felt differently if there'd been a point to her actions, but there hadn't been, she'd been cruel for no useful purpose.

When Munroe reentered the room, Bradford was on his bed, arms behind his head, staring at the ceiling. He didn't turn or acknowledge her, so Munroe picked up the last of Logan's folders, sat cross-legged on her bed with the documents in front of her, and said, "Are you okay?"

Bradford shifted to his side so that he faced her, propped his head against his hand, and said, "Tell me about Noah."

She turned to meet his eyes. "What do you want to know?"

"Why'd you leave?" he asked. "And don't say you did it for Logan or the assignment or because of the nightmares," he said. "They're reasons, but not *the* reason."

Munroe was silent for a moment and then finally whispered, "He didn't know me. Couldn't know me." She paused, and Bradford made no move to break the silence.

"For a while, I fit an image in his head," she said, "and as long as what I did and said conformed to that image, he was happy." She shook her head slightly, sadly. "But even if I try, even if I want to suppress my nature, it still surfaces. I am what I am, Miles, and the glimpses I allowed him clashed with the image he wanted. No matter how he argues it or even how he tries to accept me for me, he can't, and I can't conform, so it's better this way."

She stared out into empty space. "I already bring so much suffering into the world," she said, "I never wanted to bring it to him. We had a good run, you know? I loved him—love him—always will." She traced her fingers in a random pattern across the top of the document folder and said, "But sometimes love is its own reward, Miles. To struggle to turn it into more is to murder it slowly."

"You could go back when this is finished," Bradford said.

"I could," she said. "Although Noah made it painfully clear that I'm no longer welcome, and I don't really blame him. It doesn't matter why I had to go—a man's pride can only take so much."

She paused. "Oh, but I have considered it, you know? Going back, unwelcome as I am."

"You won't?"

"No," she said. She raised her eyes to his. "The reasons I left are there now as much as they've always been, and all I have to offer is more heartache. He can hate me—despise me if that's what he wants. I choose to treasure what we shared, no matter how it ended." She paused and again met Bradford's eyes. "And yes," she said. "It has ended. That *is* what you wanted to know, isn't it?"

It was nine in the morning and Munroe stood in the hotel foyer, waiting for Raúl. She'd left a note taped to the TV as a courtesy against Bradford's panic. He would have bolted upright the moment she slunk out the door, and her rapid scrawl would at least allow him peace and a few more hours of rest.

The next phase was set for midafternoon, and as Bradford hadn't fallen asleep until after five, she expected he'd be out until she got back.

Her first stop was Logan's hostel, where two weeks' advance payment on the rooms had been her insurance that the trio would stick around long enough for her to return. She had called ahead, confirming with the proprietor that the boys weren't in, although how long they'd be gone was impossible to gauge.

With instructions to Raúl, Munroe wound through the narrow courtyard to Gideon and Logan's quarters, and there, after confirming again that the room was empty, she let herself in with a skeleton key. Being discovered invading Logan's space ranked low on her list of potential disasters, but an encounter was something she wished to avoid, and so she moved to get out as quickly as possible.

Between the beds she shifted the middle table and, behind it, removed an electrical faceplate, fingers deftly wiring in a bug. She then moved across the room and repeated the procedure behind another. It wasn't that she didn't trust Logan—Gideon was another story—she was simply playing it smart, and Logan, knowing her as he did, would expect nothing less.

Having accomplished what she'd come for, Munroe retraced her steps, momentarily backing into an alcove to escape detection as Heidi passed. Expecting the boys to follow shortly, she paced a quick return to the front, arriving a half minute before the taxi pulled into place. Slipping into the backseat, she checked her watch. Two hours to prep for the next phase.

She returned to Paseo Alcorta for another shopping foray, this time swinging to the extreme girly side, sticking to the high-end boutiques and couture labels. The trip inside was a focused mission of matériel acquisition, a trip that under any other circumstances would have been far more enjoyable and lasted well beyond today's time constraints.

Bradford was still face to the pillow when she returned, and he did not stir as she closed the door. It was a perfect act, so well did he hide his attentive awareness and project the appearance of sleep. Amused, Munroe dropped her bags on the bed and moved to the computer.

She was fast-forwarding through video footage collected from the Haven cameras when Bradford said, "What time is it?"

Without turning she said, "Almost one o'clock." A pause, and then, "Have you seen any of this?"

Bradford slid his legs over the side of the bed, stood, and walked to the bathroom. "Nothing since daylight," he said. "But the tracker started moving after ten."

Munroe hovered over the computer, skimming through the footage, pausing as faces flashed across the screen, images of half a dozen of the Haven's children. They'd entered the yard shortly after noon, the wall-mounted camera capturing shot after shot as they played. The computer allowed her to zoom and crop the digital information, and by the time Bradford returned from the shower, she had a full array of faces.

"Anything?" he said.

"Not yet, but these all look to be around nine or ten; the others haven't come out yet."

"What about the second camera?"

"I've got a couple of the vans leaving, all adults, nobody that looks like David Law."

"Do you want to sleep?"

Munroe paused, turned from the computer, and, silent, stared at him.

"I figure you could use it," Bradford said, "and maybe if we keep it to an hour or so, you'll get enough to take the edge off without slipping into a dream."

She said nothing.

He paused, shrugged. "Or maybe not," he said. "But I can handle what you're doing there if you want to take a break."

She pushed back from the computer.

"An hour," she said.

Anything longer was not only inviting an episode but would also put her behind schedule for the afternoon.

She stepped aside to let him near the computer and, with a glance over her shoulder, turned to lie down. Bradford leaned back in the chair, watching her in a show of exaggerated observation. She grinned, shut her eyes, and allowed herself to free-fall into oblivion.

Munroe woke to the touch of Bradford's finger against her cheek. Disoriented, she turned to him.

"Hey," he whispered. She attempted a grin, and he said, "Any monsters?"

"No," she said. "No monsters. How long was I under?"

Bradford glanced at his watch. "One hour and three minutes. How do you feel?"

"A little dizzy," she said, and she sat up, shifting her feet to the floor. "What'd you get on the tracker?"

He smiled an exaggerated smile. "I think we've got the third Haven."

She attempted a return smile, thumbed-up the news, and then stood and made for the shower and what she hoped was instant clarity. She needed to be functioning at full throttle in less than an hour, and the jury was still out on whether or not sixty-three minutes of sleep was worth the cotton-headed mental fog.

By the time Munroe returned to the room, Bradford had already left, so she dressed and for added femininity liberally applied makeup. Having finished, and with Bradford still out, she turned again to the computer.

According to the data, the van had made only one stop in the hours since she'd returned from her jaunt at the mall, and she could see from the location on Bradford's map why he'd smiled. The third Haven was less than a ten-minute drive from where they were ensconced. She would forgo the dry run and get surveillance installed tonight.

The pieces were coming together.

As long as Logan's sources were accurate, as long as Hannah was truly in one of the Buenos Aires Havens, they would soon have her.

Munroe ran through visuals of the garage, located the time frame that the vehicle had left, caught a snapshot of who'd been in it, and, certain that neither Hannah nor David Law had been among the occupants, moved to the recordings captured by the laser mike. She had gotten through only the first five minutes when Bradford called.

Setting aside the equipment, she picked up her oversize purse, left the room, and joined Bradford in the lobby. He grinned as she approached, obviously appreciative of her attire, and then took her arm in his and led her to a late-model Peugeot sedan. Munroe paused to scan the car and nodded approval. He'd procured it from his local contact, and it far exceeded her expectations.

"Is it clean?" she said.

"It'll trace back to Recoleta."

Recoleta was a neighborhood of expensive apartment buildings and city blocks filled with mansions, where the most affluent of Buenos Aires congregated.

They drove through the streets of Palermo to Pascual Palazzo, which would route them to the highway that would take them out of town. It was a different route from the one Raúl had driven the evening before, but the destination was the same.

This was the first time in all of their mutual history that Munroe had allowed Bradford the wheel, and she glanced at him now, dressed up and owning the roads. She supposed that his transformation from jeans and T-shirts to sophistication and the effect it had on her were what people around her regularly experienced when she phased from one role into the next—unnerving, but in a good way.

They drove for over an hour through gradually thinning traffic before reaching the rural road that passed the Haven Ranch, and here Bradford turned off onto the gravel track that led to the buildings.

The vehicle slowed, Bradford obviously prolonging the approach.

"You ready for this?" he said.

Munroe nodded. "Born for it," she said.

Bradford stopped the car, and while he waited in the warm interior, Munroe stepped out. She stood at a chain-link gate and, hands shoved into her pockets, searched for a bell—anything meant to alert the occupants that someone waited for entry. Several dogs approached. Their ruckus, absent any other notification, would surely give notice, but after another moment, she found a press-button on a post far to the right of the gate. She thumbed it several times and then returned to the car to wait.

"Still certain they'll let us inside?" Bradford asked.

"Nearly certain," she said. "Just give them time to clear forty pairs of shoes out of the foyer."

As if on cue, a lone figure exited the front door and made the long walk toward them. Worn coat, worn shoes, dark curly hair, he appeared to be in his late twenties, and based on stories she'd collected from Logan and later Heidi, Munroe assumed that unlike the majority of those who lived here, the man was Argentine.

As he drew near, Munroe turned to Bradford, said, "Here goes," and, with a radiant smile, stepped out of the car and walked toward the gate.

Chapter 14

The wind blew against the landscape, taking the typical winter chill and turning it bitter, and painting the leaf-strewn expanse with a dreary brush. Munroe pulled the faux-fur-cuffed jacket tight round her neck, arriving at the gate at the same time as the man walking toward it.

Her expression was one of uncertainty, of innocence and curiosity. *"¿Se encuentra el dueño de casa?"* she said. "Are the owners here?"

"Le puedo ayudar si quieres," he said. "What is it that you need?"

Munroe shifted from foot to foot, gave a nervous glance over her shoulder toward Bradford, who waited in the driver's seat, and then turned back to the man. "I'm looking for God's people," she said, and after only the slightest pause, continued on in a rush. "It sounds crazy, I think crazier to you than even to me, but last night God answered my prayers and told me to come here and ask for His people—that God's people would have answers and that they needed my help." She paused. "Have I come to the right place?"

The man hesitated. In all of the scenarios he'd expected to encounter at the gate, this was probably the most unlikely. Munroe studied his face and body language for cues and chose silence. This man was not the final authority.

He looked from her to the car and then to Bradford beyond the windshield, and finally said, "Possibly the right place."

This was good, so much better than a figuratively slammed door. For the sake of her audience, her face brightened in visible relief, and then to push his hesitation toward favor, she reached into her coat and pulled out an envelope. She held it toward him. "God said that His people need this," she said. "If you really are those of my vision, the people who have answers for me, I want you to have it."

The man reached for the envelope but before taking it said, "What type of answers are you looking for?"

"I want to know how I can find peace, and meaning to life, and what comes after," she said, and then in a rush of words that overlapped and retraced, all an excited chatter, she offered little while saying much.

After a bit, he took the envelope and, interrupting her flow, said, "If you could wait for just a few minutes?"

"Certainly, certainly," she said.

He turned from her and, more quickly than he had come, walked back to the house.

When he'd made it halfway, Munroe returned to the warmth of the car.

"Did he buy it?" Bradford asked.

"I figure ten minutes and we're in," she said.

"What did you give him?"

"A thousand U.S. dollars in nice crisp hundreds."

"Cheap date, huh?"

"The answer to their prayers."

"So that's your secret to information gathering? A gold-plated envelope?"

Munroe grinned at Bradford's teasing. He knew as well as she did that Logan hadn't come to her simply because she was a best friend who could also conveniently kick ass and hand out bribes. Logan needed her on the inside, had come for the same skill that brought the highest bidders and the biggest players to her doorstep: the capacity to read people and then shift her own personality into whatever was necessary to allow others to believe what they most wanted to believe.

What happened *after* they were inside would determine whether or not she was granted access. Munroe folded her hands in her lap and turned to him with a smirk. "If I've properly analyzed, their arms will open."

"And if you haven't properly analyzed?"

She cut him a sideways glance. "Trust me."

Munroe's estimate was off by two minutes. According to Bradford's watch, the man, whose name she would later learn was Esteban, returned within eight. He inserted a key into the large padlock that kept the gate chained shut, pulled to open it, and motioned them through. Even though tree-lined, the property felt desolate, a bleakness that was possibly due to the weather or possibly not.

Bradford followed the sweep of Esteban's hand, driving to the area beside the main house, where two vans were parked in a space made for four or five. The vehicles were in relatively good condition and much newer than the overworked and run-down vans Munroe had seen both in documents and in person.

The dogs circled the Peugeot, sniffing the tires, and Bradford killed the engine. Watching the side mirror, Munroe said, "If for any reason you have to say something, use Arabic, it's the only language we share that they won't understand."

"Arabic?" he said. "It won't raise questions?"

"It's the only option," she said, "unless we play you as a deaf mute." And then, as if an afterthought, "I know you're a professional, Miles, but in the interest of covering my ass, when you hear English, no signs of recognition, okay?"

"Lakad fahimt," he said, and his reply forced from her a smile. His accent was nearly as clean as her own.

Esteban approached, and they both stepped from the car. Bradford kept a cautious distance as Munroe initiated conversation, and with the ice thawing if not broken, she beckoned Bradford closer, introducing him as her boyfriend, hopeful that the combination of Bradford's hypervigilance and his rudimentary Spanish would allow the meaning of what she'd just said to pass unnoticed. In her manner, she was wide-eyed and expectant, simple and generous, and she preempted suspicions about Bradford's lack of interaction with the truth: he wasn't from here and didn't speak the language.

Esteban led them inside the main house, where a wide foyer opened into a wider hallway that half-ended in a winding staircase, the narrower space continuing to a back door. To their right was a large living room with furniture that was newer and in better condition than she would have expected. The size of the building spoke to the ground floor holding far more than this, although the layout didn't provide for a view of anything else.

From what was visible, signs of occupancy were everywhere: cubbyholes that reached five high near the end of the hall, far too many couches in the living room, and in spite of the swept floors and washed windows, walls that had seen too many hands.

And yet, the house was eerily silent. There were no childish peals of laughter, neither the patter nor thud of little feet, and what voices did filter in their direction were hushed; all of it so similar to the descriptions Logan had given of Havens going Secret when unfamiliar visitors were on the property.

Esteban brought Munroe and Bradford to an alcove off the living room, a small space that, from its clean walls and minimalistic décor, appeared to get little use—or at the least far less than the rest of the house. They sat and Munroe attempted conversation, and although Esteban's words were casual and friendly, his body language showed increasing signs of discomfort. When, a moment later, a second man approached and introduced himself, she understood why.

The newcomer was Elijah, a balding fifty-something who, after his first words of introduction, Munroe pegged for West Coast American. He greeted her initially in English, and when Munroe shook her head and half-killed an attempt to return in kind, he switched to Spanish. His language was proficient, though not fluent, and his accent and word usage pointed to his having learned in another Spanish-speaking country.

Elijah thanked her profusely for the contribution to their home and, at times turning to Esteban for help in interpretation, asked her what had brought her and what she knew of them.

Growing up a missionary kid in the heart of Africa may not have been the logical segue to international spy and accidental assassin, but for this journey, Munroe's childhood was perfect. She knew the answers before the questions and simply reversed course, her story following the woven fabric of what she'd first told at the gate.

She was short on details and long on emotion describing a search for happiness that had taken her through travel, then work and money, and finally drugs until she was desperate. Wanting to put an end to life, she had a vision that showed her the path to the Haven.

If there was any part of this incursion that put Munroe on edge, it was the telling of the lie. Assignments had taken her across five continents, the gathering of information propelling her into multiple roles and many stories, each washing over her conscience more spot-free than the one before it. But never had she directly preyed on the spiritual faith of another.

To so easily enter this sanctum felt like a violation of what was hallowed, and in the face of this pause her mind returned to Logan's documents, to the pictures and images of true violation, to innocence and trust stolen, to the daughter kidnapped from her parents, and the nauseating rage that had consumed her at the first kindled again, bringing her fully around to the present.

At the core of every successful subterfuge lay the desire of the mark to believe, and in this Elijah was very eager. If he harbored doubts, her act of innocence and the thousand-dollar ticket at the gate had apparently dulled them. As if he'd at last found a true votary, he discoursed with her, providing answers to her questions, guidance to her angst, and introduced her to the building blocks of his faith.

From the windows the shade of the sky shifted from gray to black.

Esteban occasionally interpreted an English word into Spanish, as often getting it wrong as right, and Bradford sat silent until the middle of a lively exchange when he interrupted with but a stage whisper in Munroe's direction. She deciphered his request, Arabic to Spanish, asking for the restroom.

There was a moment of pause and the predicament washed over Elijah's face. He could let a stranger wander their house, or insist on having him accompanied and scare off the young potential proselyte who was so eager to give of herself and her fortune to God. In the end, and after an awkward silence, the man gave directions. Munroe, now certain that neither Elijah nor Esteban had understood the initial request, in turn interpreted to Bradford, adding a few words of her own.

"Try not to get lost," she said. "We know how you can be when you're in unfamiliar places."

"I'll try not to," he said.

When he had left the room, Munroe turned immediately to Elijah and rushed onward in the conversation. The move had been intended to distract from Bradford's absence, but it had little effect. Elijah after a continued pause finally said, "You speak Arabic?"

"Oh yes," Munroe replied, "and a few languages besides. It happens that way when you are a mutt of no pedigree and you have relatives around the world."

"And your boyfriend?"

She laughed, as if his question had been a joke. If they wanted to know what part of the world the Arabic-speaking, dirty-blond, gray-green-eyed stranger hailed from, they'd have to work for it. Her face drew serious, and in spite of the visible cues to Elijah's discomfort and internal debate, she pressed forward with a question that he would not be able to ignore.

Bradford returned a long ten minutes later, and after another fifteen of continued doctrinal back-and-forth, Munroe apologized and excused herself on account of a prior appointment. Elijah begged a few more minutes of her time, and although Munroe stood to leave, he called for his wife, and when she arrived, several smiling children were with her.

It felt like cheating, to know so much about them and what they intended from the encounter when they in turn knew nothing of her, but she was along for the ride and so hugged the children back as they hugged her. Munroe promised to return—tomorrow if she could.

By the time they left the Haven, they had been there nearly four hours. Four hours for Bradford's ten minutes of work, but the long wait leading up to his exit from the room had been every bit necessary.

"Four bugs," he said. "One in the kitchen, one under the stairs, one in the living room"—he shrugged—"and one in the bathroom." At Munroe's mock disapproval he said, "Hey, don't knock it. Listening to teenage boys' bathroom talk might be our best lead."

She chuckled. "Cameras?" she asked.

"Couldn't," he said.

She nodded and her face grew serious. "It's possible—highly probable, that she doesn't go by Hannah anymore. I mean, The Chosen change names often enough without being on the run, I imagine she's gone through quite a few."

Bradford nodded, and they both grew silent at the implications. They were halfway to the hotel before Bradford spoke again.

"So," he said, "how long exactly have I been your boyfriend?"

She grinned. "About as long as humans have lived on Mars," she said.

He smirked. "That's what I thought," he said, "but for a moment there it seemed I might have been mistaken."

Munroe said nothing, continued to smile, and kept her head tilted toward the window. She turned toward him to find him watching her, and this time it was she who winked.

The stoplight changed to green and Bradford returned his focus to the road, but he was grinning. "That wasn't flirting, was it?" he said.

She turned her gaze back to the window. "Maybe," she said. "I'll leave it to you to figure it out."

*   *   *

Arrival at the hotel shifted their interaction from rapport to func-
tional business partners. There were preparations to be made before
beginning the foray into the third Haven.

The nearly six hours away from the desk had allowed an over-
abundance of footage and voice recordings to accumulate, and so,
while Bradford sat on the bed, snapping equipment into place and con-
structing from obscure pieces what would eventually be the night's
placements, Munroe ran through the data, scanning, listening, ever
searching for evidence of Hannah.

Bradford completed his task and, with the equipment laid out,
stretched out on the bed, and so typical of battle-hardened soldiers
who learned to rest whenever the opportunity arose, fell right asleep.

Munroe continued on through the data, didn't stop until she came
to the end of it. She had no idea how long she'd been at the desk, her
only awareness that of muscles that had cramped and a room gone
silent.

In spite of all the information that had come in, there was still
no indication that Hannah resided at either of the penetrated Havens.
In frustration she stood and tossed the headset with more vehemence
than necessary. The desktop rattled, and Bradford, with eyes closed
and hands behind his head, said, "Nothing?"

"I think I've seen just about every child in Haven One," Munroe
said, "and unless she's never allowed out, or is lying sick in bed, she's
not there. As for the Haven Ranch, the recordings are clear, but unless
someone openly discusses kidnapping, it's still guesswork."

Bradford sat cross-legged on the bed. "There's Haven Three," he
said.

She nodded. "We'll see what tonight brings, but my gut tells me
that if she's in Buenos Aires, she's out at the ranch."

He raised an eyebrow, an invitation for her to share.

"It's a larger place," she said, "more of them are out there, and

I've also not seen any children over nine or ten at Haven One. If they congregate them, it's going to be at the Ranch."

Bradford said, "You're going back inside?"

"Of course," she said. "I'd like to get a visual setup in there, and I've got an open invitation to return—it beats getting bit in the butt by a pack of mangy dogs."

She paused, turned back to the desk. "I'm willing to stick with this as long as it takes," she said, "but I don't want to waste time chasing a phantom. Right now, all we have is the word of Charity's sister saying Hannah is in Buenos Aires. No offense to Logan or anyone else, but that's a pretty long stretch of trust. I need to establish that she's here before putting plans in place to get her out."

"I'm not keen on your returning," Bradford said.

Munroe turned, stepped toward the bed, and, with a smile that was evil, knelt on it, making a slow crawl across the mattress in Bradford's direction. She continued until she was face-to-face with him, then reached out and patted his cheek. The physical contact was soft enough to avoid implying a slap, hard enough to make him cringe in irritation.

"I'm a big girl," she said. "I can take care of myself."

"Just know," he said, "that if I feel you're under threat or in danger of any kind—physical or otherwise—the assignment or the kid be damned, I will come in, and I am prepared to use force if I must."

She continued to smile as she backed off the bed. "That's why you're my rearguard," she said, and then, having stood, and without breaking eye contact, she pulled on the black neoprene that was the base of her costume for the night.

Chapter 15

Shortly after midnight Munroe left the hotel room, and as he had the night prior, Bradford watched her go, continuing to stare at the door after it had shut.

Satellite images showed the house that they'd targeted as Haven Three to be the smallest of them all, and having already experienced the first two, Munroe had seen no need to waste time on a dry run.

Bradford opened the balcony door, stepped out, and, keeping back from the edge and her line of sight should she turn around, watched her step from the curb into the cab. Instinct said she was right about eliminating the dry run, and were their roles reversed it's how he would have called it. But a job was different when he wasn't mixed in the action. He was used to being in command, putting himself on the front and clearing the way for his men. Remaining on the sidelines left him uneasy and restless.

At least, if nothing else, the property was close enough that he could get to her in an emergency.

The taxi peeled away from the curb and Bradford turned toward the desk with its myriad pieces of equipment. He keyed in an instruction that activated one of the trackers Munroe had taken. Observing progress on a screen was a poor substitute for being there in person, but under the circumstances, watching her move through traffic electroni-

cally was the best that he could do. Astute as she was, she'd know what
he'd done and why, and would probably respond with mock chiding.

The tracker came alive, and eyeing the coordinating blip, Bradford picked up the phone. He had only a few minutes before Munroe
reached the target destination, but he needed to make the call now,
while still certain he would be connected.

It had been three days since he'd contacted Logan, and even if
Bradford hadn't already had audible proof that Logan had returned
to the hostel, it was easy to imagine that this was how he spent his
evenings: sitting, anxious, hoping for the call. Had it been Bradford
in Logan's position, the waiting would have driven him to madness.
Instructions or no instructions he would have been compelled to action,
and he understood from personal experience the restraint it took for
Logan to stand aside. But still, there was a certain vindictive sweetness
in knowing Logan's torment.

It didn't matter that Munroe was her own person and would never
have agreed to the job had she not wanted to do it. Nor did it matter that she'd taken the assignment with full disclosure, knowing well
what she was getting herself into. It mattered even less that work, with
its thrill of challenge and the intense focus it brought, was what kept
her alive and sane. None of it negated Logan having used his friendship and history with Munroe, and then Bradford's bond to her, to
manipulate the two of them into the project as he had.

It seemed a rightful return that Logan should be left blind and
forced to wade in a pool of frustration while the assignment went on
without him.

Bradford dialed.

The hostel had only one main line, and there was a wait while
Logan came to the phone. When Logan finally picked up and then
recognized the caller, his voice filled with relief.

"I haven't much time," Bradford said, "but Michael asked me
to update you." He paused, and when Logan said nothing, he continued.

"So far, she's located two of the Havens and what she believes is the third. We've got visual on one, audio on the other, and trackers on four of the vehicles."

"Is there any sign of Hannah?" Logan asked. His tone was calm, but the stress of inactive waiting was there in his voice.

"Not yet," Bradford said, "but if your daughter is in Buenos Aires, Michael will find her." The words seemed redundant, perhaps even patronizing, considering that it was precisely because of Logan's awareness of Munroe's ability that Logan had come to her for help.

There was a long pause and then Logan said, "Is there anything more?"

Bradford hesitated.

This was Logan asking. Logan. The man Munroe trusted with her life, and still he could not bring himself to divulge details that would in any way compromise the mission.

"No," Bradford said. "That's as far as we've gotten. I'll keep you posted as we progress. In the meantime, lay low, okay?"

"It's getting harder," Logan said. "Not for me—although, granted, I can't tell you how unbelievably frustrating it is not being involved—but I mean, to keep the others from taking matters into their own hands. Gideon, especially, keeps pushing for action, swearing up and down that he didn't come all this way to take a goddamn vacation. I'm not his boss, Miles, I can't make him do anything. The only thing I have going for me is that Charity's put her trust in me, and Gideon does what Charity wants. I don't know how much longer I can keep everyone here happy with promises."

"I'll talk to Michael," Bradford said, "and see what she has in mind, but, Logan, this is hurry up and wait. You and Gideon, of all people, should know how it goes, so sit tight. I'll get back to you next chance I get."

Bradford put down the phone, eyed the tracker, and leaned the chair back on two legs. Given the very personal nature of the job, he wanted a barrier between Munroe and Logan and minded not at all being the one to put it there. What he did mind was remaining still, helpless in a hotel room, nothing but a detached voice in her ear.

Bradford traced his thumb along the scar that ran from the base of his ear across his cheek. It was old in terms of injury, but it would be a long while before the pink faded into silver, longer still for the unspoken and unseen wounds to heal. He'd lost a good man in that fight, and the shrapnel from the same IED that had taken out his best friend's eye had narrowly missed Bradford's own. Some would say he was the lucky one, but what did they know about war and death?

Bradford watched the tracker come to the end of its journey. Munroe was running on empty. If there was any one person capable of going into a fight and coming out alive, it was she, but no matter how able she was, she couldn't function on nothing indefinitely—losing one's edge was how mistakes were made. Even the fittest could fail to survive when cut down by time and chance, and the way she pushed herself made him uneasy.

Her voice came online, and Bradford broke from his thoughts. Activity replaced stillness, and after a moment, visual replaced darkness. Like the foray before, the shadows were Munroe's friends, and she worked among them as if she were at home. She was sleek and efficient, and watching her from the vantage of the first surveillance camera brought on the exhilaration of observing a master at her art. Bradford worked with her, guiding her through the night, trusting her and fearing the vagaries of fate.

But there were no mishaps, no errors, and the hour it took to assemble and position the devices seemed to pass within minutes. Bradford called Raúl for the pickup, and figuring fifteen minutes at the extreme for Munroe to make her way back, he switched off and tossed the earpiece on the desk.

Tonight, she had to sleep—even if it meant medication—because tomorrow she would return to the Haven's fold, and this time, in spite of his protests, she would be going without him.

After thirty minutes, Munroe had still not returned to the hotel, and Bradford began to pace. Forty, and his forehead was to the wall while he pulled back on punches in order to keep from creating visible damage to either the wall or his hands. Fifty, and he tried to raise her on the earpiece, and when that failed, called the emergency cell phone, which went straight to voice mail.

There was a nervous edge to his movements, a disjointed lack of rationality to his thoughts. Time and chance. He cursed himself for having remained behind.

The cell phone bleeped and he lunged for it.

On the other end Raúl said, "Mister, the lady, she no come."

Inside Bradford's head, the fear chanted over and over: time and chance, time and chance.

He remained in front of the computer, stymied, struggling for clarity on where to go with the next step. He couldn't trace her because she'd left the trackers stuck to the vehicles at the Haven. For the time being, the best he could do was keep trying the phone. Beside the desk, bloodying his fist against the wall, he willed her to turn it back on.

Munroe waited for the clear, and then dropped from the compound wall to the shadows along the sidewalk. She traced her way toward the back of the perimeter, where she'd reach the narrow side street and, from there, turn again to the wider way for Raúl's approach.

This residential neighborhood was close to the liveliest areas of Palermo, and its streets, clean and small, were tinged with muted laughter and music and the scent of asado and cigarettes, which reached from indoors out into the cold late night.

Munroe drew in the evening air, and with it the satisfaction of a job gone smoothly, one step closer to bringing Hannah home. She moved steadily toward Raúl and the arranged pickup, thoughts of Bradford the worrywart on her mind, until movement along a branching side street caught her eye.

Her attention was arrested, not from the pedestrian familiarity but from the break in pattern: a parked Mercedes with two doors left open and engine idling. Beside the car were two men whose relative positions declared that one owned the car and the other the house to the right of it. Between the men, in the awkward position of merchandise being exchanged, was a child of nine or ten.

The man from the house pulled the child closer, tore open the robe that clothed her, and, apparently satisfied, handed a wad of cash to the man beside the car.

Munroe paused.

The man by the car shut the rear door.

Inside her head, the cries of duty to Logan and Hannah rose in rebellion against any detour, but her response was only to back up a pace and there, still cloaked in shadow, turn in the direction of the men.

Like the night in New York, like the nights of many kills, she felt no surprise at having once more been drawn toward the arms of evil. She felt only a consuming rage driving from within, unadulterated anger at the violation of innocence, a rush of blood so loud that it drowned out the laughter and the music.

In place of the evening's ambience came the internal percussion, the drumbeat pounding out the order to kill, the passion that would only be assuaged when blood was spilled and justice served.

Time slowed. Incremental slivers of understanding laid strategy across her mind: move against move, like a living chessboard. She had no fear of their weapons, though she trusted they were armed; neither had she fear of death nor fear of pain. The terror in the moment was failure, to inadvertently allow either of these men life, when they deserved none.

Speed.

She needed speed to reach both men, before either in their gradual pulling apart found safety; before the innocent disappeared forever behind locked doors.

Through the dark Munroe moved as a shadow across the pavement, first to the man with the car. The transaction finished, he'd walked to the driver's side. He placed a foot on the floorboard, and Munroe reached for him. He leaned down to be seated. Her two hands grasped his head.

Fiercely, violently, she twisted. Internally, pressure released with the snap of his neck, satisfaction like popping her own spine. He collapsed in the space of time it would have taken to draw a breath. Munroe followed him down to the seat, felt for a weapon where instinct told her to search, and with hands still gloved from the evening's original purpose, took the piece, checked the safety, and stashed it at the small of her back. She slipped from behind the car's door, moved around the rear.

The second man, with his back to the car, walked toward the house, toward the few stairs that led to the front door. His hand was firmly on the child's shoulder, guiding, if not pushing her forward, while she struggled, barefoot, almost naked, in the cold.

Munroe waited until the man unlocked the house door, then came again from behind. The child heard what the man did not, turned ever so slightly as Munroe drew close, and stared blankly into her eyes.

The man paused to follow the gaze of the child, and before he could react, Munroe placed her hands tight to his head. Again forceful, again violent, she twisted for the snap, for the euphoria, for a rush that sent the chemical cocktail coursing through her veins.

She let him drop to the ground and felt the rush, allowed the ecstasy to settle, and pushed past it for what was still to come.

The child stood frozen, face puffy from where she'd been struck, stained with old tears and grime, eyes wide, lips parted, head twitching slightly from Munroe to the man and back again, as if in her little mind she couldn't quite decide whether to scream or run or simply submit to what new twist fate had to offer.

Munroe felt for the man's weapon, took it.

The child began to move—a cautious step backward.

Munroe knelt and took the child's hand, but gently, so that she couldn't retreat farther. "I'm here to help you," Munroe said. "This bad man will be sleeping for a long time, so don't worry about him. Are you cold?"

The child nodded, eyes still wide, lips trembling, tugging slightly against Munroe's hold.

"Are you hungry?"

The child nodded; stopped tugging.

"I will take you someplace warm and safe where you can eat, yes?"

The child nodded, relaxed.

Munroe leaned forward and, with hands on either side of the girl's face, kissed her forehead. "You'll be all right," she whispered. "I promise you. But in order to make things all right, I need you to be very, very quiet. Can you do that for me?"

Another nod.

Munroe pressed her index finger to her lips, and certain that the child grasped her intent, she stood and with the weapon drawn opened the unlocked door.

She peered through the crack into the silent building. Pressed the door forward. Entered.

The interior was everything other than what the neighborhood promised. The foyer and the two front rooms that bordered it were bare and empty. There was no furniture, no artwork, nothing other than curtains, which shielded the windows from prying eyes. A dim-wattage bulb hung loosely from the ceiling down the hallway, casting a sick yellow hue.

Munroe motioned the child inside and again, with finger to her lips intimating silence, pointed to the tiled floor, to the corner that was least exposed to the rest of the house.

Munroe whispered, "You stay here, yes? I am coming back for you, once I know everything is safe." Such was her explanation to the child, but not her reason for entry. It was possible that this exchange tonight, money for child, was a one-off thing, but Munroe expected it wasn't; she needed to finish what she'd started, had to know if there were others.

The girl nodded a response to Munroe's request, and then, inexplicably, she smiled. Hers was a beautiful smile radiating innocence and trust, an unexpected contrast to the tearstains, grime, and torn and ratty bathrobe.

In a momentary pause from the rage and the blood, Munroe's

throat tightened and she forced back her own tears, which now threatened to surface in the wake of the child's gift.

Munroe turned again toward the rest of the house, toward the hallway that led away from the front with its open tiled rooms, forward toward whatever and whoever lay beyond.

Aside from the kitchen with its table and chairs, and one bedroom into which two mattresses were pushed against opposite walls, the rest of the four-bedroom house was empty. Anxiety rising, Munroe passed through the place a second time, certain that in the oddity of the emptiness, the completeness of the silence, she'd missed some vital clue.

Chapter 16

In the main hallway, vibration against Munroe's back caused her to pause. She placed a palm to the wall and felt it again, a solid repetitive thud, understood what it meant, backed to the end of the hallway. Knelt. Waited.

In half a minute came the scraping of a door on unforgiving hinges, a slice of the wall, moving inward, creating a doorframe where seconds before there'd been none. From within, a man's voice called out in a low bellow, presumably to summon his now missing partner.

Munroe drew and held steady.

The thud continued as the man with the voice worked up the last two steps.

He passed through the doorframe, a large man, not so much in height as in weight—his girth would have half-filled the hallway had he the opportunity to get that far, and by appearance, he'd climbed the stairs with effort.

Munroe aimed. Fired. Three shots in rapid succession.

The reports tore through the hall, their deafening aftereffects muting his yell and the thud of his fall.

She strode toward where he lay on the floor, clawing to shift position, struggling to reach the submachine gun still slung over his shoulder and now pinned behind his back. It was as if the shots had toppled him and in the fall he'd broken a leg or twisted a knee joint. He was bleeding from his side, a rich dark color that spoke of imminent death.

Around his neck was a chain with three keys. His left arm trailed into the space made by the new doorway, where tight stairs led to a fluorescent-lit basement.

Munroe put a boot on his weapon. He stopped struggling. Gaped at her. And with obvious effort, in his native tongue, whispered, "Who are you?"

In language familiar from an assignment long ago, she whispered back, "I am redemption."

She strained to hear footsteps, see motion, discover anything to indicate there'd been another with him, and after no reaction, put the muzzle to his forehead. Pulled the trigger. Yanked the chain off his neck, and headed down.

Underground, the tight hallway fronted three small holding cells. The concrete floor was damp, as if it had been recently hosed off, and the smell of bleach overpowered the scent of decay.

Munroe started with the cell farthest back, found the key, unlocked the door, and repeated this until each metal door had been opened and slid aside. In a space clearly intended to house several per cell, Munroe found only one child.

The girl cowered in a corner, a tight little ball of self-defense wrapped in dirty clothes that were still wet from hosing. Munroe ducked to enter the low-ceilinged room and then crab-crawled forward. "I'm not going to harm you," she said. "I came to set you free. Are you hurt? Can you stand?"

The girl said nothing, remained tight in her ball, and drawing closer, Munroe judged her to be around eleven or twelve. Munroe reached for her and the child screamed, hers a helpless plea, a cry, a terror to be left alone while she remained curled and shaking.

Munroe stayed low, stayed back just far enough to keep from being seen as a threat. "How many men are keeping you here?" she said.

Without moving or raising her eyes, the girl whispered, "Two."

"The fat one and the little one?"

The girl nodded.

"You are safe from them," Munroe said. "Come, come see, they are gone."

Munroe stretched her hand forward, but the girl did not move to take it. Munroe scooted closer, a cautious advance until she could touch the child. The girl flinched but didn't cry out, and Munroe, as gently as possible, brought her to her feet and pulled her along, up the stairs and over the body melting outward into pools of red; the body that, contrary to expectation, calmed the child from her shaking, the body that would forever be more fodder for Munroe's nighttime terror.

The first child had remained where Munroe placed her, and Munroe brought them both to the kitchen. "Eat," she said. "I have work to do. I'll be back as quickly as I can."

Munroe checked her watch. What felt like three hours had passed in fewer than ten minutes. Outside, the first man still sat, head lolled back, behind the wheel of the idling car. Music and laughter still tinged the winter air; life had gone on without taking notice of the dead.

Munroe reached in to shut off the ignition, took the keys, searched the man's pockets to retrieve the cash paid for the child, then dragged him to the steps and set him next to the other man so that they were tipped together like drunken conspirators in hushed conversation.

Again inside the house, Munroe searched the one occupied bedroom for money she expected to be hidden within it, and finding this in a small box stored beneath a loose tile, returned to the kitchen for the children, who had by now eaten their fill of food clearly intended for their captors.

Cautious inquiry brought forth facts about each child. The elder had been taken from her family far, far north in Bolivia; the younger had recently lost her parents and been sold by her uncle.

Outside, Munroe opened the rear door of the vehicle and ushered the girls in. She took the wheel, put the engine in gear.

Anger still raged, adrenaline still pumped, but the drums of death had gone silent. Thumbing through the vehicle's navigation controls, Munroe searched, found the closest convent, and headed toward it. She would place these daughters where men should never go, and the money that had been used to take their lives would now be used to save them.

Two hours late, Munroe returned to the hotel. Bradford sat at the desk, staring into space, and very nearly knocked over the chair getting out of it when she opened the door.

He stood at the far end of the room and said nothing. The look on his face spoke of panic phasing to anger, mixing with relief.

Munroe stepped inside and shut the door.

"Where have you been?" he said.

"I got held up," she said.

"It would have been nice of you to turn on your fucking phone."

Munroe bit down on her bottom lip. Waited. "Don't start with me, Miles," she said. "Now is really not a good time."

"Do you have any idea what kind of thoughts went running through my head when Raúl told me you never showed up for the pickup?" he said. "Do you have any idea at all, the hell I've been through over these last hours?"

"Do you have any idea what *I've* been through these last hours?" she said.

"Of course I don't!" he said. "You wouldn't pick up the goddamn phone!"

Munroe remained by the door, hands slack at her sides, adrenaline dropping, lack of sleep taking its toll, the haunted faces of the girl children staring out at her as she drove away into the night. Overwhelming conflict collided into a potent mix, bubbled to the surface, and the water of emotion, so rarely shed, began to seep.

Bradford, who had begun to pace, whose lecturing voice had risen further, stopped short at the sight of the tears. He looked befuddled, at a loss, as if he couldn't decide whether to remain planted where he was or move toward her in an attempt to comfort her. "Oh God, Michael," he whispered. "What the hell happened out there tonight?"

"I'll tell you everything later," she said, voice cracking, "I promise."

Bradford walked toward her, drew near, and she leaned in to him. He held her until the tears dried and the walls returned, until she could shut it out like she did everything else.

"You need to sleep," he said.

She sighed.

"It's been far too long," he said. "You're not helping anyone by running yourself ragged. Not Logan. Not Hannah. Not you, and you're definitely not helping me. Look," he said, pointing to his head. "Gray, gray, gray. One gray hair for every day I've known you."

His attempt at humor took the edge off. She tilted her head upward and her eyes met his. "If I have nightmares, I'm medicating," she said.

He nodded and rested his cheek against hers, wondering if his face looked as grim as he felt. "If that's what it takes," he said.

It was after five in the morning by the time Munroe settled, and as expected, she was out within seconds of having lain down. Running on empty as she was, it stood to reason that once she allowed it, her body would simply shut down, but Bradford knew as well as she did that the exhaustion wouldn't matter. The nightmares would come; it was only a matter of when.

He'd encouraged her to take this assignment, had hoped that work would ease the pressure, that being busy again would temper the inner turmoil and set her world right; and it might still, but not tonight. He sat on his bed, notebook in his lap, looking up occasionally from the rapid scrawl he put across the pages. It would be a short night, and if they were lucky, she'd get several hours of true sleep before the interruption began.

In any case, she was sleeping. That was one of two issues handled, but her return to the Haven would definitely be the more difficult to deal with.

Bradford was familiar with Munroe's patterns, had seen her in operative mode more than once, and knew how effortlessly she slipped into whatever role was needed to beguile a mark, but her interactions with Elijah and Esteban, her professed enthusiasm for the lifestyle of The Chosen and approval of their beliefs, went far beyond that.

Stress over it as he may, he could never voice concern that her apparent acceptance had not been entirely an act.

Although, personally, he could never allow another to take a wife or child for sexual pleasure, or submit to someone who ordered him away from one nuclear family and into another, and although to him the beliefs surrounding sex with Jesus, talking to dead people, and magical powers were absurd, when The Prophet called, as was evident by the large numbers among The Chosen, thousands followed.

Bradford could sense the appeal, the draw that giving up autonomy might have. To abdicate was a form of escapism. To release oneself from independence, to follow The Prophet was to be free from personal responsibility.

He thought of Munroe and felt the weight of her struggle.

In the stillness, the hours passed, and the relaxed pattern of Munroe's sleep was a drowsy background to his writing until a casual glance in her direction found his eyes locked on her vacant, unblinking stare.

The shock raced through his system and his heart hit hard in response. He knew the look, and from the last time he'd watched a nightmare surface, readied for what was coming.

Chapter 17

Without moving, Bradford scanned the bedroom surfaces, checking once again for anything that could be used as a weapon against him. While his eyes darted from Munroe to the room and back again, his hand, slowly, so as not to alert her to his movement, put down the pen and inched it underneath his pillow.

These were the actions of a man who found himself accidentally in the path of a dangerous, wild creature.

Had Munroe been awake and aware, a fight with her was a suicide gamble, but in this state of somnambulism, she moved slower, was less intuitive, and with a struggle, Bradford could gain the upper hand, as he had the time before. Munroe wasn't truly sleepwalking—at least not in any clinical sense; people who killed people in their sleep didn't do it while they dreamed. But whether it was clinically true or not, this was real, and she was deadly.

Her eyes were locked on him now. Whatever went on inside her head, whatever she lived and saw, given her predilection toward violence, she would not stop until she woke or he was dead.

Munroe sat up, swinging her legs over the side of the bed, never breaking eye contact. Her hands flexed, tensed, and then repositioned, as if they carried knives.

Bradford had the advantage of timing and awareness, and he remained still, taut, and ready. If he was careful, he could end it in a single move, but doing so required getting her on her back in order to pin her under his weight.

Her focus was singular. No matter the angle, her eyes, still glazed, still unblinking, continued to track him as she stood and took a step in his direction. He waited. She took another step. And then she struck. A slash toward his jaw that would have been lethal were she armed. He weaved and she missed narrowly.

Bradford twisted to follow the flow of her movement, intending to throw her off balance, and was met with an elbow to the side of the face. The blow came so quickly that he'd no time to brace for it, and the shock wave inside his head sent him reeling.

He shifted, prepared to block her follow-through, but it never came.

Instead, Munroe stood motionless, feet planted, staring at him with a puzzled expression. And then, slowly, she glanced down at her hands and consciously unclenched them.

They both remained solidly in place—he eyeing her cautiously, she staring at some vague point near his knees, blinking as if she were running through a memory.

Finally, she raised her eyes to his and said softly, "Did I hurt you?"

He reached for her, his hand to her waist, his touch cautious and gentle. "No," he whispered, "I'm fine."

Her eyes followed his movement, but she gave no other reaction.

"How long was I under?" she said.

He directed her toward her bed, and although she didn't resist, she cut him a wary glance. "About five hours," he said.

At his guidance, she sat on the bed and then lay back with her hands behind her head. "That's a decent night's sleep," she said.

Bradford sat beside her, elbows to knees, watching her face, and then, certain that she was fully coherent, said, "If you want to sleep more, I'll get you a bottle."

She shook her head. "Five hours is a good stretch for me," she said. "I'll save the bottle for when I really need it."

She turned toward him and reached for his face, running her fingers along the side of it. His cheek was tender, and Bradford flinched.

She pushed slightly, turning his head so that the side of his face fully reflected the bedroom light.

"I'm sorry," she said.

He smirked. "I knew what I was getting myself into."

Munroe returned a weak smile and sat up. And then, as if a switch had been thrown and the temper of the room altered, she said, "Come on, let's go find Logan." Her smile widened. "If things go well, I might even get to hit Gideon."

Bradford chuckled at her joke, but he understood fully the well-spring from which it came.

Meeting with the trio was a necessary evil, one that Munroe would have preferred to postpone until she had determined with certainty whether or not Hannah was in the city. But the confrontation couldn't wait. She knew Logan well, knew that he wouldn't have even mentioned the issue of Gideon to Bradford had he not felt the situation slipping from his grasp. Gathering with the three was more than just a nod in Logan's direction, it was a warning shot—a preemptive strike against stupidity.

The Chosen had kept Hannah on the move over the years, and if the girl was in Buenos Aires, it would take relatively little to spook them to take action once more. The pieces were currently in place, data beginning to pool, and Munroe didn't need Gideon or Heidi screwing things up in pursuit of their own objectives, whatever they might be.

They were to meet at twelve on Logan's side of town, the café chosen specifically for its proximity to the hostel. It would allow the others to get to it on short notice and provide Munroe enough traveling distance for her head to clear from the aftereffects of sleep.

They traveled first by city bus and then on foot, public transport always Munroe's preferred mode of transportation when on assignment. To center oneself in the cadence of human activity was to absorb the essence of a place, like breathing air when underwater, and so much better than the stifling confines of a taxi. Around her, conversations ebbed and flowed, the radio blared, street signage passed and blurred; the whole of the city's chaotic fragrance filled her senses and she became one with it.

They arrived at the café five minutes before the agreed-upon hour, and there Logan sat waiting at a table near the window. He stood as they approached. His eyes were ringed with shadows of sleeplessness, and when Munroe reached to hug him, his body seemed to deflate, the rigid tension going out of him.

Both hands on his shoulders, she took a step back and scanned him. "You hanging in there okay?" she asked. He nodded, and as they sat, scooting chairs up to the table, his face remained wan.

"Where are Gideon and Heidi?" Munroe said.

"I asked them to give me a few minutes," he replied, and then looked toward Bradford as if to beg for the same courtesy.

Bradford remained seated, face placid, arms crossed, and Munroe acknowledged his body language. He'd go if she asked, but she wouldn't. Her decision to keep him close wasn't personal, it was strategic. No matter how often Logan had watched her back, he couldn't help her now, and with what she was preparing to do, she needed Bradford fully.

Munroe placed a hand on Logan's knee and, as gently as she could, said, "There's really nothing we have to offer, Logan, that can't be said in front of the others."

"I was just hoping that there might be something more," he replied. "It's difficult being out of the loop."

"We're moving as quickly as we can," she added, "and you know as well as I do that to pinpoint three locations and set up surveillance in such a short time is pretty fast work."

"I'm appreciative," he said. "Please don't think that I'm not."

She said, "Signal the others, I know they're watching."

Logan, with his back to the window, stood and, no longer blocked by the signage, removed his jacket and placed it on his chair. When he sat, he was smiling. "I'm not that predictable, am I?" he asked.

"Gideon is," she said, and then, in a show of normalcy, she motioned for the waitress and ordered coffee and *facturas*.

It took but a minute for Gideon and Heidi to enter the café. Gideon, in the lead, slowed when he caught sight of Bradford. The subtle pause was a good sign. That the others were, until now, unaware of Bradford's involvement spoke volumes to the lengths Logan had gone to respect Munroe's wishes.

As a matter of decorum, Munroe reintroduced Bradford to the group, although he already knew more about Gideon and Heidi than either could possibly imagine. The small talk was short. Perfunctory. The closest she would go to preliminaries and niceties.

Her primary purpose for coming had been simple: outline the progress, make sure they understood how easily it could be undone, reiterate that they needed to back off and let her do her job. As Bradford had done before, Munroe limited information to what was innocuous. She provided no locations and kept back the details of having entered the Haven Ranch.

In contrast to Logan and Heidi, who were by all appearances accepting, Gideon exuded aggression. He finally uncrossed his arms and, leaning forward, said, "Are you certain these places you've got under surveillance are really Havens?"

Munroe nodded. "One hundred percent."

"You should let us be a part of this," he said. "We're insiders, we can verify what you can only guess, make sure you're really on the right track. We know them, know the way they talk, know who these people are, and by not letting us be a part of this you're taking a huge risk."

"It's a risk I'm willing to take," she said.

"It's not your decision," Gideon said. His tone remained calm, but his body language spoke to his anger. "This is our project. You work for us, not the other way around. We hired you, we're paying you."

"No," she said. "I don't, you didn't, and you're not."

She paused for effect, continuing before Gideon could say more.

"I'm here for Logan," she said, "end of story. You have no idea what it takes to run a project like this, but I do. It's what I do for a living. If you doubt me, ask Logan. Not only have I put more money into this than all of you combined, but it's my neck on the line if something goes wrong." She nodded toward Bradford. "At best, you're paying for my rearguard, and good luck convincing *him* that he works for you. I've given you an overview. The play-by-play is provided on a need-to-know basis, and quite frankly, you don't need to know."

Gideon's face reddened, but he said nothing. Munroe gauged him carefully. The provocation wasn't meant as a way to establish rank or to throw her weight around—she didn't need to waste words in order to achieve that—she was pushing in order to prove to Logan what she already knew.

Gideon wasn't here for Hannah. He could claim it as much as he wanted, but she was merely a cover. Sure, getting the girl would be a huge upside, but there was more that he wanted, something that required access to the Havens, and Munroe had a pretty good guess as to what it was. Gideon, just like Logan, and possibly Heidi to a lesser degree, was using the others to get to what he was really after.

When this was all over she could sit back and reminisce over it, but at the moment Gideon was kindling to a fire, a match to gasoline, a danger to the assignment and, by implication, to her.

Munroe placed both hands on the table, shifted forward, and in a near whisper said, "Look, we're all here to get a little girl back to her mother, right?"

The nods of agreement were reluctant, but there.

"Finding Hannah is why I'm here," she said, "the *only* reason I am here." She reached under her chair and retrieved a small envelope. She slid it across the table in Gideon's direction. "This is me," she said, "my professional life, facts that you won't find in any Internet search." She paused. "I deal in information. This is my area of expertise, and I have the backup manpower to get Hannah out once we find her." Munroe paused and, with a hard stare in Gideon's direction, said, "Provided she doesn't disappear while we're in the middle of this."

Gideon took the envelope and stuffed it into a pocket. He stood. "I'll read it when I have a chance," he said, "but unless you have something further to add, I'm finished here."

Munroe placed her hands on the table. Folded them. "It's all I've got," she said.

Leaving the table, Gideon passed Munroe, brushing close against her as he did. Too close. Her reaction came in a nanosecond of calculation. Instinct before thought. He was still in midstep when Munroe stood, caught him at the wrist, twisted so that she had the advantage of position, and yanked his pinkie back nearly hard enough to break it. It was a movement so sudden that Heidi jumped.

In a voice low enough that only those at the table could hear it, Munroe said, "You really have no fucking idea what you're dealing with, do you?"

Chapter 18

Gideon's mouth formed into the shape of an O, and he began to lower as a way to lessen the pain. She bent with him, her mouth following his ear, and she whispered so that only he would hear. "I don't want to kill you," she said. "I won't kill you, but if you continue to fuck with me, you'll wish I had."

Munroe's respect for Gideon had gone up a notch with his attempt at placement—he'd been swift and smooth, and had it been anyone else that he'd tried to mark, he would have surely succeeded. But professional admiration could never stand in the way of the need to assert dominance. Alpha to alpha, Gideon must never forget his place.

Logan and Bradford sat motionless, eyes wide, and it wasn't until Munroe pried the tracking device from Gideon's palm and slapped it on the table that the rest of them understood what had taken place in the space of those few seconds.

Gideon's face was red, his jaw clenched, and Munroe readied for retaliation. Instead, he straightened, turned, and left the café.

There was silence as they watched him go.

"Many of us don't take well to any form of imposed control," Heidi said. "Ours was a totalitarian life, and we're allergic to authority now." She paused. "He's a good person," she added, "just thought you should know."

"I'm in no position to judge," Munroe said. "If circumstances were different we'd probably get along fine, but right now my world revolves around getting to Hannah and defending the process. I do that by taking advantage of opportunities and protecting them from threats."

Heidi nodded, and then paused in the slow hesitation of someone who wanted to say something but was worried about doing so.

Whatever tumbled inside Heidi's head, Munroe needed to hear it, and with time at a premium, she needed it fast. In an immediate downshift and instant role change, Munroe dropped her shoulders, became visibly smaller, and followed this with a relaxation of facial muscles, all of it culminating in a wistful smile.

The response was as expected, a reciprocal relaxation on Heidi's part, and with the easing of tension, Heidi's struggle ebbed. "I was wondering," she said, "if on any of the surveillance you've done, you've come across a guy named Malachi. Well, maybe it's Malachi, maybe it's Elijah."

Munroe said, "Who?"

Heidi reached into her purse and pulled out an aged photo. She slid it across the table. "This guy," she said. "I don't know for certain what name he uses now, but the last time I saw him he'd just switched to Elijah."

The photo showed an unmistakable blond, mustachioed, much younger, guitar-playing version of the Elijah that Munroe had spoken with yesterday at the Haven Ranch.

Munroe studied the photo and after a moment slid it back. "The information is still pooling," she said. "I haven't had a chance to go through it all yet."

She'd given the truth, if not the answer.

Heidi put the photo back and nodded, disappointment written on her face. "He's my dad," she said. "I haven't had any word from him in about six years. We used to be close. In spite of all of the insanity and the times we were kept away from each other, he always found a way to make sure that I knew he was there for me. He was a good dad. That's probably the most painful thing in all of this—being cut off from my family. Not just my dad, you know. I used to take care of my brothers and sisters—well, half brothers and sisters—I was more their mom than my stepmom was."

Heidi paused, looked toward the table, and said, her voice lower this time, "I guess I hoped that maybe in the course of all of this, someone might spot him, might be able to tell me if he was still in Argentina. I'd really like to connect with him again, to see my brothers and sisters again."

"What about your mom?" Munroe asked.

Heidi shrugged. "It wasn't the same."

Munroe understood the ache of separation and, with true compassion, said, "When all is said and done, if they're here, I'll let you know."

Heidi's return smile was warm and trusting, an almost childish acceptance that contrasted with her extreme intelligence and yet was completely sincere. It was difficult not to like Heidi, and the idea of being able to fulfill such a simple hope as a by-product of finding Hannah was a pleasant one.

"Will they let you in?" Munroe asked.

"Maybe," Heidi said. "It's worth a try."

Munroe turned to Logan and said, "Walk with me for a moment, will you?"

Logan stood and grabbed his coat. To Bradford, Munroe said, "I'll be back in ten."

Outside the café, the sky was overcast and the humid chill of yesterday had taken on the aspect of a misty rain just wet enough to coat everything in a layer of teardrops, yet not quite enough for umbrellas.

Munroe took Logan's hand and led him away from the entrance until they were out of sight, and there, under a storefront awning, she sank back against the wall. He followed suit, and together, in comfortable silence, they watched pedestrian traffic.

Finally she said, "Do you still think Gideon is here to help find Hannah?"

"If that's all he wanted, he'd be content to let you do your job," Logan said. "Especially now that he knows you're capable of it."

"He wants inside," Munroe said. "I'm going to venture that the only thing holding him back from making a break and attempting to find them on his own is the risk of screwing things up for Hannah—for Charity. He wants it bad, Logan." She looked off in the distance for a moment and then turned back to him. "What's Gideon's relationship with Charity?"

"He's been in love with her for years," Logan said.

"Are they a couple? An item?"

"If Gideon had his say they would be, but Charity's not interested in him in that way."

"He doesn't know about the two of you?"

"Nobody knows," Logan replied. "Except for me, Charity, you, and"—he paused—"well, now Miles."

She nodded. "Miles is my rearguard, Logan, you know the drill."

"Yeah," he said. "I know how it goes."

Munroe stared off in the direction that Gideon had walked. "Logan, it's important that you realize the situation you're in. As of right this moment, Gideon is the biggest threat we're facing in getting to your daughter. He came down here for a reason, his time is running out, and he's not going back until he gets what he wants. If they spook because of something he does, Hannah's gone again. You know that, right?"

Logan nodded. Kicked a leg back against the wall for support.

"I know you all think that Charity needs to keep her name out of this," Munroe said, "but if you're serious about getting it done, I need you to buy me time. If Gideon will do what Charity wants, you need to get her involved."

"It won't be a problem," Logan said. "I talk to her at least once a day, sometimes more. She's biting her nails even more than I am right now."

"Tell me about Gideon," Munroe said. "What's his story?"

"Kind of like mine," Logan said. "He was tossed out of The Chosen when he was fifteen. He'd never been to the States before, had never even met his grandparents, and then one day he was dropped off on their doorstep. He tried going to school, was too far behind academically to keep up with his peers, couldn't adjust, couldn't relate, started getting in trouble, and before long his grandparents kicked him out."

Logan paused, and Munroe motioned for him to continue.

"He ended up on the streets," Logan said. He chuckled. "Remind you of anyone?"

She smiled. Logan grinned.

"I was lucky," he said. "Eric's dad took me under his wing and put a roof over my head, even if it wasn't much. Gideon didn't fare as well. He was in nonstop trouble and twice narrowly missed a term in juvie. He saw the military as a way out, and when he was seventeen tried to enlist. He couldn't without a guardian's signature. His grandparents had already disowned him and his parents treated him like a pariah and refused. Some love, huh? They'd rather have their son out on the streets than break with The Prophet's antigovernment worldview. So he survived by picking up odd jobs, eventually got into the Marine Corps, did his time, and then moved on from there. That's Gideon in a nutshell."

"What were things like for him while he was in The Chosen?" she asked.

"I don't know," Logan said. "I only knew him when we were younger—seven—eight—didn't live with him when we were teenagers, and these days he doesn't talk about it much. That's how some of us deal, you know? Pretend it didn't happen."

"Anybody in particular he might have a vendetta against?"

Logan paused. Looked directly at her. "You think that's why he wants in?"

"Gideon's got a big chip on his shoulder," she said. "He's got something to prove to someone, and he doesn't strike me as the type to want to prove it with words—maybe he wants to pound some issues out."

"I'll ask around," Logan said. "See what I can find."

When they returned to the café, Bradford and Heidi were talking. There was an intimacy to their conversation, both of them leaning in toward each other, steady eye contact, and Heidi's face was flushed in a way it hadn't been when they'd left.

It was hard not to like Heidi.

Munroe slowed. Her face burned hot. The café ambience faded. The reaction, instant as it was, came as a surprise. In split-second intervals Munroe studied Bradford. Studied Heidi. And then turned concentration inward.

Emotion on an assignment could get a person killed. She pushed it back. Each step toward the table was a conscious rejection of the intensity that had set her heart racing, each step a return to the focus on the tasks at hand. By the time she and Logan had joined the others, it was as if the moment had never happened.

The good-byes were brief, the promises short, and the return to the hotel made in silence.

For Munroe the transit was downtime, transition from one role back into another, and Bradford, aware of how she worked, seemed content to allow her the space she needed.

It w a s late afternoon by the time Munroe approached the Haven Ranch. The sky had brightened, and scattered rays of sunshine gave rise to the illusion of warmth. She rolled the Peugeot to a stop at the gate, stepped out for the push-button, and then returned to the car to wait. Gaining entry for this round should, by all expectations, be straightforward.

This time it wasn't Esteban who made the long walk to let her in but a teenage boy. She guessed him to be around fifteen or sixteen, still in that awkward stage between child and man, with limbs longer than they should be and blemishes where they shouldn't be.

When he had swung the gate wide, Munroe lowered the window and eased the car forward a few feet.

"I'm Miki," she said.

He didn't reply, merely nodded and met her eyes shyly.

"I can drive you to the house," she said, "and save you the cold walk back."

He shook his head. "It's okay," he said.

His reaction was a good gauge. They trusted her enough to send a teenager but not enough to allow him to ride with her.

Munroe parked in the same space that Bradford had the last visit, although today hers was the only vehicle. She stepped out of the car to wait, and when the boy approached, she held out her hand. "I didn't catch your name," she said.

He paused and then reached to shake it. His touch said that shaking hands wasn't an everyday occurrence. "I'm Dust," he said. Their conversation had so far been in Spanish and the English word was a jarring contrast.

Dust for Dustin or Dust for dirt? Given the nature of the rest of The Chosen names thus far, Munroe guessed dirt.

"Is Esteban here?" she asked.

Dust shook his head but offered nothing else, and not wanting to make him more uncomfortable, Munroe stayed silent, following him to the room in which she'd sat the day before.

"Elijah asked me to tell you he'll be here in just a minute or two," he said.

This was the longest string of words the boy had yet to offer, and although from his Scandinavian looks he was clearly not from here, his accent was perfectly local. He'd been in Argentina for a while.

Dust's dichotomy was part of what made The Chosen what it was. Not Argentine, nor wholly American, the group and the people within it were a hodgepodge of races and cultures homogenized into the culture of The Prophet. From Romania to Zimbabwe, Chile to Finland, The Chosen were different faces, different Havens, functioning as shell organizations under a myriad of names, but behind closed doors the lifestyle was the same: the culture of The Prophet.

Dust left the room, and alone as Munroe was, it would have been a prime opportunity for her to wander. But instinct told her to wait, and so she sat while the minute or two turned into five, and when Elijah arrived, he wore the harried look of a cook in the kitchen on Christmas morning.

Munroe stood in greeting, and he wrapped his arms around her in a tight and welcoming hug.

Her response to the uninvited physical contact was instant, a drive so intense that it required every shard of focus to keep her solidly in place. The rhythm of violence pounded in her chest and she remained frozen, fighting the urge to destroy him, to crush his head against the wall.

With fire burning a trail through her veins, she forced reciprocation.

To every single person in this commune, close physical contact was a part of everyday life, and this was a dangerous tightrope act that she had to walk. The rage had nothing to do with Logan or his daughter or even Elijah; this was Munroe's own past, a history that would forever allow but a handful of people safely into her personal space—and Elijah certainly wasn't one of them. It would be several moments until the urge to strike passed, and to remain so close to him now required pure, practiced self-control.

"We're short-staffed today," Elijah said, seemingly unaware of how near he stood to hospitalization. "Why don't you join me in the dining room? We can talk during cleanup."

Still fighting the internal pressure, still not trusting herself to speak, Munroe nodded, followed, saw in his profile and his gait similarities to Heidi that she hadn't noticed before, and was irritated for having missed them.

They passed from the alcove, through the living room, past the stairs, and out the back door to a path that led to the annex. There, Elijah slid open wide glass doors, and instead of standing back to allow her to pass, as politeness would have dictated, he walked in ahead.

The doors opened directly to a room, which by appearances accounted for half of the building. The space was lit by neon, tiled white, and half of it was filled with row upon row of rough-hewn picnic-style tables and wooden benches. The other portion was devoted to serving food—large industrial-size pots sitting on a wide counter gave testament to as much—and a dishwashing assembly line.

The only others in the room were children, eight of them, between what seemed to be ten and twelve years old, silently busying themselves clearing tables and sweeping the floor. Munroe strained to see beyond Elijah's shoulder, scanning faces, searching for a shock of blond hair, green eyes, anything that might confirm that she had come to the right place, but there was little opportunity.

Elijah ushered her to a table where a stack of papers and file folders were turned blank side up, and against all hope he motioned her to sit where his face was to the room and her back against it.

Each of these details filled in the gaps, all of them snapshots of commune life. She'd arrived at the end of either a very late lunch or an early dinner, and most of those who had once filled this hall were gone again, leaving this particular group of children to do the cleanup. Elijah, harried, juggling his paperwork and his leadership, filled in overseeing these children while whoever usually held the position was out in the vans today, and he, apparently unfamiliar with how odd such a scene would play out to fresh eyes, carried on.

Munroe listened, answered, her mind working overtime to stay in the present while thoughts pinballed through her head. That Hannah could be here, in the same room, invisible while her back was turned, made the attempt to focus on Elijah's words almost unbearable.

She waited an appropriate amount of time, waited until the sounds and the limited conversation behind her indicated that the cleaning had come to an end, and then, as Bradford had done the day prior, she requested the restroom.

Elijah motioned one of the girls over and, in English, asked her to show Munroe where the bathrooms were. He said nothing more. No request to keep an eye on her, no warnings about limiting conversations, no instructions to wait with her charge. Perhaps such things were so ingrained as to make further commentary unnecessary.

Munroe stood, turned, and scanned the room, running her eyes from face to face, but found no one resembling Charity or Logan.

The girl led Munroe through another sliding door, to a hallway, which passed three smaller rooms, each without a door in the frame, each lined with bunks that stood three beds high.

The bathroom was makeshift and tightly fitted, narrow stalls of plywood on a cement dais set across from the one sink—what appeared to have been a large bathroom, gutted and refitted to run several toilets into plumbing built for one.

Munroe didn't linger. There was no place to stash either a bug or a camera, and her reason for the trip had been to see the faces in the dining room.

The girl was still outside the bathroom when Munroe exited, eliminating any chance of poking around the bedrooms. They returned to the dining room in silence, the child offering no conversation and Munroe hesitating to initiate it lest her motives somehow be misconstrued.

In the dining room, the children sat at a table, silent, focused on small cards, and the girl went to join them while Elijah stood and motioned Munroe over.

He handed her a small book. "I want you to read this," he said. "I've got a few errands to run and then I'll be right with you."

He signaled to a boy of twelve. "Nathaniel will show you the way back," Elijah said.

Munroe knew the way. Didn't need a guide or a warden, no matter how young, in order to walk from one house to the next, and she knew that Elijah knew that she knew. Instinct screamed in rebellion, but acquiescence was his expectation, and whether this was a test or merely the way of The Chosen, she couldn't break from her role.

Showing only gratitude, she followed Nathaniel out.

The boy said nothing, and so again Munroe walked in silence, and at the alcove off the living room, Nathaniel left her alone.

She glanced around the room, sat, and made herself comfortable for the indefinite wait—by the number of pages she'd been assigned, it could be hours. She cracked open the book, and as Elijah, her new spiritual guide had instructed, she read.

Chapter 19

Miles Bradford slipped on his coat. And then, with a hesitant, backward glance toward the desk and the tenuous connection to Munroe that the array of equipment and wires represented, stole out the door.

He'd no idea when he'd hear from her or when she'd return—if she'd return—and he'd waited as long as he could for any form of communication beyond what he'd picked up from the stairwell bug when she entered the Haven Ranch.

In the unknown, it was a risk to head out. Away from the desk, he'd be unable to monitor, wouldn't know until far too late if anything eventful happened, but he wanted to see Heidi, needed to see Heidi, and the opportunity was fast slipping away.

They'd arranged to rendezvous on the sly, away from the others, had set a time and place, but in his reluctance to leave the desk he had waited too long and was now beyond fashionably late. He could only hope she'd wait, because he needed to meet now. Today. Not another day. And he had no way to contact her to let her know he was still on his way.

Outside the hotel, Bradford hailed a cab, and when he arrived at Cementerio de la Recoleta and spotted Heidi just outside the gated entrance, leaning against the wall, face in a book and the sun's sparse rays shining down on her, relief welled through him. When she saw him, her face lit into a chill-dissolving smile.

In spite of his hurry and the uneasiness that had brought him here, Bradford couldn't help but return the smile in kind.

Heidi greeted him with a hug and stepping back said, "So, tell me, Mr. Secret Guy, what it is that you need so badly that it comes to this."

Bradford smiled again, his mouth in upward movement while his eyes diverted down the lanes, searching out anything familiar, chasing body shapes and wary steps. He'd asked her to be careful, to come alone, but both Logan and Gideon had the skill to follow undetected if they wished, and to ask her now if she was certain they hadn't would only insult her.

"Thank you for meeting me," he said.

Heidi nodded, and he looped his arm in hers, diverting her down a branching mausoleum-lined lane. Here they would blend in, just one more couple among so many others taking in the dead on a pleasant afternoon stroll. He'd chosen this place because it wasn't far from his hotel, and as an attraction to both tourists and locals alike, it would be impossible not to find, thus lessening the chances of either one of them getting lost.

Bradford stopped several times, ostensibly to admire the architecture, the marble and stonework, while his eyes passed beyond the lifeless monuments to the living who came and went. He saw no sign of Gideon and, better still, no sign of Logan, although it was impossible to know for certain.

Each time Bradford stopped, the puzzlement on Heidi's face increased, but she said nothing until at last they came to a secluded alcove and Bradford headed toward it. The nook, with only one way in and out, was a field operative's suicide, but under the circumstances, perfect. One final glance back the way they'd come and Bradford said, "Look, I need your help."

"I figured as much," Heidi said.

"Off the record, okay? Logan can't know, Gideon can't know, and most of all Michael can't know."

Heidi nodded, and Bradford hesitated. "Michael speaks very highly of you," he said finally. "She says you've been brilliant in explaining the mind-set of The Chosen, and I'm hoping you can help me."

He hesitated again, and Heidi's smile radiated, as if she had all the time in the world, as if they stood waiting under spring blossoms instead of the warming winter sky.

"I haven't done the research Michael has," he said. "And I haven't had a friend to drop snippets of information over the years. My experience with groups like The Chosen is limited entirely to what I've heard through the media and in dealing with extremist factions in the Middle East. I've got images in my head of Jonestown, Koresh, Heaven's Gate, Aum Shinrikyo, and terrorists—mass suicide and murder—so forgive me any misperceptions, okay?"

Heidi nodded again, as if to say "go on," and in response Bradford again paused. He burned precious time, needed to get back to the hotel, but the thoughts that had made so much sense when faced with Munroe's solo entry into the Haven Ranch were quickly dissolving into the abstract.

He sighed and ran his fingers through his hair, fought back the urge to pace. "Hypothetically," he said, "unless we can do a snatch-and-grab, to get Hannah will mean Michael goes inside the Havens. That was the whole point in bringing her into this, right? And the way I see it, it's eventually going to come to that. But what about brainwashing? If Michael goes in, what are the chances she'll be coming out the same person who went in—if she comes out at all?"

Heidi's shoulders relaxed and, with a grin that bordered on smirking, leaned against the cold stone of the wall. "Yeah," she said. "That's kind of a misperception."

There was a long silence as she gazed first at the ground and then off into some invisible distance. Bradford knew the look, the struggle for words, and so he let her be, although as the moments ticked away it was more difficult to fight the urge to hurry her.

"What's your idea of brainwashing?" she said finally.

Bradford shrugged. "Mindlessness, I guess, from constant and repeated mental abuse. When a rational person starts doing irrational things that someone else has told them to do—things they never would have done before."

"So, going against free will and changing them into something else, right?"

Bradford nodded.

Heidi said, "It would mean that a brainwashed person would lose the capacity to reason or to make personal decisions that fell out of line with what the brainwasher wanted or programmed, that they'd kill or commit suicide if told to, even if they didn't want to do it. Mindless obedience, right?"

"I suppose," he said.

Heidi's eyes took on a note of sadness as they wandered again toward that invisible distance. "Isn't that just another way of saying 'the Devil made me do it'?"

Bradford pondered her words. "You're saying there's no such thing?" he asked.

Heidi turned toward him. "I'm not saying that brainwashing doesn't exist," she said. "I may personally doubt it, but I'm no expert. I wasn't raised in any of the groups that you mentioned. I can only speak of The Chosen, of my own childhood and that of my friends."

"There's no brainwashing in The Chosen? People actually do those things because they want to—of their own free will?"

She shrugged. "Yes and no. It really depends on how you define brainwashing. There's a lot of indoctrination, a tremendous amount of control, and so much pressure to conform to 'the new' and heed the word of The Prophet. I think a lot of people would consider that brainwashing—but that's not the same as having no mind of your own. Everyone still has free will. Any one of the adults could say no."

"But how?" he said. "And if that's the case, why on earth do people do it, why do they stay?"

Heidi shrugged again. "Sometimes they go along with things out of fear of God's judgment if they don't, or because they feel it's what God wants of them. Nobody's a zombie or an automaton." She hesitated, as if she found tedious Bradford's inability to accept what to her was so obvious.

"Look at it this way, Miles," she said. "There are two types of people in The Chosen. There are the ones who had adult or nearly adult lives before choosing to join, and there are people like me and Logan and Gideon, the children, who never had another beginning, never had a choice, who had no education, no access to television or books, little to no connection to family outside the movement, and who were terrified of what would happen to us if we were to leave. If anyone was brainwashed, it was us, the second generation.

"So then, completely cut off and indoctrinated as we were, if we are brainwashed, *how* can so many of us turn our backs on everything and walk away, sometimes even in the middle of the night with only the clothes on our back? And if we, the ones who never knew anything other than their world, can turn our backs on it, how can anyone who was supposed to know better claim brainwashing as an excuse for what they did?"

Bradford said, "So, these people on TV who say they were brainwashed into joining a cult, or that they did awful things, criminal things, against their will, that the leaders made them do it, they're lying?"

"We're all susceptible to influence to one degree or other," Heidi said. "Apparently some more than others, but that isn't the same thing as having no mind of your own. People who have sex with children, that's not brainwashing. That's not even coercion. Nobody took a bat to their kneecaps and said have sex with kids or we'll hurt you. People who beat children, starved them, locked them in closets, called them demon-possessed, that's not brainwashing, nobody *made* them do that.

"Do you know what the big punishment in The Chosen is?" Heidi asked.

"I don't think so," he said.

"Excommunication."

"Meaning?"

"Let's say a man in The Chosen is caught molesting little boys, which is against The Chosen's rules because it's homosexuality. Even though it's also a crime, members of The Chosen, even the parents of the child, are *forbidden* to go to the police about it. Excommunication, which is sometimes only for a few months, is such a big deal, they consider it to be punishment enough. By their reasoning, sending the criminal out into the Void is the worst possible thing they could do. Excommunication is the heavy stick that they carry to keep people in line, and members will do just about anything to avoid it. But if brain-washing was all that it is cracked up to be, why the need for the big stick? Shouldn't everyone automatically obey and keep all the rules?

"To say that the things done to us were done because of brain-washing is a slap in the face to those of us who were tortured. They did what they did because The Prophet said it was right in the eyes of God, because they placed a greater value on some screwed-up ideology than they did on protecting the rights of children. But they were not mind-less when they did it."

"So what you're saying," Bradford said, "is that the only way a person like Michael would end up changed or stuck inside was if what they said and how they lived appealed to her?"

"Pretty much," Heidi said.

"Does that also apply to someone who might be—" Bradford paused. "Well, someone who might be going through an emotional upheaval—would it be different for that type of person?"

"Is she?"

Bradford shrugged. "We all have our history, our scars, sometimes literally," he said. "What Michael does is highly specialized. It's not something you go to school for. The things that made her what she is left their mark, just like with you, just like with Gideon and Logan."

Heidi nodded. "If she falls for any of it," she said, "then she's not half the woman I think she is, and I suspect that in reality, she's much more than I've even glimpsed."

Bradford nodded in appreciation of Heidi's perception. He straightened and took his hands from his jacket pockets. "Thank you," he said.

"Better now?" she asked.

"Yeah," he said, "much better." Bradford paused, the running clock counting down time in his head, the pressure to get back to the hotel becoming stronger, but seeing Heidi there tipped back against the wall while her words tumbled around in his mind caused him to stop. He shoved the need to hurry aside.

"When you did finally get out, how did you manage?" he said. "Without any education or any connections, how did you start?"

"It's like being an immigrant stepping off the boat, heading into the big city with nothing but the clothes on his back," she said. "Where *do* you start? I was lucky. My younger sister had already left, so I had a roof over my head. But we were both naïve. Our behavior was weird to people, we were taken advantage of until we figured out how things work here. But at least we had each other. Some of my friends were luckier—they had grandparents or uncles or aunts who had never given up hope of bringing them home and were able to help them get on their feet. The worst are cases like Logan and Gideon who were basically dumped on the doorsteps of unwilling relatives and ended up on the streets until they were old enough to sort things out."

"Isn't there some remedy?" Bradford said. "Have you ever thought about trying to get some closure, some form of justice through the court system?"

"Sure," she said. "Lots of us have."

"And?"

"Statute of limitations. Jurisdiction. Lack of evidence. It gets pretty complex." She shook her head. "There's no legal recourse for us," she said. "The criminals polished their image, and we, the ones who tell what happened, are the bad guys." She sighed. "But you know? You do the best with what you've got. You try not to lose any more time on the ones who hurt you, try to make something good out of it—they don't deserve my future the way they took my past."

"There's so much I want to understand," Bradford said. "But I'm already running late. I have to get going."

"Anytime," Heidi said, and she reached out to give him a parting hug.

Bradford walked to the lane and, after checking for signs of either Gideon or Logan and finding the way clear, blended into the crowd. As he moved away, he glanced over his shoulder. Heidi remained with her back to the wall, staring after him, and in that look he felt the touch of her agony.

Chapter 20

Outside the cemetery, across the lawn and on the other side of the fronting street, Logan stood tucked into a doorway and out of sight. For forty minutes he'd been waiting and watching, and now patience had been rewarded. There, blending with the crowd, a furtive glance right and left as he left the graveyard, was Bradford. The movement was quick enough, natural enough, to go unnoticed by most, but Logan understood. Bradford was wary of being seen, of being followed.

And it was tempting too, the idea of tracking him back to wherever he'd come from and figuring out where Munroe was holed up.

But there wasn't any point to it.

Logan hadn't followed Heidi here as a way to get to Munroe.

Bradford's showing up was an unexpected twist that explained, possibly, Heidi's erratic behavior today. For once, she was cautious of being followed—although her attempt to lose an invisible tail had been clumsy and awkward at best.

Bradford, though, was a twist that Logan didn't understand. Especially that he, either alone or at Munroe's bidding, had so furtively sought out Heidi. Answers would have to wait. Trying to track Bradford, like attempting to figure it out, would be a waste of energy and distract him from more important issues, such as keeping Heidi under control.

Bradford headed right, down the winter-brown lawn and toward a parking area that would have been heavily shaded in summer, nearly disappearing among pedestrians, and after a short while, reemerging to hail a cab. A moment later the vehicle swerved into the stream of traffic. Bradford was gone.

Logan shifted to twist out the kinks of the last half hour and, supposing that Heidi would arrive shortly, continued to watch the exit. He counted down the minutes, and as if on cue, there she was.

For four days he'd been following as she went about town visiting one random spot after the next. He followed because he didn't trust her. By outward appearances Heidi was all-innocent and angel smiles, but behind everyone's backs she was sneaking around. Unlike Gideon, with his in-your-face attitude, Heidi was subtle enough that it had taken Logan a couple of days to pick up on her patterns: a shopping trip here, an eatery there, her absences easily explained and hardly noticeable, especially since she'd turned into an early riser, and he and Gideon tended to be out late and wake up late.

In his gut, Logan knew what Heidi was up to, though he had only suspicions to go on. They were damn good suspicions—good enough to keep him following—just not quite good enough to bring Munroe into the equation, to get her involved the way he had with Gideon. Besides, he didn't need Munroe for Heidi. He could handle Heidi on his own.

His biggest issue right now was exhaustion. Trying to juggle Gideon and Heidi, to keep an equal eye on both of them with their opposite schedules, was creating burnout, and fast.

He'd thought that Munroe's intervention, her update on the project and warning to stay the hell away from it, would have affected Heidi—put some sort of pause on whatever it was she was doing, the way it had with Gideon. But so far, nada. It was up to him to put a stop to things before the situation got out of hand, before it came back to haunt him. But for that he needed some kind of proof, and *that's* where the fine line between hope and disaster was drawn.

Logan stepped from his spot to the sidewalk and, without ever truly taking his eyes off Heidi, followed parallel to the end of the street, to the waiting cab, reaching it right about the time that Heidi found one of her own. She climbed in, and the hunt was on again.

Keeping up with her day after day seemed so melodramatic, like a movie chase scene—"Follow that car!"—but that was as light as it got. Heidi, with all of her warmth and delicate ways, had just as much potential as Gideon to blow this project, and this close to finding Hannah, there was no way in hell Logan was going to let it happen.

Heidi's vehicle led through Recoleta back toward downtown, and Logan knew now where they were headed. Not through any clairvoyance on his part, but rather because this would be the third time in four days that she'd made the trip to Calle Florida.

The shopping street was a consumer's paradise and a surveillant's nightmare: blocks and blocks of stores, cafés and restaurants, street performers, hawkers, and jostling throngs, which made it easy to lose track of a person. He knew instinctively why Heidi kept going back. If there was ever a place The Chosen would target in order to hand out pamphlets during their begging, Calle Florida, with its abundant tourists and dense crowds, was it.

The taxi dropped Heidi off near Plaza San Martín, and from there she walked the remaining distance. Logan kept behind her, just far enough back that in her casual stop-starts and occasional window browsing he remained out of her line of sight. Like on the days before, it was easy enough keeping track of her while on the nearby streets, which by comparison were relatively empty. But once she turned down Florida proper, where the crowds unpredictably ebbed and rapidly thickened, all bets were off.

Logan moved in closer, grateful for the teal in Heidi's coat, which made it possible to pick her up again after he'd lost sight for longer than was prudent. The first time Heidi had come here, she'd walked the entire length of the strip, then caught a cab and returned to the hostel. But the second and third times, she'd moved on to other locations, and he suspected today would be more of the same. For that reason he needed to stay close.

And then Heidi was gone. Just like that. The crowd had parted, then surged, an undulating wave of people that had blocked his sight for but a moment, and then . . . nothing.

Logan picked up the pace, moving past a tight pack, switching right, then left, and no Heidi. He turned a slow circle, feeling a twitch of panic, trying to figure out where she'd gone, wondering if all this time she'd known he was here and only now had decided to make a run for it. He wondered if she'd led him to this street deliberately to lose him. The crowd parted. It was for a second, but he saw her, ten feet away, stock-still, solid in place, hands clenched, staring.

Logan followed her line of sight, and in that moment he froze. A block of concrete hit him midchest and his legs locked up. Every muscle, every nerve ending called out to do what Heidi was doing right now, to stand and stare at the small group of girls up ahead, with their bags and their papers, to search out faces, and from there to move quickly in a search for Hannah, because he knew instinctively that if *they* were here, then she might be close.

But even if he found her, then what? Grab her and run? To where?

Michael was in the city, near the Havens, on her way inside, and Michael could do what he or any of them could not: get Hannah safely out of the country.

Against everything he wanted to do, every instinct, every desperate longing, on trust alone, Logan turned to face Heidi. On her he focused his frustration, and with the emotional fog lifting, anger filled the gaps. Right here, right now, Heidi could ruin everything.

Reason kicked in. He moved toward her, a rapid pace that brought him to her side within seconds, and next to her ear he hissed, "What the hell are you doing?"

Heidi jerked, spun, her face blank. This was surely a double shock. First the girls just down the street, now him, here, right beside her, while she was caught red-handed. Heidi's mouth was moving, but no words came out, and she looked ridiculously fishlike.

She turned her head back toward The Chosen. Logan grabbed her biceps, locked an arm around her waist to avoid attracting attention, and spun her around so that her back was to them.

He was eye to eye with her, and every bit of anger he felt must have been reflected on his face, because Heidi went slack.

He walked her forward, away from the girls with their pamphlets and sob stories, through the crowd, those many empty faces, one foot in front of the other while his own mind reeled out of control. He hailed a cab and rode with her back to the hostel.

She said nothing for the duration, and Logan also kept silent. He was working through the script, the things he would say once they were settled, the words that would guarantee she put off her headstrong notion for good.

There was no doubt in his mind who Heidi had spotted—the features were there clearly for anyone with half a brain to see. And he had even less doubt of the shock Heidi would experience on so suddenly coming upon her sister. Had Logan somehow spotted Hannah on these streets, there's no telling what he'd have done, and it burned, knowing that Hannah *could* have been there. Continued to burn knowing that if Hannah *had* been there, and had any one of those Chosen spotted and recognized Heidi, Hannah would be lost again, forever.

Burned.

He kept it to himself during the drive and allowed Heidi to remain lost in her thoughts, whatever they might be.

The taxi stopped outside the hostel, and Logan paid the fare. He escorted Heidi to her room but braced the door open with his foot when she attempted to shut him out. With a sigh, apparently realizing it wouldn't be over quite this easily, she let him follow.

In spite of his burning anger, the ride had given Logan time to settle, so that by the time he spoke, his voice was calm and even. "That was a nasty thing you did," he said. "Do you have any idea what would have happened if they saw you?"

Her mouth said, "They didn't." But her eyes said, *How the hell did you find me?*

"The problem with being as smart as you are," Logan said, jabbing an index finger in her direction, "is that you start to think everyone around you isn't quite up to your speed, but you know what? You're dealing with some pretty fucking intelligent people here, Heidi."

She nodded. Face grim. "I'm sorry," she said.

"Oh, really? Is that what you would have told Charity, told me, told Michael, when The Chosen packed up and shipped Hannah off again? *I'm sorry*. That's real grand of you."

"They didn't see me," Heidi said.

"What the hell were you thinking?"

"I didn't really think I would find them," she said. "I was killing time, keeping busy."

"Not anymore," Logan said. "No more traipsing around town looking for begging spots or trying to find their secret mailboxes or any of that shit. You stay put. Out of the way. That's what we've been asked to do."

Heidi sat on the bed, arms crossed, quiet, and Logan knew exactly why. From her look, her expression, maybe he was wrong to assume that he could handle her. It was touchy ground, him asserting authority over her, telling her what she could or could not do. She might take it from a boss or a boyfriend. Might take it from a stranger. But with the familiarity of their background, the terms with which they were raised, there was no way she'd take it from him or any person once part of The Chosen. And he didn't blame her. It would have been no different were their roles reversed.

Truth was, the only thing stopping her from doing anything rash at the moment was her devotion to the greater good—of finding a way to prove to the world, or anyone who would listen, that The Chosen leadership and The Prophet were scum. Getting Hannah out was a huge part of that.

After a long stalemate, Logan broke the silence. "Okay," he said. "I apologize. I have no right to tell you what to do, and can't make you do anything."

Heidi nodded. Uncrossed her arms.

"That said," he continued, "I *can* predict Michael pretty well, and I promise you that after everything she's invested in this, and after all the warnings she's given you, if you do anything that interferes with her getting to Hannah, she's going to take it personally, and she will exact a price."

"What kind of price?" Heidi said.

Logan shrugged. "Honestly, in your case, I have no idea. Something she deems a fair exchange," he said. "Set you up for a crime and watch you squirm your way through the Argentine legal process and possibly into prison, maybe. Whatever it is, I would never want to be the person to cross Michael," and then he stopped, because he could see from the shadow that passed over Heidi's face that he'd driven the point home.

Chapter 21

Elijah didn't come, and in the protracted silence, Munroe waited with the deliberate patience of a predator on the hunt. The world of information, of infiltration and surveillance, of buying and selling secrets, was a world of endless waiting, idle stress, and measured self-control, a learned and practiced skill of knowing when to move, when to stop, and how to maintain a holding pattern for indefinite periods of time.

This was a holding pattern.

Like the four hours that had been spent in this room yester-day in order to allow Bradford his ten minutes of reconnaissance and placement, the waiting would buy her what she wanted. If she hadn't already been handed a book and asked to stay, she would have requested something, anything, to prolong the visit until the missing vans returned and the house began to fill again. Elijah, with his desire to bring her into the fold, had solved that problem.

As if on cue, from beyond the front door came a mounting wave of sound, of footsteps and voices, all drawing closer to the house.

Munroe switched off the light in the alcove and moved through the darkened living room toward the front door. She chose the chair closest to the entrance, positioned so that its back was to the front of the building, and its direct view to the foyer blocked by a small wall segment. Here in the darkened corner she could see the side and back of each person who passed, and the disadvantage of not being able to clearly scan faces was compensated by placement. Unless someone specifically turned around and peered into the room, she would never be noticed.

Through the front door they came, mostly teenagers, tromping in from the cold with the weariness of a hard day's work. Based on the size of the vehicles and the size of the crowd, if this was the return of only one van, it had headed out with more people than seat belts.

There was conversation and a form of lighthearted jostling among the youngsters as they passed, and with no consciousness of noise level, the building took on a tone closer to what Munroe expected to be its natural state.

They passed in groups of two or three, loaded with coats and heavy bags, and were it not for the information she already had, by looks alone it would have been easy to assume that they were students returning from school rather than from begging in the street, which made up much of their daily routines.

From beyond the open front door and still out of sight, the voice of a woman called to several in the group. Three of the teenagers, having just passed through the foyer, paused and then turned. They stood but several feet from where Munroe sat, each face clearly illuminated by the hallway lighting.

And in that moment, time stopped.

Munroe measured out the heartbeat trying to escape her chest.

Feet away was the mirror image of a younger, female Logan.

Munroe fought the urge to stand, to snatch, to run, and made the split-second decision to hold back, based on the factors hammering their way into mental position: location to the door, number of people nearby, time needed to get to the vehicle, and, provided she could neutralize Hannah, the process of fighting her way out with a hundred pounds of dead weight.

And so Munroe stared, action held in check by the lasting shock of seeing the miniature copy, blond-haired and green-eyed, before her. Slowly, the pure focus of impartial, unemotional assignment returned.

Through the freeze-frame moment, she had nearly failed to register the weight of the words that the girl had spoken to that detached and invisible voice beyond the door.

Mom.

The child, whose true mother and father had spent the last eight years fighting to find her, had addressed another as her mother.

Munroe waited, tense, eager for the woman to pass, hoping for a sign of recognition, to know who this person was, and as the last of those who'd filled the van trailed inside, she found nothing but a female indistinguishable from any other stranger.

The foyer emptied, and Munroe remained motionless in the dark corner, pushing down the slow, smoldering burn that she'd been sitting on all day, processing the moment, running scenarios.

To strike too quickly with a lack of valid information would invite mistakes; to wait too long was to expose herself to unwanted scrutiny and suspicion. The mental chessboard set itself out; move against move, strategy to probability, chance against the known, while she counted off time in her head and waited for the next group to enter the foyer.

Another ten minutes and the procedure repeated with a second group, this time the youngsters closer to preteens and nearly as many adults as children. On the heels of this came another, and as the first two groups had done, they filtered down the hall, some heading up the wide staircase, others passing on through the back door toward the annex.

With each return, the volume in the house grew. The stairwell became a beehive of activity, the back door a constant open-and-close as the main house filled and emptied again.

If Munroe had calculated correctly, there were still two more vans to return, but there was no point in sitting here waiting for them. She'd seen what she wanted, knew what she required, and the spectrum of objectives had narrowed down to two: she needed to gain familiarity with the layout of the building and to know where Hannah slept.

The back door opened again, and instead of the steady flow heading out, a solitary set of footsteps slapped a rapid pace toward the foyer. Munroe stood, moved back across the room to the alcove, and flipped the light on. She was nose to the book when Elijah entered.

His mouth was smiling, but his eyes were worried, and his previous harried look had grown to frazzled. Something was keeping him occupied, had him stressing badly, and he perfectly portrayed the stereotype of an executive just out of a bad news conference.

"Hey," he said. "How's the reading going?"

In a contrasting calmness, Munroe looked up, her face full of peace. "It's wonderful," she said. And then, as if in a bewildered afterthought, added, "What time is it?"

Elijah glanced at his watch, a nervous movement that had to be more habit than necessity because she knew that he knew exactly what time it was. He uttered the hour, and Munroe feigned innocent surprise. "It passes quickly," she said.

He paused and then relaxed, the tension he carried fading, as if he'd shifted from work to pleasure. He sat next to her, so close that they almost touched, and he appeared oblivious to any discomfort the invasion of her personal space might cause—even less aware that his proximity might be unwanted or of the effort with which she pushed back the returning rage.

Elijah asked about the material she'd read. He fished for depth, for emotional connection, and Munroe's words flowed in response. Her answers were a cautious hot-and-cold, a drawing close, then a pulling away that toyed with him in the same way a player might keep a love interest on the line.

Elijah put a hand on her knee and said, "Why don't you join us for dinner?"

At his touch, Munroe's vision shifted to gray, and in microsecond gaps she fought back the desire to break his fingers. With a smile plastered on her face and a long pause that could only be interpreted as thoughtful consideration, she said, "I think I would enjoy that."

His hand remained on her thigh, burning a hole of violence through her core, and then, in a sudden movement, he stood.

"Wonderful," he said, and her body reacted to the removal of his hand as if she'd received an oxygen mask in a room full of noxious gases. She handed him the book, but he shook his head.

"Keep it," he said. "There's more to read and we can discuss it as soon as you've had the chance."

"Thank you," she said, and then, with another vanload of footsteps playing background music, she clutched the words of The Prophet to her chest and followed Elijah out the back door to the annex.

If the main house had been quiet, the dining room was the perfect counterpart. The room of tables that had been so empty earlier in the day now birthed life and volume, and was still in the process of filling. From the sliding door on the far right wall, a girl of thirteen or fourteen led a group of six toddlers into the room, and then, having delivered each child to groups at separate tables, joined a table near the center of the room.

Although the varied looks and racial features of each group would have implied otherwise, the scene was set as if dinner was being served in family groups, and so Munroe scanned the room, searching out Hannah. She found her several tables down with the woman she called Mother and three younger children. The woman shared none of Hannah's physical characteristics, instead sporting a contrasting mixture of nearly pale green eyes, thick lashes, and jet-black hair against skin the color of a perfect tan. There was no sign of David Law, although he was perhaps in one of the vans that had not yet returned.

Elijah led Munroe to the same corner table that they'd sat at earlier in the day; this time it was filled with the wife and children she'd met before. Three teenagers and a young couple with a baby were there as well, and as Elijah explained her presence to the others in English, he introduced the couple to her as his son and daughter-in-law, and grandbaby.

These were Heidi's people, the son and two of the girls clearly her biological brother and sisters, and the others, although half siblings and sharing the Filipina features of their mother, still showed familial similarities. Of those at the table, the teenagers spoke Spanish with perfect fluency, but the mother and younger children spoke only English.

Munroe was offered a seat that allowed her a vantage point of the room, and she took it all in, detail by detail, under the guise of conversation. Industrial-size pots again filled the serving counter, and three teenagers stood over them, scooping food onto plates as the line progressed, cafeteria style. One of Elijah's daughters brought Munroe a plate, and Munroe nodded in thanks over the indiscernible soupy contents.

The influx began to ebb, and Munroe estimated there were a hundred and fifty in the room, the majority of them children and teenagers. Her eyes scanned, running over the faces of the children, all of them young, innocent, and perfect, some fighting in their own way for a slice of limited attention spread so thin among so many, others, as with Elijah's children, appearing indifferent to their parents completely, all of it so painful to watch, but Munroe couldn't look away.

Thankfully, The Chosen didn't carry weapons. Had that been the case, should anything go wrong with extracting Hannah, the potential for collateral damage would be tremendous to the terms of unacceptable. Munroe's eyes rested at last on a young man, mid-twenties, with a guitar hung around his neck. With a perfect lack of self-consciousness he stood, strummed, and began to sing.

The eating stopped, the discussions stopped, and a hundred voices filled the room in unison. One song segued into another, and into another still, until the medley relating to food and the gratitude of belonging to this large family of believers had lasted nearly ten minutes.

When the music ended, the young man said a few words of thanks to the Lord requesting cleansing of the food from any germs, then he joined his family and sat. The volume in the room went back to its original cacophony. He had spoken in English, a clear articulation that reminded Munroe of Logan, his accent distinctly American but with twinges of Western Europe and hints of Latin America, and it seemed that most of those here shared that same accent.

Munroe rejoined the conversation and continued to surreptitiously watch the room. The influx was over and so was the singing, and the table at which Hannah sat still held no David Law.

For being the man who had kidnapped a child to bring her back into a movement, the man who was the closest thing Hannah would have known to a father and the only thing she had resembling real family, David Law was strangely absent. Munroe didn't need to know where he was in order to pull off this job, but like a wasp in the room, it was helpful to know his location.

The meal wound down, families filtered out of the room, but Elijah's remained and Munroe stayed with them, internal tension mounting while she applied focus to the moment. She wanted Hannah. Wanted to wander. Reconnoiter.

Instead she sat, plying the made-up desire to belong and feigning interest in their beliefs, sweetly conversing and answering questions, until eventually the group of teenagers who had stayed behind to clean up completed their chores, and Elijah and his family invited Munroe to join them in the living room.

There, crowded into every seat and the floor space between, were the same one hundred and fifty from the dining area. Together they spent an hour of dedication to The Prophet, songs and selected readings, and as Munroe assumed was the same for many in this room, she countered the boredom of it all by allowing her mind to wander free, wondering if they were so naïve as to fail to recognize the obvious—that even the most unsuspecting visitor would realize that this evening's show had been put on especially for her.

Chapter 22

By night-owl standards, it was still early when Munroe left the Haven, although the Haven itself, in shutting down for the evening, had already grown dark and quiet. Unlike the rest of the city, The Chosen were early to bed and early to rise.

Elijah and Esteban walked her to the car, and then with feet shuffling and this time not-so-subtle suggestions about giving to God, they prolonged the good-bye to the point of awkwardness. Munroe refused to offer, they didn't directly ask, and she toyed the issue along, string to the cat, courting an invitation, and it came right on schedule, Elijah offering to spare her the trip home if she'd like to stay the night.

Munroe appeared to weigh her options. She would stay the night, yes. But not tonight. She had prior plans with her family that she couldn't break, but tomorrow she would be free and tomorrow she would return.

Tomorrow she would steal Hannah from this place.

Munroe drove to the hotel by rote, traffic signs, lane markers, and suicidal merging processed automatically by years of Third World experience. Her mind worked overtime to deconstruct the violent mix of emotion that she'd held in check throughout the evening, piecing together the steps that must follow to bring Hannah safely out.

Bradford was at the desk when she opened the hotel room door. He stood, his face expressing genuine happiness at her return. The welcome warmed her only until she opened the closet and sensed the subtle perfume of Heidi coming off his coat.

Munroe froze in a flash of knowledge and paused for the brief moment that it took to push back the hiss of anger that followed in its wake. She returned Bradford's nod, his smile, and in a mixture of exhaustion and nervous tension, stepped to the bed and lay down, fully dressed.

"Can I join you?" Bradford said, and Munroe, hands behind her head and staring at the ceiling, shifted slightly to allow him space to sit. Legs over the side, leaning toward her in quiet company, he asked, "Have you eaten?"

"If you could call it food," she said, and then, after the slightest pause, sat upright. "Come on, let's get out of here. You've been cooped up all day and I need to crawl outside my own head and process a shit-load of information—I want to talk it out with you," she said, "and I'm sure you're waiting to hear it."

"Indeed I am," he said.

Munroe shed her clothes, changed into evening wear, and then from the hotel they found a *milonga*, one of the city's many dance halls devoted to tango. Nearing midnight, and still early by city standards, the place was only partially filled, and they easily found a spot on the outer edge of the tables, among others who had arrived as couples. Here in the thick, smoky, dark, music-filled room, they could talk, undisturbed, while watching dance partners ply their skill on the wide center floor.

Over drinks and light food, Munroe told Bradford about the day's events, taking him through the routines and what she knew of the building layouts thus far. They discussed strategy, options, and the pros and cons of a late-night extraction versus tagging a van and pull-ing Hannah off the street once The Chosen deployed their members for begging. Each option held its own series of unknowns and set of complications. They made preparations for both eventualities.

As was his reason for being here, Bradford would run matériel and specs as backup to Munroe's intel, and he outlined the protocols necessary to get Hannah securely over the border once they had possession.

"I'm considering letting Logan know," Munroe said. "If nothing else, that we've pinpointed the location."

"Another person in the loop brings another potential round of trouble."

She nodded, acknowledgment of his concern if not concession to his point.

Bradford continued. "Regarding Logan, I spoke with him just a bit before you got back today. He needs to talk to you about Gideon."

Gideon's name brought with it a different set of issues. Being this close to Hannah, the job really didn't need a loose cannon getting into the mix, and any information Logan had to offer was crucial.

Munroe checked her watch. "What's Logan's schedule these days? You think he's still up?"

"Even if he's not, I can call him," Bradford said. "I got him set up with a cell phone."

She ran a finger around the rim of her water glass. "Invite him to join us, will you?"

He nodded and stood. "Let me find some quiet," he said. "I'll be back in a bit."

When he returned, he said, "He's on his way. Half an hour, maybe," and Munroe let loose the grin she'd been holding back for the last half hour.

"There are women making eyes at you," she said. And teasing, "Why don't you dance?"

Bradford paused a moment, and he followed her line of sight down the room to a table of three single women. His expression morphed into a slow smirk, and with a sly glance back toward Munroe, said, "Maybe I will."

She hadn't expected that he would take her up on the dare, but without a hint of hesitation, he locked eyes with a long-haired brunette, and ticked his head upward in *cabezazo*, the way locals did. The woman smiled, nodded in return, and Bradford stood and made his way to her.

Munroe had observed the woman over the course of the evening, had seen her level of skill, and was certain that Bradford had as well. She wondered how the mixture would blend, how much embarrassment would ensue—but only as long as it took for Bradford to reach the center floor.

And then her jaw dropped, if only slightly, at the unexpected poetry in motion. The man could *dance* and displayed dramatic flair that she'd never before seen in this soldier of casual confidence.

The set ended, Bradford conversed with his lady friend long enough to be polite, the pain of broken English and broken Spanish etched on both their faces, and finally, catching Munroe's eye, returned to the table, grinning.

"Ah," he said, arms stretching, knuckles cracking, "that was good."

"What I don't understand," she said, "is why I'm even surprised."

"I don't know why either," he said. He held his hand out to her. "Dance with me?"

She raised an eyebrow, and he continued holding his hand in her direction.

"After that performance?" she said.

"I'll make you look good," he said, "I promise." And he motioned his fingers toward himself, as if to say "come here."

She was still smiling but shook her head.

"Oh, come on," he said, his tone wheedling and cajoling. "You, the woman who's not afraid of anything, hesitate to dance with me?"

"I'm not afraid," she said.

"Then let's have at it." The playfulness had gone out of his voice, his eyes were locked onto her, and he stood, undeterred, waiting.

She reached out her hand, and when their fingers connected, the warmth and the electricity of the moment transferred skin to skin.

In the center of the room, Bradford first led slowly, the motions of teacher to student, until realizing she was less a stranger to tango than he; he pushed livelier, harder, as the dance became magic, beat to angry beat, upper bodies taut, hips fluid and sensual, each touch alive and expressing far more than words ever could, coupled, heated and sweaty, until Munroe caught sight of Logan in the back of the room, and the spell was broken.

She nodded in his direction, and Bradford, following her line of sight, waited until the music paused and then led the return to the table.

Logan joined them a moment later. He'd been watching for a while, which was written on the cloud across his face, as if tonight's snapshot of play was somehow indicative of how Munroe had thus far spent her time in Buenos Aires.

She reached over the table and pinched his cheek, the way she would a little boy. Her gesture was an instant icebreaker, and Logan batted her away. She laughed, ignored his silent accusations, offered him a drink and antipasti, and then went straight to business.

"I got the information you wanted about Gideon," Logan said. "It might help to clarify his motives here."

Munroe nodded, motioned for him to continue.

"So, apparently, he lived in Argentina when he was fourteen and fifteen. Seems like when he first got here—right after he turned fourteen—there was a guy living in the Haven—single guy, American—don't know his name." Logan took a breath, paused long, and then continued. "He sodomized Gideon," he said. "It was a pretty frequent thing."

With Logan's words, the air split, and Munroe, drawn away from the evening, from the distraction of Bradford and the music, stood on the edge of a precipice, staring down at molten depths. Her pulse quickened. She pulled her hands from the table and placed them on her lap, where no one would see the destructive anger that worked itself out in her knuckled grasp. Logan spoke, and with the description came the flood of fire from the depths. Images. Helplessness. Hatred. Violence.

Not the events of today, but from long before.

"It went on for about a year," Logan said, "and then Gideon was moved to a different Haven, and it was shortly after that when they kicked him out."

"Why'd they kick him out?" she asked. Her words were calm. Hollow. Echoes in her ears.

"He started having emotional problems, behavioral issues; they said he was demon-possessed."

Munroe was silent for a moment, working past the rage, through to calm. She understood Gideon's anger, the passion that drove him, and the hostility with which he faced her and faced the world. She knew it. Felt it. Lived it. He and she were more alike than either would want to admit. To Logan she said, "I thought homosexuality was forbidden in The Chosen—excommunicable, you said."

"Well, sure," Logan replied, "but that doesn't mean it didn't happen. It just wasn't out in the open like all the other abuse was."

"And nobody ever stopped to think that some of these behavior issues might be trauma-related?"

"That's not the way they think, Michael. The problem is never the doctrine, never the leader, never The Chosen. The problem never has an external source. The problem, no matter what it is, is you. So they get rid of the problem."

Munroe nodded. She was running scenarios. Damage control. Not only on the project but also on her own emotions, which were charging blind like a team of bolting horses. "Why Argentina?" she said. "It's been what? Seventeen years? Nineteen? People in The Chosen move around so often, if the guy is even still part of them, there's no way that he's stayed here all these years—Gideon's got to know that."

Logan shrugged. "Maybe he has to start somewhere. Or maybe things have come full circle. Seems like he got wind of something, some piece of news worth moving on, like maybe the guy had come back here or something like that."

"Who's your source," Munroe said.

"Charity."

"She knew all of this and didn't tell you?"

"Yeah. It's personal stuff, Michael, not exactly something a guy like Gideon goes around confiding in everyone. I only dragged it out of her because I told her that if she didn't let me know, she'd quite possibly never see her daughter again."

Munroe said nothing.

"I also told her that you were getting really close and that if Gideon found out that you were looking into his past, you'd walk off the project."

Munroe gave Logan an appreciative nod. He knew the look. It wasn't gratitude, it was admiration. "You did good, Logan," she said. More than good, because she now had what she needed to neutralize any threat from Gideon.

"So here's the thing," she said. "We've located Hannah."

Logan blinked, inexpressive, as if he wasn't sure he'd heard correctly. The music set ended, and in the volume drop the table was ensconced in a bubble of impenetrable silence. Logan's mouth opened, as if his mind couldn't process the words from head to vocal cords. He paused another moment and then said, "What happens next?"

"That's what we were discussing tonight," Munroe said. "I'm torn, really torn about letting you in on this. I can't work with you stressing around me, and the last thing I need is to be worried about you getting hurt, but I feel you have a right to know. So you are to stay away, far away, you got it?"

Logan nodded.

"And whatever you hear tonight stays with the three of us, okay? If I want Gideon and Heidi to know, I'll tell them myself."

Chapter 23

*M*unroe sat on the floor, back to the wall, a blade in each hand. The only light was that which slivered in from under the door, and for the third time in the past few minutes the light had flickered with the shadows of footsteps on the other side.

They would come for her eventually, and when they did, she would be ready. There was nothing they could do to her that had not already been done, and whatever they wanted they were welcome to try to take.

She was in no hurry; time was all she had.

The ship rose and fell with the steady rhythm of the water. Reverberations from the diesel engines shuddered through the hull and into the base of her skull.

There was another flicker under the door and then the hush of whispered voices. She estimated four or five on the other side and willed them in. Expectation of the fight made her hands tingle. The adrenaline built a slow pressure that would culminate in a savage ecstasy when blood was spilled.

She flipped the knives and played them along her fingers in a pattern; the blades were her friends, they brought reassurance and continuity to a world that had otherwise been shredded.

The sliver of light went out.

In a fluid movement, Munroe shifted upright, coiled and tense *beside the door. The handle clicked and the door inched open. She sensed a presence before she saw the penlight searching the mattress. The body was fully in the room now. She heaved her weight against the door, slamming it shut, throwing the bolt.*

The room went from dark to black.

The body was big and burly and stank of sweat and alcohol. Working off instinct, she lunged forward, plowing into his stomach. The speed and direction of attack knocked him off his feet. His head slammed into the wall. He fell. She plunged her right knee into his midsection; heard the expulsion of breath. He began to pull up. She leaned hard against his chest, one knife at his throat and the other to his groin.

And then she heard the pounding, to which, until now, she'd been oblivious. The door smashed inward, and with the light came a piercing blindness. Disoriented, she braced for what was to come.

Munroe gasped, her back arched, and she drew in air, as if coming up from a water trap. She opened her eyes and, seeing the hotel ceiling, almost laughed in relief.

The replay had ended short; without the guilt and pain, without Logan dead in her arms again; without the horror. Bradford was staring at her. There was concern in his eyes, though none of the panic that had been there the last two times.

"Did I try to kill you?" she said. Her voice was raspy, and she winced at the forced whisper.

"No," he said. "Not this time."

"You didn't wake me."

"I didn't want to make it worse," he said, "and you weren't hurting anything or anyone."

She nodded and closed her eyes. Her heart was still working double time, and it would take awhile for the adrenaline to run its course.

"Who are they?" Bradford said. "The ones you see when you dream."

"My kills," she said.

"You relive them?"

"Over and over. But in the end, it's always someone I love who's dead."

"How long has this been going on?"

She allowed a moment to pass before she answered. "It started a couple of months ago," she said.

"Why now, after all these years?"

She shrugged.

"Africa?"

"I really don't know," she said.

"They haunt you?"

"Every single day." She paused, turned her head toward his; studied his face. "What does it feel like when you kill?" she said.

He was quiet for a moment, staring down at her, as if trying to decipher a true meaning or draw the hidden message from her words. He said, "I'm a soldier, Michael. Killing is part of war."

"Do they ever haunt you? The ones you've killed?"

"There's a lot that haunts me," he said, "the brutality, the children, the women, the innocent casualties—unspeakable things—holding my friends bleeding and dying in my arms, feeling them take that last breath, wondering why them and not me. I still hear the grinding of machinery, I smell the fireworks and blood and the stench of fear."

"But not your kills?"

His eyes wandered to the far wall. "I remember every face. Call me calloused, but I've no pity for them—they weren't very good people to begin with. It's the ones I couldn't protect, they're the ones who haunt me." His eyes cut back to hers. "A mechanic fixes cars, a soldier kills people, it's not pretty, but that's what we're trained for—it doesn't make me any less human."

She sighed and turned her gaze back to the ceiling. "If only it were that easy to stay human. My kills consume me," she said. "I stare into their eyes, lust for blood, take life, and bask in the rush of triumph."

She turned from the ceiling to his eyes, which watched her, absorbing, nonaccusatory, accepting. "And then it's over and reality creeps in like a rising dawn: I've done it again. It feels unfair, unjust. I can take so easily, so fast, and they are so weak—fragile playthings that fall and bleed and die. How is it," she said, "that I can hate killing so much, and yet at the same time desire it, and it comes to me so naturally?"

"In honesty," he said, "have you ever killed an innocent?"

"It's always been in defense of myself or someone else," she said, "except for the first, but that one was a long time coming, and the only one toward whom I feel nothing."

"Maybe that's your problem," he said, "the guilt."

She chuckled humorlessly. "It works well in the comics and graphic novels, doesn't it?" She paused, shifted so that she sat cross-legged on the bed and faced him directly.

"Superheroes defend what's good and destroy evil," she said. "They mete out justice, and everybody cheers. Nobody ever talks about what it feels like to kill." She turned her palms upward and stared at them. "They don't discuss the rush, the savage ecstasy of bloodlust, the sense of satisfaction when it's finished." Her eyes cut to his. "Super-heroes are glorified serial killers, Miles. Sure, they only kill bad guys, but aside from the moral labels, what makes them any different from the madmen?"

"Have you ever considered that it's not always wrong to kill?" he said. "Maybe some people need to be killed, maybe by taking them out you break the cycle of pain and suffering."

She looked toward him and said, "I get a fucking euphoric rush when I kill, Miles! What makes me any different from Bundy and Gacy and Dahmer or, for that matter, Pieter Willem?"

Bradford was silent for a moment, as if he found it necessary to choose his words carefully, and Munroe knew that he was tiptoeing around the issue of Pieter Willem, her first kill, the mercenary psycho-path who had made her what she was and whom she'd murdered in a mixture of terror and cold-blooded calculation.

"That you care," he said. "That's what makes you different. You're not Willem, you'll never be Willem, no matter how hard he worked to form you after himself. You can spend the rest of your life running from his ghost, afraid of becoming what you hated most in him, tormented by what you're capable of, or you can see your skills for what they are and use them without destroying yourself from the inside out."

"You're advocating vigilante justice," she said. Not a question or an accusation, merely a statement.

"Maybe I am," he said. "I've seen enough evil in this world to know that sometimes taking justice into your own hands is the only way. Just because killing comes easily to you doesn't make you evil, just because instinct kicks in doesn't mean you are a serial killer. You are a soldier at war. And in war, you do what you've got to do." He paused, and then softly, he said, "You have a gift, Michael, and you have a heart, let them serve you."

Silence filled the room, and after a trice, she met his eyes. In them was a well of understanding and acceptance so deep it felt as if she could fall into it and drown happy. Leaned in, breath to breath and eye to eye, they remained frozen in the moment until the trance was broken by a bleep on the desk.

Without moving, Bradford said, "It's probably Logan."

"Were you waiting on something?" she asked.

"After last night, he's checking in with me twice a day," he said.

From the bed, Munroe reached to the floor and picked up the clothes she'd shed before climbing in. "I need to find Gideon and get him sorted out before he wrecks everything," she said, "and the timing absolutely sucks. I've got to get back to the Ranch—losing a day is going to cost."

"Maybe not by much," Bradford said. He stood and leaned over the computer, keyed in several commands, and then as the screen changed, he turned the map in her direction. In answer to her puzzled expression he grinned. "Courtesy of Logan," he said. "It's in the sole of Gideon's shoe."

"Sneaky, sneaky," she said, and he shrugged in innocence.

"That will indeed shave a considerable bite off the time cost."

"I've still got stuff coming in from the Havens as well," he said. "Now that we know where Hannah is, do you want to kill the cameras?"

"Are you still going through the footage?" she said.

"Yeah, it's all routine stuff. But then, I'm not really sure what I'm looking for. And I don't understand much of the audio."

"Has David Law shown up anywhere?"

"Not that I can tell."

"Let it pool," she said. "We may not need it, but until we've got Hannah out of there, I want as much data coming in as possible. I expect to get another three cameras live tonight, maybe more. Do we have the storage space for it all?"

"Yeah, we're good," he said.

She stood and headed toward the bathroom, turned on the hot water, and then returned to the bedroom and checked the clock. Time was moving fast.

"I can handle Gideon if you want," Bradford said.

"I've no doubt that you could," she said. "I wish I could take you up on it, but this one I have to handle myself."

Chapter 24

With Bradford's guidance, it took less than a half hour to track Gideon down. Munroe trailed him until he stopped for lunch at a park-side café. He took an outside table in the sun, in the warmest weather they'd had since their arrival. She waited only until he was seated and then approached from behind, tapped him on the opposite shoulder, and as his head turned away from her, slid into the chair next to him.

"Hey," she said.

Gideon flinched, reacting to her presence like a finger to a bee sting.

Prepared for this, she spoke quickly. "I have a story to tell you," she said. "All I ask is that you sit and listen, and after you've heard it, then you decide if I'm the bad guy here, or if maybe, just maybe, I can help you get what you want."

"You have no idea what I want," he said. His tone was spiteful, but his shoulders relaxed and his hands lost some of their tension.

"Let me talk, and then you be the judge."

Gideon made no reply. He would listen, couldn't help but listen, because even if he'd never admit it, he wanted to know what she knew.

Munroe shifted forward, and with her eyes searching and her face not far from his, said, "Once upon a time there was a little girl whose mother and father were so intent on serving the Lord, they forgot to be parents to their unexpected daughter."

Munroe paused a beat. "For the sake of simplicity, let's say that the girl was me, and that since my parents were so busy doing whatever they did, they sent me away, putting me on my own at the age of thirteen.

"They thought I was going to school and living with close friends in a nearby big city," she said, "and I did for a while, but they didn't check, and what did they care? I was fourteen when I walked away. I found full-time work as an interpreter for the friendly local gunrunner, and he moved me to his house. Those were good times, running the bush in Central Africa. Backward as it sounds, I was happy. There was challenge, and focus, and a lot of laughter when the jobs were done.

"He was my friend," she said. "He was eleven years older than I was, and yet somehow we got each other. It was a symbiotic relationship—he needed me, I needed him, and I thought I'd found a home. That is, until a year and a half later, when a pair of mercs joined our team, and life became a garish nightmare."

Munroe waited for Gideon's reaction. Subconsciously mirroring, he leaned in to listen, and with this confirmation from his body language, she continued.

"One of the mercs was a little wiry guy from South Africa," she said. "Charming. Smooth. Personable. Smart, but evil. On the sly he was abhorrently ruthless, the kind of guy who secretly tortured puppies as a child.

"He singled me out for his sadism, and every day, no matter what else happened, there was one thing I could be guaranteed to experience—me, flat on my back with his knife to my throat while he raped me. He taught me to fight," she said. "It was more of a challenge for him that way, you see? First it was weaponless, and then as I got faster, smarter, dirtier, he brought in the knives. It was always hand to hand. Up close. Personal. He fought for the thrill, I fought to kill him. And the better I got, the harder he came at me. The sex was the icing on the cake for him, what got him off was making me bleed.

"He threatened to kill my family if I tried to get away," she said, "and although I wasn't close to them, they didn't deserve what he would do—not for something that had nothing to do with them—so I was trapped in his presence with no one to protect me, and the only thing I could do was learn fast, learn well, and fight back. I want to show you something."

Munroe stood, and fully aware of those around, lifted her shirt high enough for her torso to show, high enough for Gideon to catch a glimpse of the slivers that crossed her body.

His eyes betrayed the shock.

"His mementos," she said, and then slyly, "there are more, but there's no point in stripping down here and showing them off."

Having made her point, she returned to her seat. "For two years, there was no safe place," she said. "When we were camped or back at base, and I kept to the jungle, he would track me. I would stay around others, he would wait. He almost killed me on a few occasions, but in my mind, I died five hundred nights."

"How did it end?" Gideon asked.

"I killed him," she said. "In his moment of weakness I followed him into the jungle. I took him down with a tranquilizer gun, and when his eyes lulled in their sockets, I stood over him and slit his throat. I was seventeen."

Munroe's speech had trailed into monotone, and she waited for the words to sink in.

Gideon stretched back and let out a low whistle. "Wow," he said.

He was silent for a long while, and although Munroe could only guess at what was going on inside his head, it would have been clear to anyone who looked at him that Gideon was struggling with something.

Finally, his eyes cut back to hers. "That's completely fucked up," he said. She ignored his words for the tone, which carried in it the seeds of change that she'd been working toward. The door had been opened, she'd proven that she was capable of giving him what he wanted, and this was the groundwork for getting what she wanted in turn.

"Is that what got you into this line of work?" he asked.

"Partly," she replied. "I came to the States after that. Put myself through school, got a degree, tried the corporate route and failed miserably at it. Lots of people wish their bosses dead, but do you have any idea how difficult it is to stay on a normal job when you've got the skills and mind-set to kill your evil supervisor and get away with it?" She paused and, with a smirk and an exaggerated roll of her eyes, said, "I don't do normal very well."

Gideon let out an involuntary laugh and then, in seriousness, said, "Logan says you're getting close. He seems pretty hopeful."

"Yeah, I am," she said.

"Are you going inside?"

"That's the plan."

"I wonder if much has changed," he said. "They say it has, and that's great for the younger ones if it's true, but that doesn't do much for me, does it?"

"No," she said. "I imagine it doesn't do much for you at all," and between them, there was a moment of understanding.

Munroe shifted toward him, hands folded, elbows on the table. Gideon's size and short fuse made it easy to dismiss him as a hulking brute, but bully strength wasn't what got a guy from where Gideon had started to where he was now, heading up a large IT department. His well ran deep, and Munroe needed him to talk himself completely empty, because until he'd thoroughly vented, not one word she'd said would make a damn bit of difference.

So she sat, quiet and waiting.

Gideon stretched out, legs forward, one arm looped over the back of the chair, and he looked toward her in a long and drawn-out silence.

"All most people know is what they see on TV," he said finally. "And for the most part, TV news stories are nothing other than sensationalism and pandering. Have you ever seen a segment done on The Chosen?"

Munroe shook her head.

"Probably better that way," he said. "Every last one of them takes our pain and makes a mockery of it for the sake of ratings. You'd think after getting burned once or twice, me and my friends would figure out that nobody really gives a damn, huh? Every time we think we find a reporter who might actually care, who is willing to tell our story as it truly is, they stab us in the back and turn it into more of the same lurid entertainment. That's all we are to them, you know? A juicy paycheck. They get paid and we get screwed. Again.

"Don't get me wrong," he said. "There was sexual abuse. Lots of it. But that was just one of so many dishes served on the smorgasbord of my childhood. Just one. Nobody reports about the extreme discipline, or being separated from our families, or education deprivation, or the lack of medical care, or the unquestioning obedience, or that we're thrust out into the world to fend for ourselves after being kept from the world our entire lives. That's not entertaining enough, so it's just, 'Sex, blah, blah, blah. Blah, blah, blah, sex,' and in the end, we just look like freaks—damaged goods that people can tsk-tsk over before they move on to the rest of the evening's titillation. Do you have any idea how that translates for me into everyday life?"

He leaned forward and pointed a finger in her direction. "Not only am I forced to pay for the mistakes of my parents," he said, "not only do I struggle to recapture and put to use the human potential stolen from me, but I have to carry through it in secrecy, as if there was some shame in my past, as if somehow I'm responsible for what was done to me, because nobody, not law enforcement, not academia, and certainly not your all-American Joe, can wrap their heads around what actually happened. Do you have any idea what the typical response is whenever I do give someone a glimpse of my life?"

Gideon paused, as if he waited for her to answer, and Munroe hesitated. Yes, she did know. She knew, because it was the same response she would get if she chose to let down her own guard—hell, it was practically the same response Miles had given the night she had told him the unadulterated truth of her past.

She shook her head again.

"Standard response," he said. "I swear to God. First thing out of their mouths, is, 'Wow, it's shocking you're so normal.' What the fuck?

Do I *have* to be damaged for my past to make sense? And what the hell is 'normal' anyway, and does white-bread America have dibs on it?" Gideon stopped talking, crossed his arms, and the look on his face said that he regretted saying as much as he had.

Munroe mirrored his silence, hoping that he would continue without the need for her to poke and prod, but when he leaned back with an air of finality and she knew he would go no further without provocation, she said, "Can't you just let it go? Move on?"

His face darkened, his eyes glared in response, and he was silent a long time while his jaw worked over a toothpick.

She'd used the same line that The Prophet and his Representatives had been using for years. *Even if these things did happen, there's no point in being bitter. You should forgive and forget and let bygones be bygones.* Kind of galling, considering the insistence upon forgiveness was being made by the people who'd done the hurting and done nothing to make up for it, but then, that was the standard, blame-the-victim, abuser mentality, and to be expected.

Gideon seemed to work through the slap in the face and let it slide. He said, "For a while I thought maybe, you know, if I could talk to the people responsible, if I could show them how difficult life has been because of them, that maybe they would care. I don't know, I thought maybe if they apologized it would be so much easier to forget this shit, you know? To do what they say and let it go? But nobody will take any personal responsibility. My own parents have nothing to offer but a bunch of whiny excuses. They try to convince me that my life wasn't as bad as I remember it. Fuck that," he said. "They weren't even there. They don't even know what went on with me. I just—" He paused and pulled his fingers through his hair.

"Christ," he said. He paused again, eyes to the sky, and then back to her. "Even the people who never personally raised a hand against me still propped up the regime that made it happen. They stood by and allowed it, played a part, all of them. Every single one was a participant, either directly or by looking away. Institutionally, doctrinally, they abused us, sent us into the streets to beg, denied us an education, had us beaten, starved, exorcised, and separated from our parents; they broke up our families, gave our bodies to perverts, and stole our future, and then they turn around and say we're supposed to just forget it happened and move on from it.

"If instead we bring up the past, then they'll call us liars, say we're exaggerating or making it up completely. Why the hell would we make any of this shit up? What's the point in that? To make our lives seem worse than they were? Not that I would, but do you have any idea how much exaggeration it would take for the average person to even begin to grasp how fucking miserable it was? And then, if they ever do admit to any of it, they say that mistakes were made. Mistakes!" he said.

He was leaning forward again, punctuating the air with his finger. "Michael, they commit crimes against children! You know, those things people in society go to jail for when they're caught? And then to the public they do what they always do, 'deny, deny, deny,' and we're left more raped than ever, victimized first by what they did and again by their refusal to admit that it happened. They paint us as bitter apostates and liars to a world that not only doesn't give a shit but also couldn't possibly understand even if it did."

"I do," Munroe said, and Gideon stopped.

In his eyes were tears. He shook his head and took a cleansing breath. "I don't understand why you are doing this," he said. His words were sarcastic and threatening, but his tone was sincere. "Why do you even care? At first I thought you were here for money and I really didn't get Logan's attachment to you, but obviously it's not about that."

Munroe reached her hand across the table, placed it on top of Gideon's. "Because of the bond you share with those raised like you, I think you can grasp this in a way most people can't," she said. "For years, Logan has been the only one who has really understood me and accepted me for who I am, and for that acceptance, Logan will always have a piece of my heart, my life, and I will always have his back."

"So you're doing this for him, for friendship?"

"Initially," she said. "I started on this assignment for him, for Hannah, and because I needed to work." She paused. "You see, Gideon, like you, I have my own rage issues, my own rapid pace toward self-destruction, and if I'm still for too long, I become very dangerous. So I started out doing this for Logan, and for myself, and for a little girl that reminded me of me."

Gideon watched her, eyes narrow, jaw thrust forward. "That's how it began, how does it end?"

Munroe sat back and held steady eye contact. "I don't know how it ends," she said. "The story is still being written, and I'm inviting you to write it with me. I need time," she said, "just a little bit of time. I know you're here for more than just Hannah, I know you're looking for something—someone—and in your own search, you have the power to disrupt everything. If you back off and give me time, when my part of this story is finished, I'll give you everything I have on the Havens, everything I know, so that you can find your own path to justice."

"How long will it take?" Gideon said.

She shrugged. "A few days, maybe. If we're lucky."

Gideon looked off into the distance, and Munroe shifted forward again, elbows and forearms to the table, as they had been previously, hands folded in front. She waited.

"You've killed people," he said finally. Not a question but rather a realization that surfaced slowly and audibly.

"Is it so difficult to believe?" she asked.

Gideon turned toward her, and while Munroe remained quiet, he studied her face for a long while. "I think I understand why Logan trusts you so much," he said.

"Because I've killed people?"

"Because you're like us," he said. "You're different. You understand our pain."

"And you understand mine."

"I think I do," he said, and then after a long pause nodded in acquiescence. "I'll give you the time you need," he said. "I won't interfere, won't do anything to hinder getting Hannah out, even if it means I came down here for nothing."

"Who do you want to find?" she asked.

He shook his head. "It doesn't matter."

"Fair enough," she said. "What's forcing you back? Is it work? Money?"

"A little of both," he said. "I have limited paid vacation time, and tickets to Argentina aren't cheap."

Munroe nodded. "Let's see how things play out here, and when it's over, find me, okay? I'll see how I can help you."

"I don't want a handout," he said.

"If we get to that point, just consider it a reimbursement for your wasted time and your travel expenses."

The corners of Gideon's mouth turned upward, almost shyly, and for the first time since Munroe had known him, there was a genuine smile in his eyes.

Chapter 25

The big room emptied, and the hallway and stairwell filled with the footsteps and commotion that always came when everyone filtered out from morning Instructives to their different ministries.

Hannah kept her eyes low and followed the footsteps to the schedule board. She wanted to be small, invisible, didn't want anyone to talk to her because, being on silent punishment as she was, she wasn't allowed to return the conversation, and that was embarrassing.

The assignment board said she was in the kitchen again, and for this, Hannah almost smiled. Normally, when you were in trouble, except for the days of raising money, you were put to cleaning toilets, scrubbing floors, or any other of the yuck jobs around, usually for weeks at a time. But since Morningstar was her full-time Keeper, and maybe because Morningstar didn't deserve to do the low jobs, they'd let Hannah stay on normal assignments instead, which was a relief.

Hannah pushed open the kitchen door expecting to find Morningstar waiting, but so far, only Uncle Hez was there.

Hannah nodded. Hez already knew she was on silence, so he sent her to sort vegetables in the lean-to pantry. That was the yuck job of the kitchen, sorting vegetables. It meant digging through what was rotten, sometimes even with maggots or other bugs, to find what was still worth eating. It was a little tricky to find the balance, because lots of things Hannah didn't want to eat were still considered edible, and if you threw away too much, Hez got mad.

She was sorting through a box of tomatoes, fingers covered in mush, when the screen door banged open and Morningstar stepped into the lean-to.

"Elijah wants to see you," she said. "He's in his room."

Since Hannah was allowed to talk to Morningstar, she said, "Should I finish this first?"

"No," Morningstar said, so Hannah put down the bucket, turned on the tap of the outside sink, and washed her hands.

She didn't look up when she walked back through the kitchen. The rest of the crew was there. They knew she was in trouble, and Hannah was pretty sure they also knew she'd been summoned for another talk, and she didn't want to see them stare after her as she went.

Hannah walked slowly to the back door, her stomach turning cartwheels, the sick feeling coming all the way up to her throat. Her heart was pounding very hard, as if it were beating against a wall and trying to escape through it. In her mind a thousand thoughts flew by, every possible thing she could have done wrong in the last few days. She'd not talked to anyone. She'd not disobeyed. She'd shown a meek and humble spirit. She'd written good and honest reactions to every Instructive in order to show that she'd truly taken in the words of The Prophet. And she had been very, very yielded.

But, even still, it could be anything, and there was nothing good that ever came out of a talk.

Elijah's room was in the annex, around the corner from the ten-to-twelves, and when Hannah reached it, she knocked quietly on the door.

He said, "Open," and she stepped inside.

The room had a double bed, and very close, with almost no walking space, a small desk. Elijah was sitting on the chair beside the desk, and Auntie Sunshine was sitting on the bed. Seeing Sunshine here was a surprise.

Sunshine patted the bed and said, "Sit down, sweetie."

Hannah's stomach jumped again. Nice words or even nice gestures were often the thing that came before trouble. She sat slowly, folded her hands in her lap, and waited for someone to talk.

"I have a letter from your dad," Elijah said.

Hannah nodded, and reached for the paper that he held out to her, which was really a printed-out e-mail that Elijah and Sunshine had obviously already read. There was no way they would have called her in here just to give her a letter, but still, it felt good that her dad had written, and since Elijah and Sunshine still didn't say anything, she knew they were waiting for her to read what it said before they started talking.

There wasn't much to the e-mail, just a couple of paragraphs about how busy he was and how much he missed her, how proud of her he was for letting him go do the Lord's work, and that he had put her in the Lord's hands and trusted those who made decisions for her, that they were doing what was best.

That's how all her dad's letters were, they never really said anything, and even if she really, really tried to read between the lines, she might only find a possibility of some extra meaning. But it was nice to hear from him, nice to be remembered, and it made her throat hurt and feel all tight.

She put the page down on the bed so that Elijah and Sunshine would know that she had finished, and then, right on time, Elijah said, "Honey, we're going to be sending you away from the Haven for a little while."

A million questions danced around in Hannah's head, but there were very few she would be allowed to ask, so she paused, and with what she was sure would be seen as a humble spirit, said, "Because of my sins?"

Elijah smiled, and it was a funny smile, almost like he was laughing at her, but it was better than if he was angry.

"No, sweetie, not because of that," he said. "Our vicious enemies, the ones who have spent so much time trying to get you, are on the attack again, and there might be raids. We want to keep you safe and away from it all, so that's why."

Hannah felt sad, repentant, and it was such a heavy weight.

The Havens and The Prophet suffered so much because of her, and because of her evil mother from the Void who used the police and Antichrist governments to persecute The Chosen. She and her dad had to move often, and the Havens went to great lengths to keep her safe from the Void. Even The Prophet knew about her situation, and that made her current sins so much worse, because it showed she didn't appreciate the sacrifices made for her.

"Is it my Void mother again?" Hannah asked.

"We're not really sure who it is this time," Elijah said, "but the Lord and The Prophet showed us to expect it, so we are making preparations."

"Where will I go?" Hannah said. "Will I travel without my dad?"

"Your dad's given his blessing," Elijah said. "But since he can't travel with you, you'll stay in the city—just not in a Haven, and Sunshine will go with you instead."

That explained why Sunshine was here.

"Right now?" Hannah asked.

"We have Sponsors stopping by sometime today or tomorrow, and they'll take you to a safe place."

The experience of what had happened the last time Hannah had visited Sponsors with Sunshine was still fresh and raw, and the memories wrapped around her neck like two large hands that cut off her air, and made her feel as if she would suffocate.

She wasn't supposed to ask questions, but the fear of one overpowered the fear of the other, and without thinking she blurted, "Will I have to share the Lord's Love again?"

The response to her question was silence.

Sunshine's face clouded, and Hannah recognized the look—it was what adults did when they were thinking about how to get out of a sticky situation. But Elijah's expression really scared her, because he looked absolutely puzzled, like he had no idea what Hannah was talking about.

This meant two things. The first was that maybe Rachel hadn't reported on her. Maybe it was some other disobedience she was in trouble for. But worse, it meant that Sunshine, even though she lived in this Haven, was higher than Elijah, and the only way that could happen was that she reported directly to The Prophet. That meant that if Hannah were to leave the Haven with Sunshine, Sunshine basically owned her, because nobody would cross someone who reported directly to The Prophet.

The fear was overwhelming and Hannah fought back the tears. She was more helpless than helpless. She didn't want to leave the Haven. Didn't want to go anywhere alone with Sunshine, and Hannah wanted to believe that if her dad were here, this would never happen. At least with her dad, she could beg him to intercede, beg that he be the one to go with her instead of Sunshine, which was something she couldn't do with her mom, because her mom would just tell her to be yielded and to obey.

These insights came in a flash, and Hannah, frantic to find a way to appease Sunshine, to get on the good side of this woman, who, after today or tomorrow would have full and single control of her life, began to try to back out of her question, but Sunshine spoke first.

"Oh, sweetie," Sunshine said, "it's nothing like that. We're going to go to a hotel for a few weeks, just to keep out of sight and keep you protected because the Lord and The Prophet told us to prepare for raids, that's all."

Hannah nodded. She wanted to believe. Sunshine wouldn't lie, would she? They could lie to outsiders in the Void, but Chosen didn't lie to Chosen. If the adults didn't want you to know something, they just rebuked you for asking. But maybe this was different. Maybe Sunshine would lie because Elijah was here, and it was so obvious that Elijah wasn't supposed to know anything. Did adults lie to adults?

Elijah cleared his throat, like apparently he was done with the topic and ready to move on to something else. Hannah tensed.

He said, "You understand, sweetie, that moving outside the Haven doesn't change the lessons that you need to learn, right? We're still very concerned about your spiritual health, and from some of the reports that I've received over the last few days, it seems you're still letting the Devil into your life."

Hannah didn't say anything. Whatever it was she'd done this time, she was completely unaware of it. Maybe the confusion showed on her face, or maybe a look of pure innocence, because Elijah continued.

"Many people have noticed a gloom on your countenance," he said. "When you are full of the Lord's spirit, it shows, and you've not been letting Jesus shine through you. You need to smile more, Hannah, and let others see Jesus in you."

Hannah nodded. There hadn't been a whole lot to smile about lately, but that was never a basis or justification for letting her countenance darken. No matter how sad, you couldn't show it, it was very important that you smile and let Jesus shine through you always, and with so much going on inside her heart these past few days, she had been careless about what showed on the outside.

"You can pack after lunch," Elijah said. And when she'd nodded again, he said, "Now come give me a hug and show me that you're right with the Lord."

Hannah stood, leaned toward him, gave him a hug. Elijah reached around, squeezed and patted her bottom, more of that uncomfortable kind of touch.

"The Bible says, 'Whom the Lord loves, He chastens,' " Elijah said, "and we only punish you because we love you and want you to be the best that you can be for Jesus."

Hannah returned to the kitchen as slowly as possible. The only thing waiting for her was rotten vegetables, so there was no reason to hurry, and Hez couldn't be mad if it was Elijah who'd called her away. Maybe, if she was lucky, Hez needed them right away and so had already sent someone else to do the sorting.

Hannah thought about all the things that Elijah had said, and as she always did whenever she was taken for a talk, or when any other piece of news came her way, she searched out whatever good she could find, so that she could hold on to it and convince herself that everything was okay. As long as she could make herself believe, then the sick feeling was controllable.

Hannah reached the kitchen, but before opening the door, she paused to make sure her countenance was right. A half-smile would be enough. Too much would look fake and make it seem that she'd gotten into more trouble, and that would cause just as much of a problem.

Hand to the door, Hannah pushed it open, and every part of her body and every secret prayer reached toward Heaven in the hope that Sunshine had told the truth.

Chapter 26

orking with Gideon had set Munroe back two hours, making it midafternoon before she finally rolled the Peugeot to a stop outside the Ranch gate. The routine for getting inside was the same as it had been since the beginning: a wait at the gate, a slow drive to the house, and another wait for Elijah.

But three days in, and her arrival had become routine enough that Dust, the teenage boy, accepted her offer of a ride to the door and was not nearly so reticent as he'd been at the beginning. Having the boy in the car was the first time that Munroe had been entirely alone with one of the younger set, and although a dozen questions ran through her head, the ride was too short for any of them, even if it was long enough for her to try to ingratiate herself.

Eyes fixed ahead on the gravel road, the better to avoid intimidation and to pass off the illusion of innocence, Munroe said, "You must be special; not just anyone gets to manage the gate, do they?"

In her peripheral vision, Dust grinned. "I'm a Greeter," he said. "Not really anything special." But his voice betrayed the pride he held in the position—even if he was but a helper—trusted only enough to open the gate for people known to the Haven, not enough to take on strangers the way Esteban was trusted.

Munroe stopped next to parking spaces that should have been

empty but weren't. The vans were gone, and in their place stood two late-model Mercedes sedans, black and imposing with windows tinted nearly as dark as the paint. These weren't the kind of vehicles that could inconspicuously transport fifteen people around town, nor the types of cars bought on the Haven's very limited budget.

Munroe exited the car, walked to the rear of the sedans, stood still and stared, a deliberate gesture meant to provoke an explanation from Dust without having to ask for it.

The boy turned back, said "Visitors," and waited for her to follow.

The likeliest explanation was Sponsors, those the Haven courted for money and protection, and this was a twist. Depending on who the Sponsors were and what connections they carried, any number of complications could be brought into the equation.

The one-word response was the best she would get from Dust without prying, and as with any grab for information, holding back for a score was better than ruining an opportunity over a tidbit. The boy could have his silence; she'd get a trace on the visitors as soon as she could get the license-plate information to Bradford.

Munroe left her overnight bag on the backseat of the car and followed Dust inside. Instead of leading her to the alcove as she expected, he took her up the stairs to a small plywood room that walled off part of the landing near the stairwell. Dust knocked to announce his presence, Elijah's voice called them inside, and the boy poked his head beyond the door. Dust motioned Munroe onward, then turned and left, returning to whatever kept him occupied all day—certainly not waiting for the gate bell to ring.

The little room, crowded with shelves and all the paraphernalia of a home office, was clearly shared space. Elijah sat at a makeshift desk on a metal folding chair, laptop in front of him, and a stack of papers on the side. When Munroe entered, he stood to give her a hug, blocking the way before she got far into the claustrophobic space.

She bristled at the uninvited physical contact, and once again, against visions of inflicting bodily harm, forced a casual reciprocation.

Directly behind Elijah were three rows of shelves only partially veiled by a curtain, and books of Instructives visible beyond it. This was why he'd blocked her way.

Elijah still bore the distracted, frazzled look of yesterday and motioned toward the door, so that they both returned the way she'd come.

"I had another dream last night," Munroe said, and before he could reply, handed him an envelope. "God told me to give this to you."

Elijah took the envelope with an appropriate pause, a glance long enough to ensure gratitude and appreciation, quick enough to avoid appearing money hungry. Without opening the envelope, he said, "Thank you," and then, guiding her back toward the stairs, said, "The Lord could use you in his service today. If you are willing, there's a need in the kitchen."

"I'd love that," she said, and notwithstanding that within The Chosen willingness was never a choice, there was more truth in her simple statement than in anything she'd said to him thus far.

The kitchen was on the ground floor, far back along a hallway that ran behind the stairs, cordoned off from the rest of the house by a solid door that remained closed.

Elijah opened the door, and Munroe entered a room much warmer than the barely heated house. Whatever had been going on came to a near stop, and in the quasi-silence the hiss of large pots simmering on an industrial-size gas stove was louder than it should have been.

In the center of the kitchen, allowing minimal walking space around it, was a makeshift wooden island with enough counter space to accommodate the three teenage girls who stood chopping vegetables. On the far wall were large stainless-steel sinks, in front of them a teenage boy, and beside him a guy in his early thirties whom Munroe assumed was responsible for orchestrating whatever went on inside these walls.

Elijah introduced Munroe, spoke in English, and said little. The thirty-something introduced himself as Hez, to which Munroe guessed

Hezekiah. The boy, Jotham, faced the door only long enough for an introduction, then turned his back to the room and his hands to their labor. The girls smiled, if somewhat shyly, and moved closer together to make space.

On the other side of the island, between Morningstar—Elijah's daughter of the night prior—and a new face called Sarai, stood Hannah, who introduced herself as Faith.

In Munroe's mind, this should have been the moment of the great escape. This was where the good guys finally got close to the target, whipped out the guns, and dragged the kid safely out of the compound.

And technically, Munroe could do it.

All it would take was a quick stroll to the car, a click of the trunk, and a return with a weapon. The gate out front wasn't much of an obstacle, considering that her car's air bags had already been removed for such an eventuality. If the little band in the kitchen chose to fight instead of cower, it might be a struggle to hold on to Hannah and fend off the other four, but it was possible.

Not possible without firing a round or two, which given the potential presence of Sponsors on the property would be an unwise course of action.

But this wasn't the movies.

These were real people, with real lives, real teenagers who, among all else, didn't need the traumatic emotional damage of witnessing that type of violence. Especially not on top of what they already experienced in daily life. These were the brothers and sisters that Heidi and Logan and Gideon cared so intensely about, and to harm any of them as a way to rescue another was to inflict pain in the course of healing.

If violence was the only way to get Hannah out, Munroe would act. But there were other, cleaner ways. Tonight, while the Haven slept, she would plot the house and call Bradford in. Together they would extract the girl and be done with this place for good.

In the meantime, the kitchen provided the perfect opportunity to develop familiarity, confidence, and camaraderie, not only with Hannah but also with Morningstar, Heidi's sister. Through Morningstar, Munroe could delve further, and better understand what tack to take with Hannah once she was successfully pulled.

Hez, in Spanish that was poor at best, gave Munroe a brief rundown of what the kitchen needed to accomplish in the next two hours. She nodded meekly, and when he was finished, she shrugged out of her coat, glancing around for a place to set it.

As she'd hoped, he recommended that she keep it in the living room, and so Munroe left the kitchen, moving slowly only as long as they watched. When the door shut, she headed to the big room at a near run. She dropped the coat on one chair, placed a bug underneath another, and then mounted a microcamera close enough to the floorboards so that it was almost unnoticeable.

The camera was small, with limited battery life and limited range, but provided she didn't go far, the receiver in her purse would pick up the signal, boost, and transmit. She aimed the lens toward the front door but had no time to check for accuracy. She'd try to fix it later.

Munroe knelt by the chair, said, "Take note. I need you to run these license plates," and to the quiet living room recited from memory the numbers she'd taken from the black sedans.

Even if Bradford wasn't at his desk when the bug had gone live, he'd be eager for any data coming from the Ranch and would find it soon enough. Munroe left it at that. Bradford had what he needed to get to work, and if he turned up anything urgent, he'd call the cell phone set up for that purpose, although, for the sake of appearances, outside of an emergency, it was best that she avoid calling him.

Munroe returned to the kitchen and stood at the island with the girls. Morningstar pushed a bowl of potatoes in her direction and handed her a cutting board and knife.

With a silent sigh, Munroe turned to the knife, bulky and dull. Had those in this room any inkling of what the predator inside her could do with this clunky kitchen blade, they would never so blithely carry on. Her fingers closed around the handle and the knife became one with her body, an extension of her arm. On instinct she measured the weight and balance, pulled a potato from the bowl, and, as she was shown, cubed it.

English was the lingua franca, the conversation casual and at times even irreverent. From the sporadic banter, Munroe learned more about The Chosen and their ways than she had in all of her conversations with Elijah. Occasionally Morningstar would pause and, in turn, interpret selected phrases into Spanish, unaware, because of Munroe's pretended ignorance, that everything said was not only understood but also recorded.

It also quickly became clear that when Spanish was spoken, Hez and Jotham understood little of what was said and cared even less.

The dynamic of the kitchen was a lesson in the division of power. This was Hez's domain; he was responsible for making miracles with the food supplied to him, and each person yielded to him in matters of the work being done. But in all else, Morningstar, Heidi's sister, held sway. Morningstar was the one trusted with guiding Munroe, the one from whom the others guarded thoughts and conversation, and to whom they deferred when talking with this stranger.

Time progressed, and the little group grew more comfortable with Munroe's presence. She was integrated into the conversation, cracking quips that made the girls laugh, and asking the occasional question. Not the uncomfortable topics that were standard fare out in the Void; nothing about what they did for fun or their favorite subjects in school, and definitely no discussion about college or their career choices—as if such decisions were theirs to make. She stayed within familiar territory where there were no traps or pitfalls, or topics tiptoed around in order to make their way of life more palatable to an outsider, and thus they felt less reason to guard their conversation.

These three teenagers were no different from even the hardest of marks with secrets to keep and the moral upper hand in keeping them. Flip a mark from offensive to defensive, poke at his softest spots and put him under attack, whether real or imagined, and barriers are lowered and information becomes available.

Munroe bent the conversation offhandedly, focusing on their church,

as they called it, on the joys of serving the Lord and the blessing of sacrifice, reflected on the sacrifices made by those who'd given up everything to serve God, and then she pushed on, asking the young ones
to explain how, having been blessed to be born into the movement,
they could possibly match or appreciate what the first generation had
given up.

The segue came so subtly that the girls never saw the angle. Morningstar and Sarai spoke freely of their own lives, their own sacrifices, and Munroe waited patiently, absorbing, while oddly, Hannah
remained silent.

Munroe said finally, pointedly, "What about you, Faith?"

Hannah gave a furtive glance in Morningstar's direction, and then,
after what seemed like but the slightest nod of assent, Hannah said, "I
sacrificed my dad for the Lord's work. He serves in a special way,
which means I don't see him anymore—haven't for a few years, so just
like the first generation that joined and gave up family, I've done it too.
I know what it's like. It's hard. But the Lord will bless me for it."

Hannah's words were confirmation of what Munroe suspected
regarding David Law, but the blatant truth brought with it a pang of
agony. Munroe's face mirrored the placid reaction of those around the
table while her own inner cauldron began to bubble once more. Hannah was a child that mattered enough to steal, enough to kidnap and
remove from parents who loved her and who would have given her the
world, but she didn't matter as much as service to The Prophet.

Morningstar shot Hannah a withering look, and Hannah paused in
her explanation. Munroe moved to salvage the moment. "At least you
have your mom," she said.

Hannah nodded. "She's my mother in the Lord—kind of like an
adoptive parent."

"Is your real mom together with your dad?"

Hannah shook her head. "She's in the Void, she's an Enemy of
God. We're not yoked with unbelievers."

Munroe knew the scripture and what that meant, and this was an
opening to run in a million directions. She chose the path least natural

and most sympathetic to The Chosen. "So it's for the best," she said. And then, after a pregnant pause, "Do all of you have unbelieving family outside The Chosen?"

"Not all of us," Hannah said, "but Morningstar does."

Munroe expected another look of reproach from the nineteen-year-old, but instead the girl sighed and set to work mincing onions. The sting was powerful enough to set eyes watering around the table. "I have a couple of sisters in the Void," she said.

"Older sisters?"

Morningstar nodded. "But I don't talk to them, not just because they're unbelievers but because they're liars."

"What do they lie about?"

"Things that didn't happen in our church that they say did happen," she said, "things that we believe and things that we don't believe— stuff like that."

"Like what, for example?"

Direct probing was a tactic Munroe generally tried to avoid, but here, Hez and the boy paid no attention, and it passed unnoticed by the girls.

"They say that children in The Chosen are abused and that we have no education and that adults have sex with kids," she said. "Obviously, looking at me, you can see I'm not abused. Personally, this life is the best education any teenager could hope for, and no adult has ever had sex with me."

Across the island, Hannah shifted her eyes. Her glance was barely noticeable, the type of look a guilty man gets when his subconscious overrides a lie and awareness quickly overcomes it. It was a split second of recognition, but it was all that Munroe needed to draw the connection. Her stomach dropped and her pulse rate rose. Instant. Calm to rage in a split second.

She put the knife down and slid it point first under the cutting board. Not because it was what she'd been instructed to do when it wasn't in use, but because getting the knife out of her hands was the fastest way to keep from shedding blood.

Chapter 27

Munroe's heart pounded. Her mind reeled, working at double speed not only to maintain control but also to process what she'd just heard. She only half-listened as Morningstar's explanation continued, and then, in the resultant silence, without truly thinking of the potential repercussions, Munroe said, "It's possible for things to have happened to your sisters, even if they never happened to you."

Morningstar, caught up in the moment, and oblivious of both Munroe's reaction and her undercurrent of challenge, plunged on. "I have hundreds of friends," she said, looking like a younger, harsher version of Heidi. "And these things never happened to any of them. I can guarantee you that none of us are abused. It's impossible to live this close to each other and not know what's going on—surely out of all those hundreds, someone would have said something to me." She paused, deliberated. "I'm sorry," she said. "I just can't accept those stories as true."

Munroe nodded. She knew the drill, had read it all before. This response was standard Chosen mind-set—one person's reality used to reject anything other than the official truth, and the term "abuse" so easily denied because it held a different meaning for the children than it did for those out in the Void. Same word, different language. Munroe grew dizzy.

Yes, it was possible for this to happen in such close quarters and to never know. The proof was there, right in front of them all, young and blond and innocent, with eyes on the zucchini, chopping away with not a word spoken to correct her elder in the Lord. Hannah's truth was so obvious to anyone who truly cared to look—who truly cared at all.

The pounding in Munroe's head was extreme; the knife in front of her a rapturous way to salvation. Munroe fought back the urges. Fought back the rage. Fought to maintain focus. "I have to use the restroom," she said.

"It's the first left down the hall," Morningstar replied, and Munroe was already on her way to the door before the sentence was finished.

In the bathroom, Munroe pounded the back of her head against the wall. Eyes to the ceiling, she took in air but could not calm the burning. The lust for blood was there, pure and unadulterated; the desire for revenge; to bring redemption and right wrongs that should have never been committed. She'd planned to avoid violence, to wait for the night and take Hannah away quietly, but she could not. Her head beat against the wall, a quiet thud, thud. Could not. Could not.

And then the fire, raging out of control, collapsed in on itself into a heat of pure focus. Munroe moved from the bathroom toward the kitchen and the hall that would lead to the foyer. She would grab a weapon, pull Hannah out, and be done with it all. Five minutes. The rest of them could pick up the pieces, and to Heidi, Gideon, and Logan—well, screw it all, she'd tried—they had her condolences for the fallout to come.

She strode past the kitchen and around toward the main hallway, moved steadily toward the foyer, and as she came to the stairwell, stopped short.

At the foot of the stairs and still descending was a group of five men and three Chosen women. It wasn't the numbers or the odds that gave Munroe pause. She could get out, could get Hannah out no matter what the numbers, provided fatalities were an acceptable by-product. She slowed because of the men. These were the visitors, the owners of the black cars outside.

They wore tailored suits and expensive shoes, and three of the jackets bulged inconspicuously where there should have been no bulge. The three women, better dressed and groomed than any of the other Chosen Munroe had yet encountered, doted on the center two, who were at most early forties and easily brothers. The smiles were flirtatious, the conversation light, the entire crowd oblivious to Munroe's presence until they'd all reached the lower stairs.

In slow-motion clarity the picture snapped into place. Posture. Positioning. Mannerisms. Airs. These were businessmen, yes, but more than that. Munroe had spent enough time greasing the palms of society's underbelly to know corruption when she saw it, and this was it—two of them with their bodyguards, with courtesans provided courtesy of The Chosen—and the explanation for the Ranch's better furniture and newer vans.

The group was on the ground floor now, between Munroe and the door, in no hurry and perhaps not even going anywhere in particular. They remained in the hallway, and when there was a pause in their conversation, Munroe continued forward, pushing toward the right wall as a way to get past.

Her slow progress came to a complete stop when one of the two bosses reached for her. He moved in a playful yet proprietary way, as if somehow he had a right to touch her. "Hello, beautiful thing," he said, and Munroe smacked his hand away in a move so sudden that none but he and a bodyguard were aware of it.

She had acted without thinking, rationale and logic clouded by emotion, and the shock of it pulled her back. As the others turned to see whom he addressed, she softened into the meekness of damage control and instantly shifted roles. She stared at him now, under lowered eyelids, her body speaking submission to everyone else, but her eyes glaring at him, daring him to try it again.

Munroe waited a beat and, receiving no reaction from the others, attempted to move forward. The bodyguard who'd seen her act blocked the way.

Under other circumstances this scenario would have propelled her to a different sort of action, but today she wanted none of it. Her focus

was on getting Hannah out, and getting her out now; but her immediate plan to carry it through was rapidly deteriorating, not because
of the manpower that stood in her way, but because as long as these
armed men were near, there was no longer a quick and clean way out.
Someone would be shooting back, and Hannah could get killed in the
process.

The boss man whispered to one of his men, who in turn whispered
to one of The Chosen women. Munroe remained where she was, her
way still blocked, the boss man eyeing her like party food.

The woman's face clouded when she realized what the men wanted,
and once the response filtered down the line, the bodyguard stepped
back and allowed Munroe to pass.

At the car, she walked to the trunk and stood there, motionless,
staring at everything and nothing for a long while. The pause in the
hallway had forced her back to reason, and with that reason returned
the chessboard, the strategy, the plan that had already been laid out
if she could maintain composure and hold it together long enough for
the night to come.

She left the trunk and opened the driver's door, slipped inside, and
shut herself in. She took from her pocket the emergency cell phone and
dialed.

Bradford picked up on the first ring.

"I've only a minute," she said. "Did you get the information; did
you run it?"

"Yeah, I just got my query back," he said. "The vehicles belong
to the Cárcan family, they're business owners in Buenos Aires, highly
connected, powerful, their names linked to organized crime. Most of
it is high-level money laundering, although they're suspected of far
more. They work below the radar, definitely not friendly, definitely not
to be trifled with."

In Bradford's subtle pause were many questions—like where she'd
gotten the plate numbers and what the hell was going on, but he didn't
ask. "You've run into a vipers' nest," he said. "Please be careful."

Munroe paused, thanked him, and shut the phone.

Beautiful.

She stared toward the front door.

The scions of the Cárcan family had not yet exited the Ranch, and Munroe had no desire to still be sitting here when they did. Until they were off the property, extracting Hannah was out of the question, and if she wanted to keep the option of a late-night job on the table, Munroe had no choice but to return to the kitchen.

The hallway was empty when she walked back through it, and with each determined step to the kitchen, she worked herself backward, reverting to the same frame of mind she'd had before Hannah's private revelation had set her off.

The kitchen was as she'd left it, busy and warm, and now down to the final fifteen minutes before the food was expected in the serving area. When Munroe entered, there were no questions other than to assure that she was okay, and on her affirmative response, all was as it had been when she'd first walked out the door.

Munroe moved on autopilot, her face a placid veneer to the simmering inner turmoil, grateful for the quickening pace in the kitchen, which left little time for any nonwork-related talk. And then, the pots and trays were out the door, servers from the dining room came to collect them, and the kitchen, which just a moment before had been nearly frenetic with activity, went suddenly silent.

With a theatrical sigh, Morningstar turned to Munroe. "My dad said you're staying the night," she said.

Munroe nodded, ersatz smile still painted on her face.

"We've got ten minutes till dinner," Morningstar said, stepping toward the door. "Let's get your things, I can show you around, show you where you'll stay." She opened the door for Munroe to follow.

This should have been a moment of exultation, the perfect opportunity to plot the house, the whole of it presented without ever having asked and without the need for subterfuge. But Munroe was emotionally tethered to Hannah, and to leave the room, even for much needed recon, put her further on edge. With tense reluctance, Munroe picked up her purse from the floor and left the three teenagers to their cleanup.

Munroe and Morningstar walked to the car, and there, outside, under the dimming sky, and next to the ever present sedans, Munroe pulled her overnight bag from the backseat. Morningstar watched with veiled curiosity, and her look gave Munroe pause. Morningstar's glance at the car and then at the bag wasn't the observation of a Keeper but that of a questioner, as if she were truly seeing the car for the first time, connecting its ownership to Munroe, and from there to the previous conversation about sacrifice.

Munroe set the small suitcase on the ground, expanded the telescope handle. Morningstar eyed the luggage—a little piece that probably cost more than Morningstar brought into the Haven through begging in an entire month.

"Do you like it?" Munroe asked.

Morningstar's face darkened with the embarrassment of one caught peeping. "It's very nice," she said.

"You can have it."

Morningstar paused and said, "Really?"

Munroe held the handle outward. "You can have it now, if you like," she said. "I'll get my stuff out of it later."

Morningstar hesitated, and then with a beaming smile that screamed of Heidi, she reached for it.

Offering the suitcase was the easiest bribe Munroe had yet made.

The upstairs portion of the main house was divided into quadrants, one for rooming the teenage boys and younger single men, a second for the teenage girls and single women. The third housed a younger group, which was not segregated by gender, and the fourth, according to Morningstar, was divided into smaller rooms for several couples.

The entire upstairs had only two bathrooms, and much like the toilets that Munroe had seen in the annex, these also had been modified to accommodate an extra number of people.

The girls' room, as it was called, was similar to the bedrooms in the annex and was lined and filled with homemade narrow bunk beds, three high, forming tight corridors for passage. Suitcases were stored underneath the bottom beds, and a row of built-in cupboards along one wall functioned as additional storage. All of the beds were tightly made with no personal items strewn about, the top covers home-sewn and matching. The only additional piece of furniture in the room was a tall, lean shelving unit covered with a curtain that fit between two of the bunk beds.

Here in this place, where space was at a premium, Munroe grasped the value held in the small suitcase she'd given to Morningstar. All told, if the number of beds were any indication, this unheated room of twenty by twenty feet housed fifteen girls.

Morningstar pointed up to the top of one of the bunks. "That's the only one we have empty right now," she said. "Because Crystal is on a trip. If you think you'll have trouble getting up and down, I can trade with you for the night."

Munroe glanced at the bed and shook it some. Considering the center of gravity on this monstrosity, the bed was sturdy enough. "I'll give it a try," she said. Not because she wanted to sleep there, or even would be, but because next to the bunk was the shelf unit, which was prime real estate for mounting a hidden camera.

Munroe utilized the bunk's end boards as a ladder, and with far less agility than she was capable of, made her way slowly upward. She sat, her head slightly bent to the ceiling, grinning, and said, "Where do you sleep?"

Morningstar pointed to a middle bed against the far wall.

"And Sarai?"

The bottom beneath Munroe.

"Faith?"

Morningstar nodded to a middle bunk, one over.

All of this for that little piece of knowledge—to know where to find Hannah at night. But this was how it went in the world of information. And this was good. In one turn she had received confirmation of her target's location, a layout of the upper floor, and full access to it all. For the price of a carry-on suitcase.

The most difficult event of the evening would be getting out of this bed without waking the ones below. Munroe wiggled to shake the bed and in turn elicited a smile from Morningstar.

"I might get used to this," she said.

Morningstar's smile lingered. "I've got to take care of something real quick," she said. She pointed to the curtained shelves. "You can use Crystal's shelf for anything personal you need to set out. Why don't you get situated? I'll be back in five minutes and then we can head to the dining room."

Munroe nodded, baffled at how The Chosen so easily incorporated her, a criminal for all they knew, into their personal spaces; they trusted her to stay with their children, but not to read their disciples' Instructives. Their twisted priorities made sense in a Chosen kind of way, if you understood The Chosen.

Morningstar left, and with the room empty, Munroe mounted a camera atop the shelving unit, finishing as the teenager returned.

The dinner scene was as it had been the night before. The noise of a hundred fifty voices in multiple conversations. Singing. Prayer. Then cacophony again. And again, Munroe sat with Elijah's family, only tonight Hannah was there too, even though across the room her adopted mother, Magdalene, was sitting at a table with the three younger children.

Hannah's presence gave Munroe pause, a mental double take, a rerun through scenarios and precautions, private assurances this wasn't some form of setup, that they truly had no idea why she was here, that their act wasn't better than hers; that it could only be coincidence.

Elijah was late in joining the table, and as he slid onto the bench opposite, he squeezed next to Hannah and put his arm around her and to Munroe said, "I see you've met my adopted daughter."

"I'm still trying to understand all the family connections," Munroe said.

"Her father is serving the Lord in another Haven," he said, "and so Faith is with our family a few nights a week."

His arm stayed around Hannah's shoulder far longer than what seemed normal, and Munroe would have written it off as simply part of The Chosen were it not for the pained discomfort on Hannah's face.

It was the second time Munroe had seen that look today. This was a child who had grown up among such close contact, who had shown no aversion to the physical touch of any other person, yet she was clearly distressed and wanted nothing to do with him. Munroe glanced from Elijah, to Hannah, to Morningstar, who sat opposite Hannah. This girl so proudly proclaiming that none of her friends were abused was oblivious to the dynamics in her own family and the deeds of her own father.

The embers of today's earlier fire rekindled into a full flame. Nausea swept in, Munroe's eyes smarted with the sting of anger, and her mind worked overtime, analyzing, rationalizing. That Hannah was being molested in this Haven, Munroe had no doubt. But that it was Elijah?

Munroe wasn't infallible. She read the body language, but there was room for error. It wasn't safe to assume. Not with something like this.

She sat. Breathing. Calm. Controlled breathing. Whatever was said around the table was lost to the filters of internal dialogue. Time slowed. She watched the interaction. Studied. Observed. And again the evidence was there, so obvious in the way he touched and interacted with her, so obvious in Hannah's distaste and the fear in her eyes.

This man, this leader of the commune, was Hannah's surrogate father, authority figure, teacher, leader in the Lord, and her abuser. And Hannah, stolen from her parents, abandoned by her kidnapper, and passed from hand to hand like a pet from owner to owner, had no safe place to turn, if she even understood these things to be the crimes against her person that they were.

Munroe's inner guidance screamed, her violated childhood rose like a primal creature from the magma of the earth.

Even when Hannah was gone from here, it wouldn't end. There would be another innocent to fill her place. But Munroe could put an end to it all. Kill this man tonight before leaving the Haven and break the cycle for good. In the scorch of each passing second came the personal conflict of vigilante justice. Break one cycle only to start a new one.

These were not strangers in a darkened alley. Elijah was a husband, parent, and granddad. This was Morningstar's father, Heidi's father, the only person these children who sat around the table had to protect them from becoming more Hannahs, and their innocent eyes, staring curiously at her from across the table, made very vivid and personal the effects of whatever she chose to do.

Control. Munroe fought for control. Breathe. Listen. Talk. They were talking to her. Answer the questions being asked.

"I'm fine," she said. "Maybe a little dizzy from the heat of the kitchen."

Chapter 28

Munroe processed through the evening, seeing and experiencing everything as if through gauzy curtains, interacting by rote and, through force of will, betraying no sign of the turbulence beneath the façade.

As per the night prior, dinner segued into further discussions, and as the conversations lengthened, those at the table slowly drifted away. Munroe watched Hannah warily, anxious about not letting her out of her sight, yet knowing there was no option but to do so.

They congregated again in the living room, another evening of songs and motivational words, another act from The Chosen, all of it fast becoming tiresome, especially after the events of today. Munroe wanted this over. Wanted to escape to the top-tier bed, where she could stare at the ceiling in darkness and her mind could churn and analyze unhindered, and from where she could observe Hannah until the night lengthened.

After a final round of singing, the Haven's members dispersed in their many directions, and Munroe walked with Elijah to the makeshift office. There he pulled out another book for her. He suggested she read until lights out, and Munroe was happy to oblige. Not the reading per se, but the escape to the girls' room and the sanctuary of the upper bed.

Unlike earlier in the day, the beds were now mostly filled. The girls wrote in journals, read, or talked quietly, bunk mate to bunk mate, the sleeping places used like personal pods on some alien craft. Touches of individuality were tacked to ceilings or posts here and there, these small spaces the only thing uniquely theirs, as if in this crowded house, the boundaries of each one's personal universe extended only to the four borders of her bed.

Munroe recognized some of the faces from time spent around the Haven but knew none of the names. Their expressions were welcoming, and as no one moved to challenge her presence, Munroe assumed they were at the least aware in some general sense of who she was and why she was here. Introduction and some form of familiarity with these eager teenagers would have been the better course, but Munroe wanted only quiet, and so instead she headed up the end boards.

Neither Morningstar nor Hannah was in the room. Given that several of the beds were still empty, it was safe to assume that all was in order, but their absence was anxiety inducing.

Munroe wanted Hannah where she could see her.

On her bed Munroe waited, eyes closed and mind running, scattered. Her priority was Hannah, but Hannah was not the only child in this Haven at risk, and that burden, the conflict of retribution, weighed heavily on her. No matter the choice she made tonight, there would be suffering, and although it would be easy to ignore the decision completely and leave the outcome to fate, fate like the other options bore its own implications.

According to plan, she would wait until after one in the morning to contact Bradford, and from there she'd guide him in. Getting past the gate and the dogs would be a nonissue for him, and the front doors had no security beyond the inside dead bolts. Once Bradford set foot on the property, she would already have the girls in this room unconscious.

Time passed, the room filled, Morningstar returned, and by the time the lights went out, Hannah was still not in her bed. The violence that had been brewing throughout the day, the death and vengeance that had thus far been held in check by willed control, pressed relentlessly against restraint.

Munroe climbed from the bed, and Morningstar sat up when she did.

"I left my phone in the car," Munroe said. "My parents were supposed to call and I forgot all about it—if they can't reach me they get panicky—I think I need to check."

Morningstar slid out of bed. "I'll go with you," she said, and Munroe nodded, expecting nothing less.

The goodwill purchased earlier in the day was still between them, and as they walked, Munroe, in as casual a tone as she could conjure, said, "I thought all the girls are supposed to follow the lights-out rules."

"They are," Morningstar said. "But we won't get in trouble if you need to get something from your car."

"I was thinking more of Faith," Munroe said. "She seems like a special exception."

"Oh, that," Morningstar said, and in those few words, Munroe caught the darkened tone of envy. "No, she's not staying here tonight."

That simple sentence changed everything.

The excuse of needing the phone was meant to be but a way out of the room and alone with Morningstar. Now the little device was burning a hole in Munroe's pocket, screaming to be used.

"Where'd Faith go?" Munroe asked.

She'd asked a direct question with no couching, barely concealed under the guise of innocence, a tactic that would normally shut a mark up faster than any other and was typically best saved for interrogation.

Morningstar paused, and after a long hesitation said, "She's staying with friends."

Outside, five vans were parked under the stars and both sedans were gone. Munroe opened the passenger door of her vehicle, and by sleight of hand pulled the phone from the glove box. She flipped it open, and with Morningstar curious and watching closely, sighed heavily and said, "God, I feel stupid. Several missed calls."

She went through the act of listening to voice mail, and when all was done, concern set across her face. "I need to return this call," she said, "it's my boyfriend, and it's urgent."

Morningstar made no move to reenter the house or to allow Munroe space or privacy, and so with the girl standing there, watching and listening, she dialed Bradford.

"*La youmkinouni an atakalam be houriya,*" she said. "We've got a problem, and I need you to work fast. Have you gotten any of the footage from the front-door camera?"

"I've gotten it," Bradford said. "But only hips, legs, and feet."

"I'm looking for a teenage girl heading out the front—I suspect she's accompanied."

The last time Munroe had seen Hannah had been during the evening vespers. "Start scanning at eight-thirty," she said.

There was silence on the line, the quiet broken by the barely audible clicks and beeps of Bradford searching through footage.

"I think I've found it," he said. "There are only a few ins-and-outs after eight, and of those, the only one that seems to fit what you're asking for shows a group—two sets of female legs—one of them definitely a girl—and a couple of suits."

There were no words for this. Munroe stood stupefied and, caring nothing for how it might appear to Morningstar, swore silently. Everything was wrong. Very wrong. Wrong on the macro level, in the screwed-up-strategy, something-critical-had-been-overlooked sort of way. For whatever else Munroe didn't understand, two things were immediately clear.

This had nothing to do with keeping Hannah away from her—her masquerade was as of yet uncompromised, and Hannah going away for a night was by no means routine or normal.

Munroe had seen firsthand the proprietary nature of the Cárcan boss men and knew from the documents how easily The Chosen shared their women with those in power. Hannah, though young, was a beautiful girl, and even though providing underage girls was officially forbidden, that didn't mean it didn't happen, as was clear from Gideon's experience.

Until Munroe had more information she saw only two viable possibilities: Hannah was being handed over to the Sponsors as a plaything, or The Chosen were pulling her out of the Haven—hiding her. If it was the latter, if it was the result of Gideon having spooked them, she was going to break his fucking neck.

"I'm coming back," she said to Bradford. "There's nothing for us here tonight." And she shut the phone.

To Morningstar, she said, "I have a family emergency, I need to leave."

Morningstar looked puzzled. "Let's go talk to my dad," she said.

Elijah's reaction was as Munroe expected, confused and disappointed, and the only reason she stood here now in his presence, even bothering to explain that her mother was in the hospital, was to keep open the option of returning to the Haven in case it proved necessary.

"Put your mother in the hands of the Lord," Elijah said. "His work, His plans for you come before anything else, and if you do what He wants of you, He will take care of your mother."

Munroe grit her teeth and forced to the surface the closest illusion of calm she could manage. "She's my mom," Munroe said. "She needs me, and my family expects me to be there."

The door opened, and Esteban stepped inside the room, making it now three Haven members to her one. It should have been intimidating, and as they saw her as nothing more than a girl, perhaps it was intended to be so.

"By staying in the center of God's will," Elijah said, "you can have perfect peace that no matter what the outcome is tonight, it's according to God's plan. God wants you to stay. And you have to ask yourself, who is your mother or your father? Who are your brothers and sisters? Your true family are those who do the will of God. We are your family, Miki, here is where you belong."

If there was anything that Munroe knew and knew well, it was scripture; voices from the Book were so branded onto her consciousness that until recently they were a background whisper that permeated her everyday life. She understood upon what Elijah based his values, and trying one last tack before she cut him off, said, "She may die tonight. I need to go."

Elijah responded in a flat patriarchal reproach. "Jesus was once faced with that same issue," he said. "One of the men who came to him, who wanted to be a disciple just like you do, begged for a little time so he could first bury his father, and Jesus said, 'Let the dead bury the dead.' Are you one of the spiritually dead, Miki?"

"No," Munroe said. "I'm very much alive, but I need to go."

Without allowing for a further response, she turned toward the door. Morningstar stood by with mouth agape, and Esteban was close enough to the exit that he seemed to be blocking the way. Munroe didn't wait for him to move. She strode past, brushing against him as she did.

Outside the doorway she turned. "I am ready to give everything I have to the Lord's work," she said. "But if I'm not there at that hospital and my mother dies, there will be nothing for me to give."

With those two sentences, they would forgive her anything.

She returned to the girls' room long enough to grab her purse and then headed down the stairs to the foyer.

Morningstar ran after her, and as Munroe stepped out into the night, she paused to give the girl a genuine hug. "You can keep the suitcase," she said, "and if I don't make it back, the clothes are yours as well." And then, after another pause, "Let me drive you to the gate so that you can open it."

Morningstar hesitated and then got in, and they rode the few hundred yards to the gate in silence.

When Munroe opened the door to the hotel room, Bradford was pacing. He stopped when she entered but remained planted in the middle of the floor, like some battle-scarred statue. His expression was hard. Pure business. And it softened only slightly as she dumped her coat on the bed and strode toward the desk.

He said, "Michael, what's going on?"

She leaned over the desk and loaded the footage, then sat down and stared as the segment played. According to the time stamps, while she had been upstairs being handed a book of indoctrination, Hannah had gone out the front door. She restarted the piece, and then played it again.

In the nightmare scenario of having the child spirited away, there was a ray of hope. Munroe's first set of fears—that the child had been handed over to the men for entertainment—was calmed somewhat by the details on the screen.

The luggage pointed to a protracted stay away, and the frayed and worn clothing was nothing even close to what the women on the staircase had been wearing. There were no guarantees, but by all appearances, The Chosen were moving Hannah out and away from the Havens.

And after a third time through the footage, Munroe stood, and without facing Bradford, she answered his question. "I don't know what's going on," she said, "but I'm sure as hell going to find out."

She pointed at the screen, made a tap toward it. "Those license plates," she said. "Wherever those plates lead, that's where I'll find Hannah. I need everything you've got." She paused, turned toward Bradford. "Is Logan still carrying the emergency phone?"

He nodded.

She stood with her arms crossed, mind racing. "Arrange a meeting," she said, "as soon as possible. Tonight. All three of them. There's something someone's not telling me."

Chapter 29

Bradford stood motionless while the full meaning of Munroe's words sunk in. She would follow the license plates as far as the information took her, and this was the way of madness, the way of death. He sat on the edge of the bed, raked his fingers through his hair, and didn't move to make the call Munroe expected him to make.

After a moment of silence, she turned the desk chair to face him, sat, and in her typically intuitive way, joined him in the quiet until he'd gathered his thoughts.

"Look," he said finally, "pulling Hannah out of a sleeping commune, or snatching her off the street, that's one thing. But going after the Cárcan family? An operation like that is a whole different caliber. I understand you feel an obligation to finish what you started, you made a promise to Logan and you gave him your word. But this changes everything. We're looking at an entirely new sitrep. We have none of the same targets, none of the same risks, we'd be going in blind against a group of ruthless people who are on their home turf and are well armed and well connected. This isn't something the two of us can take on with just a day's notice."

Whatever reaction Bradford expected after having vented, it wasn't to find Munroe in his lap.

She'd sat for a moment, still and thoughtful, and then rose from the chair and stepped to the bed. She placed a knee on either side of his legs, held his face in her hands, and kissed his forehead.

"I won't argue with you," she said, "because you're right."

She remained like that for a moment, her cheek to his hair, and he closed his eyes and breathed her in, hurting and happy in the same moment. He wanted to hold her, hold on to her, protect her from herself and from the world, but she wasn't his to protect and never would be.

She let go and backed away, walked to the window, and stared out. "I have to finish this," she said. "I'll get it done one way or the other, and if I have to, I'll go alone." She turned from the window. "I'm not threatening you, Miles, and I'm certainly not trying to manipulate you. I know you. I know that if I say I'm going, then you believe you have to go, if for no other reason than to watch my back. But I don't want that. This might very well be a suicide mission, but it's my mission, not yours, and I accept that fully."

"Why?" he said. "For God's sake, why, Michael?"

She quoted his words back to him. "I have a gift," she said, "and I'm letting it serve me."

Bradford sat silent, the timpani of frustration building into a crescendo. Her decision was about Logan, it had always been about Logan. And some misplaced loyalty and her bullheaded stubbornness and refusal to know when enough was enough simply because her life didn't mean as much to her as it did to other people. He paused and measured his words carefully.

"Logan would throw you under the bus in a minute to save his daughter if it came down to it."

"Yes, I know," she said. "But Hannah's his daughter. Who is there to look after a child if not her parents?"

"Well, sure," Bradford said, his voice rising slightly. "But if Logan is truly what he means to you, then he should have your back, not use you as some form of human shield. That's what this is coming down to. You've become a human shield. Can you even see it?"

She shrugged, as if the implications of such were not even worthy of consideration. "I can take care of myself," she said. "I don't need someone to protect me."

"And yet you do this willingly, knowing that you're his tool."

Munroe paused, and then turned slightly so that she faced him dead-on. She stared. Long. Hard.

"Yes," she said. "I do it willingly, knowing that I'm a tool, because my decisions have nothing to do with reciprocation. I choose to do this because it suits me. I choose to help Logan because I want to. I choose to save his daughter because I can. I choose to care. Do you understand the difference? It's a choice, Miles, not an obligation. Not a burden. Not emotional blackmail. Not something I *have* to do simply because Logan needs me. I don't do it for gratitude or for quid pro quo. What Logan does, how Logan feels, how Logan reacts, has no bearing on my decisions. They're my choices, not his."

Bradford stopped, said nothing more.

He understood, then, her bond to Logan, her continued love for Noah, and so many of her life's decisions. Self-preservation for her was instinctive, feral, and wild, inevitably bringing death to those around her, instinct that controlled her body and kept her alive, and she refused to allow that instinct to encroach upon her heart. She acted and loved who she wanted, when she wanted, and how she wanted, and having made those decisions consciously, for reasons that were her own, even against self-preservation, she would abide by them, even if it killed her.

"Okay," he said. "I won't try to stop you or convince you not to go. I'll get you all the information that I have, get you whatever you need."

"Thank you," she said.

"On one condition."

She paused. Stared at him sharply.

"I'm going with you," he said. And then as she'd done to him earlier, he quoted her words back. "It's my choice," he said. "Not a burden, not an obligation, not emotional blackmail or something that I have to do. I do it because I choose to."

*   *   *

They gathered at a watering hole off one of the many side streets in San Telmo, near the hostel, nothing more than a room fifteen feet wide, no windows, dim, smoke-hazed and crowded all the way to the bar counter on the end wall. The place was chosen because it was where Logan and Gideon already were when Bradford called, and for what Munroe needed, here was as good as anywhere.

Munroe stepped into the din, Bradford at her heels, and spotted Logan and Gideon in the front corner. The boys were nursing the local brew, had been for a while by the looks of it, and although Munroe would have preferred they be solid and completely sober, she'd take what she could get.

Logan spotted them, stood, and motioned them over. They made small talk for the few minutes it took for Heidi to arrive, and then, with the five of them pulled tightly around the table, Munroe said, "Unless one of you has done something really, really stupid, there are factors in play that you've failed to mention."

There was a shock of silence around the table, and Gideon put his hands up in a defensive position. "I gave you my word," he said. "Whatever it is you're going on about, it wasn't me."

"Maybe you should start from the beginning," Logan said. "Because, for the most part, we haven't been included in your chain of 'need to know.' "

Bradford tensed.

Logan's sarcasm was an obvious dig at Bradford and the way Munroe had allowed him to usurp Logan's position on the assignment. Under the table Munroe placed a hand on Bradford's knee to quiet him.

She was silent for a moment, not because of Logan's snipe, but to plot her way through several days' worth of details to the precise moments that would encapsulate where they now stood.

"I've been inside The Chosen for three days now," she said. "Welcomed, and for the most part blending into the scenery—close enough to Hannah to snatch and pull her out the front door, which I didn't," she said, "in order to limit damage potential."

She paused, took a sip of water, and forced silence on the table.

"Tonight was the go night," she said, "with everything in place for a clean extraction. But since I'm sitting here and I'm not smiling, you can bet things didn't go as planned. I'll give you one guess as to what happened."

Gideon looked at Heidi, who looked at Logan, and among the three there was a form of baffled confusion until Gideon said, "They pulled her out?"

"Yes," Munroe said. "They pulled her out. Anyone want to tell me why they would do that? I was spending the night one bed over, so I think it's safe to assume it isn't me they're hiding her from. Why'd they pull her out, guys? Why now, all of a sudden, are they spooked?"

There was a subtle exchange of glances between Logan and Heidi, a sort of knowing between them, and Munroe paused. "What?" she said. "What aren't you telling me?"

"Heidi ran into a group of The Chosen," Logan said.

Munroe bit back spite and mulled over this unexpected piece of news, because even out of the blue like this, it still didn't quite fit. "Why didn't you tell me?" she said finally.

"They didn't see me," Heidi said.

Munroe nearly stood and pointed her index finger in Heidi's direction. "I told you to stay away," she said. And to Logan, "You were aware of this?"

Logan nodded. "I saw it happen."

"When?"

"Yesterday," he said.

"You can verify, without a doubt, they didn't see her?"

"I would have called immediately," he said, and Munroe calmed. With Logan so thoroughly vested in finding his daughter, he would be hyperattentive to the details, and so she trusted him completely. More so, if The Chosen had spotted Heidi yesterday, Hannah would have been gone that same night.

Munroe leaned forward, elbows on the table. "We're back to the original issue," she said. "If they didn't see Heidi, why are they suddenly spooked?"

She allowed the ambience of the bar to engulf the table, allowed them to mull and stress over the answer to the problem at hand, an answer that so obviously stared them in the face. She waited, hoping that at least one of them might fall into it before she had to articulate it, because if it had nothing to do with any of them, then in her gut she knew the answer, if not the details, and what she needed before she could figure out what to do next were the details.

Logan spoke first. He was staring at the table, the look on his face reflective of the mental obstacle course his mind was running. "They are preparing for something," he said. "They're bracing for a move on Hannah, and they're getting her out of the way, they just have no idea that it was you."

Munroe nodded, wasn't going to help him out yet, wanted to make sure all three fully grasped the complexities they were dealing with.

"Why now?" she said.

"They knew we were coming," Logan whispered. He said it more to Heidi and Gideon than he did to Munroe, and it came out more as an uncertain question than a statement, but the glances exchanged by the three spoke to the realized horror that passed among them.

Munroe said, "So here's the thing. If the three of you are certain— and I mean certain with not an iota of room for error, certain because you *know,* and not because you're afraid I'll break your legs—that this thing has nothing to do with anything that's happened in the city, then I can work with it, but if it has something to do with any of you I need to know now or we could all end up dead."

"It wasn't anything on my part," Logan said. Heidi shook her head as the answer, and Gideon put his hands up once more. "Not me," he said.

"Okay," Munroe said, and she was silent for a long while, allowing the weight of the situation to spread. "If it's not you, then I can posit two possibilities, neither of which matter much to me at this point, but it might be helpful for you to be aware of them. One: someone you've talked to, someone in your close circle who knows what you're up to, has said something they shouldn't to someone they shouldn't."

She waited a beat. Held up two fingers. "Possibility two," she said. "The information on where to find Hannah was fed to you deliberately to bring you—something—to their doorstep."

The first possibility brought with it a round of sighs that spoke to the high potential for such a calamity; the second resulted in a round of simultaneous response, all three of them answering at once, all three expressing pure incredulity. So Munroe probed at the disbelief.

"You said your source was Maggie, Charity's sister," she said to Logan. "That she's the one who contacted Charity with the news?"

Logan nodded.

"Does Maggie live in Buenos Aires?"

"I'm not sure," he said. "I mean, we've been working a lot of contacts for a long time, and Maggie was just one of many—we don't always know where to find people, just how to get in contact. E-mail. Networking. Friends of friends. That sort of stuff."

"It came unexpectedly, though, right? I've seen the way siblings react to news of their estranged sisters." Munroe gave a subtle nod in Heidi's direction. "I'm guessing Charity's sister wasn't exactly at the top of the list of people you'd expect to cough it up, was she?"

"Correct," he said.

"What's she look like? Does she strongly resemble Charity?"

Logan paused, as if he wasn't completely sure, and Gideon answered for him. "No," he said. "They have different dads."

"It would be too much to hope for a photo, huh?"

Gideon paused and said, "Maggie has dark hair, she's shorter, and she's more Asian-looking—I think her dad is half-Japanese."

Hannah's adopted mother.

Munroe swore silently and said, "But she has really light hazel-green eyes like Charity."

The three hesitated, at first as if they were puzzled as to how she could possibly know and then because they realized why.

"You guys have been the perfect tools," she said. "And the only reason you're even close to getting Hannah is because you did the unexpected. You found a way to the inside."

Logan was the first to protest. "It doesn't add up," he said. "Even if Maggie is here, isn't it possible that she was sincere in wanting to help? It doesn't have to be a setup. She could have wanted to help her sister, wanted to make things right."

"If Hannah were still in the Haven tonight, you might have a valid point."

"What could they possibly hope to gain from this?" Heidi asked. "Why would they deliberately invite trouble? It's completely counter-intuitive, and it can't be a setup without a motive."

Munroe turned to Bradford. "She's very good, Miles. If I had a company like yours, I'd offer the lady a job." And then to Heidi, "You've got to ask yourself, in cases like this in the past, what typically happened when an abducted child was located?"

"There's been government intervention, usually police raids on the Havens."

"And eventually the dust settles, charges are dropped, and the kids go back home, right?"

Heidi nodded.

"Has someone ever infiltrated a Haven to kidnap the kid back?"

"No."

"Is it fair to assume that looking to the past as a guide to the future, they've moved Hannah out because they're bracing for a raid? One that they themselves are trying to provoke?"

Gideon said, "Are you crazy?" and both Logan and Heidi simply stared at her as if she'd sprouted a horn in the middle of her head.

Munroe shifted back, the preliminary movement to leaving the table. "Look," she said. "The biggest mistake you can make is to underestimate your opponent. At this point, it makes no difference to me one way or the other, but it might to you—or to your friends. From a purely analytical, disinterested point of view, The Chosen have expended considerable resources to keep Hannah hidden, and now out of the blue have tipped you off, as if they're setting the kid up as perfect bait, expecting someone to come looking for her and being able to show a clean bill of health when all hands turn up empty. Is there anything going on in your community? Custody battles? Upcoming TV shows? Something that might make them look bad if it were to come to light?"

"Maybe," Heidi said. "I mean nothing specifically, but last I heard from my own connections inside, The Prophet is making a push toward mainstream acceptability and image improvement. As a whole, they're trying to bury unpleasant issues and show themselves as merely a different sort of church. But people like Charity, they don't go away, and as long as they're in the media, the negative spotlight continues to return. It's possible that The Prophet—The Chosen—the local leadership—would want something flashy, a raid perhaps, something that media outlets couldn't ignore, as a way to prove that their ex-children are a bunch of crazies, that we're liars who exaggerate and whose word couldn't be trusted. It would be a dramatic way to prove that they are being persecuted and vilified."

"Well, there you go," Munroe said. "There's a motive."

"But in that case, why not tell us she's in Jakarta or Mumbai or even Asunción and send us on a wild-goose chase? Why take us to where she actually is?"

Munroe shrugged. "Maybe they think you know more than you do and didn't want to risk you calling their bluff. I mean, from everything I've read, The Prophet is a narcissistic nut job. Do his reasons even have to make sense?"

Munroe stood and Bradford did as well, and she dropped a wad of pesos on the table.

Heidi said, "But wait, you just leave it at that?"

"It's not my fight," Munroe said. "I'm going after Hannah."

Chapter 30

Munroe and Bradford stepped out of the bar, and Logan followed them, calling for Munroe to wait. She paused on the street corner until he caught up, and when he reached her, he was breathless and strained, and didn't bother with niceties.

"Where did they put her?" he asked.

"I don't know," Munroe said. "I called you guys in as soon as I found out she was gone. I haven't had a chance to start digging yet. But I know who she's with, and with that I'll find her."

"Tell me truthfully," he said. "No padding, no sparing my feelings, no trying to protect me. How bad is it?"

Munroe blew imaginary strands of hair out of her face, debated against going back inside the bar, where they could sit and she could lay it out for him. But there really wasn't any point. She didn't know enough to do anything more than scare him.

"We're back at the beginning," she said. "Not square one exactly—maybe three or four—but at least I have something to work with. No padding. We're dealing with a whole new animal. An animal with teeth. The Chosen have some strange bedfellows for Sponsors."

Logan began to speak and then stopped, as if he was now finally grasping the situation for what it was. "What are they? Military? Police? It wouldn't be the first time."

"Organized crime."

His lips drew taut, and he didn't even pretend to be calm. "I can be an extra set of hands," he said, "another pair of eyes, one more set of feet on the ground. I can help you."

"No," Munroe said. She crossed her arms. There would be no discussion, no room for argument, no area for debate. Just no.

"Michael, please," he said. "Not only am I highly motivated, I've done this with you a dozen times. I'm an asset, and you know it—it's not like I'm some outsider to this game."

She paused, put her hands on his shoulders, and held him at arm's length. Stared at him eye to eye. "You are an asset," she said. "No question. No doubt. And under any other circumstance we'd be in this together. But not this time. I can't. It's too personal to you, and too personal for me." She paused, fighting for the words to explain the blade of pain that pierced each time she slept.

"I need you alive," she said. "I can't afford to lose you, and even more than that, Logan, I won't have your blood on my hands."

She paused again, and then in almost a whisper said, "I can't."

She stopped. Cleared her throat and upped the volume. "If you go into this, my attention will turn toward keeping you safe. You will distract me, and what I really need right now, more than anything else, is the ability to focus. It's in your best interest, Hannah's best interest, and my own best interest to keep you as far away from this project as possible."

Logan took a step back. His face creased with a mixture of frustration and resignation. "Okay," he said. And then he turned from her toward Bradford, jabbed an index finger in Bradford's direction, and said, "If anything happens to her, what she just said goes out the window. I'm the Reserves. You'd better fucking call me in."

"Nothing's going to happen to me," Munroe said, and she steered Bradford toward the street before the two alpha dogs could tear into each other.

To go after Hannah meant finding Hannah, and finding Hannah meant the possibility of breaking kneecaps. The vehicle plates led to home addresses, the home addresses to people, and where people lived, information could be forcibly extracted, although ideally, it would never get to that. If things went the way of the backup plan, something said within the Haven and picked up by one of the listening devices would point them in the right direction.

But so far, things weren't ideal and hadn't exactly gone according to plan.

In the hotel room Munroe headed for the desk. She was in predator mode, hunting and out for blood, and with her back to Bradford she said, "Get some sleep, you'll need it."

Her manner was brusque, and after the display of care and emotion she'd given Logan, probably hurtful. He'd have to deal, and the kinder, gentler moments would have to wait for better times. Bradford wouldn't fight her over the suggestion of sleep, not only because she was right but also because at the moment there was nothing further he could do. At two in the morning his contacts and connections were all in bed, and what she needed was both quiet and time to listen through several days' worth of data.

Behind her the blankets rustled, followed by the quiet of Bradford's settling. He switched off the bedside lamp, and the room was bathed in the computer screen's ambient glow.

The window of time was narrow, and in these hours of darkness Munroe would—had to—find what she needed. It was either that, or the kneecaps. She placed the headset over her ears, and in a purity of concentration that only focusing on an assignment could bring, allowed the rest of the world to fade away.

Collectively, pooled over the past two days were twenty-eight hours of voice, split unevenly among the three Havens, a lot to cull through, but not nearly as much as it would have been had Bradford not already clipped out the extended silences and unintelligible chatter.

The bulk of the recordings came from the Ranch, which was good in that it increased the odds of finding what she wanted, but daunting for the amount of time it would take to locate it.

She started with the two hours from Haven Three, the smallest and nearest, with only one channel open for audio. She expected to find little there, and wanting to eliminate this chunk before moving on to the rest, Munroe set the software to allow for listening at a distorted high-speed, closed her eyes, and ran it.

The recordings were an aural version of voyeurism, peeping into the lives of those exposed, and the momentary snapshots, as they filled the hour, confirmed what she'd supposed. There was nothing of value.

Of the remaining twenty-six hours, eight were from Haven One, and like those she'd just scanned, she expected nothing and set them aside.

Munroe paused before the machine and took the headset off, feeling comfort in the darkness of the room and in the rhythm of Bradford's sleep. She waited, listening, falling into the cocoon of silence, willing her mind to emptiness, and then turned again to the headset and the voices.

The hours from the Ranch were divided among six channels, one for each of the listening devices placed by either herself or Bradford. She started with what would have seemed the most obvious, the device on the stairwell, listening to gibberish and group talk, picking out snippets in Spanish and English and the occasional stray conversation in Finnish or German. Time passed.

She moved to the girls' room, to the living room, and finally on an urge to clear the smallest channel, found the first clue. In a fitting form of irony, it came from the bug Bradford had planted in the electric socket of the boys' bathroom.

The voices of the visitors filled the headset—their words, more than tone or accent, had given notice to the change in speakers, and the difference was enough for Munroe to recognize what she had. She reset the software, slowing to normal speed.

The conversation from the hallway, picked up but not perfectly clear, was a discussion of Hannah, what appeared to be a restated agreement to take the girl and a guardian away for an indefinite period, but there was no indication as to where, and nothing more was said about it.

The only other piece to go on, a hint of what would come next, happened in the moments when Munroe had left the kitchen. The talk between Morningstar and Hannah was of packing, of a stay, and no answer to Hannah's question of how long. They hadn't discussed the why, but then, for Hannah, that was probably never much of a question.

Munroe set the headset on the desk and for the first time noticed the change of light in the room. Small rays creeping past the curtains announced that day had come. She turned. Bradford lay on the bed, arms behind his head, watching her.

"How long have you been awake?" she said.

"Half an hour."

"Hungry?"

"Starved."

They took breakfast at a café down the street, coffee and croissants with the sun coming in off the window, and the warmth comfortable and drowsy.

"How good is your guy?" Munroe said.

"Guys," Bradford said. "Plural. It's been a long time since we've worked together on anything big, but if the past is any indication, they're solid."

"Connected?"

"I expect so."

"I've got a lead on Hannah," she said. "Not much, but something. If it was me, I could work with it, but I don't have the time to entrench and do it myself. If your guys are worth anything, it'll be faster to go through them."

"What did you find?"

"Hotels."

"Hotels?" he said.

She nodded. "Hotels. Bed-and-breakfasts. Inns. Youth hostels. Anything of that nature within the boundaries of the city."

"It's a wide net."

She shrugged. "Maybe, maybe not. They might own one, they might own three dozen. It's still a smaller net than the entire city. I'd like to put out a line, see if we can draw a bead on anything in particular."

"There shouldn't be a problem to throwing it out there."

"How fast till we get something back?"

"That I don't know," he said. "But I can push. What about you, are you going back to the Ranch?"

"I need to sleep," she said. "I can feel myself slipping, losing my edge. If what we're going up against is even half as bad as you say it is, I need to be at full capacity. I can dose enough to take myself out for eight hours—and it'll free you to work without worrying about me."

He cringed.

"I haven't medicated for over a week, Miles, one day isn't going to make me an addict. It's either that or you lose a day of work and take the risk of me trying to kill you again."

"The risk I can handle."

"Go work," she said. "I'll sleep."

He didn't say anything, and so she stood. They returned to the hotel in silence, and once in the room, she moved to the bag that lay slumped against the foot of her bed. As much as Bradford would have wanted to dump the bottles in her absence, he wouldn't have. She unzipped it and rummaged through the contents, knowing they'd still be there.

She grabbed a bottle and broke the seal. Tipped the liquid into her mouth and then, matching his stare and with a hint of defiance, wiped the trace of syrup off the corner of her lip. "One day," she said.

The potion was a sweet seduction as it trickled down her throat. Not nearly as strong or as addictive as hydrocodone or morphine, the codeine still did the trick. The warmth of the opiate was a heady relief from pressure and pain and responsibility, a relief from feeling anything at all, a rush, not unlike adrenaline, coursing in the opposite direction toward repose. Had Bradford any idea how strongly Munroe fought the desire to live in a perpetual state of this bliss, he would have tried to fight her, perhaps even attempt to remove the bottles by force. And that would have been a mistake.

But he hadn't. And she'd drunk. And now on the bed with a smile on her face, she closed her eyes and descended into the ecstasy of oblivion.

When she woke, it was to Bradford's touch on her shoulder. Perhaps more than a touch. Maybe he'd been shaking her for a while. Awareness came slowly through a haze, and even if she'd wanted to react, her only response was to smile a drunken smile. She rolled on her back, still smiling, still stupid.

She laughed at the look of concern on his face, ran her finger along his cheek, and said, "How's it going?"

"I think I might have what you're looking for," he said.

She nodded, pressed her lips together to suppress the internal laughter.

"Maybe I should get you some coffee," he said, "and a heavy meal."

"I'll be fine, just needs to wear off. How long has it been?"

"Five hours."

"It's a big dose I took," she said. She closed her eyes and resisted the urge to drift back into the web of darkness. "Give me what you've got. I'm not functioning at a hundred percent, but the brain is still working, even if my lack of sense of humor is impaired." In the wake of his silence, she soughed at her joke, and then she laughed.

Bradford sighed. "Okay," he said. "The Çárcan family does have an interest in a number of hotels around the city, most of them are midsize, one step up from the Budget Inn–type places. But those are all owned by companies and partnerships, nothing privately held, everything out in the open and legal. Except for three smaller places that belong to one of the sons—a little side project of his, you could say."

Munroe scratched the back of her neck, her eyes still closed. "Sounds like a good starting place," she said. "We'll need to get some form of surveillance set up on each—some way to find out if that's the right direction—if she's there in one of those."

"Go back to sleep," he said. "I've got some ideas. I'll let you know what we've got to work with."

It was dark when Munroe pulled out of the haze. She'd been asleep and was then awake. Just like that. Light off, light on. Bradford was still gone and his phone was missing. She assumed it was with him. She reached for her watch. Seven o'clock. Doing the math, she figured it had been around three when he'd woken her. He'd been gone four hours. A little long for a drive-by.

She stepped from the bed to the shower, turned the water fully cold, and the shock against her skin was an unpleasant return to the land of the living that took away with it the final effects of the bottle.

There was still no sign of Bradford when she came back to the room.

She dressed for recon, pulling on pieces that belonged to the night and the dark alleys. They felt good, like a second skin, the stuff you wore when scaling walls, walking ledges, and sliding into tight spaces, nothing like the upscale feminine clothes of the last few days.

And still no sign of Bradford.

She didn't need him in order to make the next move. The information he'd gleaned during her hours asleep had been left on the desk, his notes clearly legible and obviously intended for her benefit as much as for his. She could set out to gather her own intel and at worst double on Bradford's effort, but it was uncomfortable not knowing where he was or what he'd been doing since he'd left.

Munroe stood in front of the mirror, face-to-face, eye-to-eye with herself, as she plotted through the events to come. One way or another, Hannah was hers. Recon or no, Bradford or not, alone or together, she was going after the girl, and if she returned to the Ranch, she wouldn't be going as a guest.

From a pocket in her overnight bag Munroe pulled out one of the several purchases from her shopping spree. She unwound the cord. Snapped the plastic guard into place and switched on the buzzer. Head over the sink, she sheared off the last remnants of femininity, and years of practice left a young man with a military buzz cut looking back at her. He wore an evil smile.

She cleaned the mess and packed away the machine, and still no Bradford.

Munroe trusted his judgment, his survival instinct, assumed that when he said the Cárcan family was not to be trifled with that the warning applied to himself as much as it did to her. He would be careful. She checked her watch. It was late by what he'd told her, still early by the city's standards.

Munroe sighed and returned to the desk. As odd as it was to allow another her role, she would let Bradford work. If he wasn't back by early morning, she'd try to raise him on the phone, and if she couldn't contact him then, she would go alone. In the meantime, there were the last of the audio tracks.

Chapter 31

The clock had passed midnight and the voices with their worthless conversations were coming to an end when Bradford finally walked through the door.

Munroe turned to face him, an accusation almost to her lips until she saw him. She stopped and forced back a laugh.

"Where the hell have you been?" she said, but this time she was smiling.

Bradford was dressed in old clothes, ratty and tattered, the kind of getup you'd see on a kid who'd spent the last four months hitchhiking the continent. The boots on his feet were beat up and worn through, and over his shoulder he carried a small backpack. This wasn't the Bradford who'd headed out at midafternoon.

"I've been hobnobbing with the base and seedy," he said. He shrugged off the backpack. Held it out, as if the grime were contagious, and dumped it on the floor. "There wasn't really any way to call. I'm glad you waited for me—hope I didn't worry you."

Munroe nodded at his outfit. "Talk to me," she said.

"We're in," he said.

"You found her?"

Bradford shrugged and smiled a bragging smile, an actor's grin. Munroe let him have the moment. She moved from the chair to the edge of the bed, audience to the stage, and motioned for him to continue.

"Out of the three hotel-slash-hostels on our radar, two are normal run-of-the-mill-type places," he said. "Not a whole lot happening. Quiet. Empty. Clean. And from what I saw, there didn't appear to be any Cárcan henchmen around. Now, if I were a Cárcan big shot, and I were going to stash a kid like Hannah as a favor, I'd wonder what exactly my friends were up to, and I'd put her where I could keep an eye on her. Which brings me to the third location.

"This one is different. It has three stories and borders one of the rougher neighborhoods, and rumor has it that a lot of the guests are not as transient as you'd expect—that the Cárcans use it to house short-term employees. You know, the kind who are in town for a special job before moving on? Definitely more up our alley and closer to what I expect we're looking for.

"Whatever else the place may be, it's also open for regular business, and it seemed the easiest way inside was through the front door, although not the way I was dressed. I found a kid a few blocks away who liked my offer of clothing and shoe exchange. I had to pay extra for the luggage." He shook his head theatrically and rubbed his finger along the shirt's frayed collar. "I checked into the Cárcan family suites. The place is a dump, but the rooms are clean and the doors lock. There's a small cantina downstairs. Metal tables, folding chairs, tepid coffee, local TV. I'm sure you know the drill. Hung out there for a while, and eventually me and my trusty guidebook made some new friends."

Munroe raised an eyebrow, as if to say *And?*

"Hannah's a real cute little lady," he said. "Looks just like a miniature Logan. That woman who's with her, though—" Bradford grimaced and shook his head.

Munroe's face remained deadpan, and her voice monotone. "You have target location?"

"No need to thank me," he said. "But yes, we have confirmation." He paused. "And I love what you've done with your hair."

Munroe grinned and, without breaking eye contact, stood. She moved toward Bradford, slow and languid. He remained motionless, eyes tracking her as she drew near, head turning slightly to follow her approach until she was close against him, mouth to his ear, her lips close enough to graze his skin.

"Not bad for a night's work," she whispered.

The hair raised along Bradford's neck. Munroe continued on past, and he, with a deer-in-the-headlight glaze, turned to follow her.

Leaning against the wall, she said, "Considering the type of neighborhood, I'm surprised two women would be socializing late at night with a strange man."

"They had reason to feel safe."

"I assume it wasn't because you're such a great guy."

Bradford shook his head.

"Lay it out for me," she said.

Bradford's time in the hotel had allowed him to plot the floor plan; his time at the table discussing first the country and then religion had gotten him Hannah's room number.

On a piece of paper, Bradford diagrammed the access points, the blind spots, and the sticky issues. Hannah was on the third floor, and the only way to her was through the front door, past the front desk, and up the stairwell that wound from the rear of the tiny lobby through the center of the building. There were no elevators or fire escapes or emergency exits. Not in this part of town, or this building.

The hotel's desk clerks were gatekeepers rather than humble staff. Shift change showed each man as beefy as the other, with weapons behind the counter and no subtlety in the handoff. There were no security cameras, but two of the Cárcans' foot soldiers traded off in a leisurely form of round-the-clock, patrol-the-hallways, keep-an-eye-on-things security. From the condition of the hotel and the sidewalk out front, the measures did well at keeping the local riffraff from messing with the place. Whatever street crime occurred in the area wasn't happening there.

Up the stairs, branching right and left off the stairwell, were two floors of short hallways, four doors to a side, sixteen rooms to a floor, and Hannah's was at the far end of the hall. The entire third floor, Hannah's floor, housed only the Cárcan's people, although, as far as Bradford could tell, Hannah was only being hidden, not specifically guarded.

Getting past the desk going in was a nonissue. Coming back out with a drugged teenager who also happened to be the personal guest of the hotel owner and the Cárcan family was another story altogether. As far as extractions went, it wasn't as simple as it would have been had they pulled Hannah out of the sleeping Ranch, but it was far easier than a hostage rescue.

Pinpointing the new location as quickly as they had was a lucky break, and Munroe wanted nothing more of waiting. That said, her world was one of information and intelligence, stealth and smarts over guns and door kicking, and by that token, it might have been the wiser choice to acquire more knowledge, to get a personal feel for what she was going into, because Bradford's point of view, no matter how accurate, could never substitute for her own.

But at this stage, she no longer cared.

It was impossible to guess how long Hannah would remain holed up in the hotel, and the Cárcan family inevitably had plenty more places to stash their charge if The Chosen got jumpy. More still, Munroe was wary of what men like those she'd met in the hallway would do if they got their hands on a young girl like Hannah, and Hannah was now surrounded by an entire hotel floor of them.

She had no more patience for being Mr. Nice Guy, was all out of caution and concern over avoiding collateral damage. This time the bets were off. The projection was smash and grab. Get in, get the girl, get the hell out.

A hefty payment to Raúl, and the taxi driver was willing to let go of his cab for the rest of the night—maybe forever. Bradford drove it, navigating the chaos and suicidal maneuverings of Buenos Aires traffic with the skill of a local, while Munroe followed in the Peugeot.

They stopped at a parking area a crooked half mile from the hostel, a place where the streets were still well lit and the vehicle was safe enough from vandalism during the hopefully brief time away.

Munroe stepped from her car and into the night. She pulled a nearly empty duffel bag from the passenger seat, tossed it into the back of the taxi, and locked the Peugeot by remote. She joined Bradford in the cab, handed him the keys, and they rode in silence to the hostel.

The building was sandwiched between others, fronting a two-lane road in a part of town where sidewalk traffic never died. On either side, up and down the street were mom-and-pop restaurants, tailors, repair shops, secondhand shops, all closed and dark, the street traffic coming from the many bars, all with their light and noise and smoke spilling onto the otherwise darkened sidewalks.

By contrast, the hotel was quiet, if dimly lit, a beacon of order in the midst of confusion.

Bradford stopped the cab a half block away from the hotel. Munroe slung the bag over her shoulder and stepped out.

"Ten minutes," Bradford said, and she nodded.

Going in, she was carrying two blades and a Bersa Thunder 9, one of several firearms that Bradford had already picked up locally. Considering the hotel's management and clientele, it would be insane to enter unarmed, but the plan was to move fast enough to avoid having to utilize any weapon at all.

The tiny hotel lobby was as Munroe expected. To her left as she entered was the open doorway to the cantina, and after only a few steps in, the hotel desk. The man behind it was easily six-foot-four, and half as wide. He was polite and deferential, and he treated her request for a room with the courtesy expected of any proprietor. She filled out the paperwork and he handed her a key, an old-fashioned-looking thing that hung on the end of a four-inch strip of wood.

The room was as Bradford described: clean, spartan, tiny, and, ironically, on the second floor directly under where Hannah slept. Munroe moved to the window and stared down at the rear alley only long enough to draw the image of the taxi out of the darkness.

Pulling Hannah from the third floor of this building required supplies that they didn't have, and Munroe had been unwilling to wait to procure them. Like so many parts of an assignment that required split-second changes and last-minute improvisations, the extraction would be makeshift and sloppy, executed with what was already at hand.

Bag on the floor, Munroe tossed the bed, pulled both sheets off, and far corner to far corner, knotted them. Double-checked the tensile strength, checked against slippage, and then shoved them into the bag.

Door locked, she walked to the end of the hall and rapped a pattern against Bradford's door.

He opened, and she stepped inside.

His bed was tossed, his sheets knotted. She checked his knots and said, "No offense." He shrugged, and in turn checked hers. Munroe connected the two pieces, and together they worked the length of it. They moved fast. Thorough. And when complete, she stuffed the finished product back into the bag.

They left his room together, listened for the footsteps of the patrolman as he walked the halls until they placed him on the first floor. Bradford headed down the stairs, and Munroe headed up.

She had no business being on the third floor, no business standing in front of Hannah's door, and Bradford, with his limited Spanish and necessary questions, would buy her time from prying eyes.

The door locks were basic and old-fashioned, the rooms without backup chains or dead bolts, and it took but a moment to work the mechanism and slip inside to the black of the room. Munroe relocked the door from the inside.

The click of the latch was a subtle sound. Not so subtle that Munroe or Bradford or Logan would have slept through it, but then, these two in the bedroom were not war hardened and at three in the morning were dead to the world.

Munroe paused long enough to allow her eyes to adjust to the room's minimal light level, then lowered the bag to the floor and pulled from the side pocket a bottle and cloth.

On the bed and closest to the door was the woman Bradford had scrunched his face over. Munroe recognized her as one of the many from the dining-room scenes, one of the few who hadn't had children about her. She was early fifties—possibly younger—and the years and the poor quality of life hadn't been kind.

Munroe wet the cloth and placed it over the woman's nose and mouth. The woman's eyes opened, panicked for a moment, before they shut again.

On a foldout cot that barely fit between the bed and the window was Hannah.

Munroe stared for a moment while Logan's daughter slept in innocent bliss. Then she knelt, placed the cloth over the girl's face, and watched her eyes flutter open and the same terror settle into them before she too drifted back into oblivion.

With both of them unconscious, Munroe shifted the nameless woman off the bed and settled her on the floor. She tore the sheets off the mattress and added them to the chain that she and Bradford had already assembled.

Hannah was a much lighter load, and instead of lifting her out of the bed, Munroe curled her and took the four corners of the sheet, knotted them into a sling, and repeated the procedure with the second sheet, a backup in the unlikely event the knots on the first slipped.

The window was waist high, a narrow opening that did not give easily when Munroe tugged at it, and when it moved, it did so loudly and grudgingly. Munroe paused; listened to the night; listened for a response; heard none. Below, Bradford burst a quick flash of light in her direction. All clear.

Getting Hannah to the window was easier said than done. Although she was an easy ten inches shorter than Munroe, and even thin for her height, she was still a heavy weight to be safely raised and then lowered along the outside wall.

Bradford would have been the better, stronger choice for this part of the job, but to put him in this room with two women carried its own risks. While he might hesitate to use physical force against either of them if necessary, Munroe would not.

Munroe knelt with one knee to the floor, tight against Hannah's cocooned body. She took the sheet's tail, wrapped it around her forearm, and then around her torso, allowing the remainder to trail along the floor. Using her knee as a brace, Munroe pulled Hannah toward her, cradled her, and with all of the weight centered at her hips, stood.

There was only a step between where Hannah had lain and the window where she must go, but in that step came the reverberation of a door being slammed directly below. Inching backward, Munroe tipped her head toward the night and heard the window ten feet down scrape shut.

Munroe paused, arms beginning to shake from the weight they bore. Bradford flashed again from below, and feetfirst, Munroe tipped Hannah out the window. The sling held, tightened, and Munroe let go the remaining side. With the last of Hannah's body through the threshold, the tightly wound sheet and the weight pulled Munroe hard against the wall. She braced, knees bent, pulling backward, allowing the sheet to unwind inch by inch, while counting down minutes until whoever had been downstairs was at the door.

There was no good explanation for why someone had been in her room. Best case was statistical crime. Theft, vandalism, even intent to rape or murder were better possibilities than that of the front-desk and security guys comparing notes. But barring the unlikelihood of the downstairs incursion being bad timing on the part of a common criminal, the sheetless bed would only confirm whatever suspicions the Cárcan foot soldiers had originally had for entering.

Given the proximity in timing between her predawn request for a room and Bradford's return to the hostel, it wouldn't take long to draw the connection. After that, it was merely a matter of minutes before the bad guys headed this way. If she and Bradford were lucky, there were rooms and things in this building that ranked higher in order of priority and would be checked on first.

Hannah was five feet down the thirty-foot drop when the first knock came at the door. Munroe ignored it, ignored the anxiety of having her back to the room and her hands tied, closed her eyes and continued to feed the cocoon toward Bradford.

The knock was louder, a pounding that couldn't help but roust adjoining neighbors from their beds. Bradford's light clicked a rapid succession. He'd heard the noise. Munroe slowed in feeding, pulled the flashlight from her teeth, and replied.

Company.

Hannah was ten feet down. Still too high to drop. Munroe's back remained to the door, her hearing taking over where sight was absent. The door handle shook. And then came splintering as the door slammed inward.

She continued to feed. Fifteen feet. Halfway there.

They paused at the door, and Munroe didn't need to see them to follow their movements. Long years spent in the night of the jungle, years of tracking in the dark, of hiding in the dark, of avoiding the worst kind of predator, had primed her for moments like these. She knew them by the rustle of clothing, the weight of foot to floor, and the carelessness of their breathing.

There were two of them, paused at the sides of the doorway, as if these thin walls would protect them from any return fire.

Seventeen feet.

Against the ambient light of the window, Munroe made a perfect target silhouette.

She fed the line. Eighteen feet.

One intruder knelt in the doorway, weapon trained on Munroe. The other moved into the room, nudged the woman on the floor with his toe, and then low and calm came the order for Munroe to raise her hands and to turn slowly.

Munroe ignored them. Nineteen feet. At twenty-four feet, Hannah would be close enough to the ground for Bradford to break her fall.

The order came again, this time not so low, not so calm.

Munroe continued to feed, calculating distance and accuracy. From fifteen feet behind, the chances of even a mediocre shot landing

a fatal wound were high. It would be tragic to end it here, like this, but
if this was how she went, so be it. She wasn't turning, wasn't letting go
of Hannah.

Twenty feet.

A warning shot shattered a window pane above her head. Shards
of glass fell away. From below Bradford muffled a yell.

"Drop her," he said. "I've got her. Drop her!"

Twenty-two feet.

Footsteps crossing the room.

Munroe released the sheet from her forearm and it slipped slowly
from her grasp. The full weight of Hannah wound around her waist,
slowed only by Munroe's weight against the windowsill.

"Follow the plan," she yelled.

Bradford's beam pointed upward.

Munroe took a step from the window, let go, and the sheet whipped
wildly. From below came first a thud, then a grunt, a pause, and then
a door slam.

The cold of gun metal pressed against the back of Munroe's head.
She raised first one hand and then the other until her fingers joined
behind her head.

Tires peeled, and in her mind's eye, Munroe saw the taxi launch
forward.

Hannah was away, and every moment here, every moment stalled,
facilitated that escape. Munroe filled with a mix of elation and regret.
The sadness wasn't for herself but for Bradford, because no matter
what happened tonight, she knew well from personal experience the
torment to come: he would feel helpless to protect her, he could do
nothing but watch and wait; he would curse himself for his weakness,
torture himself while wondering if he had done the right thing.

The muzzle stayed pressed to Munroe's head, and she stared forward, out the window, into the night, a sad smile on her face while the
other set of hands, rough and angry, patted her down.

Eventually Bradford would realize that there was nothing he could
have done differently. She'd gone into the hostel, this third-floor room,

fully aware that she was walking into a box. She had made the choice consciously, and her refusal to resist or fight was more of the same, this time to allow Bradford the opportunity to gain distance from the hostel. But in the end, no matter tonight's outcome and no matter what her reasons, Bradford would ache, and this was the one thought that pained her.

The hands found the Bersa, found the blades. Took them. Munroe braced. Waited. And then the world went black.

Chapter 32

Bradford fishtailed out of the alley and onto the narrow connecting street, the street that led away from the hostel, away from Munroe and toward the objective.

He was breathing hard. Too hard. He needed to slow down, he couldn't think, couldn't focus. She'd been clear on what she wanted. *Follow the plan.* And so he followed, driving on instinct, moving on autopilot, every muscle, every nerve screaming the contra-order.

He'd left a man behind. And not just any man; he'd left Michael.

This was not the way things were done. Not the way it should be. Wrong. He had to go back, fight, protect her the way she refused to protect herself. Michael was the important one, not this girl she was giving her life to save.

Bradford swung a left, side street to boulevard, one more taxi blending into the city's late-night or early-morning traffic. He eased off the pedal if only slightly. Every second took him farther away from Munroe—if she was even still alive.

Reason kicked in.

Of course she was still alive. She'd walked into the big dog's den and taken his bone, and now that dog was going to want to know where to find it and how to get it back.

The realization was a double-edged sword. There was relief in the knowledge that Michael was alive, and would still be alive for a while; but there was torment knowing what would come when she refused to divulge any information. Not only because she wouldn't, but because she couldn't.

She'd foreseen this. It's why she'd left the finer details of getting Hannah out of the country in Bradford's hands, why even she had no idea how he was transporting the girl, or where in neighboring Montevideo he would take her.

More, she knew the way the game was played. As long as they thought she had what they wanted, they would continue to try to break her. The longer she lived, and the more they focused in the wrong direction, the safer Hannah would be.

Bradford pulled into the parking area next to the Peugeot and shut off the engine. He turned to the backseat where the little body was still bundled, and after staring at the girl for several seconds, he stepped from the cab and opened the rear door.

He sliced through the knots in the sheets and let the material fall. The girl looked so small, so fragile, sleeping as she was. She was unmistakably Logan, and the similarity brought on a surge of anger that crested above the tormenting conflict.

Bradford remained motionless, caught in the crosshairs of duty.

The child breathed a steady in-and-out, and his mind found the pattern, working through the maze. He would find a way both to fulfill his obligation and to avoid abandoning Munroe to the vises of the Cárcan family.

He lifted Hannah and transferred her from one car to the next. Left the items in the trunk where they were. Tossed the keys to the cab under the cab's front passenger seat and climbed into the Peugeot.

He would do this.

Against his strongest instinct he would follow the plan. But he would add his own twist. This was the only way his conscience would allow him to both move forward and give Munroe what she wanted.

The time had come for Logan to pay his dues.

Bringing Logan into the mix wasn't a decision made lightly, nor was it based on emotion, although granted, emotion ran high. These were Bradford's terms. If he was to sacrifice Munroe to save another's child, then everyone would pay a price. A life for a life for a life.

And that, exactly, was the risk of bringing Logan or even Gideon into the fray. Sure, they were both kickass in their own little worlds, but that wasn't the same thing as living on the edge. Skills got rusty, muscles got weak, and for whatever else, they were still living the civilian life. Munroe had a reason for wanting to keep them out of the fight—not just so that she wouldn't worry—but because of the higher likelihood of one of them getting killed.

Life for a life for a life.

Bradford picked up the phone. Punched in the number.

"I've got Hannah," Bradford said.

The relief on the other end was palpable. "Where are you?" Logan said.

"They've got Michael."

Silence.

"I can't go after her," Bradford said. "Not if I'm to get Hannah safely out. The situation is volatile."

More silence.

"You can either track Michael or I'm leaving Hannah where she is, right now, and going back myself." Bradford stopped, waiting for the venom in his voice to fade.

"Why don't you give me Hannah?" Logan said.

"Not an option. It's either all or nothing. The people we just took her from are powerful, connected, and vicious. I have pieces in place to get your daughter safely out of the country, and my window of opportunity is closing. I don't have time to dicker around with you. Either I do this or I don't."

Another pause, and Logan said, "Tell me where I should start."

Bradford gave Logan the address of the hostel, provided general directions, told him how to find the taxi and what he would find in the taxi. Explained the layout of the hostel, the patterns of security, and what Logan could expect. He told him to move fast. Munroe was there right now. There was no guarantee for how long.

"Last thing," Bradford said. "Tell Gideon the only way he's ever going to get the information Michael had for him is if she's alive to give it to him herself."

Bradford shut the phone without waiting for a response, tossed it on the seat, and pulled out of the parking area into the thin stream of traffic. Gideon might have gone along anyway, simply to watch Logan's back, but there was no motivator like self-interest.

Logan stared at the phone in his hand, held it out as if it were toxic, his mind blank, in shock. The news that he'd waited eight years to receive brought with it an unbelievable anguish.

He stood and climbed back into the clothes he'd shed only an hour earlier. On the opposite bed, Gideon stirred and said, "Was it Michael?"

"Miles."

Gideon tossed, turning from his back to his side. "Good news or bad?"

Logan moved steadily through the room, collecting items. Belt. Shoes. Wallet. Watch. "Both," he said.

Gideon turned on the light. "What's going on?"

"Miles has Hannah," Logan said. "That's the good news. He's on his way to moving her out of the country as we speak." He paused, turned to face Gideon, and, as if his mind couldn't quite comprehend the reality of his words, said, "Michael was taken in the process of getting Hannah. Not by The Chosen but by the Sponsors they'd handed Hannah off to—a big-name local crime family." Logan stood, momentarily blank, and then clasped his watch into place. "She'll probably be tortured for information if they don't kill her outright."

"Sucks for her," Gideon said, and then, realizing that Logan was preparing to leave the room, sat up. "Where are you going?" he said.

"To find Michael."

Gideon lay back down and pulled the covers up to his chin. "Good luck with that."

Logan paused and stared at Gideon the way he'd stared at the phone. "Incidentally, a little message to you from Miles," he said.

Gideon rolled back and blinked an eye open.

Logan knelt and tied his laces. Tight. Old habits. "Michael not only had the locations of all of the *puerteño* Havens," he said. "She had days of video and audio, a hierarchy map, and lots and lots of names. Whatever arrangement she made with you was between the two of you. Miles says the only way you're getting anything that she had is if she's the one to give it to you."

Gideon swore. Flung the blankets aside and stood, muttering about blackmail. "So what are we supposed to do even if you do find her?" he said. "Just go marching in like two idiot targets, saying, 'Here shoot at us, and let her go'?"

"Apparently, Miles left us a gift. It's in the back of a car, and we're going to go find it."

Logan stopped. He stood square in front of Gideon, didn't move, just stood until Gideon raised his head and said, "What?"

"Michael is my best friend, Gideon—more than friend—she's the only family I have. She's saved my neck more than once and put her life on the line to get Hannah because I asked her for help. Whether you come or not, I'm going after her. She deserves at least that from me. And you? You can either put up or shut up."

Gideon raised a hand. "It's cool," he said. "Let's go kick some ass."

They found the taxi where Bradford said it would be, and the parking area not as empty as described. The morning was coming quickly. Logan fished the key out from under the seat, opened the trunk, and almost cautiously unzipped the long duffel bag.

There was a long moment of silence as he and Gideon stood side by side, mouths open, staring at what waited for them.

Logan took a quick look over his shoulder, checked again that they were alone in the parking area, pulled the bag to the ground, and then shut the trunk.

Gideon said, "Where the hell did he get that? And how, with all of this shit, did Michael manage to get taken?"

"Weapons are what Miles does," Logan said. He grunted, heaved the bag onto the backseat, and closed the door. Slow and firm. "Miles has connections all over the place," he said, and then paused, thoughtful, piecing together the unknown events of the darkened morning. Logan didn't know much about Miles, but he knew Michael better than anyone else ever would.

"She didn't want to go in shooting," Logan said, "for Hannah's sake. And Michael has always been more about stealth than bullets." He nodded at the bag. "That was Miles's doing—she probably didn't even know it was back there."

They climbed into the cab, Logan in the driver's seat, Gideon riding shotgun. After another thoughtful moment, Logan turned the ignition key and pulled into the thickening traffic. It took several passes to find the hostel, and on the way, the boys discussed strategy. Logan outlined all he knew of the hostel and its security, a repeat of everything that Bradford had told him.

Gideon climbed from the front seat into the back. Pushed the bag to the floor and culled through it until he'd found what he wanted, then searched on Logan's behalf. Most of the lighter pieces were Argentine made, an assortment of Bersas, reliable 9 mms, even if not well known outside of South America. There was a pair of Spanish Star Z-84 submachine guns, also 9 mm, a block of C4 with ample det cord, timers and remotes, smoke grenades, live grenades, night vision, and what had to be at least two thousand rounds of ammunition.

The sky was breaking into dawn, and day had come by the time they reached the neighborhood. Logan broke from the journey long enough to transfer the bag and its remaining contents into the trunk and then made his way to the hostel, parking the taxi just beyond the front door.

He shut off the ignition. Nodded at Gideon. "Ready?"

Gideon returned the motion. "Let's do it," he said.

They exited the cab, both doors slamming at the same time, walked the two steps up the hostel entrance, and once inside, separated. No point in creating a single target.

The desk clerk looked up, and his face clouded. Any idiot who'd been in the building within the last few hours would have reason to mistrust two men walking solidly through the door. The clerk's hands fell below the counter.

Gideon drew, his weapon trained on the man's chest. The clerk froze. And why not; all he had to do was wait for the backup that was somewhere upstairs and would soon be down.

In Spanish fluent from his years in South America, Gideon stage-whispered a demand to the man to place his hands where he could see them. When the clerk obliged, Gideon crossed the lobby, a few quick strides, and slid in behind the counter. He stood behind the man and out of reach, with the weapon still trained on him.

Gideon nodded to Logan, who had waited at the base of the stairwell.

Logan slipped behind the counter, rooted out the weapons from underneath it, and handed them to Gideon. He stepped back to cover the clerk while Gideon zip-tied the man's hands behind his back.

With the clerk secured and still behind the counter, Logan returned to the bottom of the stairwell and, as casually as possible, weapon out of sight, waited. Disarming and securing the clerk had gone quickly—better than anticipated—almost like clockwork. This next part wouldn't be as straightforward.

The hotel's guests were beginning to stir, and Logan's judgment call said that the first steps down the stairwell toward the cantina would not be those of the foot soldiers. He had little to go on in pin-pointing the hotel security other than Bradford's descriptions, which, admittedly would probably now be different, but something about the posture of the man on the stairs was wrong. Like Munroe, Logan knew the subtleties of facial expression, knew body language, skills highly attuned after years of trying to avoid trouble in the ever-changing, arbitrary structure of The Chosen.

Another set of footsteps came down the stairwell, and again Logan ignored them. The man passed through the lobby to the outside, but there would be more coming, others who would go instead to the cantina. The hotel guests, although guests, still mostly worked for the Cárcan family, and each provided his own separate threat level. Bradford had made that clear. The more of them that congregated downstairs, the harder it would be to pull off a repeat performance of securing the desk clerk.

Without turning, Logan said, "Change of plans, Gid. One of them should be enough. Let's take him now while we've got a chance."

"If we fail with him," Gideon said, "we can't come back for seconds."

"We won't fail."

Logan waited until he was certain the lobby would remain empty for the time they needed to get out, and then with the stairwell silent, he gave Gideon the all-clear.

Gideon nudged the man out from behind the counter. Halfway across the small space, the clerk, realizing what the two intended, realizing his partner would not be there in time to save him, began to yell. Gideon struck him, and Logan pushed him forward. The combined movements threw him off balance.

He stumbled out the front door. Tripped. Fell. Struggled to get up, to get away.

They each grabbed an arm and, straining against his weight, hustled him up and forward. Gideon yanked open the back door of the cab and, together with Logan, against the man's struggling and continued clamoring, attempted to shove him inside.

Logan ran for the driver's door. "Just shoot him," he yelled.

Gideon put muzzle to the man's struggling leg. Pulled the trigger.

The power of the weapon's report was matched by the man's bellow and followed a second later by the spit of return fire coming from the hotel's front door. Gideon pushed. The man caved. Gideon threw himself on top of the clerk, slammed the door.

"Drive," he yelled. "Drive!"

The rear window shattered.

For the second time in less than three hours, the taxi peeled away from the raunchy neighborhood of the Cárcan hostel.

Logan drove blindly. Madly. Weaving through traffic until Gideon's voice finally registered.

Gideon was on top of the clerk, head inches from Logan's, yelling, "Slow the fuck down, they're not following us and you're going to get us killed!"

From the tone, Gideon must have been repeating that mantra for a good minute now. Logan nodded, eased off the gas.

This was what adrenaline should be. This was a jacked-up heart rate, and nothing at all like the rush he got racing motorcycles or BASE jumping.

There was a moment of silence, and then as the reality of the moment sunk in, both he and Gideon burst into laughter. Their cackle was manic, the hilarity of insanity that calmed only when Logan said, "We're drawing attention, get off the guy."

The clerk, face to the seat, hands still behind his back and legs at an odd angle, had stopped struggling. Gideon shifted. Made sure the guy was still alive, and then with one hand, did a quick inspection of the leg. The wound was a clean through-and-through, muscle tissue, the slug somewhere in the seat cushion. Blood was pooling, but not fast enough to be serious. The clerk would live. Maybe.

Gideon tore the guy's shirt, took what he wanted, and wrapped the leg to stanch the bleeding, and then slid into the front seat. The clerk turned so that his face was to the front.

"*Sos un hombre muerto,*" he hissed at Gideon. "A dead man. Both of you."

Gideon pointed the gun at the man's head. He said, "Bang," and then ignored the insults that followed.

Logan got his bearings and changed course. They were heading out of town. Someplace deserted and quiet. Someplace where screaming wouldn't raise an alarm.

Chapter 33

Awareness came slowly, a haze of sensory pulses that invaded the darkness and brought Munroe fully awake. She was seated. Chin on her chest, feet bound to the legs of a metal folding chair, hands secured behind it. Not by handcuffs, duct tape, or zip ties.

Her mind worked. Struggled toward lucidity.

Rope. Thin rope. Lots of it.

Idiots.

Whatever was wrapped around her eyes had been bound tight, and not even a kiss of light reached her eyelids. To her left were voices, raucous conversation, men sitting around a nearby table. Their volume and language spoke to playing cards or some other game of chance. These men—four of them, by the distinctness of tone—were unconcerned with her. They were killing time. Waiting.

Each sound, each smell brought with it a mental snapshot to create a composite of what she couldn't see. There was no tell of a nearby guard, no restless feet or fidgeting fingers, no rustle of clothing, no breathing.

Cigarette smoke hung in the air, not heavy, as it would be in a small space; it dissipated in the same way the voices did. This place was large. Cavernous. Munroe gauged ten feet between her and the men at the table, maybe fifteen, no more than that. They'd set her off to the side, alone, with her face toward them, trusting that she was secure.

Such basic blunders made it easy to lower the estimate of threat, but she wouldn't make the same mistake these men had. They would learn that to underestimate an opponent was the fastest route to getting dead.

Chin to chest, as if she were still unconscious, Munroe's fingers worked, wrists twisted until they found the slightest bit of slack, pushing, prodding until she had enough play to slip free. Well-oiled rollers slid along tracks somewhere across the cavern behind her, pausing the escape.

She stopped to listen.

Doors easing open.

This place was a warehouse.

Only the faintest noise filtered in from the outside, no cars or horns, no pedestrians, no music.

A warehouse outside of town.

The rollers made a return trip, and the purr of a well-machined car engine drew close, shut off. The conversation around the table stopped. Chairs scraped against the floor. Feet shuffled. A car door opened. Shut. Followed by another.

Footsteps drew away from the table, toward the chair, and then fingers, hands, released the blindfold.

Munroe blinked.

The lighting inside the warehouse came from industrial lamps beside the worktable, and although the glare was easily swallowed by the building, the wattage was painful after having been forced into complete darkness.

Munroe winced, staring at the man in front of her.

She had expected someone from the Cárcan family to show, had planned on it, knowing that until the boss had a chance at her they'd keep her alive, a deliberate delay that would buy time not only for Bradford and Hannah but also for herself. That the tormentor had to be the guy who'd groped her in the Ranch hallway was an unfortunate twist.

He stared at her now, looking down in a long-drawn-out silence that spread to the men on either side of him. Munroe's face relaxed from wince to deadpan. The boss man grinned, and his men remained motionless. He then stood back, forefinger and thumb to chin in an exaggerated pretense of thought.

He wagged his finger at her. "I know you," he said.

Pulling at the knees of his slacks, the man lowered to a half-squat so that he was eye to eye.

"Yes," he said. "I do know you."

Munroe stayed silent, eyes glazed over in a stare of noncomprehension and ignorance. Her eyes didn't track him when he stood, didn't follow when he turned to whisper to one of the men that remained behind him. Now that she could see, could fully assess the situation, this Cárcan son was the least interesting object in the vast empty space.

Instead, her eyes darted to the table and then searched upward along the walls and around the circle, seeking out a way to escape, scouting for anything that could be turned into a weapon: instantaneous survival assessment of who, what, when, where, and how. She already knew the why.

The floors were smooth concrete, the walls cinder block, and the roof, fifty feet up, was of corrugated metal. The direction of echoes spoke to the warehouse being empty; the worktable near the wall and the lights around it seemed to be the only objects there.

The four men who had originally sat around the table had been joined by two more who'd arrived with the boss. All six stood on either side of him in a hungry, uneven semicircle, each carrying firearms, most of which were holstered and a few held in waistbands.

The men were similar only in their build—thick and stocky from too many hours spent in the gym. In contrast, their boss was slight and otherwise undistinguished apart from his expensive clothes and what Munroe already knew was an overdeveloped ego.

She absorbed the placement of men and weapons, each detail filtering into awareness with the accuracy of echolocation, an appraisal that was swift and instinctual, made in less time than it had taken for the boss man to turn and speak.

It was difficult to predict the odds of survival. She'd fought against larger groups, but never in such a defined space, and never from a position of weakness. Speed was her friend, was always her friend, speed born from the will to survive when night after night she was hunted down and forced to defend herself in order to live. Agile and able to move faster than expected, she could handle four or five who were not trained military but thugs. Seven was pushing against reason.

Munroe's eyes returned front, to the boss man's second, the one to whom the boss had turned and whispered, the one who now strode toward her.

The second was the broadest and shortest of the seven, and he didn't pause in his approach. When his feet stopped moving, his arm continued on, fist connecting with Munroe's face. The blow, hard and dizzying, would have knocked her off the chair had she not braced for it, and were she not strapped to the chair.

Munroe shook her head to clear the dizziness. The telltale trickle flowed from the corner of her mouth, and the stabbing pain brought a hint of smile to her lips. Her heart began to beat the march to destruction.

The boss came close again to look at her swelling face, and she studied his. Her vision blurred to gray, the borders of sight narrowing to feral focus, the lust for blood, for retribution, rising, while long years of practice in pulling back the urge kept her from striking.

Bradford's words scrolled against the back of her mind.

Have you ever considered that it's not always wrong to kill?

The boss said, *"¿Donde está la niña?* Where did you send her?"

Munroe's eyes glazed again, stayed focused ahead, as if his words held no meaning. The boss nodded to his second, and the man stepped forward again, struck again. The hit was harder. Set her ears ringing.

Maybe some people need killing, maybe by taking them out you break the cycle of pain and suffering.

Munroe's eyes remained to the front, centered on what would appear to be some invisible distance. The boss stepped back into the semicircle. Whispered again. His third placed a spring blade in his waiting hand. The boss switched the knife open and squatted again, eye to eye with Munroe. He took the blade up, underneath her chin, pointed into that sweet spot so favored for the kill. He pressed so that in order to avoid puncture, she was forced to tilt her head upward and back, and when she had lifted as high as she could, had tightened all the skin along her neck, he flicked.

The blade took a quick slice, not deep, but enough to feel, enough to draw blood. "Where did you send the girl?" he said again, only this time he spoke in nearly unaccented English.

"I didn't send anyone anywhere," she said.

The boss stood. Turned to the men behind him and let out a half-laugh. "English?" he said, as if surprised to discover that what he thought was a long shot turned out instead to be true. English was correct as far as he knew. He could have used Italian, German, Turkish, Ibo, or any one of twenty-something languages, and the result would have been the same.

"But you didn't speak English when you were around my friends."

"What friends?" Munroe said.

The boss shook his head. His was the look of impatience, the look she wanted.

He motioned a finger upward, and two of his men left the half circle for the chair, knelt, sliced at the bonds on her ankles. Beefy hands closed around each of her arms. They jerked her upward and shoved her toward the boss man. Munroe struggled to maintain footing. Her hands were still palm to palm, and the rope still slack.

Munroe breathed in the aura of this man and his intended violence, absorbing until he blended with the memory and musk of Pieter Willem, until they were one inside her head.

The boss drew the knife up toward her face, smiling as her eyes tracked it. He pointed it down toward her chest. In a quick movement he sliced the material of her shirt; sliced through the undershirt. The clothing fell away, leaving her chest exposed.

The boss man turned to his men, jerked his thumb toward Munroe, and said, "See, I told you she was a woman." He drew close, his breath hot against her neck. Ran his finger along her nipple. Tweaked it.

"I was right," he whispered. "I do know you." He took the blade and played it against her skin. "And now that you're no longer their guest but mine, I will treat you as I please."

He paused when he saw the slivers that marked her torso, stared at them a moment and then his face creased into a half grin. "I see I won't be the first," he said. "Did he make you cry, the one who did this? Did he make you bleed?"

He stretched closer, sniffed her neck and her hair, licked her, his tongue running from her ear to her cheek and over her eye. "Did he make you suffer the way I will make you suffer?"

The rush of blood was loud in Munroe's ears, a heavy pounding that drowned out the world, drowned out everything but the man in front of her, and shouted the command to kill.

Instinct.

Timing.

Calculation.

In a last effort toward reason, she forced it back, fought against the urge, offered a way of escape to someone who deserved none.

"Let me go now," she said, her voice low, nearly a monotone, "and I won't kill you."

In response, the boss laughed. His bark was hard and unfeeling, a mockery. "Please, little girl," he said. "You go ahead and try to kill me. It would make for an entertaining morning."

She sighed.

Wrong answer.

It was always the wrong fucking answer.

Her eyes closed as pleasure flowed through her system. This was the point of no return, the pre-rush of a killing. There was no going back. She had no regrets, had made her peace, would die happy if such was the outcome. She'd traded her life for an innocent child's, and it had been an even trade.

"I will tell you what you want," she said.

"Yes," he whispered, his eyes on the knife as it caressed her skin. "You will."

He paused, broke from his trance, and slipped the knife into his jacket pocket. Sudden and violent, he drove a fist into her stomach and knocked her to her knees. He leaned over her and ran his fingers along her cheek.

Time slowed. Motion was broken into the fragmented jerking of strobe-light speed. Munroe's fingers worked, wrist passing, bonds loosening. She looked up, and this time, she smiled death.

One movement, solid, fluid, fast. Knees to feet. Upward. Forehead into his face. Fast enough to break his nose, hard enough to whip his head backward. Her hand to his pocket. His knife to her palm. Arm around his neck. Blade to his throat.

In the time it took for his bodyguards and bullies to draw their weapons.

The boss man's arms flailed, trying to get a grip, trying to gain balance as she dragged him backward along the far side of the semicircle toward the table and the wall that lay behind it. He was strong. Nearly her weight. Equal to her height, and such was the beauty of adrenaline and the rush that it bore that she didn't feel his strength, didn't know his weight, and pulled him along like a ragdoll.

The men, afraid to fire and hit their leader, followed instead, tightening the circle and drawing near.

Munroe flicked the boss man's neck, drawing blood.

"Back," she hissed, and each of the men from the semicircle paused in their encroachment.

Her cut had been more carefully placed than his had been. She'd struck the jugular, like putting a hole in a dike, and he, still flailing, not yet accepting his fate, seemed unaware that the harder he fought, the faster he'd die. He got hold of one of her ears. Began to dig, tear, pull.

She stabbed his hand.

He screamed.

"Right now you're just in pain," Munroe said, "but if your men don't put their weapons down, you'll be dead."

He hissed an unintelligible response.

She reached the table. Stepped around it. The wall was solid, cold against what was left of her shirt. No one would be coming at her from behind, and the table forced at least six feet of space between her and the others.

To her captive Munroe whispered, "You're bleeding. Badly. At this rate you'll be dead in twenty minutes. Do you want to make a trip to the hospital or do you want to make a trip to the morgue?"

She'd spoken a lie to keep him motivated; at the rate he was bleeding, he'd be lucky to last ten.

He stopped struggling. She could feel his body weakening, either through defeat or because with his neck held in the vise of her arm, she'd slowed the blood supply to his brain. The reason mattered little.

"Drop them," he said to his men. His voice was low, a whisper.

"They can't hear you," she hissed.

"Drop your weapons," he said again. Not much louder, although this time he flailed one arm up and down to emphasize the point.

In case there was any doubt, Munroe repeated the command, and when the men hesitated, didn't move at all, she dropped the tip of the knife into the tender of the boss man's shoulder joint and yanked.

He screamed again.

The men placed their drawn weapons on the floor.

"Scoot them under the table with your feet," Munroe said, and then added to the boss man's driver, "You. Fat guy. Toss the car keys on the table."

When they'd done as instructed, she nodded to the two closest to the warehouse entrance. "Get the doors," she said.

Munroe couldn't reach for the weapons on the floor, couldn't collect them and maintain her hold on the boss. They knew it. She knew it. They knew she knew it. She counted seconds as the two faded in the dimness toward the sliding doors.

Now was the moment of weakness, when the four still standing on the other side of the table would begin to close in.

Across the warehouse, the gate men slowed. Dawdled. They were killing time, keeping the escape route sealed off while they waited for their counterparts to take action. She was losing the upper hand, the window that she'd gained by surprise was closing.

The four around the table fanned out, inched forward, moving in a way that was far too confident for unarmed men, no matter how loyal they might be.

Instinct again. The fastest way to survival. Munroe dropped the boss—just let go and let him fall. He collapsed under his own weight, and she went down with him. Pulled two weapons off the floor. Dip and grab. No time to look, just take what she could get, then point and click.

Her fists closed around a pair of Bersa Thunder 9s, identical to the one pulled off her earlier. If the magazines were full, and they would be, they afforded seventeen rounds apiece. If that didn't cover what she needed, she deserved to get shot.

Still lying on her side, she fired. A warning discharge, aimed toward the floor in front of the men nearest the table. The report was a loud echo in the emptiness. They jumped, crouched, backed away only to the edge of the light. Time continued to move in split-second intervals, body language screaming in a way that words never could. The men were each reaching.

Backup weapons.

If she was going down, she wasn't going down alone. Munroe paused. Calmed her breathing. Double tapped. The closest man yelped. Fell. Wounded but alive. For now.

The boss moved to get up. She drove an elbow into his face and then downward against his cut shoulder. He screamed again.

She slid over the top of him so that his body remained a shield between the shooters and the wall, and with one weapon pressed into his spine, said, "Move again, and you're paralyzed for life. Understand?"

He groaned.

The three men remained on the periphery of light, inching forward again, trying to find a line of sight between the legs of the table and chairs and past their boss. The warehouse doors were still closed.

Munroe yelled into the darkness, "One minute to get the doors open or one of your people dies."

This time the shooters backed fully into the darkness; nobody wanted to be first. The occasional shuffle, toe scrape, and rustle betrayed position. They were close, just out of sight. The distance would make it difficult for them to shoot with accuracy, but there was always dumb luck and shrapnel. Especially when the lights blinded Munroe to what lay beyond the table area and made her an easy target.

She shifted forward. Aimed. Popped the lights, and the warehouse went completely black. Her eyesight ringed with the burning images of the powerful lamps, but even effectively night-blinded as she was, the darkness was still home.

Their eyes would have adjusted first, it would make them brave. Brave enough to crawl in close where they could see. She knelt. Waited. Listened. Then stood to a crouch, fished the keys off the table, and ducked back down to where the table and chair legs provided a modicum of cover.

She whispered to the boss, "You've been deserted." She punched the muzzle of the gun to the back of his head. "Get up."

He struggled to push upward to hands and knees. His breathing was slow, shallow. He'd lost a lot of blood, wouldn't last much longer. She needed to get to the car before any collateral she held in him ran out.

Chapter 34

Logan brought the taxi to a stop several hundred feet from the warehouse. The building was impossible to miss. Even in this remote industrial area, with fewer buildings and ample land between them, it still stood out from the rest, an easy story or two above the other buildings on the street. And from this distance, with the exception of an SUV parked just off to the side at the front, the entire structure appeared quiet and empty.

Unlike the other buildings set off from the road, there were no trucks idling or laborers milling about, no activity at all. And although Logan would have assumed it to be an illusion, the wide sliding doors were open and welcoming to the world.

"What do you make of it?" Logan said.

Gideon shook his head, as if pondering a puzzle for which he had no answer. He reached to the backseat and grabbed the desk clerk's shirt, pulled so that the man's line of sight was above the dashboard. "Are you sure that's the right place?" he said.

The clerk, gagged and swollen, nodded, and Gideon said, "Look at the doors. Is it normal for them to be open like that?" The clerk shook his head for no, and Gideon let him drop back to the seat.

They believed he'd led them to the right spot, and believed his answers. Not because he was a trustworthy guide, but because two hours ago his self-interest had aligned with their own. They'd taken him out of town and, in the dark of a field, with his body spread-eagled and staked to the ground and a gun muzzle pressed to his hand, threatened to shoot off one finger at a time until he told them what they wanted. It wasn't fear of pain that spoke to him as much as reassurance of release. They wanted their friend, their predicament was that simple, and when he brought them to where she'd been taken, when they knew without a doubt where she was, they'd let him go. That was all. It was either that or the fingers, and then toes, and whatever else it took to get what they wanted.

Logan took the cab another several hundred feet forward before stopping completely and shutting off the engine. Here at this vantage point, not far from the warehouse entrance, they sat, watching and waiting.

The area was quiet, the street traffic slow, and after a half hour had passed with no movement, Logan reached for the door handle.

"We're burning daylight," he said. "She's either in there or she's not."

Gideon turned to the backseat. "We live, you live," he said, and the desk clerk nodded. They knew he'd try to get loose while they were away, any sane person would, but he wouldn't succeed.

From the trunk Logan and Gideon pulled out the submachine guns. The pieces were too large to conceal under their jackets, and with the building set back off the road, they still had a few hundred feet to cover, but the security of having the higher-powered weapons overrode the little risk of being seen carrying them.

Gideon, whose hands were in the bag, tossed three loaded magazines at Logan and awkwardly shoved an equal number into his waistband and pockets. Any more and the weight would drag them down.

The clerk seemed to think they'd find between five and ten men with Munroe, but even if he was off in his guess, or if he'd lied to skew the odds, unless a small, well-equipped army waited on the other side of those doors, what they carried should be enough.

Gideon closed the trunk, and Logan stopped at the front passenger door. He kicked at the side mirror until it came loose, picked it up, and carried it with him. They walked in silence until they went off the pavement and Gideon stooped to gather several pebbles. Logan didn't bother asking what for. He knew.

They came at the building from far off the street, from the side where their approach would be unseen from within the windowless walls. Gideon neared the SUV, walked backward along half the body, peering into the windows, confirmed it empty, and signaled Logan forward. The only sounds were the light crunch of their boots against the gravel.

Logan followed the building's front wall to the edge of the open door, and there he tipped the mirror forward in a crude form of periscope, reflecting back what images he could gather. The mirror showed no movement. Along the vast, empty floor were lumps here and there. Bodies, perhaps. The lighting and angle made it difficult to tell.

He nodded at Gideon, who in turn tossed a pebble through the doors. The clack of the stone was hard against the floor, a repeated echo while the little rock bounced several times before settling.

Still, there was silence.

Gideon repeated the procedure. Again they listened.

No gunfire. No footsteps. No voices. Nothing.

Together, they rounded the open wall and flattened along its inside seam.

Daylight from the doors lit the interior nearly a hundred feet inward, and although the building continued on past the light, the bodies were out in the open, visible from where they stood.

There were seven, all men, strewn across the floor with wide spaces between.

Gideon stood still, staring, mouth slightly agape. He walked toward the center of the violence, and there turned in a slow circle. "This is the right place, isn't it? She was here, wasn't she?"

The tone of his questions framed the level of his disbelief.

Logan reached the first body. Knelt. "Yes," he said. "It's the right place."

"You should get a picture of this," Gideon said. "Miles will never believe it."

Logan felt for a pulse. Expected nothing, got nothing. The man's skull was shaped wrong; his body appeared broken and disjointed, as if he'd fallen from the rafters of the building—or been hit by a car. "Miles will believe it," Logan said. "He's seen this stuff firsthand, up close and personal."

Logan stood, turned to face Gideon and continue his explanation, but when he saw Gideon's face, he remained silent and went on to another of the bodies.

He was allowing Gideon space to process the scene that surrounded them. It wasn't the carnage, Logan knew that much. Gideon had seen—experienced—far worse. But there were seven dead, Munroe was missing, and Gideon would gradually realize that all of this had been caused by the same woman that he had tried to bully into a fight just days before.

The awareness of what he'd escaped was a little late in coming, but better late than never. "What do you think happened here?" Gideon said finally.

Logan shrugged. "At this level of violence, I think someone probably touched her. You know, sexually." He strode to the next man, knelt again, and felt for a pulse as he had the first two. The bodies were cooling but not cold. "She tries to avoid bloodshed," Logan said. "Especially so much of it. But there are a few things that will completely set her off and cause something like this, and if someone gets sexually violent with her, he's soon a dead man."

"All of them?" Gideon asked.

"I don't know," Logan said. He paused, turned a slow circle, and then pointed at a man pooled in blood and crumpled up against a wall riddled with bullet holes. "That guy," he said, and walked toward him. "It looks like he bled to death from the knife wounds. I don't know about the others, but this one carries all the hallmarks of Michael. Whoever he was, he really pissed her off. I venture he's the one in charge."

Logan pointed at the scars on the wall. "They were shooting at something or someone—not this guy." He ran the back of his hand along the wall and checked his fingertips. "No blood spatter," he said.

He searched the floor for spatter beyond the congealed pool. "I don't think they hit whatever they were shooting at," he said. "I want to bring that clerk in and verify the ID on these guys."

"What about Michael?" Gideon asked.

"She's not here, and all seven of these guys didn't arrive in that one vehicle outside. There had to be another, and it's gone. So, either she's dead somewhere else or there were more people and they took her somewhere else. But if that guy over there is the boss, then my guess is that she's free and on the move. If that's the case she's going to be heading in Miles's direction as quickly as she can. We should probably do the same."

Logan paused, stared at the scene across the floor, and then stood. If the head of a local crime family fell off the radar, sooner or later someone was going to come looking. "I'm going to check out the back of this place, just to be sure Michael's not here," he said. "Go get the clerk. I want to identify these guys, and then I want to get the hell out of here before reinforcements show up and we take the heat for this."

The morning was still early, city traffic still light, and Munroe drove as slowly as was possible to drive on Buenos Aires streets without attracting attention. Moving through town inconspicuously wasn't easy when driving a car dented from where she'd hit the warehouse wall, or a front grille spattered with blood, and a rear passenger window spiderwebbed from the absorption of several rounds against bulletproof glass. A few more miles and she could ditch the thing.

She'd seen the SUV sitting by the side of the warehouse only after she'd spun out onto the road, and although in retrospect it might have been the smarter option to go back for it, at the time going back wasn't a consideration.

In the ebb and flow of changing lanes, Munroe's mind ran in circles, attempting to put into place the series of steps that she would make next. There were loose ends, pieces to be ordered, and like a house of cards, each one balanced on the ones below. She needed clarity, but the adrenaline dump was slowing her down and making it difficult to focus beyond getting the car safely from point A to point B.

She had to get food into her system, had to pump up blood sugar levels, and she craved sleep too. Food would be the faster and easier option. It had to wait just a little longer. First a trip to her hotel room to confirm that Bradford was safe, that he'd followed the plan. She needed to see it, know it, not only for personal assurance but also for guidance in deciding which direction to turn. Because the way things stood now, she had to get to Bradford as quickly as possible, or locate and then rescue Bradford. One or the other.

If Bradford was alive, if he'd been successful in getting Hannah to safety, Logan would want his daughter, and Bradford would refuse. This was the way it had to be. Bradford was neither Hannah's guardian nor the one legally assigned to take her home; he had no authority to do anything other than deliver the girl to her mother and would want her off his hands as quickly as possible.

Once successful, Bradford would be driven to return to Buenos Aires, to search for Munroe, no matter how long it took, and continuing this mess was the last thing she wanted. She had to reach him before Charity did, and for reasons of her own had to reach Hannah before Charity did. On both counts, time was running out. It would take time, a day perhaps, for Charity to get to Montevideo, if she wasn't already en route.

Munroe entered the hotel with her head tucked down and one hand holding her sliced shirts closed. She made directly for the small ground-floor restroom. She'd seen her face in the car's rearview mirror, and it wasn't pretty. Her lips were swollen, both eyes blackened, and her cheeks and forehead bruised and mottled. All told, the facial coloring was far better than the sheet-white alternative, but it made blending in nearly impossible.

She pushed into the unisex bathroom and locked the door. Facing the mirrors, water running, she scrubbed the blood off her face, hands, and arms, and plunged her head under the water to wash everything out of what was left of her hair.

The best she could do about the slit shirts was to strip out of them, reverse the undershirt so that the opening faced the back, and pull the top layer back on over it. Blood had dried on the clothes, had drenched the arm she'd used to create the chokehold, and there wasn't much she could do about that. Against the black, the stains weren't obviously blood, they could be anything, and although she would have preferred to wash them out, or at the least scrape the residue off into the sink, this was a procedure that would take more time than she had, and she'd already been in the bathroom long enough to attract attention.

She bathed her face in the cold water once more and patted herself dry. The water wouldn't help much with the swelling, but it made her feel better.

Munroe left the restroom for the front desk and, amid curious stares at her battered face, requested a key to the room. As was standard procedure, she'd carried nothing on her during the extraction. Her passport, money, and all personal effects had been left behind. And although she expected the room had since been cleared out—for Bradford's sake, she hoped that it had been—she was compelled to make sure.

The desk clerk did a poor job at concealing his disgust at her mangled face, and made no pretense of helping. Yes, the room was still paid a week in advance, but as she could not prove that she was one of the occupants, and he certainly didn't recognize her, there was nothing he would do.

The dangerous chemical cocktail brought on by the morning's events still percolated through Munroe's system, and any ability to maintain cordial interaction with a snot-nosed brat had ended hours ago.

Chapter 35

On the best of days Munroe had little patience for power-playing tug-of-wars with ignorance or arrogance, and today was not the best of days. She flipped the boss's blade into her palm, sprung it open, leaned over the counter, and hissed a vivid description of what she would do to the desk clerk once she found him alone after work, and it took but a moment for him to compromise.

Key in hand, Munroe took the stairs up, two at a time. She worked against the clock, against private security, which would soon be on their way, and the police that might eventually come.

Munroe opened the door to an empty room. The place had been cleaned out. Not in a housekeeping sort of way, but in special-ops style, where no hint was left that either she or Bradford had ever been there. Munroe made directly for the bathroom, ignored her reflection, and lifted the toilet-tank lid. Disappeared with everything else was her money and her identification.

She replaced the lid with relief. Bradford was gone. He'd followed protocol. Without money or documentation, getting out of the country and finding him was going to be a bit of a bother, but she wouldn't have had it any other way.

Munroe tossed the keys on the bed, blocked the door open an inch, and ducked into an alcove before the stairwell. She'd been in the room a minute and a half, an entire minute longer than acceptable. The elevator opened, and a pair of uniforms rushed past. They stopped at the room door and kicked it inward, and Munroe slipped into the stairwell.

She ran the way down, rushed the lobby to the sidewalk, turned left, and head down, moved forward at a brisk pace. She didn't pause when she came to the stolen vehicle but slowed to a quick walk, heading past it toward a man several spaces down who was getting into his car.

Knife to his side, she ordered him across the front seat and slid in next to him.

The decision had been made in a split second and was one Munroe detested. Under conditions like these, getting across town shouldn't have required carjacking; whatever she was, she wasn't a thug, and preying on random strangers who had nothing to do with her predicament was not her way.

Procuring a ride should have taken only a careful study of body language, a few smiles, and a sob story. But nobody wanted to play host to Frankenstein, and with her face as it was, her options were reduced to forcing a ride or driving the streets in a moving target.

Munroe peeled into traffic, sped away from the hotel only far enough to put distance between herself and whatever security was up to, and then, safely gone from the place, slowed to the speed of acceptable insanity.

In the seat next to her, the man's eyes were wide. He'd pushed himself as far away as he could, as if it were possible to become part of the door, and staring directly at her, with terror on his face, he stammered nonsense, as though he were speaking to an imaginary friend.

"I'm not going to hurt you," she said, but he continued on, as if her words held no meaning.

He was a slight man, mid-fifties, gray hair, mousy suit that read bureaucrat not businessman, and from his lack of Spanish, was clearly not from here. Staying in the flow of traffic, Munroe focused on his blubbering, gathering a snippet here or there until recognition struck. His words were an incantation; the same few sentences whispered over and over. In Russian. The oddity was disconcerting, and barely escaping a collision, Munroe returned her focus to the road.

"*Ya ne sdelayu vam nichego plokhogo,*" she said. In the stress of the moment, the switch from one language to the next came without thought, like flipping stations on a remote or shedding a jacket after arriving home.

"I just need to get from one part of town to the next," she said to him, "and then I'll give you back the car. I promise."

The man's eyes widened farther, if such were possible, and his mouth dropped open an inch.

At least this was a predictable reaction: It happened often when others heard their mother tongue spoken in a foreign land and believed they'd found a compatriot. It didn't typically happen under these circumstances, but was familiar territory nonetheless, and she'd have been able to answer questions as a matter of rote had he asked them.

But he didn't.

The incantation stopped, his hands relaxed, he didn't try to fight her, and she was able to drive in silence. For these, Munroe was grateful.

On the street outside Logan's hostel, Munroe stopped short at the curb, hopped out of the car, slammed the door, and paused just long enough to reopen the door, lean her head back inside, and apologize. She shut the door again, turned, and headed for the courtyard at a near run.

Munroe moved through the inside area, didn't bother finding the proprietor or asking for a key. These rooms had thinner doorframes, smaller locks; a solid strike to each, just left of the handle, would give her entry. Munroe reached Heidi's room first.

Knocked. Waited.

Pounded. Waited.

And then kicked.

The frame splintered, the door swung inward, and not quite unexpectedly, the room was empty. Not the special-ops empty of the last hotel, but left-in-a-mighty-big-hurry kind of empty.

She moved down the hall to Logan's door, where she expected the same, but the need for certainty compelled her toward it. The door flung inward and she checked to a stop. Bradford had cleared out, Heidi was gone, but Logan and Gideon's room still showed signs of occupancy.

Munroe entered the room and closed the door, fiddled with the latch until it held in place. She stepped to the beds, felt them, and found them long cold. Among the items that had been left behind were computers, portable electronics, and on Gideon's bedside table a book that he'd been reading.

The boys were still in town.

Munroe felt under Logan's mattress for the money belt that should be there, snagged it, and pulled it out. He'd left his passport and several hundred dollars, half of it in Argentine pesos.

With all of the other evidentiary pieces, there was only one reason these two hadn't gone. Munroe would have laughed if she wasn't so conflictingly angry about it.

Bradford had followed the plan—to a point. Then he'd sent Logan and Gideon after her. The situation was beyond frustrating. People she loved and cared about were spread around the city. She had no idea where they were. No idea if they were safe, and she wanted nothing more than to track them down and protect them. But like a kid lost in a haunted amusement park, the only thing she could do to keep from making the situation worse was to follow the plan. Get to the meeting point and hope that they did too.

Munroe took a portion of the pesos and thrust them into her pocket. Found a pen, scrawled a note to Logan, and placed it under the front cover of his passport. She shoved it all back under the mattress where she'd found it, then stripped out of her clothes, pulled replacements from Logan's suitcase, and changed. She dumped the bloody items into a backpack and slung it over her shoulder. She'd been inside the room a total of four minutes.

Inside the main house, she searched out the proprietress, ignored both her reaction and that of some of the guests, and left a message for Logan and Gideon. Provided the boys were still alive, they would be checking out soon, and assuming Logan with his emergency phone was still in contact with Bradford, this would be the fastest way to let Bradford know that she too was alive.

The money she'd taken from Logan was enough to get a cab to the port, and from there to buy a one-way ferry ticket to Montevideo, the capital of neighboring Uruguay. The trip was only a three-hour skip over the water, but money to pay for a ticket was useless without documents for travel, and as such, the trip would predictably be a whole lot longer.

When Munroe stepped outside, the Russian was still in his car by the curb where she'd parked. He'd switched to the driver's seat but turned off the engine, and was now staring out the windshield. It had been fewer than ten minutes since Munroe had rushed inside, but to a man who had, by his own interpretation of events, narrowly escaped a violent act, ten minutes were ten lifetimes, and she would have expected him to have used that time to put as much distance between himself and the hostel as possible. And then maybe down a stiff drink.

The man didn't have the look of a trauma victim, and other than that he still sat where she'd left him, he didn't appear to be in shock. Munroe cursed inwardly and made a slow, cautious return to the car. There wasn't time to waste, but the Russian was there, and as she was at fault for bringing him to this point, she couldn't just walk away.

Munroe rapped knuckles on the passenger window, and the man turned as if he'd been waiting for her and was happy she'd come back.

"What happened to you?" he asked. "Are you in trouble?"

His questions weren't what she'd expected, but she wouldn't turn down an opportunity. "I could use a ride," she said.

He reached to open the passenger door, and she slid inside.

"We Russians must stick together," he said, and Munroe, following the path of least resistance, simply grinned. Her nonverbal response was neither acknowledgment nor contradiction, and he would read from the look whatever pleased him. Ambiguity was so much easier than truth and the exhaustive amount of time it would take to explain that she'd never even been to Russia, that she had a gift for languages, that the only reason he mistook her for one of his own was because in her second year of college she'd spent four months dating a boy from St. Petersburg.

Better just to grin.

The man turned the ignition key and Munroe asked for the Buque-bus terminal, the lower end of the port, south of the commercial shipping docks, where the ferry lines to Uruguay were found. The Russian seemed familiar enough with the location and the route. He pulled directly into traffic, asked no help with directions, and drove the first several minutes in silence.

"If you're in trouble, maybe I can help," the Russian said, "so far from home, we must ally."

"It's been a bad morning, that's all," she said. "I've friends to meet up with and once I find them, everything will be well."

"You're certain?" the man said.

Munroe nodded, and he said nothing more.

The port abutted the wide, busy avenues of Puerto Madero, as if the city had decided to end things by jumping into the chocolate-toned water and then at the last minute would rather tiptoe in, adding a few more buildings before the very end.

The Buquebus terminal, with its modern glass design and Jetway-style boarding, which ran from the second floor down to where the ships would dock, seemed more like an airport than a ferry transport.

Munroe asked that the Russian drive beyond the parking area, with its policemen and security, just a little farther down the branching road, and so he continued beyond the terminal and ticket office, stopping as requested along a rusted fence that separated the docks from city traffic.

She offered to pay for the ride, and he refused.

With a good-bye full of unasked questions, and a reassuring hand-shake on her part, he pulled away from the curb, and she remained rooted, watching as the vehicle shrank away and then blended with traffic to vanish completely.

Munroe turned from the road to the fence and headed farther back, to the run-down end of the wharf, where the buildings were old, the security lax, and where fewer pedestrians mingled. There she found a spot to hop the wires in order to gain access to where the employees gathered: a place where she could sit and observe without being noticed while cars lined up and the baggage men with their little tractors and trailing carts made ready for the next departure.

The ferry to Montevideo was scheduled to leave in an hour, and one way or the other, she would be on it. The issue wasn't ticketing per se, it was getting identification to purchase the ticket—and then proceeding through the appropriate immigration procedures—as if her face, messed up as it was, wouldn't create unnecessary complications.

Up top, through the glass, she could see the shadows of passengers as they gathered and prepared for embarkation, but they held no interest to her. Passports were only as good as their original holder, and as such had the possibility of bringing the bearer unforeseen trouble. Ideally, she would swipe a national identification card; this was all that an Argentine would need to cross into Uruguay. No questions. No suspicions. Simply an open door to the country across the border.

With emotionless calculation she studied those mingling about the dockside, judging the quality of each, passing them over in turn. This was that dangerous place where the predator overrode empathy, where, like the Russian with his car, solving need and want blurred the boundaries between right and wrong, and the uninvolved suffered on behalf of those to blame.

Munroe stood and slipped closer to the work area, watching, waiting, searching out opportunity amid the bustle of dockside readiness. Suppliers, dockworkers, and the occasional crew member came and went, and Munroe tracked them with dispassionate interest.

It took twenty minutes to spot the mark. He was part of the ferry staff, early thirties at best, and both his body language and the menial tasks he performed pointed toward his being low man on the totem pole. Unlike any member of the crew, he wouldn't be overly missed if he failed to show up for embarkation, and better still, his position as a

Buquebus employee would not only solve the issue of documentation but also eliminate the need for ticketing and much of the immigration and border protocol that went with the journey.

The ferry was in the final stages of preparing to set out, the stream of passengers that had been steadily boarding over the past ten minutes began to ebb slightly, and the target had already made several trips over the service gangplank and back, carrying an assortment of boxes on board.

Munroe loitered, waiting until he'd moved most of them, timing each trip in and out until, with only one load left, he was swallowed by the interior of the ship.

Much could be assessed from a person's walk, from their build, and the level at which they observed their surroundings, but appearances were often deceiving. The sweetest old lady might think nothing of sticking you with a shiv, and as such, taking on an unknown opponent, no matter how docile and defeated he might appear, always carried an element of risk.

On the man's return, as he prepared to lift the final box, Munroe casually approached from behind, across the dock, amid the commotion, as if she rightfully belonged there. At the periphery of her awareness remained a counterweight to the savage, the ever present caution that there was no point to eradicating evil if in the end she would only replicate it.

She took the knife to the side of his lower back, tip pointed upward, far enough through his clothes that he would feel the thrust of it. "I don't want to hurt you," she whispered, "and I don't want to steal from you."

He tensed, let go of the box, and straightened. His breathing shifted, and it wasn't a rapid pant of fear. His were the slow and measured movements of a man who had been down this path before, a man who understood the leverage he held in this crowded area.

With her free arm wrapped around his waist, she steered him back the way she'd come, under the upper floor, toward the staff door along the outside of the ticket building wall. She wanted him off the wharf and into privacy as quickly as possible.

"Walk with me and listen to my proposal," she said.

The man did as she asked, moved with her for the moment, acquiesced, perhaps to put her off her guard, because several paces forward he drove his elbow into her side so hard that it knocked the knife from her hand.

Chapter 36

It was speed that saved her, was always speed that saved her. Munroe drove a responsive fist to his kidney and a boot into the back of his opposite knee. Followed him down when he stumbled. Scooped the knife and pulled him upward, all in the time it would have taken for him to trip and catch his balance.

Those mingling along the dock were none the wiser.

He had spoken, and she'd replied, hers the stronger message of the two. She forced calm against anger. There was no reason to fault him for trying, she would have reacted the same way, and the only thing he'd done to deserve this treatment was having been in the right place at the wrong time.

"I swear I don't want to hurt you," she said. "But if you force my hand I'll have no choice, you understand?"

He nodded, and at her nudge they continued across the way, to the end of the building and the inconspicuous door from which staff had filtered in, but over the last thirty minutes, mostly out.

The small interior was limited to a narrow hall and two small rooms branching off on either side. The clutter of papers and the smell of stale coffee and food spilled beyond the open doors into the walkway. The hallway continued to a closed door that could be only a bathroom or a utility closet, and from there turned a sharp right toward the remainder of the building. Munroe walked him to the dead-end door.

"Open it," she said, and then followed close behind into the one-stall bathroom, locked the door, and motioned him to the toilet. It had no lid, no seat, and in order to keep from sliding into the water, he had to straddle it, legs held wide.

"I need your jacket and identification," she said. "I can either take what I want by force, which will be painful for you and messy for me, or you can give them to me in exchange for what money I have on me—not a lot, but more than what it will take to replace your ID. Either way I'm going to tie you up and leave you here. If you fight me, I'll do it because I have no choice. If you give me what I want, it will be so that when you are found, your story, whatever you decide to tell, will be believable."

The man stared at her, his jaw working back and forth in what she read as anger or deep thought, probably both.

"How much money?" he said finally.

Blade in her right hand, eyes always on him, guarding against any movement, she reached with her left into a pocket and pulled out two-thirds of what she'd taken from Logan. She dropped it into his out-stretched hand, and in response he reached for his back pocket.

She said, "Stop."

He put both hands up. "My wallet," he said, and she nodded.

The man pulled out his ID card and held it toward her.

"Drop it on the floor," she said. He did as she asked, then shrugged out of his overshirt and theatrically dropped it on top of the ID. He raised his eyebrows in a look of "Now what?"

She wanted his T-shirt, and he peeled it off to reveal a well-toned torso underneath. She placed a boot on his groin, shoved dangerously downward, and reached for the shirt.

"Don't move," she said.

With the knife, she slit the material, one ribbon after the next, then pushed his head between his knees. Boot to his neck, she secured his wrists behind his back, then tied a gag between his lips. Certain he couldn't easily free himself, she ordered him to stand.

She loosened the buckle of his pants. A look of horror crossed his face and he began to crawfish backward, a blinded, crazed attempt to escape when there was no escape.

Munroe's laugh was spontaneous and she shook her head. "Calm down," she said, "I'm just making sure you remain secure." Never mind the explanation that she was female.

His eyes remained wide, but he stopped struggling. Hands to his shoulders, she moved him back into a seated position, and with his pants around his ankles, she secured his feet, one to the other, with strips she'd taken from his shirt, the improvised bonds running behind the toilet from one foot, back again to the other. Once she was gone, he would struggle, but the restraints would hold until after the ferry departed, and that was all she needed.

She slipped into his work shirt. Picked up the ID. Slid out of the bathroom and shut the door.

Munroe moved back onto the dock and next to the ship, shouldered the remaining box still there on the ground and, five minutes from start to finish, carried it into the belly of the ship.

Only after she was on board, out of the light and out of the fight, did she realize the severity of her shaking. She'd gone from adrenaline rush to adrenaline dump, to adrenaline rush twice over, and was beyond spent. She needed food. Needed a place where she could lay low for the length of the trip.

She was on the ship's lower level, the hollow space where vehicles were stowed for the duration of the trip and where the air was foul with fumes and machinery. The last of the luggage trolleys had returned to the dock, passengers who'd driven the vehicles on board were sent upstairs, and only a few crew members remained below.

Munroe slipped between the cars. On a ledge, next to life vests, was a small container, like a lunch box, temporarily set aside, and without breaking stride or letting go of the load she carried, Munroe picked it up and continued on, beside the vehicles to a windowless door.

The interior was dark and small, an empty storage area.

She slipped inside, dumped the box onto the floor, sat on it, and shoveled food from the lunch container into her mouth faster than she could chew, gorging on it as if she were starving, craving protein when there were only vegetables and potatoes and a flavor that said meat, although there was none to be had.

The food was sufficient to slow the shaking, but not nearly enough to satiate the craving for sustenance. Munroe slit open the box, found it filled with an assortment of packaged desserts, and although she knew that she would later pay the price for dumping sugar into a system that badly needed nutrition, she opened and ate several.

In the wake of ebbing hunger, the full weight of exhaustion descended, and in the dark, warm cocoon of the closet, Munroe fought to stay alert, to stay awake. She didn't need a nightmare now. Not on top of everything else, and if she slept, completely fatigued as she was, it was also possible she might sink so fully that she missed port call on the other side.

The rumble of the ship played melody to the beat of its rocking, and against Munroe's mental protest, her body, drowsy, weak, and demanding that its needs be met, was lulled into a complete shutdown.

The night was black, the sky starless, and from across the length of sand came the rhythmic wash of waves upon the shore. It was deserted here, no light of civilization, no intrusion of humanity into this quiet. Alone, with only the smell of fish, salt, the subtle fragrance of jasmine, and the warm ocean breeze kissing her skin, Munroe rocked in the hammock.

It mattered not that she couldn't see or that the cadence of the water completely muted all other sound, because she could feel. In this space of complete darkness there was only tranquillity. Here was a haven of nothing, nothing that could go on, and on, and on . . .

The voice of rhythm shifted to a low grumble, Munroe's eyes blinked open, and she drew in air as if she'd been long without it. Her surroundings were still dark but no longer tranquil. Disoriented, she struggled to give place and meaning to the confines of this space and then calmed, remembering where she was and realizing that the shift had come from the ship's engines reversing.

The ferry was pulling into port. She'd no idea how long she'd been under, and at which port was anyone's guess.

She felt through the darkness, and with relief, her fingertips returned an uneventful story. The knife was still in her pocket, the container on top of the box where she'd left it. There were no fragments of clothing, no shards of destroyed property. Uncomfortable as it was, shoulder propped against the wall for a pillow, she'd slept soundly and, for the first time in three months, had slept without dreaming violence.

Footsteps and voices filtered in from beyond the door, and the sounds of car engines coming to life indicated that passengers were disembarking. Munroe stood, smoothed down the wrinkles that would inevitably be on her clothes, ran her fingers across her head, and cracked the door a sliver.

Munroe waited for an opening, drew back the door, and as if she had every right to be there, stepped alongside traffic. Without looking back, and ignoring the occasional stare in her direction, she made for the dock and strode down the gangplank.

Montevideo.

From the wharf, the cityscape poked above commercial transport containers stacked three and four high, and in the cool of the lengthening afternoon, Munroe paused to take in the air of the place. The city was so much smaller than its sister capital three hours west, but still nearly two million strong, and had she not at least an idea of how to begin searching for Bradford, her path would have been one more needle in a very large, very time-consuming haystack.

The Buquebus terminal in Montevideo shared space with commercial shipping, although the passengers disembarked on the second floor, as they had in Buenos Aires. Munroe bypassed immigration and customs controls by wandering directly off the dock, deeper into the containers, eventually moving on foot beyond a cursory security checkpoint and into the streets of the oldest part of the city where buildings, centuries old, were arrayed in a matrix on a peninsula of sorts.

Munroe hailed a taxi, the same bumblebee black and yellow of Buenos Aires, and with nearly the last of her money caught a ride to the central post office. There was but a mile to travel, a short jaunt between the ferry and the center of the old town, but she was short on energy and short on time; she wanted this over, and even with the ride, she stepped through the doors dangerously close to quitting time.

Montevideo's primary post office was small compared to the stately building that housed it: one large room lined corner to corner with antique mailboxes, and in the center was a counter that made a smaller square. Behind it, three postal workers went about their business.

From the nearest woman, Munroe asked for *poste restante,* and she directed Munroe to the side and asked her to wait.

Here was where letters written to those without an address could be sent and held for a month or more, though what Munroe hoped to find would have arrived today at the earliest, hand delivered. Palms to counter, she waited for service. Her nerves were still raw, but food and three hours of sleep had worked their magic, and now only patience would buy her what she wanted.

Against the urge toward motion, she forced her body to stillness and brought placid indifference to her face. The clerk was a plump woman in her mid-forties who returned in no hurry. Munroe requested mail held in her name, and the woman searched through several boxes sorted alphabetically. She finally pulled one lone envelope.

At the sight of the white rectangle the weight of the last twenty-four hours and all of its unknowns slid off Munroe's shoulders.

The woman asked for identification, and Munroe had none.

Bradford wasn't an idiot, he'd taken her ID, knew she'd need it to retrieve any message he'd left, and would have compensated. With what little charm Munroe could muster, and with a heavy dose of flattery, she requested to see the envelope first. The woman raised an eyebrow in mock reproach and, not letting go of the corners, held it address forward.

Munroe stared for a moment and then sighed in dejection. "It's not for me," she said, and leaving the confused woman standing, Munroe turned and walked away.

Outside the post office, she flagged another taxi, and to the driver gave the address that had been written as the return on the envelope.

The Palladium hotel.

She'd find Bradford and Hannah on the eleventh floor, in the presidential suite.

Like in the heart of Buenos Aires, Montevideo was a city of tree-lined boulevards and European architecture, a smaller, calmer, cleaner version of its sister to the west, and in spite of its size and the belching buses that flew down otherwise quiet streets, it still held an Old World sleepy-town charm.

They continued east, outside the old town and into the new. Blocks from the coast, the Palladium was modern and sleek with rounded lines and inlaid glass, one of several of the relatively higher-end hotels the city had to offer. Munroe took the elevator up and followed carpet and sconce lighting in Bradford's direction.

With the same prescience that he'd always displayed when they were together, Bradford opened the door before she reached it. His expression read relief and happiness, and there, subtly, under the initial layers of natural caution, something more.

Munroe paused at the door's threshold, and Bradford reached for her, pulled her toward him, and wrapped his arms around her, tightly. She understood the desperation: She'd frightened him badly, but in the moment he said not a word of reproof, and there was relief in his acceptance of her entirety, personal risk and bodily damage included.

Munroe leaned into him, put her head on his shoulder.

Bradford smelled of joy and pleasure and belonging, and the tension, the anger, and all of the rage of the past days dissipated.

Bradford released her, stepped back a foot, and put hands to her face. "What the hell did they do to you?" he said.

"You should see the other guys," she said.

He pulled her to him again and kissed her forehead. "Logan told me about the other guys."

Head still on his shoulder, still standing at the door's threshold, Munroe said, "Logan made it to the warehouse? Is he okay?"

Bradford nodded, his whisper soothing against her skin. "He and Gideon got into town a couple of hours ago," he said.

That Bradford had sent them after her remained an unspoken understanding.

"They tracked you from the hotel to the warehouse, and considering the state of things, figured you were alive and moving in this direction." He wrapped a hand around the back of her neck, kept the other around her body, pressed his cheek against the side of her head, and then shifted.

One arm behind her knees, he picked her up, brought her into the foyer, and knocked the door closed with his foot.

She laughed, hooked an arm around his neck for support, and said, "What are you doing?"

"Depositing you in the bathtub," he said. "You need it." And he carried her forward.

The suite had two rooms, separated by a solid wall and a series of doors that provided a division of space and a sense of privacy. Bradford would have wanted it that way, as much for himself as for Hannah, who was in the bedroom, sedated and asleep, still in the same nightclothes she'd been wearing when they'd taken her from the third-floor room. He was a grown man with a kidnapped and drugged thirteen-year-old girl in his possession and no official authority to have her; it couldn't have been a comfortable situation.

Munroe, still in Bradford's arms and straining for a look around the corner, said, "Has she woken at all?"

"Yes," Bradford said. "Run the water. I'll get you clean clothes." He paused. "And if you don't mind, I'll tell you about it while you soak."

Chapter 37

Munroe was smiling again, an ear-to-ear, shit-eating grin that Bradford could only return in kind. To see that smile, even with the damage that had been done to her face, made him damn near euphoric, and having her here, having her safe after so many tortured hours of the unknown, was such a giddy relief that it cloaked the anger that had fast followed the assurance that she was alive and okay.

He wanted to kiss her, wanted to hold on to her, but then shake her and ask what the hell she had been thinking—yell out the frustration so that she'd understand the nauseating ache that had been with him all this time.

But he didn't.

Wouldn't.

As she'd said, sometimes love was its own reward, and to struggle to turn it into more was to murder it slowly. No matter how badly he hated that she played so easily with risk and thought nothing of living on the blade of danger, he accepted this as the only way. He couldn't protect her, wouldn't attempt to change her, and if acceptance was the price required to stay within her orbit, he would pay it gladly.

Bradford set Munroe's legs on the bathroom floor, put her upright, and stepped out of her way. He waited just outside the door until the tub was full and she was in it, and then with a slight knock at the door brought in his only change of clothes and set them on the edge of the sink. But for these, which had been in the trunk of the car, everything else had been left in Buenos Aires.

According to the plan, he and Munroe would have traveled to the charter together, and then, once she and Hannah were safely ensconced, he was to return to the hotel and clear it out.

That was the plan.

What he'd been left with was the need for improvisation: putting boot to Logan's butt, rousing Heidi out of bed and getting her on her way, and then pulling in one last middle-of-the-night favor from his local connections. By his best estimate, the hotel room had been scrubbed clean right about when he was strapping Hannah into the seat of the Gulfstream that would carry them into Uruguay.

Everything taken from the room was still in Buenos Aires, the clothing, equipment, data, money, and identification, all of it secured and waiting until ready for retrieval. They'd have to head back, probably sooner rather than later, if for nothing else than for their documents and to recover the data that Munroe had used as her bargaining chip with Gideon.

After all of the buildup prior to Hannah's extraction, and after the horror of having Munroe snatched from him, getting Hannah out of Buenos Aires had been a straightforward nonevent, executed flawlessly, the end result of meticulous preparation. The charter had been fueled and waiting, and although Bradford carried a valid passport for Hannah—something Charity would need to get the girl out of Uruguay—neither he nor Munroe had planned to travel documented, and arrangements had already been made to bypass official exit and entry.

The girl had woken on the way to the airport, and although it had taken less than a minute to put her back under, that had been a painful minute. The kid was terrified. She'd gone to sleep in a bed, in familiar surroundings, and woken in a car with a strange man. Sedating her had been not only a necessary part of transporting her but also a favor.

Once they'd reached Montevideo, he'd put a very slow drip into her to keep her hydrated and asleep and had kept her under ever since.

But sooner or later they were going to have to wake her, and then what?

Bathwater splashed against the other side of the shower curtain. There was joy in that simple sound, and then more of it in the ensuing silence while he waited to give Munroe information. She wasn't ignoring him, she knew he was there and probably also knew that his patient waiting was really just a cover for a truth he'd never voice. He wanted to be near, didn't want to let her out of his sight, not for a very, very long time. And although that was a wish that would never be granted, for now he had her cornered, and for the moment it was enough.

Arms crossed, Bradford leaned into the wall opposite the tub, and after several more minutes, content to simply be, he finally spoke. "I know we did the right thing in taking Hannah from The Chosen," he said. "But for all the time we've spent discussing the strategy of extraction, we haven't talked much about what to do with her once we have her. The kid's going to be traumatized, you know? One moment she's asleep in her bed with someone she knows, the next minute she wakes up surrounded by people that she's spent her whole life thinking were the Devil. Even if we wait until the last minute to wake her and give her directly to her mom, that's not going to make it any better."

"How long was she awake?" Munroe said.

"Not long, maybe a minute, but if you could have seen the look on her face, it was heartrending."

"I kind of figured that's how it would go," Munroe said. "Is Charity already in town?"

"Tomorrow afternoon," Bradford said. "But Logan's been pushing nonstop to have me give Hannah to him. I had to turn off the phone."

"I can only imagine how difficult this is for him," Munroe said. Logan had waited eight years for his daughter, and now that she was in custody, he couldn't even come to hold her hand while her mother

traveled down. But it was the way it had to be. Kidnapping and transporting a child across international borders was a serious crime. That
they were doing so under the auspices of the child's legal guardian was
something of a gray area, and in order to fly under the radar of the law,
they had to wait for Charity.

"It can't be helped," Munroe said. "But maybe it's for the best,
because I need to talk to Hannah before she meets any of the others. I
don't know if it'll go any better than it did for you, but I'm no longer a
complete stranger, and I have something that she needs to hear."

Munroe let the water out of the tub, stood, and turned on the
shower. From beyond the curtain her body was a vague silhouette, and
Bradford watched with unabashed appreciation as she stretched her
neck long and let the water beat against the back of it. Then, shutting
off the water, she said, "We'll bring Hannah out of it in the morning.
That'll give me several hours at least before her mom gets here."

Munroe reached her hand beyond the curtain, fingers wiggling
expectantly, and Bradford grinned and handed her a hand towel. She
laughed and tossed it back. "Give me," she said, and he gave her a
bath towel.

"I got another bit of information out of New York this morning,"
he said. "A decent-size update on the investigation that's under way
up there."

Munroe stepped from the shower, pink from the heat and towel
wrapped around her. "Oh?" she said.

"Yeah," he replied, smiling, saying nothing more.

She smacked the back of her hand to his biceps and, smirking,
said, "I'm not going to beg you for the details, Miles, no matter how
much you want me to."

"We'll see," he said, but his voice trailed and lowered, and had
none of the bravado that he'd intended. In front of him, she stood
warm and wet, and no matter how untoward it might appear, he
couldn't avert his eyes. To believe that he had lost her forever, only
to have her gifted back, had altered any sense of propriety, and took

from him all the reserve and control that thus far had kept him from pursuing her.

He reached out, put a hand behind her neck, pulled her close, and kissed her.

She could have pushed him away or gone cold, gone deadly, and he would have suffered the consequences willingly, if only to have that taste. But instead she put her hands to his face, let the towel drop, and kissed him back.

He grabbed her to him, fingers and mouth hungry, wanting, and in full reciprocation her hands found their way underneath his shirt and began to pull it off.

They had started in the bathroom and ended on the living room sofa. Munroe had no idea of the time, only a vague notion of how much had passed, and that it was now dark outside. The suite was lit by ambient light from the windows and what little seeped from under the bathroom door.

Bradford lay with his back flat to the couch, and she was beside him, on her side with her head on his chest, listening to the rhythm of his breathing. He'd drifted off to sleep, and although the idea of joining him in dreamland, joining him for longer, was tempting, she had work to do.

As close as they were to handing off Hannah and finishing what they'd come down to accomplish, the assignment had loose ends. Munroe's dilemma at the Haven Ranch hadn't ended simply because circumstances had forced her to move away from it in the middle of the night. Elijah was far out of sight, but his treatment of Hannah wasn't out of mind, nor was the convoluted way that everyone was connected, each relation turning in on another like an endless loop.

Munroe slid over Bradford, making a halfhearted attempt not to wake him, though she gladdened when he did.

"Where are you going?" he whispered.

"I need to talk to Heidi," she said. "And then I need to find Gideon and Logan. But first, I really need to eat."

Bradford was silent, and she knew the struggle. He didn't want her to go without him, but neither could they leave Hannah unattended—even though she continued unconscious.

Munroe stood, went to the bathroom, and retrieved the clothes that had never made it on her the first time. She slid into pants that, though a bit large, didn't fall around her knees, and left the shirt hanging baggy over them.

Bradford remained on the couch, eyes tracking her movements until she had fully dressed and her boots were back on, and then he stood. He walked to one TV desk, his naked physique a beautiful shape against the moonlight. He picked up the cell phone and tossed it to her.

"It would make me feel a whole lot better about staying behind," he said, "if you'd meet them at the restaurant downstairs."

She nodded. "I can do that," she said, although they might, perhaps, suspect that Hannah was in the hotel, and Logan's tenaciousness could become an issue. "Is the room in either of our names?" she asked.

He shook his head and held up empty hands. "No identification or credit cards. I arranged it long before we ever flew, just had to know where to find the keycard."

Munroe smiled. This was one of the many things she liked about Bradford, that his mind worked so similarly to the way hers did, that he was able to plan and process in several directions at once, many moves in advance of where they stood.

"This phone goes to Logan, right?"

Bradford nodded.

"How do I reach Heidi?"

"She's at the Balmoral Plaza," he said, and Munroe left unspoken the dozen personal questions unspooling in her head.

Getting the number for the hotel and then Heidi's room was easy enough, and from there Munroe made two calls. The first was to Heidi, the second to Logan, and with each she arranged to gather at the hotel's restaurant. But she gave Heidi a different time. Munroe wanted her there first, wanted her alone without the others, every second discussing details that she'd no desire to relay, a necessary evil that she would have avoided if she could.

She'd run the scenarios backward, forward, and around again. She'd come to Argentina, accomplished what she'd set out to do, and these loose ends were extraneous—not her burden to bear. Yet in good conscience she couldn't walk away. She'd seen, was aware, and to refuse to act, to turn her back completely and ignore what lay in plain sight, was to become a complicit part of it all in the same way that each person within The Chosen had become complicit.

Munroe could see only one clear path toward extricating herself from a responsibility she'd never wanted, and this was part of it. Heidi had to know. And no child, no matter how adult, or how long estranged, would willingly bear the news that the father she loved and longed to reconnect with was potentially a child molester.

Heidi's own childhood experience would speak to the truth in what Munroe would say, and yet the human condition was so strong that it would force her into denial. She couldn't accept it, wouldn't want to, and the emotional conflict would over time become extreme. It would be far better if Heidi heard the news and confronted the initial round of disbelief with Munroe instead of hearing it later from Logan or Charity, when the truth eventually surfaced.

And it would surface, of this Munroe was certain. Because even if Hannah didn't tell her parents what had been going on, Munroe sure as hell would. Unlike the tarnished history of The Chosen and their older children, right here, right now, there were no expired statutes of limitations, no possibility of hiding and protecting the criminal, and if jurisdiction became an issue, Munroe would personally rendition Elijah back to the United States and dump his ass on the courthouse steps if that's what it took. And maybe, just maybe, this time the legal system would work to protect those it was designed to protect, and save Munroe from being forced to take matters into her own hands.

She left the hotel room, found a table at the restaurant, and ordered. She ate heartily, her body still craving true sustenance, and had nearly finished when Heidi arrived.

Less than forty-eight hours had passed since they'd last met at the bar in San Telmo, and still it felt like a lifetime. As was Heidi's way, she greeted Munroe with a hug and then, full of genuine concern, asked about the bruises.

"I almost didn't recognize you," Heidi said. "Not with the clothes and your hair and your face like that." She paused. "Just like you said it would be." Without waiting for a response she handed Munroe a small plastic bag with a change of clothes. "They were the smallest things I have with me."

"I'm sure they'll be fine," Munroe said. "I just want her to have something available if she wants it, so she doesn't have to face strangers in her pajamas."

Heidi nodded and looked around the restaurant. "Where are the guys?"

"They'll get here as soon as they can," Munroe said, her answer the truth, if not completely.

She invited Heidi to sit, and they exchanged small talk until Munroe, in as offhanded and casual a way as possible, segued into the events of the last week, a setup for what was to come, all of it necessary to take Heidi off her guard. She told first of what it had taken to get Hannah out of the country, and then how the Havens had been located and the methodology of gaining entrance once they'd known where Hannah was. All of this was new to Heidi, who sat wide-eyed, full of questions and tangible energy, which grew even more intense when Munroe spoke of Heidi's siblings.

"I expect that we'll eventually hear from Morningstar," Munroe said. "When she finally goes through the bag I left behind she'll find a bit of documentation that she doesn't believe exists, and there's also a prepaid phone and my number." Heidi's expression, full of joy and expectation, was as Munroe had anticipated, but she followed this with the news she'd no desire to deliver. "The other thing is that sooner or later you'll probably hear things about your dad."

Munroe paused, waited a beat, and continued. "I don't want them to be a shock to you when you do."

"What kind of things?" Heidi asked. Munroe didn't answer, and when the silence became tangible, Heidi appeared to grasp the unspoken allegations.

"I'm not going to give you specifics," Munroe said, "because I don't have them. But you need to brace yourself for when they inevitably surface, okay?"

Heidi nodded, and was still silent, still processing, when the boys arrived. They both stopped short when Munroe turned to face them, Gideon's reaction far more cautious than Logan's. In response Munroe said, "Yeah, but you already saw the other guys."

They sat, relaxed, and in order to allow Heidi time alone with her thoughts, Munroe repeated for Gideon and Logan most of what she'd already relayed. The boys, in turn, gave their version of events, and when playing catch-up was over and Munroe had thanked them for coming after her, she turned to Logan and said, "You've heard from Charity, right?"

He nodded. "I'll be there to get her when her flight lands, and then we'll head over to wherever you are."

"Miles will get you the information," Munroe said. And then, "Look, Logan, I know that all of this waiting is incredibly difficult for you, but when Charity gets here, I think it's best that she meets with Hannah alone first—before the rest of you, okay?"

"It'll just be me and Charity."

"You're part of the 'rest of you,'" Munroe said, and when Logan began to protest she shook her head. There was no point in having this discussion in front of Gideon or Heidi—there were things Logan wouldn't want discussed—and as frustrating as it would be that he was being forced to wait yet again, when all was said and done, he'd understand and perhaps even thank her for it.

Munroe turned to Gideon. "I need to talk to you," she said.

"Alone?"

She shrugged. "It's your call."

He stood, and leaving Logan and Heidi to their individual silences, Munroe and Gideon stepped outside the restaurant to the carpeted elevator foyer.

"A deal's a deal," Munroe said. "Everything I told you I'd give you, I'll give. The catch is that it's all still in Buenos Aires. As soon as we get Charity and Hannah on their flight home, Miles and I are catching a charter back. You're welcome to come along if you want, or I can deliver everything to you back in the States."

Gideon was silent, as if he was truly weighing the options.

"I don't need an answer right this second or anything," she said, "just wanted to let you know where things stood." She paused and then straightened, standing taller and closer. Her movements were subtle, meant not to intimidate but for emphasis.

"I'm not going to pressure you about what you're up to," she said. "That wasn't part of the bargain, but it is within my rights to know. By giving you all of this information I become a participant in whatever it is you're setting out to do." She paused. "What is it you're after, Gideon?"

Deliberating, he shifted back against the wall. "I'm looking for someone," he said finally.

"Who?"

"A woman."

The vagueness didn't surprise her, but based on the story that Logan had told about Gideon's past, the gender did.

"Who?" Munroe said again.

"It doesn't really matter," Gideon said, "and talking about it isn't going to change anything."

"I know a lot more than you think I do," Munroe said. "Talking might change everything."

Gideon was silent a long while, and Munroe didn't rush him. She stood beside him, back to the wall, mirroring him breath for breath. When he finally spoke, his voice was low and tranquil. "When I was living in Argentina as a teenager," he said, "it was a pretty rough time. A lot of stuff happened. I mean, you've read the documents, so you know it wasn't a picnic for anyone, but stuff happened to me that even the hard-core survivors have a difficult time believing."

Gideon paused again, perhaps contemplating how far he would go with the explanation, and in response, Munroe remained quiet.

"Anyway," he said finally, "when it was all going on, there was this woman who lived there, and she knew about it. She was involved in the—" He broke the train of thought, as if unsure of the appropriate word usage. "The excommunication process," he said, "against one of the people who hurt me. You know what excommunication for The Chosen is, right?"

Munroe nodded.

"So she knew everything. Years later, when a lot of the adult children were leaving and a lot of the horrors of our lives were being brought to the public's attention, I spoke about some of the things that happened to me. It's hard to talk about these things publicly, you know? But a few of us were willing to do it. We thought it might make a difference—that maybe someone would do something about it, law enforcement or something—or at least people would know who they were and what they were doing and stop giving them their money. It was horrible, you know, making a public spectacle of myself, but I thought it would do some good. But that same woman who was there, who saw it, who knew what had happened to me . . ." Gideon's voice cracked. He coughed and cleared his throat. "On national television, she told the world that I was making it up, and then went on to tell a whole round of lies about me, things I'd never done, or vicious twists to things that had actually happened. But she knew the truth, no excuses, she was there, and straight to the interviewer's face, without batting an eye, she lied!"

Munroe was silent a moment, and finally, with a low voice that matched his, said, "You think she's in Buenos Aires?"

"I know she's there. I don't know why, exactly, but she's there."

"And what will you do when you find her?"

"I don't know," he whispered. "I want her to suffer. I want her to look into my eyes while I'm hurting her and tell me again that I'm lying. Honestly, I really want her dead, but as much as I would like that, I don't know if I could kill her." Gideon cut his eyes to Munroe, and there was an unveiled terror in them because he knew he'd said too much.

Munroe put a hand on his shoulder and turned so that they were eye to eye. "I understand the pain and I know the rage," she said. "Just remember that some things are impossible to undo, and you'll carry those burdens to your grave, because everyone is someone's daughter or sister or mother."

"She's no one's mother," Gideon said, and with his words a chill of recognition ran through Munroe. A childless woman inside The Chosen was a rarity. How many of them were in Buenos Aires at the same time?

"Describe her to me," Munroe said.

Gideon shrugged. "Sandy blond hair, buck teeth or an overbite or something like that, brown, murky eyes, about five-foot-five, maybe. Kind of homely-looking."

Munroe shook her head in a mixture of amusement and anger. Gideon had described Hannah's nameless companion, the woman who, assigned as guard or chaperone or whatever she was, had accompanied Hannah to the Cárcan hostel, another connection that folded in on itself.

Chapter 38

The necessities of the evening over, Munroe took the stairs up; ten floors in a slow climb that allowed her mind to purge everything left after those two hours at the restaurant. Of the four who'd gathered at the table, Munroe was undoubtedly the only one who had stepped away with a lighter burden.

Predictably, Bradford opened the door before she reached it. He'd taken time to put his jeans back on, although the rest of him was still bare. She reached the threshold and he grasped her hand, drew her to him, pulled her inward and down to the sofa.

The door shut.

She laughed, and he, hands wandering and mouth grazing hers, said, "I missed you."

Those three words, so basic in their simplicity, encapsulated far more than either would admit. It felt for the moment as if language could never suffice for what touch communicated. Bradford's hands roamed, hers reciprocated in kind, and she kissed him with the same intensity with which he'd drawn her to him.

His skin was warm against hers as the clothes fell away, and again their bodies tangled on the couch, each moment timeless, until they were spent to exhaustion and lay wrapped in each other's arms.

Munroe rested her head on Bradford's shoulder, body up against his while his fingertips stroked through what was left of her hair, the silence long until Bradford finally spoke. "The guy's name was Patrick," he said.

Munroe shifted, chin to her hand atop his chest so that they were face-to-face. "The guy I tossed into the garbage?"

Bradford nodded. "Devin Patrick. He carried a badge, but he wasn't NYPD."

"What then?"

"An impersonator," Bradford said. "He used the badge as a weapon, and he's been at it for a few years now. The more the department digs, the more they find, and the less they like what they see—so, in a way, you did them a favor."

"Are they burying it?" she asked.

"I wouldn't go so far as to say burying," he said. "Back shelving, maybe. But unless someone throws some evidence in their direction I don't think they're planning to look hard."

Munroe returned her head to its resting place. "It's good news," she said. "Not necessarily that they aren't looking, but that what I did might have been justified."

"You already know it was justified," Bradford said, "but I'm sure the confirmation is welcome."

Munroe allowed the silence to swallow her. Bradford was right, the confirmation was welcome. More than welcome.

"Will you sleep?" he said.

"No," she whispered, "not tonight." And it wasn't that she was afraid to fall asleep, afraid to dream or of the nightmares. She was nearly certain that the dreams weren't coming back, but not certain enough to tempt fate tonight. Not with Hannah sleeping in the other room, and not when they were so close to the assignment's end.

The nightmares had vacated, leaving a delicious weightlessness in their wake. Perhaps the change had come because she was back on assignment or that so much killing had caused a pressure release, but she knew better. For the first time in as far back as she could remember, she had allowed herself to feel the one thing she desperately craved from those closest to her but never afforded herself: acceptance.

She had a gift, and without fighting against it, without loathing her own nature, she'd let it serve her. Bradford's insight—his words—had meant something, and although she'd never been and would never be one to need approval or another's validation to be whole, in this one weakness, where she was so desperately alone, another hunter had shown his face.

Sometimes it's not wrong to kill.

There would be time later for sleep. For now, the gift had saved a child, and then she'd lived to tell of it, and if the pieces fell into place as Munroe planned, tomorrow the last of the remaining strings would be brought tightly together.

Bradford shifted into the rhythm that had come to symbolize peace, and Munroe slid off the couch, squeezing his hand in reassurance as she left.

She pulled her shirt over her head, found a blanket, and placed it over him, and wandered into the other room of the suite. She sat on the edge of the bed, and, her mind draining itself empty, watched Hannah sleep while the clock made its rounds and the predawn eventually arrived.

At six Munroe stood, removed the IV, collected the paraphernalia, and pulled it into the living room. Her call to room service brought Bradford's eyes open, although she expected that he'd been awake from the moment she'd begun moving about. He joined her at Hannah's bedside a few minutes later.

"Why don't you go clean up," he said. "It'll be a few before she starts to pull out of it. I'll keep an eye on her."

Munroe nodded, headed to the shower, and a long, hot ten minutes later, returned.

"It'll be soon," Bradford said, and they both turned toward the door and the heavy knock that reverberated from it.

Hannah's eyes twitched.

"I'll get it," Munroe said. "Take a shower while you can, because once she fully wakes, I want you and all of the equipment permanently out of sight until her mom gets here."

Bradford nodded and turned. Munroe followed after him toward the door, collected the tray, and returned to the girl. Only these last remaining hours until she fully discharged her duty, to Logan, to Charity, to Heidi and Gideon and to all of the children of The Chosen.

The bathroom door opened and closed, followed shortly by that of the main door as Bradford left the suite. With this last, Hannah's eyes rolled open. Her eyelids fluttered in the gradual open-and-shut of groggy cognizance until she slowly turned to face Munroe.

The room was still dim, and Munroe knew from experience that focus would come slowly. Hannah would sleep and come back again several times before she was fully aware. Munroe took Hannah's hand and squeezed it.

Hannah's first instinct would be to question, but her body's physical needs would beg priority, and this was to Munroe's advantage.

"How do you feel?" she said.

Hannah turned toward the sound of her voice. "I have to use the bathroom," Hannah said. "Really, really bad."

"I'll help you up," Munroe said. "We're going to go slow, okay? Because you're weak and woozy, and if you're not careful you'll stumble."

Hannah nodded and licked her lips in that dry fuzzy-mouth way of having been under the influence of the chemicals in her blood. The girl struggled to sit, and Munroe slipped an arm behind her, helped her to her feet, and kept her balanced. In the bathroom, Munroe held the door open for light and kept the fluorescents off. Not only to spare Hannah the harsh glare, but so that the girl wouldn't catch a glimpse of Munroe's face and be prematurely frightened.

Mission accomplished and the return made less wobbly than the way there, Hannah lay back down and, eyes closed, said, "Where am I?"

"Montevideo," Munroe said. "Are you hungry?"

"Starving," she whispered.

Munroe brought the tray to the bed and placed it where Hannah could both easily see and reach it.

Hannah turned toward Munroe and said, "Who are you?" but the intensity of the question was quickly dispersed when the girl caught sight of the assortment of *facturas* on the plate.

"My name is Miki," Munroe said. "We spent the day together in the kitchen, do you remember?"

There wasn't any reason to spell out the amount of time that had since passed. Being put under wasn't like waking from sleep. Hannah would have no awareness of the lost hours, and as far as the girl knew, it was now the morning after.

Hannah nodded at the familiar reference, and as the mental fuzz faded, creased lines of worry crept to her face, but panic didn't set in. This was the bonus of having kidnapped a child who'd spent her life being shuffled from one place to the next, and handed to one stranger after the other.

"You look different," Hannah said. "What happened to your face?"

"I got in a big fight," Munroe said, and she smirked. "The other guy was ten feet tall, I had to climb on a chair to reach him, but I beat him up anyway."

Hannah smiled. "Maybe a ladder," she said, and she ate. Between bites, the questions came. "Where are we? Why are we here? Where is Sunshine?"

Sunshine? Ah, Sunshine, the name of the woman that Gideon hunted.

"She didn't come with us," Munroe said, the kinder, gentler version of *she had no right to keep you*.

Hannah took another bite, and then another, eyes down toward the bed, processing, thinking. "Why am I here?" she said. "I shouldn't be here, I don't have permission. Where's Elijah, where's Morningstar? Where's my mom?"

"There are some people who love you very much who want to meet you."

Hannah was quiet again, putting away more food than any child her size had a right to consume, but then, food like this didn't come often in the Havens, and that had been part of Munroe's reason for having ordered it.

An easy bribe.

"Are you the reason they sent me away from the Haven? Did you take me away from Sunshine?"

"Yes," Munroe said. "I did." Her voice was soft. Tender. Provoking what was to come wasn't easy, but she had to do it.

Hannah's face reddened. Tears welled. "Why? Why would you do that? I need to go back."

"Tell me about your dad," Munroe said.

Hannah's voice went up a notch. The tears gave way to anger. "If you're trying to find out where he lives, you'll never get that from me. I don't know where he is, but even if I did, I wouldn't tell you. I would never. That would be—" Her voice broke, as if fighting for the right word. "That would be disloyalty to God and to The Prophet."

"All right," Munroe said. "Tell me about your mom."

"Which one?"

"Your real mom."

Here, Hannah grew silent. She wasn't the confident, defiant child from the kitchen, nor the angry one of a second ago. "My mom didn't want me," she said.

"Do you remember her?"

Hannah began to cry again. Hearty drops trailed a line from her eyes to her chin and down her neck. In spite of the bravado she'd displayed in the kitchen, Hannah was an abandoned little girl aching to be wanted, yearning to matter to someone. Munroe reached out and pulled the girl to her shoulder, held her tight until the tears subsided, and then whispered, "What if I told you that your mother wanted you? That she wanted you very much?"

Hannah sat up and pushed away, wiped a defiant hand across her face. "It wouldn't matter," she said. "She's of the Void."

"The Void is a scary place, isn't it?" Munroe said.

"God can't protect you or keep you safe in the Void," Hannah said, "and even worse, when you're outside The Chosen you can be taken over by the Devil."

"Like your mother?"

Eyes to the bed, Hannah nodded.

There was no point in countering the fear or the belief; anything said would only create mental dissonance and be rejected out of hand. Hannah would learn in her own time and through her own experiences which fears were founded and which weren't, and that was the only way it could be. What the child needed now was only to be heard and to have her current emotions validated, and she needed this before she was reunited with her mother.

"It's scary to think that it could happen to you too, isn't it?" Munroe asked.

Hannah nodded.

"But even if she's of the Void," Munroe continued, "it still feels better knowing that she wanted you, doesn't it?"

"Even if it doesn't change anything, it still feels better."

"Your father wanted you too," Munroe said.

Hannah sniffed. Wiped her nose along her sleeve. "I know. But God's work comes first."

"I meant your real father."

"He is my real father," Hannah said. She paused, looked to Munroe, as if she wasn't completely sure, and added, "Isn't he?"

Hers was the tone of hopefulness, the voice of an abandoned child setting aside everything she believed to be true, even against the path to her own salvation, in the hope that maybe there were parents somewhere who truly wanted her. This was dangerous ground, to be trodden carefully.

"I don't have all the answers," Munroe said, "but I have known your mom and dad—your real dad—for a very long time. In fact, your real dad is my best friend."

"Did they send you to come get me?"

"They did," Munroe said. "They've been looking for you for a long time."

Hannah started crying once more, this time a slow silent well of tears that dripped steadily onto the bedcover, and Munroe understood the tormented conflict. There was relief in the idea that she was wanted,

but this was overcome by the terror of the Void and being taken outside the protective covering of The Chosen. Munroe placed a hand on
top of Hannah's, and the girl, eyes red and swollen, looked up.

"I don't know your life, Hannah," Munroe said. "I don't know all
the places you've been or the people you've met, who you've lived with
or who you haven't, but I can tell you what I know, the things that
happened before and things that you probably don't remember. I can
tell you that Magdalene is your aunt—your mother's sister, and that
David kidnapped you away from your parents, and that he was only
your mom's boyfriend at the time."

Hannah's eyes glazed in disbelief and she returned her focus to the
bed. "My dad and I look the same, we have the same last name, and
Magdalene may be my aunt, but she's American and I'm Venezuelan,
and so is my dad."

"I have passports from three countries," Munroe said, "and I don't
carry a passport from where I was born and raised, so what does that
make me?"

Hannah was silent, her eyes still on the bed, and Munroe said,
"Have you ever wondered why you move around so much?"

"We all move."

"But you have moved more, haven't you? Did you know that David
is wanted by the police or that he used to carry an American passport,
but he couldn't get it renewed without getting arrested? Did you know
that you used to carry an American passport too?"

Hannah looked up again, eyes accusing. "Is that true?"

"Yes, it's all true. And although I don't have the proof with me, it's
easily found if you are willing to look for it."

Hannah was quiet again, sullen.

"I'm going to tell you a little story," Munroe said. "After that, if
you have any questions I'll answer them. And then, if you would like to
get cleaned up, I have a change of clothes for you, because in about"—
Munroe paused and stretched for the clock—"I guess in about an hour
or so, your mom will come walking through the door—your real mom,

the one who never wanted to let you go, the mom who has spent eight years trying to find you and who has saved up all that love just for you."

Hannah was fighting back tears again, but she did well at putting on an air of bravery. She crossed her arms. "And this guy you say is my dad?"

"He'll be here soon after."

"And then what?"

"What would you like to happen after that?"

Hannah looked toward the window. "I should go back to the Haven," she said.

Should.

Munroe said, "But is it what you really want?"

She'd asked a question Hannah couldn't answer without betraying The Prophet and The Chosen.

In giving Hannah the opportunity to meet parents who loved and wanted her, Munroe had offered the largest apple this little Eve could desire. But the apple was in the Void, a forbidden fruit, the great unknown: the evil fear. And to a child raised in The Chosen, it was much better to return to the Devil she knew than to face a Devil she didn't. Hannah had no concept of free choice, hadn't the ability to grasp that it was permissible to want what her heart wanted, and so Munroe pressed on.

She told of David Law and the steps he'd taken to steal Hannah away from Charity and Logan. She spoke of the events that followed, and went on to describe Charity down to the intricacies of her personality. Munroe followed these with stories about Logan, shenanigans that a child could appreciate, until Hannah began to smile naturally and occasionally laugh. When Munroe was certain that the girl's defenses had been lowered, that a small bond had been forged, and that Hannah felt comfortable with the territory they would soon cross together, Munroe gathered the change of clothing that Heidi had brought and nudged Hannah toward the bathroom.

They were sitting cross-legged on the bed, picking the best parts from another round of food that Munroe had ordered, when the phone rang. Hannah's eyes grew wide, and the worry creases made an instant comeback. Munroe stretched to reach the bedside cradle, and in response to Bradford's voice on the other end said only, "Yes, go ahead."

To Hannah, Munroe said, "In just a minute the front door will open and your mom will come in. When she does, I'm going to step around the corner to give you two some privacy, okay? But I'm here, and if you need me, you call for me, right?"

Hannah nodded, the fear self-evident. On instinct, Munroe ruffled the child's hair. Hannah squirmed to get away and ran her fingers over the top of her head to straighten out the mess.

Munroe laughed. "Just like your dad," she said.

Chapter 39

The departure area was filled with those waiting to board the non-stop flight to New York. The crowd was a mixture of teenagers and twentysomethings, with their scruffy clothes and beat up backpacks, interspersed among the well-heeled and the economy tourists, all of them jammed into a small space that, in spite of appearances, amounted to little more than a cattle car.

Munroe and Bradford stood at the departure gate, watching the last of Logan, Charity, and Hannah as they continued down the Jetway. The perks of being a recovered abducted child were few, but priority boarding that put them first on the flight was one of them.

And then they were gone.

The assignment was finished.

The pressure was over, and the resultant vacuum was like a stadium of shouting people gone instantly quiet.

Munroe tipped her head against Bradford's shoulder. They stood there a moment, staring after the empty space, and then Munroe turned to Heidi and Gideon, who had remained several feet away. She offered Heidi a hug and Gideon a handshake. "We're heading out of here," she said, and after the expected reciprocal niceties, turned to Gideon. "Last chance to come with us."

He shook his head. "I'm good," he said.

Munroe looped her arm in Bradford's, and together they strode toward the exit.

Gideon called after her. "Hey, Michael!" he said.

She turned.

"Thanks," he said. "Not just for getting Hannah, but you know, for everything else."

She nodded. "A deal's a deal," she said. "You know where to find me if you change your mind."

Gideon tipped his index finger from his forehead toward her.

There was always the chance he'd come for her, but Munroe held out for him finding peace through Hannah's homecoming and the changes it would bring.

International child abduction was no small crime, and proof was ample that Sunshine, or whatever the hell that woman's name was, was directly tied up in Hannah's trail. For the first time in nearly a decade Gideon had hope, and when Charity and Logan were ready to move forward, they might all experience a shared taste of justice.

The reunion between Hannah and her parents had been tear-filled and charged with drama—Charity first, and then a near repeat with Logan twenty minutes later. But it came, it passed, and if there were any parents better suited to deal with the issues their daughter faced, Munroe would be hard-pressed to find them. Charity and Logan understood The Chosen, understood from personal experience both the mind-set and the process a child went through in shedding the upbringing. They would know how to work through it. It would take time, but Hannah would heal; she'd be all right.

From inside the helmet, the world took on that muted tone that amplified the clarity of adrenaline. White stripes pulsed beneath the wheels, a rapid sequence that nearly blended into a solid line as Munroe kept the speedometer climbing. It was that earliest hour of the morning when the sun had yet to crest the horizon, and she was flying toward it on open, empty road. The bike was there beneath her, driving her forward, but she didn't feel it. Felt only the exhilaration of freedom, of power, and of flying.

When Munroe opened her eyes, Bradford was next to her, propped on an elbow, watching her with a curious smile.

"You were dreaming," he said.

She returned the smile, that groggy, satisfied smile of deep, comforting sleep.

"Yes," she whispered, and then smiled again. "I was."

Acknowledgments

To my agent, Anne Hawkins, my editor, John Glusman, publicist Sarah Breivogel, and everyone at Crown Publishers who, through efforts seen and unseen, have sped this work along its way: Thank you. Thank you also to the staff at the Palladium in Montevideo for allowing me access to their hotel, and especially to the individuals at The Palace who made it possible for me to conduct research in New York City, and took the time to walk me through the triplex suites.

About the Author

Born into the Children of God, raised in communes across the globe, and denied an education beyond the sixth grade, TAYLOR STEVENS broke free of the cult in order to follow hope and a vague idea of what possibilities lay beyond. She now lives in Texas, and is writing a third Vanessa Michael Munroe novel.